By Terry Miles

The Quiet Room
Rabbits

THE
QUIET
ROOM

THE QUIET ROOM

A Rabbits Novel

TERRY MILES

NEW YORK

Published in the United States by Del Rey, an imprint of Random House,
a division of Penguin Random House LLC, New York.

DEL REY and the Circle colophon are registered trademarks
of Penguin Random House LLC.

Hardback ISBN 9780593496404
Ebook ISBN 9780593496411

Printed in the United States of America on acid-free paper

randomhousebooks.com

1st Printing

FIRST EDITION

Book design by Simon M. Sullivan

For Maisie

THE
QUIET
ROOM

"People disappear every day."
"Every time they leave the room."

—*The Passenger* (1975)

1

WHAT'S YOUR FAVORITE COLOR?

THE NIGHT WAS CLEAR AND COOL, and although the distant lights from a handful of determined stars did their best to cut through the dense urban haze of the city, it was dark.

The kind of dark where all kinds of horrible shit could happen.

The tester stepped from the passenger door of a black SUV and instinctively pulled up the collar of her gray jacket against a light rain that hadn't started to fall, but would do so presently.

She was on her way to administer the test.

She hadn't tested anyone new in over a year. The fact that she was doing so now was none of her concern. She was hired to administer the test, nothing more.

Ask the questions.

Record the answers.

Submit the card.

Glass of wine.

That last one wasn't part of the protocol, of course, but it had been a long day and she hadn't had a drink for weeks. She'd asked for something on the plane, but they weren't serving alcohol for some reason. The lack of alcohol wasn't the end of the world. It was a short flight, two hours from San Francisco to Seattle, but still, flying without drinking felt almost uncivilized.

She'd been to Seattle once before, as a child. It was the first time she'd seen an ocean. She remembered picking up broken seashells and flipping over rocks to chase the tiny crabs that would appear from the sand beneath the rocks as if by magic.

She wondered, as she approached a wooden door in the middle of a low red-brick building, if she'd have time to visit the Pike Place Market. Or maybe the Space Needle? She knocked twice, and waited for a response.

"Come in," said a low raspy voice from the other side.

She opened the door and stepped into a small waiting area.

There was a man standing there. He was about forty years old, tall and athletic, with a thick frame and curly black hair. He looked like a generic government agent straight out of central casting except for the fact that his dark gray suit fit him a whole lot better than she'd ever seen on an agent. There was something sharp and dangerous about his eyes.

He handed her a clipboard that included a pen along with a Phase Four testing form, then turned and started walking away.

Phase Four. They didn't get many of those.

She pressed the clipboard against her leg and followed.

The man led her down a dark, narrow hallway that eventually dog-legged into another slightly wider and much brighter hall. There were a number of doors on either side, each labeled with a wide strip of white tape featuring a collection of arcane symbols written in black Sharpie. The tester thought she may have recognized some of the symbols, but she wasn't really paying attention. She knew the rooms were empty.

That wasn't why she was here. Not this time.

Her guide stopped at the end of the hallway in front of a wide gray metal door, knocked, and then nodded at the tester.

"How long?" she asked.

"As long as it takes." He turned and walked back down the hall.

When she could no longer hear the sound of his footsteps, the tester took a slow deep breath and opened the door.

It took her eyes a moment to adjust to the darkness, but eventually everything slipped into focus.

The room was about twenty-five feet square. A small rectangular metal table with two matching chairs sat in the center, and the walls were covered with dark gray soundproofing foam. Seated at the table in the metal chair farthest from the door was the subject of the test: a woman wearing black-framed Ray-Ban glasses, faded jeans, and a loose-fitting cream-colored long-sleeved shirt. Her long auburn hair had been pulled back into a thick ponytail, her arms were crossed, and she looked pissed off. The tester figured she had to be somewhere between thirty-five and forty years old—thirty-seven, she thought. She could check the file, of course, but she liked to guess.

The tester took a seat across from the subject, set the clipboard down on the table, and removed a pen from where it had been clipped against the testing form.

"Who the fuck are you?" the subject said, shifting slightly in her chair.

The tester removed a small tablet from her pocket, hit a few virtual buttons, and set it down on the table between them.

"I'm sorry to keep you waiting," the tester said. "I had to fly in from California."

"What am I doing here?"

"Please, just do your best to relax, this won't take very long. I'm here to administer a quick test."

"What the fuck are you talking about? What test?"

"All we need you to do is look at a few photographs, answer some questions, and you'll be free to go."

"That's it?"

"That's it."

"You know I'm going to call the cops as soon as I get out of here."

"Of course. Do you mind if we get started?"

The subject leaned back in her chair. "Fine."

"What's your favorite color?"

"Really?"

"I just need to get a baseline."

"Children have favorite colors, not adults."

"I'm afraid I will need an answer. It's actually not—"

"Green."

"Great. Thank you." The tester picked up the pen and checked a couple of boxes on the first page of the form, then swiped up on the tablet to reveal a photograph of a man wearing wraparound black sunglasses.

"Do you recognize this person?"

"Seriously?" the subject said.

Nothing from the tester.

"That's Bono. From the band U2."

"Great." The tester swiped to the next photo: a modern house on a lake surrounded by dense, dark green woods. "And this?"

"That's my house. I grew up there."

The tester nodded, made a couple of notes on the form, then swiped to the next photo: a lime-green AMC Pacer with Washington plates.

"That's my car. I mean, it was my car, in high school. Why are you asking me about this shit?"

The tester ignored the question, made a couple of notes, then swiped again, this time revealing a photo of a small ceramic tray. It looked like it had been designed to hold soap, but it was filled with a variety of tarnished silver rings.

"Looks like a soap tray."

"That's it?"

The subject nodded.

"It doesn't look familiar?"

"No. Should it?"

The tester smiled. "There is no should or shouldn't, only what you remember."

She swiped to the next image: an extremely detailed abstract line drawing featuring tiny shapes and symbols that upon closer examination appeared to compose a dense, intricate maze.

"I bought that at an auction last year in Vancouver. It's hanging in my bedroom. How the fuck did you get these pictures?"

"Just try to focus on the test, please."

"Why did you say 'remember'? Am I supposed to remember that soap tray?"

The tester smiled. "This is going to go a lot faster if you do your best to remain calm."

The subject jumped out of her chair and stood. "No way, lady. I need you to tell me what the fuck is happening. Right now."

"You didn't react this way to the first four pictures I showed you."

"What do you mean?"

"It took you five pictures to get angry. Why do you think that is?"

"What?" the subject said, her voice cracking as she stared down at her hands, which had begun shaking. She slowly sat back down. "I don't know what's happening. I find it hard to remember certain things. I was kidnapped, I think."

"Would you like a glass of water?"

"Is that part of the test?"

The tester just smiled.

"What's going on?"

"If you just relax and answer my questions to the very best of your ability, you'll be out of here in ten minutes. You have my word."

The subject took a deep breath and exhaled. "I'm fine. Let's just get it over with."

The tester thought that the subject looked worn out and made a note to speak with the administrator about the manner in which the woman had been secured and transferred for the test.

The subject shifted in her seat. "Please, hurry the fuck up."

The tester swiped up to the next photo. It was a medium-sized dog with a ball in its mouth. The photograph looked like it had been taken on a beach somewhere.

"It's a dog."

"That's all?"

"Some kind of spaniel—a springer, I think."

The tester made a few notes on the form, then flipped the page and made a few more.

"Can you please hurry?" the subject said as she brought one of her knees up to her chest.

"Do you need a break?"

The subject brought her leg back down and leaned forward. "I'm fine."

"Picture somebody drowning. Now, you're the only person who can save this person, but you know that, if you rescue them, they will go on to harm a number of animals. What do you do?"

"What the fuck kind of question is that?"

"I don't choose the questions, I'm afraid."

"That's easy. Let the fucker drown."

The tester checked a couple of boxes on the form, then continued. "Are you now, or have you ever been, pregnant?"

"Brittany."

"Pardon me?"

"Brittany spaniel. The dog. It's not a springer spaniel, it's a Brittany."

"Anything else?"

"What do you mean?"

"You don't recognize that dog?"

"No. I mean . . . Can I see it again?"

"I'm afraid not."

"I'm not pregnant."

The tester made a few notes, then swiped to the next photo: a close-up of a tarot card or something similar, labeled The Traveler.

"Do you recognize this card?"

The subject shook her head.

"Could you please answer verbally?"

"Why? You're not recording this, are you?"

"No, we're not, but I am measuring and recording your physiological response to each of the questions."

"How the fuck are you doing that?"

The tester smiled. "That's my job." She tried to make her smile as unthreatening as possible. A welcoming and authentic smile was something she'd been working on for a while. She made a note to check her smile when she watched the footage later.

Of course they were recording the interview.

The subject appeared unnerved. She was visibly agitated, fidgeting in her chair.

"Just two more questions," the tester said.

"Thank fuck."

The tester smiled and leaned forward. "Are you playing Rabbits?"

Something flashed across the subject's face, just for a second—maybe not recognition, but something else. The tester made another note to check it out when she reviewed the footage later.

"What the fuck is Rabbits?" the subject asked. "How can somebody play an animal?"

"Okay," the tester said. "We're almost finished."

The subject exhaled slowly and finally nodded. She appeared to be doing her best to remain calm.

The tester turned off her tablet and smiled. "Last question. What's your name?"

"My name is Emily Connors. What's your fucking name?"

The tester stared at Emily for a long moment, then slipped the cap onto the felt pen she was holding, with a click that sounded much louder than it seemed it should.

"Thank you so much for coming."

At this point, the man in the dark gray suit reentered the room and handed Emily a black hood. "You'll need to put this on," he said.

"No way."

"Option two it is." He pulled out a syringe and took a step toward Emily.

"Fine." Emily snatched the hood from the man's hand and slipped it over her head.

The tester leaned back in her chair and rubbed her eyes. She was going to have to hire a dogsitter. It looked like she wouldn't be heading home to California anytime soon.

This one was going to be trouble.

2

THE PENIS MIGHTIER
THAN THE SWORD

ROWAN CHESS HAD BEEN having the strangest dreams lately.

Last night he'd dreamt that he was composing an opera about an unhatched dinosaur egg. The night before, he'd had a nightmare. Unlike the dinosaur egg, the nightmare was connected to something that had happened in real life.

Rowan was nineteen years old at the time and living in Vancouver, Canada. One night, while he was walking home from rehearsal listening to a song that his band had recently recorded, he felt a rush of water splash his face. He was startled, but it wasn't unpleasant. The night was cool and dark, and the water was unexpectedly warm. But when Rowan touched his cheek and pulled back his hand, he realized that it wasn't water.

It was blood.

He looked down at the sidewalk.

There, on the concrete directly in front of him, was a person—or rather, what had once been a person but was now just a pile of broken meat and shiny white bone.

The spray of blood hitting Rowan's face must have been preceded by some kind of sound, but with his band's music blasting in his headphones, he hadn't heard a thing.

Rowan turned and was surprised to discover that he wasn't alone.

He was looking into the faces of four or five other people who'd clearly seen what had just happened. They just stared—mouths open, eyes wide—seemingly searching for anything that might help them make sense of the tall, long-haired young man standing in the middle of the sidewalk, completely covered in blood.

Rowan sidestepped the mess of wet and bones and kept moving. He didn't hear the people calling after him as he walked away.

After a long shower followed by a pot of ramen noodles and frozen vegetables, Rowan read half of a graphic novel about a couple of sexy teenage serial killers—called, imaginatively, *Sexy Teenage Serial Killers*—and went to bed early.

He never mentioned the incident to a single soul.

Rowan grew up in a small two-floor bungalow on a heavily wooded three-acre lot just outside of Bellingham, Washington. His father was a geologist who specialized in industrial minerals and their applications, and his mother kept the house together and worked as a part-time cruciverbalist, designing crossword puzzles for local and national newspapers. She'd experienced a brief moment of notoriety when she used the clue: *"The___ mightier than the sword,"* which resulted in the word PENIS appearing at the top of the puzzle. She said it was accidental and promised her editor that it wouldn't happen again, but Rowan could tell by the expression on her face when she was apologizing to the man on the phone that his mother had done it on purpose.

Sometime around the age of fifteen, Rowan began experiencing a nagging and persistent feeling that something was wrong.

He'd started to suspect that he didn't fit into his own life.

He confessed this feeling to his mother, who just smiled and told him everybody went through it; that what he was experiencing was simply the onset of puberty.

But it felt more than biological to Rowan.

It felt primal.

Sometimes it was intense, like there was an ocean waiting to break free from his mind, and other times it was nothing more than a slight sense of unease. But the alienation was always there—a constant gnawing pressure.

Rowan's sense of disconnection from both himself and other people continued well into adulthood. Once, when describing the feeling to a therapist friend of his mother's, Rowan said it felt like he was living in a photograph that was just a little bit blurry—not indistinct enough to completely lose the outline of the subject, but fuzzy enough that you'd have trouble focusing. The therapist nodded thoughtfully, asked questions in all the right places, and then prescribed a mild antidepressant.

Rowan spent the next few years learning how to pretend he belonged, and by the time he'd graduated university—a few years after the incident on the sidewalk—he was able to fake it pretty well. After school, when Rowan moved to Seattle and rose to the top of his field in architectural design with a focus on theme parks and immersive theater experiences, nobody seemed to recognize the fact that, deep inside his heart, Rowan continued to feel like a stranger in his own life.

He'd had few meaningful relationships over the years. There was Mona, his first kiss in seventh grade, followed by Monica, the bass player from Boulder, Colorado, he'd lived with for a couple of years in Vancouver, and, finally, a woman named Madison whom Rowan had briefly dated while working on a monorail station enhancement project a year and a half ago.

There had been no one since.

He'd never tried online dating, but when Taylor—a friend from way back in their band days—suggested it, Rowan agreed to give it a shot. Taylor had met her wife through an app, and even if Rowan didn't find his soul mate, Taylor said, at least Rowan had a shot at finding somebody whose name didn't start with the letter M.

So Rowan tried swiping right for love.

He met dozens of women through the two most popular online dating apps, and some of the introductory dinners had gone so well that Rowan (or his date) had suggested they do it again.

After one extraordinary dinner followed by half a dozen pretty good drinks, Rowan ended up getting intimate with one of the women: a DJ named Hank (short for Henrietta) from somewhere in Michigan (Ann Arbor, maybe?).

They'd had a lot of fun and agreed to meet up again the following night.

The next evening, Rowan was sipping a glass of wine and watching Hank get ready for dinner in her apartment—which looked like it had been decorated using cast-off furniture from the set of *Boogie Nights*—when he started imagining a life with her. She was unconventionally beautiful, with big, fuzzy blond hair, sharp blue eyes, and a hypnotically curvy figure. Rowan watched Hank apply her mascara, and as she moved her hips back and forth to "The Long Run" by the Eagles, he imagined what it would be like to have this woman come home and kiss the back of his neck while he was barbecuing cedar plank salmon and sipping a beer. He smiled. She was incredible. That's when she turned to him and said, "We're going to do a shitload of coke tonight."

Rowan swore off online dating forever.

But a few months later, after a couple of glasses of small-batch whiskey at a friend's gallery opening, Rowan found himself unable to sleep. He opened one of his (now five) dating apps, and began to swipe.

After exchanging a few messages, a woman named Ramona invited Rowan to an escape room dinner party in an extremely wealthy gated community called The Highlands. Apparently the emcee, a television actor, was a friend of hers.

Rowan wasn't sure about Ramona, but there was no way he was going to turn down an escape room. The party aspect he could do without, but the possibility of taking part in any kind of puzzle-solving was exciting. His mother's love of puzzles and games had been amplified in Rowan, and he almost never turned down an opportunity to play.

"The rules are simple, but this isn't a conventional escape room mystery party." The tall brunette was impressive in a tight, two-toned dark gray tuxedo that made her look a little like James Bond—if James Bond were played by a six-foot-two Natalie Portman. "This is a Heist-and-Seek Party, which means you're not trying to escape anything this evening. Rather, you'll be trying to find something very special."

There were murmurs from the crowd.

Rowan looked around. There were somewhere between fifty and a hundred people gathered outside an enormous residence that reminded him of a crime lord's mansion in an old Michael Mann movie. There was a pool, some fake palm trees, and an elaborate fountain featuring a ten-foot-tall marble angel with long, thick arms that didn't quite match the scale of her body.

About thirty yards away, a whole bunch of shiny vintage cars were parked in front of a large six-door garage. Rowan wasn't an automotive expert by any means, but he thought he recognized a few iconic makes and models, including a red Ferrari, a silver Aston Martin, and some kind of shiny black American muscle car from the sixties.

Rowan figured that whoever built the place must have made their money in the late eighties or early nineties, and although the current occupants were clearly trying to downplay the ostentatious excess connected to the era of its construction, there was only so much you could hide when you were dealing with gaudy Corinthian pillars and marble fountains. A very strong current of "eighties drug dealer kitsch" ran underneath the almost tasteful veneer.

"Can you believe we're actually here?" Ramona said, grabbing Rowan's arm like they'd been dating for years. He didn't appreciate the faux intimacy. They'd just met outside, when Ramona handed Rowan his ticket.

He was already annoyed.

Ramona was a little over five feet tall, early thirties, pale and thin, with straight dark brown hair and soft blue eyes. She wore too-tight faded jeans with the top button undone, dark red cowboy boots, and a Black Sabbath T-shirt (from Target or Urban Outfitters). She spoke with a light accent—possibly Mediterranean or maybe somewhere in New England. Rowan couldn't quite place it.

"I hope we win," she said. "I heard the prizes are insane. Chris Martin sang to a girl at the last party."

"You've been to one of these things before?"

"No, but my friend Lilith works them all the time. That's her over there." Ramona pointed at the tall woman in the tux.

"You are going to be presented with ten exciting and engaging challenges," Lilith continued. "Inside the foyer, you'll find your welcome packs, which include everything you'll need to solve the mystery." She bowed deeply at the waist before dramatically tossing her hands into the twilit sky, as if starting an illegal drag race. "Good luck, everyone!"

The enthusiastic crowd started moving toward a set of large open French doors that led into the foyer of the house.

"Let's go," Ramona said, grabbing Rowan's hand. "I don't wanna miss out. These swag bags are bomb."

Rowan did his best to keep up as she pulled him through the crowd. Ramona was a people-parting professional—focused and incredibly adept at avoiding collisions while continuing to press forward. They made it into the foyer in less than a minute.

"Whoa, those look big," Ramona said as she elbowed her way past a couple of the other guests in order to gain access to a long wooden table filled with the welcome packs Lilith had mentioned in her speech.

Ramona snatched one of the dozens of medium-sized black-and-white reusable bags from the table, handed it to Rowan, and then grabbed another bag for herself.

Inside the bag was a bunch of free stuff, including two half bottles of wine, caviar, a Swiss Army knife, a Kindle, and numerous gift cards to places both useful and completely impractical but cool. The centerpiece of the gift bag was a small, rectangular dark wooden box. A tiny flower symbol had been stamped onto the lid in shimmering pearly white ink.

Ramona leaned over Rowan's shoulder as he opened the box and revealed its contents. Inside was a small postcard. Written inside the lid, in a font that looked like Futura Bold, was a three-word message in white ink: "Find the Orchid."

"What the hell does that mean?" Ramona asked.

Rowan didn't answer, because the question didn't warrant a response.

She eventually answered her own question with another. "I guess we try to find an orchid?"

Rowan was beginning to feel like the date was a mistake.

Rowan found Ramona somewhat attractive physically, but she was irritating. He briefly considered making some excuse and leaving, but there was another matter to consider.

He wasn't going anywhere until he found the orchid.

Once his imagination had been fired up by something, Rowan was the kind of person who needed to see things through.

"I think we should work together," Ramona said as she shoved her own gift bag into an enormous black leather purse.

Rowan forced a smile.

It looked like he'd have to deal with Ramona, at least for the time being.

On the front of the postcard was a symbol synonymous with army hospitals and other medical institutions: two snakes winding up a pole surmounted by a pair of wings. On the back, written in freehand script, was a message: *Follow the map, find the orchid.*

"What map?" Ramona asked, leaning her chin on Rowan's shoulder.

"It must have something to do with this image on the front."

"You wanna skip the scavenger hunt thing and get a drink?" Ramona asked, a hopeful, almost pleading look in her eyes.

Rowan shook his head.

Ramona grabbed a couple of glasses of champagne from a nearby server's tray and handed one to Rowan. "Okay, then, let's Indiana Jones this fucker. What's with the doctor snake symbol?"

"It's a caduceus."

"If you say so, smarty-pants."

She was infuriating.

"Hermes carries it, in Greek mythology." Rowan flipped the postcard over.

"What are you doing?"

"Checking for hidden text or images."

"Look at you, so professional." She took a huge sip of champagne and then burped quietly into her clenched palm. "So, you think we need to find a medicine cabinet or something?"

"Too obvious. Do you see anything related to Hermes anywhere?"

"Hermes? Like a bag or a scarf or something?"

He was about to admonish her for mispronouncing the designer's name, but she was actually on to something. An Hermès bag containing the next clue would be perfect. "That's a good idea," he said. "Let's take a look around."

Ramona smiled and squeezed his arm. "We're totally gonna win."

Rowan didn't mind the feeling of her touching his arm.

Maybe she wasn't so bad after all.

Rowan led Ramona through the foyer, looking for anything that might provide some kind of clue. The only way to leave the foyer and progress into the house proper was to pass through an impromptu checkpoint that had been set up specifically for this event. Two large security guards loomed, looking bored as hell, one on either side of the checkpoint—an access card reader on a stand between them.

"It looks like you need a card to move on to the next clue," Rowan heard someone say.

"You sure you don't wanna hit the bar for a couple of stronger drinks?" Ramona said. "It might help us think."

Rowan ignored her and made his way over to a number of small dioramas that had been set up on faux marble pedestals at various points around the room. There was a bear threatening a member of the Royal Canadian Mounted Police, a shark turning to attack a large fish Rowan didn't recognize, a small model of the solar system, a Nativity scene, and a few others. There didn't appear to be anything medical or Hermes-related.

Rowan approached the pedestal that contained the model of our solar system.

"Mercury," he said.

"What?"

"Hermes is Greek. Mercury is the Roman equivalent."

"Is that helpful?"

"Maybe," he said. "I'm going outside."

"Oh," she said. "Okay."

They made their way out of the crowded foyer and back onto the wide lawn where the woman named Lilith had addressed them earlier.

"There." Rowan pointed in the direction of the garage. "That car on the far right, do you recognize it?"

"The Cougar?" Ramona asked.

"Yeah. Is that a Mercury?"

"Sure is," she said. "1967."

"You're positive?"

"Could be a '69, if you're lucky."

Rowan ignored her joke and started walking over to the garage area.

"I grew up with two older brothers. They know a lot about cars," Ramona said as she jogged to catch up with Rowan.

"There." He pointed through the open passenger-side window of the car. The glove box was open, and there was a stack of security access cards sitting on the edge atop a small handwritten sign that said: TAKE ONE.

"You're a genius," Ramona said.

Rowan smiled. He didn't know much about cars, but it had been a simple connection to make. He was proud of himself. He hadn't solved a puzzle like that one in a long time. He glanced back in the direction of the main house. There was nobody approaching the garage area. It looked like Rowan had been the first person to figure it out.

Back in the foyer, Rowan swiped their access card through the security card reader and a tiny light turned from red to green. The two security guards stepped aside and allowed Rowan and Ramona to pass between them into a wide hallway.

In the middle of the hall, just past the checkpoint, was a small wooden table. Sitting on the table was a small stack of postcards.

On the back of the postcards, written in the same freehand script as before, was the message: *Follow the map, find the orchid.* Rowan flipped over the card to reveal a second image. It was the graphic of a tiny blue-and-white HELLO, MY NAME IS _____ sticker with the name left blank.

"What do you think it means?" Ramona asked.

"No idea," Rowan replied.

There were murmurs and rumbling from the crowd as they noticed that somebody had made it past the first security checkpoint. It wouldn't be long before other people started to put it together.

Rowan grabbed Ramona's arm and led her down the hall. If they were going to win, they would have to hurry.

At the end of the hallway, a set of double doors opened into a large game room. There was a collection of old stand-up arcade games against the far wall, including Ms. Pac-Man, Tempest, Galaxian, and a bunch of pinball machines Rowan didn't recognize. In the center of the room was an enormous billiards table, covered by dark red felt that made Rowan think of blood. On the right-hand wall was a set of double doors flanked by two more security guards, and a second card reader sitting on a pedestal.

But it was the left-hand side of the room that was clearly the focal point.

It was an exact replica of the bar from Stanley Kubrick's *The Shining*.

"Ooh," Ramona said. "I'm going to play Pac-Man."

Rowan didn't bother to respond. He knew Pac-Man wasn't related to what came next. It had something to do with the bartender, dressed exactly like the character from *The Shining,* in a burgundy tux with wide red satin lapels, a black bow tie, and a white shirt.

Rowan walked over and sat down on the barstool directly across from the bartender.

"Hi, could I please get a couple of gin and tonics?" Rowan asked.

No response from the bartender.

"Oh, I get it. There's a code or something I have to say?"

The bartender remained silent, a wry smile on his face.

Rowan looked over at Ramona, who had already moved from

Ms. Pac-Man to one of the pinball machines, then he turned back to the bartender."

The Shining was one of Rowan's favorite films of all time. He toyed with the postcard from the wooden table as he admired the authentic details of the bar from the Overlook Hotel. Whoever had designed the space had done an amazing job. The commitment to detail was incredible. As Rowan was looking over the bottles behind the bartender, it came to him. He glanced down at the image on the postcard: the tiny blue-and-white HELLO, MY NAME IS sticker.

"Hi, Lloyd," Rowan said, using the name of the bartender from *The Shining*.

"Hello, Mr. Torrance," the bartender responded immediately. "What'll it be?"

"Gin and tonic?"

"I'm afraid all we have at the moment is this, sir," the bartender said, and passed Rowan another security card.

"Is this why we're here?" Rowan asked.

Nothing from the bartender.

Ramona came bouncing over from the arcade games.

"What does a girl have to do to get a drink around here?"

"I think we've found the next clue," Rowan said, holding up the security card.

"Cool. How the hell did you do that?"

"You have to know the bartender's name from *The Shining*."

"That's a movie, right?"

"It's also a novel."

"Did you google it?"

A man and woman entered the room laughing. They'd figured out the first clue.

"No," Rowan said. "Come on. We need to hurry."

Rowan used the security card to get past the guards standing on the right-hand side of the room, and led Ramona through a set of wide double doors into another long hallway.

That hallway led to a bathroom where they found another postcard. Rowan solved that puzzle using a rudimentary code he discovered in the pattern of the shower curtain, and they were on to the next clue.

The next four postcards led to a series of fairly simple clues that Rowan solved easily, but the eighth postcard was open to two completely different interpretations and Rowan ended up choosing the wrong one, which allowed another couple of guests to catch up.

By the time Rowan figured out that the eighth clue referred to a garden gnome and not garden gomae (Japanese spinach salad), two other couples were right behind them.

Rowan and Ramona were still in the lead, but barely.

The garden gnome clue led them past another checkpoint into another long hallway (this house was filled with long halls).

In the middle of the hallway was an old vending machine, or, more precisely, an old cigarette machine. Rather than buttons, this machine had nine long handles that you were meant to pull after you'd inserted the requisite number of coins. The handles of these types of machines normally represented different brands or strengths of cigarette, but in this case, they all contained the same thing: a postcard. Above each of the handles was the message that had been written on the back of every postcard they'd discovered so far: *Follow the map, find the orchid.* There was a sticker just above the ninth lever that read: OUT OF ORDER, AUGUST 2006.

Written on a card in the middle of the machine was the following message:

Pull the lever that represents your home. You may pull one lever only.

"What the hell is this shit?" Ramona asked.

What the hell indeed, Rowan thought, as he went back and forth over the levers. They appeared to be identical except for the sticker above the ninth lever.

It took him a few minutes, but he eventually figured it out.

He smiled and then pulled the third handle from the left.

A postcard popped into the tray at the bottom of the machine, followed by another security access card.

"How did you know which lever to pull?" Ramona asked.

"Earth."

"What about it?"

"It's the third planet from the Sun."

"And?"

"The ninth lever."

"What about it?"

"It says it's out of order and the date is August 2006."

"So?"

"So, that's when they decommissioned Pluto as a planet."

"Pluto's not a planet?"

"No."

"What the fuck is it?"

Rowan ignored her question.

The back of the postcard was identical to all the others: *Follow the map, find the orchid*. He flipped it over. On the front was the image of a man who looked a bit like Robin Hood or one of his band of merry men, drawing a bow.

This was the tenth and final clue.

They used the security card and passed through the next checkpoint into what appeared to be a sort of guest suite, featuring a small living area, a bedroom, and an impressive bathroom. Inside the bathroom, an enormous Victorian clawfoot bathtub was filled with hundreds of small, opaque white plastic balls, each with something stenciled on it: a number, a word, an image, or a phrase. On the wall behind the bathtub was a sign that read: YOU MAY OPEN ONLY ONE BALL.

"My first boyfriend had only one ball," Ramona said, "but he never said anything about it. Didn't mention it at all. Hey." She laughed. "Doesn't that sound like a song?"

Rowan blinked. He had no response.

"I knew boys had two balls," Ramona continued. "Everybody knew that, so for the longest time I thought that's how y'all worked down there—one big ball, and one really tiny one that you couldn't even feel."

In an attempt to avoid thinking about Ramona and her one-balled boyfriend, Rowan held up the postcard and stared at the image.

A person holding a bow.

There were no obvious identifiers, no Greek letters or symbols to suggest that the figure might be Artemis or Eros. As far as Rowan could tell it was just a person with a bow, wearing a brown tunic, leggings, and boots. It couldn't be as simple as Robin Hood, could it?

"Maybe it's that elf guy from Lord of the Rings?" Ramona offered.

"Maybe," Rowan conceded. Legolas wasn't actually a bad guess, although this person's ears looked human.

The only thing Rowan could point to of any interest was the fact that two different colored pins held up the person's plain brown tunic. The pin on their left shoulder was black and the pin on their right shoulder was red. Other than that, it was just a plain graphic of a relatively generic archer.

"Check out the balls," Rowan suggested, then immediately regretted his choice of words, but Ramona didn't make a terrible joke. She just smiled and took his arm.

"Good idea."

Together, they began examining the symbols and images that had been stenciled onto each of the balls. While he tried to figure out what the markings might mean, Rowan started to imagine a second date with Ramona. Maybe they'd catch a movie or go to a live comedy show. She'd chuckle awkwardly in the same strange places as Rowan, and the two of them would share another laugh about it over a beer later.

Maybe they'd actually end up making out, and possibly more.

"There's a lot of repetition, but it looks like there are at least fifty different images on these things," Rowan said as he held up two of the balls, one stamped with the image of Beethoven, the other featuring the Cat in the Hat.

"Look at these." Ramona held a ball in each hand. In her right hand was a ball marked with the image of an arrow. The ball in her left hand had a tiny black-and-white-striped Michael Keaton, from the movie *Beetlejuice*. "Beetlejuice, Beetlejuice, Beetlejuice," she said. "Get it?"

"I do," Rowan said.

"I love that movie," Ramona said as she discarded both balls and continued to rummage through the bathtub.

Rowan reached in and pulled out the ball Ramona had discarded that featured the image of an arrow.

Could it be that simple?

The images ran the gamut from astrological symbols to pop culture characters and all points in between. As with the arrow, Rowan was able to make some broad connections between a few of the images on the balls and the postcard, but none of them felt right.

"You think it's that one with the arrow?" Ramona asked.

"Maybe," Rowan said. But he knew that wasn't it. That would be too easy.

He was missing something.

What was it?

"I really think we should just pick one of these balls and go grab a drink," Ramona said. "What do you say? No point in an open bar if you don't take advantage, right?" Ramona was getting antsy. "Heads up," she said, and tossed him two random balls from the tub.

Rowan somehow managed to catch both balls, but he had to drop the postcard to do it.

As he glanced down at the postcard, now lying on the floor, the thing that stood out the most was the bright red pin on the archer's right shoulder.

Rowan grinned, and started digging around in the tub until he found one of the balls with Michael Keaton on it.

"It's this one," he said.

"Beetlejuice?"

"The archer is Orion, the hunter, and the red star that makes up his shoulder is called Betelgeuse."

"It's named after the movie?"

Rowan couldn't bring himself to answer Ramona's question. The possibility of a second date was definitely off the table.

Rowan opened the Beetlejuice ball. Inside was a tiny USB drive.

"What the hell is that?" Ramona asked.

"Congratulations. Your challenge is now complete," said a disembodied female voice from somewhere overhead—probably a hidden speaker in the ceiling.

"We won!" Ramona screamed as she jumped up and hugged Rowan.

"I guess we did," Rowan said with a smile.

He was energized.

He wanted to do it again.

With the challenge over, Ramona got her wish, and the two of them finally ended up at the bar. While Ramona argued with the bartender about whether or not an annual Costco membership was actually worth the money, Rowan nursed his drink and weighed the benefits of getting away from Ramona versus sticking around to see if there might be another set of puzzles to solve.

"This challenge was one of the hardest we've ever done."

It was a woman's voice, and it sounded like she was addressing Rowan, so he turned around.

She was medium height, with shoulder-length curly dark hair and deep brown eyes. When she smiled, the corners of her mouth turned up into curvy little lines. She held out her hand. He thought her face looked a bit familiar, but he couldn't place her. Maybe she was an actor from one of the HBO shows he was currently binge-ing?

"I'm Helena," she said. "Welcome to the party."

"Is this your place?" Rowan asked, although he was pretty sure he knew the answer before he'd asked it.

She nodded politely.

There was something about this woman. It wasn't just that her voice, clothing, and bearing emanated power and wealth. There was more. "Elegant" was the best word to describe her, Rowan thought. She looked like European royalty.

"I trust you're enjoying yourself?" Helena asked as she took a quick glance in Ramona's direction.

Rowan nodded. "It's been fun, thanks." He took a nervous sip of his drink, and once again he was overcome with the feeling that he'd seen this woman somewhere before.

Ramona turned her attention away from the bartender and back to Rowan. "Hi," she said to Helena, sounding surprisingly possessive. "I'm Ramona. I'm a friend of Lilith's."

"Do you mind if I borrow your date for a moment?" Helena asked. "I promise I'll return him. I just want to ask him a few questions about how we might improve our upcoming challenges."

Ramona looked at Helena for a moment and then nodded. "As long as you promise to bring him back in one piece."

"I promise," Helena said as she led Rowan away from the bar.

Rowan followed Helena up a sloped and tightly mowed lawn that reminded him of a golf course putting green. They walked for another minute or so before they reached a low set of gray stone stairs that led up to the front doors of another section of the enormous house.

"Don't worry about your shoes," Helena said as she opened the door and stepped inside, the sharp click of her heels reverberating through the empty space.

Rowan wiped his shoes on the welcome mat before entering the room.

It was a bit smaller than the foyer in the other wing of the estate, but just as anachronistically opulent, with the same white pillars, elaborate moldings, and black-and-white-tiled slate-and-marble floor.

"We're just through there." Helena motioned toward a set of French doors to the right. "In the library."

Rowan followed her through the doors and into another world.

Except for a small fireplace set into a brick wall to the right, all four walls were covered, floor to ceiling, with books on dark wooden shelves. In the center of the room was a circular table large enough to sit at least a dozen people comfortably. Rowan thought the table would be perfect for planning the invasion of a small neighboring country, or playing Dungeons & Dragons, a game Rowan had been obsessed with when he was younger.

This room, with its dim, flickering yellow-brown light and endless walls of books, felt completely different from the rest of the house.

Rowan actually felt comfortable here.

"Please, sit," Helena said as she gestured toward a small black leather sofa set directly in front of the fireplace.

Rowan took a seat, and Helena joined him.

"It's a digital asset called The Orchid and some brand-new kind of cryptocurrency."

"I'm sorry?" Rowan asked.

"The prize." Helena nodded to Rowan's hand.

"Oh, right." Rowan was still holding the USB drive he'd taken from the ball. "Thanks, I can't wait to check it out."

Helena shrugged, as if the entire situation was the most quotidian thing in the world, and then stood up and walked over to a mid-century teak cabinet that had been converted into a small bar.

As he watched her walk across the room, Rowan once again had the feeling that he'd seen her somewhere before.

As if reading his mind, Helena turned and stared at Rowan for a moment, and as she did, an overwhelming sense of connectedness passed over him. And he realized that, ever since he'd stepped into the library, he'd been experiencing something he hadn't felt for as long as he could remember.

Rowan Chess almost felt like he belonged. The distant, disconnected feeling he'd been living with for so long had lifted, just a bit.

Rowan was elated.

Then he remembered where he'd seen her face before. Her name was Helena Worricker. Her father was Hawk Worricker, the man who created WorGames, one of the biggest and most popular video-game and virtual reality companies in the world.

"I'd like to ask you a question," she said, "if you don't mind."

"Of course."

"We're working on something in the desert outside of Las Vegas, a new kind of immersive real-world gaming experience. I was wondering if you might be open to consulting on the puzzle side? You would, of course, be well compensated."

"That sounds interesting," Rowan said, "although I am fairly busy at the moment."

Helena walked over and handed Rowan a gin and tonic, then

clinked his glass with her own. "They say if you really want to get something done, give it to a busy person."

"So they say."

"I'll call you."

"That would be great," Rowan said. "I'd love to hear more." He was busy at work, but he'd drop almost anything to work with Helena Worricker at WorGames. Rowan was fairly well known in his field, but WorGames was the top of the creative mountain as far as immersive gaming experiences went.

This was turning into one hell of a night.

"Great," Helena said. "Oh, and there is one other thing."

"What is it?"

"I'd like to invite you to try something we're working on, a beta test project."

"Does it have something to do with tonight's games?"

"Not at all. It's actually something brand-new. We've been developing some advanced tech through a number of our high-profile Silicon Valley partners. This beta project is a dating app called Find Your Person."

Rowan nodded. That was definitely *not* what he was expecting. "Thank you so much for the offer," he said. "I'm positive your app will be a tremendous success, but I'm afraid I'm finished with online dating."

"And yet here you are," Helena said with a smile.

"I suppose," Rowan said, spinning the glass tumbler between his fingers as he tried to imagine what kind of top secret thing WorGames was working on in the desert outside of Las Vegas.

"I understand your reticence," Helena replied, "but I think you'll find this app is unlike anything else in the space. Find Your Person uses proprietary-algorithm-based software and is absolutely guaranteed to produce results."

"Guaranteed?"

"Yes, or your money back. Of course, you'll be signed up for free." She handed Rowan a small plastic card with a URL and an access code.

"I'll definitely keep this in mind, thank you," Rowan said with every intention of throwing the card away as soon as he could. "Speaking of dates, I should probably go and find mine. I think I'm going to call it a night."

"I understand. And please, think about signing up for the app. You won't regret it. I promise."

"Okay." He nodded.

"It was nice to meet you, Rowan."

It took Rowan ten minutes, but he was eventually able to track down his date. He found her orally servicing the bartender in a stall in the men's bathroom, where he politely informed her that he'd be leaving the party alone.

Later that night, Ramona didn't enter his mind at all. He was too excited about the possibility of working for Helena Worricker. But there were a couple of things Rowan couldn't stop thinking about: He'd never once mentioned his name, or the fact that he'd met his date through an online app.

3

DIMENSIONAL DRIFT
IS A REAL ASSHOLE

EMILY ROLLED DOWN THE WINDOW in an attempt to clear the fog that had started spreading across the windshield. The glass cleared up almost immediately, and the seemingly endless ribbon of asphalt was once again visible, stretching from the front of the truck all the way to the horizon. The sounds of countless tiny bits of gravel pinging and banging against the bottom of the vehicle grew louder as she pressed down on the accelerator.

Emily was in a hurry.

She tried to recall where she'd come from, but all she could remember was driving down the road.

This road.

It looked familiar, but she couldn't quite place it.

In addition to the vague familiarity of the road, Emily had the feeling that she was late for something, but, like everything else, she couldn't remember what that something was.

Where the hell was she going?

As she continued to guide the truck along the road, Emily finally remembered something. There had been a woman. An irritating woman asking questions about Emily's dog.

Ruby.

And her favorite color.

Green.

The radio turned itself on with a bright pop and click, and a loud static buzz filled the interior of the truck. Emily thought she heard a voice somewhere deep within the static, but she couldn't be sure it wasn't just a combination of the noise of the truck, the tires on the road, and the rhythmic crackling of the old speakers.

Emily was about to turn off the radio when the truck's headlights died and the world turned black. She could feel the rumble of the pavement through the soles of her feet as the truck continued to speed forward into the darkness.

Emily pulled her foot off the accelerator and reached for the lever that controlled the headlights, but she was unable to find it, and even though she'd taken her foot off the gas, the truck continued to gain speed. She slammed her foot down, aiming for the brake pedal, but it wasn't there.

Fuck.

She squinted through the windshield, trying to make out the road, but there was nothing but darkness. She did her best to calm herself and keep her hands at ten and two on the wheel, as the old truck continued to accelerate.

The static was so loud that Emily had to fight the urge to yank her hands off the steering wheel to cover her ears. It was at that point, speeding along that country road in complete darkness, that Emily remembered the woman had asked her about something else.

Rabbits.

Why did that sound so familiar?

Emily reached down again, and her hands finally discovered the lever that controlled the lights. She yanked it as hard as she could and the truck's headlights cut through the darkness, once again illuminating the road.

Standing directly in front of the truck, about ten feet away, was a girl.

It was Emily's little sister, Annie.

Emily yanked the steering wheel hard to the right, and the truck flipped.

Broken glass poured into the cab like rain, as the truck flew through the air toward the pavement or the ditch or wherever it was going to land.

And in that moment, flying through the air in the old truck, Emily remembered something.

The people asking her questions had given her a choice. Put a hood over her head or receive an injection.

She chose the hood.

But they'd lied. They put the hood over her head and gave her the injection anyway.

Once again, she tried to remember the last time she'd been there, driving on that road, but her memory was fuzzy. She knew she hadn't been alone. There was somebody beside her, somebody she loved. But no matter how hard she tried, she couldn't make out that person's face.

Then the truck hit the pavement. Everything exploded.

And Emily woke up.

She was at home in her bed.

There was no irritating woman asking questions, no cold metal table, and no man holding a syringe. There was also no sound.

Then, slowly, as if somebody were turning up the volume, the silence inside Emily's head was replaced by the familiar thrum of distant birds and traffic.

She reached for her phone and checked the date.

Fuck.

She looked down at her hands. They were shaking, and she could feel the rest of her body falling into the same state.

They'd kept her for eleven days this time. That was way longer than normal.

She took a few deep breaths, doing her best to slow her heartbeat and steady her nerves, and then, with practiced precision, as if she'd done it a million times before, Emily stood up and made her way to the kitchen, popped out her phone's SIM card, tossed it into the microwave, and pressed Start. Then she grabbed a small backpack from the hall closet, threw in a couple of changes of clothing, some pepper spray, and a taser, and carried the bag into the bathroom. There she packed some toiletries and scissors, then pulled down a wall-mounted space heater to reveal a hidden compartment that contained two dozen or so small USB drives, a scanning wand, a new phone, and a passport.

After running the wand over her entire body to check for any unwanted electronic signals, Emily grabbed everything and set the space heater back in place.

She shuddered at the thought of those people moving around her apartment while she was sleeping. One of those assholes had changed her clothing and tucked her into bed.

Ew.

That flagrant invasion of personal space was upsetting.

They had a name for these invaders. They called them the Rabbits Police, and Emily had been dealing with them ever since she'd slipped into this dimensional stream eighteen months ago.

The last thing Emily remembered before she woke up in this stream was driving down a dark country road with her ex, K, seated beside her. They were traveling the very same road where Emily had lost her sister decades earlier while trying to access a mysterious radio signal connected to Rabbits: The Night Station. But this time, they were driving that road in an attempt to use Rabbits to manipulate an interdimensional repair mechanism—connected to invisible lines of energy known as the Meechum Radiants—in order to try to win the game known as Rabbits, and save the world.

There'd been a flash of light, a deafening sound, and then Emily was no longer driving down that long country road. Suddenly, she was lying in bed in the guest room of her friend Alan Scarpio's minimalist mid-century residence on the lake.

After determining she was alone in the house, Emily switched on an iMac she'd discovered on the dining room table and loaded a Web browser. She needed to find out what the hell had happened. Where was she? Where were K and Scarpio? And what had happened with Rabbits?

It took only a few minutes for Emily to discover that something was wrong.

She typed *Rabbits game* into her search engine and pressed Enter. Nothing but fuzzy bunnies.

Further research had revealed that there was no website at abbeysskirt.com—a Rabbits information site that players used to communicate—and no mention of the list of Rabbits winners, known to players as The Circle.

After a series of unsuccessful online searches for K, Chloe, the Magician's arcade, and the rest, Emily realized that there was only one explanation.

She'd slipped into a different dimensional stream.

It was more than just the lack of Rabbits information online. She was already starting to feel the familiar itch and tickle of a confusing sensation known as dimensional drift.

Soon, some memories of the stream she'd left would fade in order to make room for the reality of the new stream, and Emily would feel untethered and confused.

Dimensional drift was a bitch.

But dimensional drift or not, Emily had never woken up in a world completely devoid of any mention of Rabbits. This was new territory.

Where the hell was Rabbits?

And what had happened in the dimensional stream she'd just left? She was still alive. Did that mean she and K had been successful? Had somebody won the game, and if so, who?

Not every Internet legend or conspiracy blooms into a full-blown mythology. These things need to be constantly watered and, compared to all the other wild online conspiracies out there, the game never seemed to get all that much attention. But, still, Rabbits was a fucking succulent. It seemed to thrive no matter how little water or oxygen it received.

Emily had always been able to find something about the game online, some vague mention in a forum, a handful of posts on the darknet, a sensationalist podcast or two, copies of The Circle, but there was nothing.

It was as if the game had been completely wiped from the world.

Emily tried a couple of breathing exercises.

She always felt unmoored when she slipped streams, and she'd just been through the most intense experience of her entire life.

What had happened to K?

Was the multiverse still in danger of collapsing?

She took another look at her surroundings. She was definitely in Alan Scarpio's house. That was good. Scarpio was a friend, and the fact that she'd woken up in his house was comforting. Now all she needed to do was track him down and ask what the hell was going on.

It was always the same when you slipped streams. Everything had changed, but most of it looked exactly the same. In fact, one of the weirdest parts about dimensional drift was that the more familiar everything looked, the stranger it actually felt.

Emily had no idea where she was, dimensionally speaking, but she felt like the fact that she'd ended up someplace physically familiar had to be a good sign.

Didn't it?

She shut down the computer and took a long shower.

Once she'd finished washing her hair, she closed her eyes, tilted her head back, and did her best to clear her mind as the hot water ran down her body. The scent of eucalyptus and sandalwood coming from a small bag hanging over the showerhead reminded Emily of the month she and K had spent at Scarpio's lake house shortly after their wedding. That scent, along with the familiar décor, helped Emily relax, and by the time she'd finished showering, she was feeling a bit more like herself.

Then Emily stepped out into the hallway and saw a man aiming a silver revolver at her head.

He was five foot ten, Caucasian, with wild, wavy light brown hair. He wore faded jeans, a white button-up shirt, and brown boots. Emily thought he looked tired, like he'd aged at least five years since the last time she'd seen him.

"Jesus Christ, Emily?" Alan Scarpio lowered his gun.

"It's me."

"I thought you were one of them," he said, rushing forward to embrace her.

"One of who?"

"Wait," he said, stopping just short of Emily's outstretched arms. "What's my name?"

Emily stared. "Are you serious?"

He nodded.

"Alan, but you hate that so we call you Scarpio."

He smiled, and the two of them finally embraced. "I am damn happy to see you."

She couldn't remember the last time they'd been in the same room. That was most likely due to dimensional drift, but that didn't matter. She knew that Scarpio was a good friend, and they'd been through some serious shit together.

She was damn happy to see him too.

"How long have you been here?" he asked.

"In your house?"

"No, here, in this stream."

"I think I just arrived," she said.

"When was the last time you saw me?" Scarpio asked.

"I'm not sure, exactly," she said as an image popped into her mind of Alan Scarpio docking a boat. Emily opened her mouth to describe the scene, but realized she had no idea where to place that memory temporally speaking. It could have been days or years ago. She was unable to tether the recollection to any specific time. She shook her head. "Drift is bad at the moment. When's the last time you saw me?"

"Your wedding, maybe? A trip to Hawaii in search of a clue related to the game? A bunch of memories play in my mind like scenes, but when I try to put anything in order, it just gets lost. My head's been a jumbled mess since I landed here."

"Is there anything that I should know about this place?" she asked.

"Dimensional drift is a real asshole here," Scarpio said. "I've been writing things down, which has helped a bit, but you know how it goes."

Emily nodded. She could feel it growing stronger. The familiar disorienting pull of dimensional drift was all around her. The worst part was the constant feeling that she needed to be somewhere else. She knew that it would pass eventually, but that didn't make it any less disconcerting.

"The most alarming thing is the fact that there's no game," Scarpio said. "Rabbits doesn't appear to exist, nothing online, no Magician's arcade, and the people I know who are definitely playing Rabbits in other streams claim to have never heard of it."

"I took a look when I woke up. I couldn't find anything either."

"But it's worse than that."

"How so?"

"A few weeks ago, I stumbled upon something familiar—a path, something I felt might be a way into the game, so I followed it."

"Wait, does that mean Rabbits *does* exist here?"

"Maybe, but I didn't actually find the game."

"What happened?"

"I was captured. They took me in my sleep. I woke up in a warehouse. There were four of them. They kept asking questions. It took me a while to figure out what they knew and what they were looking for. As far as I've been able to determine, they belong to some kind of organization tracking down people they believe are looking into the game. They seem to know about dimensional drift, but they don't call it that."

"I don't get it," Emily said.

"Me either. Yet. I've only been taken twice."

"Twice?"

"I kind of let them kidnap me the second time."

"What happened then?"

"They kept me for two days and let me go. That was just a couple of weeks ago. That's probably why I'm still a bit jumpy."

"This is . . . a lot to take in."

"I stashed some recording devices in my things the second time. They found everything except for a tiny GPS chip that I implanted under my skin, so when I got back here I was able to track my location to a generic building in the warehouse district. When I came back the next day to confront them, the entire building was empty."

"That's weird."

"Yeah, and I mean *completely* empty."

"That doesn't seem possible."

"In a city like Seattle? It's not. So I looked into the building, even contacted somebody about leasing one of the floors. I told them I needed to speak with the owner before pulling the trigger. I jumped through hoops, made dozens of calls, but was never able to track down the registered owner. It looks like it was acquired by a blind trust, which is owned by a numbered corporation in Malaysia, which is in turn owned by a conglomerate in Japan. The only other company I could find connected to these people led me to nothing but a few lines of code in a computer in Bangladesh."

"Is there anything else about this dimensional stream that feels off?" Emily continued. "You know, aside from the fact that the game doesn't appear to exist and there are people who kidnap you for looking into it?"

"Everything else seems familiar—although, like I mentioned, I've been experiencing some serious drift, so I'm not sure if the things I'm remembering are truly native to this stream or not."

"Do you mind if I ask you a couple of questions?" Emily asked.

"Not at all."

"Do you remember visiting the Magician's arcade and asking K for help because you thought something was wrong with the game?"

Scarpio shook his head. "The clearest memory I can come up with of you and K is the two of you at your wedding."

Emily felt a surge of emotion. All of a sudden she and K were dancing on the beach to "The Killing Moon" by Echo & the Bunnymen, the smell of the ocean filled her head, and she could feel the wind in her hair and against her cheek.

Scarpio must have known that Emily was about to burst into tears, because he mercifully changed the subject. "Was there something wrong with Rabbits in the stream you just left?"

"Definitely."

"What happened?"

Emily had told Scarpio her story, how she'd sent K into another dimensional stream in order to stop the man named Crow from potentially destroying the entire multiverse, how Scarpio's asking K for help set off a string of events that led to Emily, K, a man called the Magician, and a woman named Chloe playing the eleventh iteration of Rabbits, and how—with the entire world collapsing around them—Emily and K had traveled to the place where Emily's sister, Annie, had been killed so that they could try to slip dimensional streams to either win or reset the game or both.

"You must have been successful," Scarpio said, "if we're still alive."

Emily nodded, but the untethered feeling remained. She couldn't remember a time when she'd felt this disconnected after slipping dimensions. "Maybe everything's okay," Emily said, "but like you mentioned earlier, there's something off about this stream."

"You feel it too?"

"Big time."

Scarpio leaned back in his chair. "I've found it impossible to think about anything but the game since I landed here."

Emily nodded.

"What are you thinking?"

"I'm feeling like we definitely need to find Rabbits, but can we get something to eat first? I'm fucking starving."

4

FIND YOUR PERSON

Rowan Chess navigated the crowded sidewalk, doing his best to reach the crosswalk before the green numbers counting down to the red light reached ten. After that, he'd have to wait. Ten seconds was barely enough time to make it across a street as wide as 4th Avenue.

Nine seconds.

Shit.

He was going to be late.

He checked the time on his phone. He was on his way to meet a woman for dinner, and he really wanted to make a good first impression.

He'd set up the meeting through Helena Worricker's dating app.

Initially, of course, Rowan had no intention of installing another app. After his recent experiences in that arena, he'd been considering chucking his dating apps entirely. He would just have to meet somebody the old-fashioned way, through friends or at work. But there were at least two major problems with that method. Rowan had very few friends, and his current contracts involved remote communication almost exclusively.

So Rowan decided to give the app a try and swiped right on Eliza, an attractive woman with an interesting profile. He wasn't planning on actually meeting up with anyone, but there was something irresistible about Eliza's profile. It wasn't anything he'd have been able to accurately describe if asked. Maybe he'd mention a kind of knowing, adventurous gleam in her eyes, or the way she appeared to be smiling even though a smile barely registered in the corners of her mouth. But whatever it was, Rowan was intrigued.

The app was called Find Your Person, and it was extremely well designed. The user interface was intuitive and easy to navigate, and the "get to know you" section was fun and comprehensive—even a brief series of strange questions near the end that felt a bit like a personality test from a Scientology textbook were thought-provoking and engaging. He found the entire experience quick and painless—and although he was pretty sure there was no way this app was actually going to help him "find his person," he enjoyed being proactive.

In the beginning, he'd been thrilled with the ease and fleetingly positive results of online dating, but after a few dozen dates—including Hank the cocaine girl and a handful of others—that optimism faded, and Rowan found it increasingly difficult to sit down in front of another stranger and relive his life story, or worse, listen to his date go on about rock climbing, Acro-Yoga, Burning Man, or Machu Picchu.

Still, he needed to try.

Rowan Chess felt like an outsider in his own life.

He really did want to find his person.

"Sorry I'm late," Rowan said as he slipped into a vinyl booth across from his date.

"Two minutes late isn't late."

"Thank you for being so understanding," Rowan said, then took a closer look at Eliza.

In real life, she looked even better than her pictures. She was mixed-race—partly South Asian maybe, although the word "Polynesian" popped into his head for some reason. She was thin, with a round optimistic face, thick, curly black hair, glowing brown skin, and large almond-shaped eyes.

She tucked her hair behind her ear and smiled. "You look just like your pictures."

Rowan believed she was telling the truth. He'd followed the dating site's instructions to the letter. Recent photos, full body, a few different angles. He'd always taken meeting new people very seriously, even as a teenager. He respected other people's time.

They met at a restaurant called Kiruto Choir that Rowan had almost visited a few times but for one reason or another had never actually made it inside. It was nice. He found it a bit formal for a first date, but Eliza had insisted on choosing the venue.

They each started with a glass of wine, then ordered a bottle. The conversation moved from their mutual love of literature (they both really liked Haruki Murakami and Amy Hempel) to music (she loved rap, he was more indie rock), sports, family, the weather, and pretty much everything else. They steered clear of politics and religion, not because they held different views (they actually didn't) but because they found those topics uninteresting.

They discovered they'd both grown up playing games (she'd been in backgammon club, he was into tabletop role-playing and video-games), and although each of them had cultivated at least one close friendship over the years, they'd both grown up as thoughtful loners.

After a series of adventurous seafood appetizers, the two of them sat together in comfortable silence as their server refilled their wine glasses. Rowan couldn't remember the last time he'd actually felt relaxed having a conversation with anyone.

They shared a toast to the future of mankind, even though seconds earlier they'd both agreed that the human race was almost certainly doomed, and then Eliza stared at Rowan for a long moment.

"I'm going to suggest something a bit . . . radical," she said, finally.

"Um . . . okay. Sure." Rowan couldn't stop smiling.

"It's actually a time-saving device."

"How does that work?"

"You need to tell me something."

"What?"

"Let's say I end up faced with both you and your evil twin on a rooftop somewhere. I'm going to need to know which one of you is the real you."

"Wow."

She smiled. "What?"

Rowan found himself speaking before he had time to think. "You're amazing," he blurted out, and he meant it. He'd been in this woman's presence for less than half an hour and he was already falling for her. Maybe Helena Worricker's dating app's algorithm was actually as good as advertised.

"You're right. I am amazing. Thank you very much. Now, I have to pee, and you've got a lot to think about." She winked, then stood up.

Rowan watched, transfixed, as she made her way to the bathrooms at the back of the restaurant. He thought he'd never seen anybody move so gracefully in his life.

As he watched the bathroom hallway, waiting for her return, he considered what he might be able to tell her that she could use to tell the real Rowan apart from his evil twin, but he was having trouble. This was because Rowan had felt out of place for as long as he could remember.

In his mind, he *was* the evil twin.

Maybe he should tell her how to identify *him* in order to continue her relationship with the other Rowan. Maybe that other Rowan would feel like he actually belonged in the world.

He eventually came up with something. He'd suggest that he and Eliza each come up with a unique phrase—something that they could use to trick their evil twins into revealing themselves. Something that only the two of them would know.

"Your pancakes are ready" was the phrase he came up with. He smiled at the thought of her face when he eventually said it. He knew she'd laugh.

He knew that she'd get it.

Rowan continued to stare at the small hallway that led to the bathrooms at the back. It had been at least ten minutes. She was probably touching up her makeup or something, but whatever she was doing, it did seem to be taking a long time. Rowan took a sip of wine and continued to watch the entrance to the bathroom area.

No sign of Eliza.

After twenty minutes or so, Rowan stood up and made his way to the back of the restaurant. He thought about sending a text, but didn't want to embarrass her. They'd just met, and he really didn't want to do anything that might jeopardize the possibility of a second date. He'd spent most of the past twenty minutes trying to formulate a plan to make sure he'd be able to see her again. He wasn't willing to entertain the idea that she'd taken off due to lack of interest. They definitely had a connection. There was no mistaking it.

"Hello?" He knocked gently on the door to the ladies' room.

No answer.

Rowan knocked again, then carefully pushed the door open.

There was nobody standing in front of the sinks, and there was no other door. The room, which appeared to be completely empty, was still and quiet. Rowan bent down so he could see under all four stalls.

No feet.

"Eliza?" he called.

No answer.

He stepped out and moved across the hall into the men's bathroom, which was completely empty as well. Again he called out Eliza's name, and again there was no response.

He examined the small hallway. There were no emergency exits. Just the two bathroom doors.

Rowan had been looking in that direction the entire time. Unless she'd sprinted away when he glanced down to check the time on his phone, or she'd climbed out a window, it was extremely unlikely she could have left the room without him noticing.

What the hell was going on?

Rowan rushed back into the restaurant proper and bumped into one of the servers. He grabbed the young man's shoulder to stop the two of them from falling over.

"My . . . date is gone," Rowan said.

"I'm not sure I understand," the server replied.

"She went into the bathroom, and now she's not there."

"And you've looked in both restrooms?"

"Yes."

"She probably just stepped outside for a moment. I'm sure she'll be right back. Would you like me to check?"

"I was *watching* this hallway," Rowan said, confused.

He shook his head and went back into the ladies' room, where he once again called Eliza's name. Again, no response.

He went through the stalls and pushed open the doors, one by one.

There was nobody else in the bathroom, but Rowan did find something in the final stall that he checked.

Somebody had written something on the back of the door in thick red lipstick. It was a simple four-word message.

The Door Is Open.

5

I WAS REALLY LOOKING FORWARD TO THE CEVICHE

EMILY STEPPED OUT of her apartment building wearing a black café racer–style motorcycle jacket and faded jeans, and took a final look around. Then, she slung the backpack over her shoulder, slipped on some mirrored aviator sunglasses, and jogged across the street to the apartment building directly opposite her own, where she used a key card to open the parking garage. As soon as the gate started to rise, Emily bent down and slid inside.

The garage was small. Inside were a dozen or so cars, a rack of mountain bikes, an old Vespa, and a motorcycle covered with a gray tarp. Emily walked straight over to the motorcycle and lifted the tarp to reveal a silver Triumph Street Twin. She tossed the tarp to the ground, pulled a helmet from beneath the seat, hopped onto the bike, and started the engine.

Emily expertly guided the motorcycle through the city, checking her rearview mirror every once in a while for followers. She lost the first car five minutes after leaving her building, and the second when she illegally cut through a residential park using a narrow bike path. She didn't think there were any others, but she needed to be sure. She sped up as she switched lanes and started moving across the bridge that would eventually lead her to the water.

The air was cool and tasted like it was about to rain.

The weather in the Pacific Northwest wasn't all that great for motorcycles in general, but late at night, when the roads were clear and dry, there was nothing Emily loved more than speeding through nocturnal Seattle.

Finally certain that she wasn't being followed, Emily did her best to forget everything that she'd just been through, the kidnapping, the questions, and the rest of it, and simply focus on the wind, the pavement, and the power of movement.

She was in complete control; the shaky feeling from earlier was gone.

She never wanted to stop riding.

After traveling east for about fifteen minutes, she turned down Lake Washington Boulevard and drove south along the water for a mile and a half before she eventually guided the motorcycle off the road and into a small carport.

She parked the bike, covered it with a nearby dark green tarp, then stepped onto a conveyor belt sidewalk that took her up to a small white concrete structure. Inside was an elevator. There was no call button, but Emily kneeled and flipped a hidden switch located beneath one of the rocks next to the pathway.

The elevator doors opened.

After a brief ride up, Emily stepped out of the elevator into Scarpio's lakeside house.

Huge floor-to-ceiling windows provided an incredible view of the lake. The entire space was elegantly furnished with all of the staples of mid-century design: cork floor, Florence Knoll sofa, Eames lounge chair, and all the rest.

If you had a mid-century modern bingo card, all your spaces would be covered.

Emily kicked off her shoes and moved into the kitchen, where she opened a double-wide Thermador fridge filled to capacity with fresh food and drinks. Whoever had stocked it had done so recently and had spared no expense—and left no room.

"Are you fucking kidding me? Heineken?" she said as she pulled out a bottle.

"I told them to pick up some Corona."

Emily closed the door of the fridge to reveal the man who'd spoken.

"Thank fuck you're here," she said as she rushed forward to hug Alan Scarpio.

"Where the hell else would I be? I've been waiting for you. I was worried."

"They took me for a long time," she said, finally breaking the embrace.

"Eleven days," he said, his eyes wide with worry. "Are you okay?"

She nodded, but she was still pretty fucking far from okay. Her body continued to vibrate beneath her skin in a way that made Emily feel exposed. It was as if a type of invisible confidence and protection she'd taken for granted had suddenly vanished.

She'd be fine, but it was going to take a bit of time.

"They're getting bolder," Scarpio said as he reached down into the fridge and pulled out a Corona. He twisted off the cap and handed the bottle to Emily, along with a precut slice of lime from a bowl in the crisper. Then he took the Heineken from her other hand and opened it with a fizzy click.

"Thank god," Emily said, pushing the lime into the bottle with practiced precision.

"Cheers," he said, gently tapping Emily's beer with his own.

Emily smiled and the two of them drank.

"How do you feel?" Scarpio asked as he sat down beside her at the dining room table.

"I woke up pretty rough, but I'm starting to feel a bit better."

"Your apartment?"

"Burned. Stripped clean," Emily said. She pulled her passport and all of the USB drives out of her pockets and set them on the table.

"What are those?"

"Crypto."

"You know, if you need money, it's yours—always."

"That's great, but what if something happens to you?"

"I'm careful."

"Yeah, well, sometimes shit happens that even you can't control."

She grabbed a couple of the USB drives and slipped them into her pocket. "Do you have a safe?"

"There's one in the guest bedroom," he said. "It's hidden behind the Cecily Brown print. You just have to set the combination."

"Cool."

"I'd like to show you something."

"Now?"

"Are you hungry?"

"I'm fucking starving." Emily stood up and drained her beer. "Five-minute shower."

Scarpio smiled. "Take your time."

"Thanks."

"I had them pick up a bunch of clothes. It's all your size."

"You don't think your picking out clothing for a woman might look suspicious?"

"Not at all. I may have had a few houseguests recently that wear the same size."

"Gross."

"Please hurry up," Scarpio said. "I'm fucking starving as well."

"So." Scarpio leaned forward in his chair. "Did you learn anything new this time?"

The two of them sat across from each other in a dimly lit restaurant. There were a half dozen or so low wooden tables set directly below beautiful green living gardens hung high on polished concrete walls. Tasteful rice paper and bamboo accents lent the place a distinctly Japanese flavor.

"Just like before, it was mostly new faces," Emily said. "The primary examiner was a woman this time, although there was a man in the room for a while as well. Him I remember, but she was new. There were a few others. I'll record their descriptions in the ledger as soon as we get back to the house."

"Good," he said, and then added, "Are you sure you're okay?"

Emily nodded.

"But, Jesus Christ, eleven days."

"The questions were the hardest. This time they treated every single day like it was the first. I almost fucked up a few times."

"I don't know how you managed it."

"Next time, I think I should stop pretending and just tell them the truth."

"You're not going back in," Scarpio said. "No way."

"We just need to find somebody in charge and get them to tell us why they're doing this shit."

"Did they refer to the game?"

"Yes. And this time the woman actually called it Rabbits."

"Shit. That's new."

"These people are our only real lead. We have to go back in."

He shook his head. "That is *such* a bad idea."

Emily was about to protest again, but Scarpio was probably right. Something felt different this time, scarier. From what she could re-member, the accommodations themselves were fine, almost pleas-ant, but if she ended up back in that interrogation room, she wasn't sure she'd be able to keep it together. But worse than that, if she was taken again, she had the distinct feeling that they might not let her go. She took a sip of wine, and changed the subject. "So, what the hell did you get up to while I was away?"

Scarpio grinned. "I got a flat tire."

"Doesn't your super-secret prototype SUV have special tires that don't lose air or something?"

"I was driving the Corvette."

"The midlife crisis?"

"How dare you."

"So sad."

"It's one of a kind and I'll never get rid of it."

Emily shook her head.

"Anyway, I got a flat and pulled over to the curb. I was right in front of the big thrift store—you know, the one near Pioneer Square?"

"I know it well."

"So, I go inside to kill some time while I'm waiting for my me-chanic to show up. I'm flipping through some vinyl when I look over and see a drawer filled with old cassette tapes."

"Cassettes are back. They sell them at Urban Outfitters."

"Right, but not these. Most of these were mix tapes and home recordings—you know, with handwritten song lists and band names?"

"I do. I still have a bunch of mix tapes from the early nineties."

"Well, here's where things get a bit strange." Scarpio reached into his jacket pocket, pulled out a cassette tape case, and set it down on the table in front of Emily. "I made this when I was in college."

"What is it?"

"It's genius."

Emily looked over the track listing. "Liz Phair, Pavement, Wilco, Queen, Guided by Voices . . . Who the hell is Saturnhead?"

"They were Canadian. It took me all day to come up with this masterpiece."

"I don't get it. Why are you showing me a mix tape from your misspent youth?"

"Because this tape was stolen from my mother's car twenty-five years ago."

"What?" Emily sat up straight and took a closer look at the cassette.

"Yeah, so imagine how surprised I was to see it just sitting there among all of those other tapes in the thrift store."

"That's quite a coincidence."

"Isn't it? And look at this." He pointed to the final song on side two. It was a track called "Play the Game" by Queen.

"Holy shit. Was there anything else?"

"Not at first, but later that night I ended up going out for dinner with a friend. We came to this place, and I sat exactly where you're sitting now."

"Suddenly I don't feel so special."

"You will in a minute," Scarpio said. "I asked them to have this curtain closed when we arrived, so you wouldn't be able to see outside."

"Okay . . ."

Scarpio reached across the table and pulled back the curtain.

The sounds of downtown Seattle—just background noise before—

were now paired with their visual counterparts. Passing headlights matched the low sonic ebb and flow of car engines, horns and distant voices became an ambient soundtrack. Everything was suddenly more alive and immediate.

But there was something else.

Directly in front of Emily, visible through the window, was an enormous gray concrete office tower with green-tinted glass. Suspended on the side of the building was one of those billboards that took up the entire wall—the kind of thing you'd see on Sunset Boulevard in Los Angeles. It was a collaboration between Seattle's most popular sports team and the biggest sports apparel company in the world. The image featured a quarterback, in silhouette, getting ready to throw the ball. Visible, in huge red letters underneath him, was the apparel company's brand-new slogan: PLAY THE GAME.

"What do you think?" Scarpio asked.

"That's pretty wild," Emily said. "But the magical phrase that normally kicks off Rabbits is 'The Door Is Open,' not 'Play the Game.' That billboard probably doesn't mean much of anything."

"You really believe that?"

"Sometimes it's important to remember that both coincidence and confirmation bias do actually exist," she added.

"I'm not sure this can be tossed off as confirmation bias."

"Me either—at least, not all of it. That cassette tape showing up definitely feels significant."

"I think so as well."

The two of them were examining their menus when the sounds of numerous, simultaneous text alerts broke the silence. It sounded like every single patron had received a text message at almost exactly the same time.

Emily and Scarpio jumped as their phones beeped and vibrated on the table.

"That's weird," she said, picking up her phone. "It's a spam message from someplace called Agatha's Used Furniture."

"I got the same one."

"So did everybody in the restaurant, apparently."

"Do you still think that billboard is a coincidence?"

Emily was starting to come around to Scarpio's point of view on the billboard and everything else. This many strange events all at once was highly implausible.

At that point, a man rushed out of a hallway near the back of the restaurant and grabbed the shoulder of the closest server.

The man was tall with dark brown hair and wild eyes that were filled with what looked to Emily like existential panic. "My . . . date is gone," he said.

"I'm not sure I understand," the server replied.

"She went into the bathroom, and now she's not there."

"And you've looked in both restrooms?"

"Yes."

"She probably just stepped outside for a moment. I'm sure she'll be right back. Would you like me to check?"

"I was *watching* this hallway," he said.

"What the fuck is Agatha's Used Furniture?" a nearby woman exclaimed as she picked up her phone and handed it to her date.

"Shit," Emily said. "This isn't good."

"Let's go." Scarpio stood up, almost knocking a glass of water to the floor. "They'll be here any second."

"You really don't think we should follow them one more time?"

"No. You just did eleven days. We're not going back."

Scarpio was right. No matter how much she wanted to find out who those people were, the part of her that she'd need to access in order to make it through another round of kidnapping was completely exhausted.

"Shit," she said. "I was really looking forward to the ceviche."

"If we make it out of here, we'll find some."

"Promise?" Emily stood up.

"I promise. Let's split up and meet at the market."

Scarpio rushed through the crowded tables toward the main entrance, while Emily took off in the direction of two wide swinging doors that led to the kitchen. On her way, she slapped a small adhesive camera on the mantel of the fake fireplace.

"She was right here," the man who'd lost his date exclaimed, shaking his head, as she passed him. "There's no way a person can just vanish, is there?"

Emily thought about that man as she made her way through the kitchen toward a small neon green exit sign located above a metal door on the far wall.

She knew what it was like to have somebody just disappear and never come back.

It fucking sucked.

6

SCOTT 5

EMILY CONNORS WAS TWENTY YEARS OLD when her parents were killed by an avalanche while skiing in the French Alps. Her younger sister, Annie, had died three years earlier in a car accident, which meant that Emily no longer had any immediate family.

She hadn't been close with any of her aunts and uncles, and although she almost always remembered to send her cousin Zoe a Christmas present, Emily felt like having a family was part of an earlier life.

In her new world, Emily was completely alone.

She'd inherited a bit of money from her parents' passing, which she used to pay for the rest of her tuition and living expenses at UCLA, but that money didn't last very long.

Emily had been excited to make a new start in Los Angeles, and she'd immediately fallen in love with the spirit of the people. Their carefree California attitude was a refreshing change from the dark seriousness that ran through the heart of the Pacific Northwest. But she'd had a hard time focusing on her studies in the midst of all the change, and eventually, the hidden layer of insincerity running rampant beneath the cloying optimism of Los Angeles—not to mention the relentless, glorious sunshine—took its toll.

And Emily found herself missing the rain.

She dropped out of school just a few credits shy of a degree and spent the last of her savings on her dream car, a 1977 International Harvester Scout. There was nothing left for her in Lakewood, so

Emily drove the Harvester Scout from Los Angeles up to Seattle, where it died a few weeks later.

Emily took a job at an independent record store and rented a large one-bedroom apartment in the Coryell Court apartment building in Capitol Hill with another girl who worked at the store, Monisha Sidhu. The apartment complex's claim to fame was the fact that it had been the location where Cameron Crowe filmed *Singles,* a classic 1992 grunge rom-com that would provide the inspiration for a very popular television show called *Friends*. Monisha was an aspiring chef with an amazing wardrobe, so Emily ate gourmet meals at home and had somebody cool and creative to get dressed up and explore the city with.

It was an incredibly energizing time. Emily's work days were long but filled with hours of amazing music, and the late nights spent running around Seattle with Monisha were some of the most carefree moments Emily could remember.

But like everything else in her life, it didn't last.

Emily had been living in Seattle for six months when she encountered the anomaly that would drag her back into a world she thought she'd left behind forever after her sister's death.

It was an album called *Scott 5* by an English singer-songwriter.

"Do you have any Scott Walker?" The woman's voice was kind of husky—not deep exactly, just a slight rasp around the edges. She was in her mid- to late-twenties, maybe a few years older than Emily. She wore low-rise dark blue jeans with a brown leather belt buckled along her hip rather than in front. On her feet, a ripped-up pair of black-and-white-checked Vans were minutes away from falling apart, and a faded leather camera case hung loose over her shoulder. Curly light brown hair popped out around the edges of a fauxhemian furry cap, and a peace sign on a thick leather strap dangled over a wolf-howling-at-the-moon T-shirt that she wore beneath an almost-too-small black leather biker jacket.

"Scott Walker is under W in Pop and Rock, right before the Walker Brothers. I think we have pretty much everything," Emily replied.

"We'll see," the woman said with a wink that left one lone bright gray eye sparkling under the pale fluorescent light.

Emily watched the woman make her way over to that section of the store. The look in her eyes and the way she moved reminded Emily of something. It took her a few seconds to come up with it, but she eventually figured it out.

She reminded Emily of a shark.

Emily had been watching a TV show called *Apex Predators* that morning, and there was something about the way sharks slid through water. This woman moved like she was looking for food or maybe some shiny hidden treasure near the bottom of the ocean, not obscure English chamber rock from the 1960s in a middle-of-the-road record store in Seattle.

"You don't have *Scott 5*," the woman called out from the W section.

Emily went over to help.

"There's no Scott Walker album called *Scott 5*," Emily said, "You're probably thinking of *'Til the Band Comes In*. That's the album he released after *Scott 4*."

Emily had become a fan of Scott Walker—and his four numbered albums in particular—after learning that Radiohead, David Bowie, and Pulp all referenced those albums as key musical influences.

"No, I'm talking about *Scott 5*, the album that opens with 'The Logic of Despair.'"

"I've never heard of it," Emily said.

"He's wearing sunglasses in a field of flowers on the cover. It was released in 1970."

"I don't remember seeing that one." Emily knew that album didn't exist, but she kept the condescension from her voice. She liked this woman.

"Which I don't get, because you've clearly heard of Scott Walker."

"I'm a big fan, actually," Emily replied. "But I think you might be confused about the title, maybe it's something else?"

The woman bit her lip and stared at Emily for a moment. Emily had the feeling she was sizing her up for some reason.

"You're right," she said eventually. "I think it probably is something else. My name is Pepper."

"Emily."

"Thanks for the help."

"Anytime."

The two women stood facing each other for a moment. Emily thought Pepper was just about the coolest name she'd ever heard in real life.

"Where the hell do you keep Elvis?" a lady called out from the next aisle, breaking the spell. "There's nothing under E."

"Costello is under C, Presley under P," Emily replied.

"I didn't ask for Abbott and Costello," the lady replied.

"You should probably attend to that moron," Pepper said.

Emily smiled and then walked over to help the lady track down her Elvis. As she approached the Elvis lady, Emily could see Pepper in her peripheral vision. She'd just pulled out a sparkly pink phone and was making a call.

"Elvis should be under E," the woman said as Emily arrived to help.

Emily politely ignored the woman as she led her over to the P section.

"Yeah," Pepper said into her phone, "they don't have *Scott 5* either. I think we're on the right path."

Emily focused her attention on the sound of Pepper's voice, which was louder and clearer now that the Matthew Sweet album Emily had put on earlier was between tracks.

"I think it's Rabbits."

Emily momentarily forgot how to breathe.

The Elvis lady was flipping through records and complaining about something related to parking at the back of the store when Emily walked away from her mid-sentence and returned to Pepper, who was now standing beneath a huge Amy Winehouse poster near the store's entrance.

"I'm sorry, did you just say Rabbits?" Emily asked.

Pepper stared at her for a moment, then shifted her weight to her back hip and crossed her arms, still holding her phone. "Maybe."

"It just seems like a strange thing to say about a Scott Walker album."

"Does it?" Pepper stared at Emily with a look that felt like a challenge.

Emily shook her head. "Never mind, I thought maybe you were talking about something else."

Emily turned and headed back to try to patch things up with the Elvis lady, when Pepper's voice rose from the other side of the store.

"What if I *was* talking about something else?" Pepper said.

Emily turned back around. "Were you?"

"How about you tell me."

"Were you talking about Rabbits, the game?"

Pepper smiled. "Well, holy shit."

"What?"

Pepper spoke into the phone. "I think we may have found another one."

"You wanna get a coffee or something?" Emily asked.

"Oh," Pepper said as she hung up the phone, "I think definitely something."

Emily hadn't thought about Rabbits for a long time, but when she overheard Pepper mention it, she was right back in that truck with Annie and a tagalong family friend named K, driving down a pitch-black country road on the night of the accident that took her sister's life.

Emily had discovered her parents' secret basement office while looking for Christmas presents when she was a kid. It wasn't that Emily didn't like surprises; it's just that she liked hunting for hidden gifts a whole lot more. And besides, if her parents weren't going to go through the effort of properly stashing her gifts in the days leading up to Christmas, wasn't it their fault if Emily figured out where everything was kept?

One day, while searching behind the old tiki bar in the basement for hidden gifts, she found something else. One of the tiles on the floor was slightly loose and a bit darker than the others. Emily lifted it up and discovered a small, dark green metal lever. She pulled the lever and half of the wicker-and-mirror panel that made up the wall behind the bar popped out with a muted click.

After double-checking that her parents weren't home, Emily carefully opened the section of the mirrored panel that had popped open—which, as it turned out, was the hidden door to a small office.

Inside the office, which was about eight or nine feet square, was a blue iMac computer on a desk, a half-sized bookshelf overflowing with novels and games, a small filing cabinet, and a corkboard covered with scraps of documents, photographs, stickers, and other seemingly unrelated material. It reminded Emily of a much smaller version of her English teacher's office at the high school—but this was way better.

This was a secret forbidden space.

Emily loved it.

She started spending time in the hidden office behind the tiki bar.

She'd run down and slip inside while her parents were out and her sister, Annie, was upstairs, reading or playing videogames. And she'd sometimes use the space to hide from Annie and her friends, who were always bugging Emily to tell them about boys or help them apply makeup.

But Emily was never able to figure out why the secret office was there. As far as she could tell, outside of a couple of shuffled books and papers and the occasional repositioning of a chair, the contents never really changed.

The most interesting things Emily discovered were a stack of old 8mm films and a pile of research documents that appeared to be tied to sleep studies and behavioral pattern analysis at somewhere called the Gatewick Institute. She tried to dig up some information on Gatewick using the computers at school, but it looked like it had been shut down years before Emily's family had moved into the house.

So why the secrecy?

Emily felt like the hidden office gave her parents an aura of mystery and intrigue, but she couldn't figure out why they kept it from her and Annie. The material in there was interesting, but not all that exciting—at least not in the eyes of a teenage girl—so, after a while, Emily stopped spending time down there.

One morning, a few months after the last time Emily had visited the hidden office, she heard noises coming from the basement. It sounded like 8-bit audio from a children's toy. When Emily went downstairs to check it out, she discovered that the sounds were coming from behind the tiki bar.

Emily's parents and sister were out horseback riding, so Emily opened the door and stepped into the hidden office.

She immediately noticed something had changed.

There were two identical medium-sized grayish-brown plastic robots on the desk, and another one lying on the floor. Each of the robots had a sticker with the name 2xl above a pair of red eyes. The robot on the floor was responsible for the noise. It was talking, repeating the phrase "Please follow all of my instructions. It is important." The message appeared to be coming from an 8-track cassette tape that had been shoved into a slot near the robot's base.

Emily lifted the robot from the floor, pulled the 8-track tape out just enough to stop the thing from making noise, and placed it in between the two others on the desk. She was about to leave, when she noticed something else that hadn't been there before, a powder blue file folder titled: RABBITS GAME.

Inside that folder were dozens of printed documents—mainly photocopies of things like catalogs, take-out menus, photographs, and other seemingly random material.

Emily had no idea what her parents were doing with those plastic robots, but it was the contents of the folder that grabbed Emily's attention. That folder felt different from anything she had ever found in the office.

It felt exciting.

Most of the stuff in the folder was concerned with things labeled ANOMALIES. For example, in four seemingly identical menus for the same Chinese restaurant, item number 62 had been circled in red felt marker. In three of the menus, number 62 was Chicken Chow Mein, but in one it was Kung Pao Shrimp.

In addition, there was an ad for two Hot Wheels cars with a printed letter from Mattel paperclipped to the ad indicating that those two particular toy cars had never been officially produced, and a pair of photographs featuring the same rather famous English spy novel with identical cover images but two different titles.

A one-word question had been written, in blue ink, just below the photographs of the novels.

Rabbits?

Emily was intrigued.

What the hell was Rabbits?

That question would lead her into a world of half clues and blind alleys, culminating in Emily joining an online bulletin board group dedicated to exploring bizarre Internet mysteries.

Although online mysteries wouldn't really come into their own until things like Cicada 3301 and Webdriver Torso more than a decade later, a series of messages posted to Usenet in 1996, known as the Markovian Parallax Denigrate—and Publius Enigma, a mystery connected to the band Pink Floyd—were keeping amateur online detectives busy when Emily had joined up looking for information about a game called Rabbits.

Emily posted a question to the Publius Enigma newsgroup a couple of days after joining, asking if anybody had heard about a mysterious game called Rabbits. A few people replied looking for more details, but nobody appeared to know what she was talking about. Eventually Emily gave up and stopped logging in to that bulletin board to check if anyone had answered her question.

She'd forgotten all about the bulletin board and the mysterious game known as Rabbits until a couple of months later, when she received an email from somebody calling themselves Pretzel. Pretzel's email to Emily read:

TO: EmandEm@yahoo.com
FROM: Pretzel@aol.com
SUBJECT: Down the RH

Rabbits is real. There's a documentary called *The Last of the Wild.* I've been searching for almost a year, but have been unable to find a copy. Apparently, that movie includes the key to finding something called The Night Station, which is supposed to provide a clue to the location of the game.

Rabbits was back.

Emily immediately began working to track down that film.

It took about a month of research, but she eventually found somebody who claimed to have seen it. That person pointed Emily to a flea market on Bainbridge Island, where she found a high school yearbook. The yearbook led her to somebody who had allegedly digitized a version of an 8mm film print of that documentary.

The person who eventually gave Emily a digitized copy of a portion of the film was named Robert Walton. He told Emily that he believed government agencies used the game to attract secret agents, and that the prize for winning was millions or billions of dollars, but playing Rabbits had become incredibly dangerous and she should stop looking into the game immediately. When she asked him why, he said that the person who'd secured the 8mm print of the movie had disappeared shortly after sending it to Robert, and that other people had gone missing under bizarre circumstances as well.

But Emily ignored Robert's warnings.

She was on a quest.

If Emily had known how everything was going to turn out, she would have heeded those warnings—or at the very least taken a few more precautions before diving in. But at the time, all she could see was the mystery.

And she wanted more.

Somewhere out there, a strange radio signal known as The Night Station was broadcasting secrets on an unknown frequency about a game unofficially called Rabbits—a game with prizes rumored to include millions of dollars, a job with the CIA or FBI, or perhaps even the secrets of eternal life itself.

Emily's need to unravel this mystery eventually led her to a lonely country road where she would finally figure out how to tune in to The Night Station.

It was there, speeding along that long road in the dark, that Emily's obsession with the game called Rabbits would claim its first victim. Emily's quest to uncover the secrets of The Night Station led directly to the accident that took her sister's life.

Annie's death was something Emily would never be able to get over.

After the accident, Emily Connors didn't think about Rabbits for a long time.

But the game came rushing back into her life when a woman named Pepper Prince dragged her from that record store in Seattle into a world of hidden secrets, unbelievable coincidences, and—if you happened to be a believer in those kinds of things—perhaps even other-dimensional planes of existence.

7

IS THIS A HACKER THING?

"Eliza Brand." Rowan spoke slowly into the phone. "I can send you her phone number and picture from the dating app, if you'd like. I'll just need an email address."

"Let me just confirm a few details first." The woman's voice on the other end of the line was professional, but there was a perceptible impatience to her tone that indicated to Rowan she believed she had more important shit to deal with.

"Are you going to file a missing persons case?" Rowan asked.

"You're saying that she disappeared from the restaurant while you were on a first date?"

"Yes."

"I'm going to be honest with you, Mr. Chess."

"Rowan, please."

"A missing persons report is normally something filed by close friends or family."

"She entered the bathroom and never came out."

"I understand, and that's what I've written on my report."

"Okay."

"Now, just to make sure I have this right, you're saying there was no other door, no fire exit or anything this Eliza could have used to leave the building without you seeing her?"

"That's correct."

"Okay, then. If you could just send the photograph and phone number you mentioned, along with screen captures of any interactions between you and this woman, to the following email address,

I'll open an incident report and attach that information." She dictated the address, and Rowan scribbled it down while flipping through his phone.

He'd only exchanged a couple of cursory messages with Eliza on the app before they shared their phone numbers and switched to text messaging. He didn't think those brief messages would be much help, but he opened the app to take a screen capture of them anyway.

There was nothing there.

What the hell was going on? Did the application auto-delete messages after people met in real life? Was it some kind of error?

"Mr. Chess? Are you still there?"

"What about the message in the stall?" Rowan asked.

"The door is open?"

"Yes. Does that mean anything to you?"

"I'm afraid not."

"Are you sure you don't need me to send you anything else?"

"We have your contact information, Mr. Chess. If Eliza's friends or family report anything, we have a really strong starting point for any missing persons investigation."

Rowan could tell that this woman believed Eliza had simply changed her mind and taken off in the middle of their date, but that's not what had happened.

They had been really hitting it off.

Rowan hadn't felt a connection like that for a long time, and he knew that Eliza had felt it too. Although he had to admit that it was *technically* possible that she could have slipped out while he was looking down at his phone or glancing around the restaurant, he knew that wasn't the case.

Something had happened.

But what?

"Mr. Chess?"

"Thank you for your time," Rowan said, and hung up.

The next morning at work, Rowan couldn't concentrate.

He kept getting distracted and found himself staring through the window. The sky was overcast, but the sun had managed to find its way through a triangular section of clouds directly above his building, warming the wet pavement in front of Rowan's office and lighting up the passing cars.

Rowan had a preliminary design presentation due for a new project he was working on—a vertical theme park in Macao related to a popular manga series called *Cowboy SpaceMan*. But he was having a hard time coming up with a central unifying idea for the park—something he could use to both ground and inspire his imagination. His last large-scale project had been spider-themed, and Rowan structured everything around the number eight. As the centerpiece of that park, Rowan had designed one of the biggest and longest amusement park rides in the world: a roller coaster just under two miles long called the Circle Eight. He won multiple design awards and wide acclaim within his field for both the simplicity of that ride's design and the way he had perfectly integrated it into the overall design of the park.

Rowan had moved from middle-of-the-road designer to theme park superstar. But now he was stuck, and he was finding it increasingly difficult to focus on cowboys or spacemen or roller coasters. The only thing on his mind as he stared out the window was Eliza Brand and the connection he'd felt with her.

Before he knew he was doing it, Rowan grabbed his jacket.

As he approached the door, a thirtysomething wide-hipped blond woman with bright red lipstick poked her head out from the back room. "You headed out for lunch?" she asked. This was Rowan's assistant, Valentine.

"I'm going to take off for the day," he said.

"Cool," she said. "You want me to stick around?"

"No need. I'll text you if anything comes up."

"I sent an updated itinerary for the panel in Hong Kong, and the *Cowboy SpaceMan* creative meetings got moved around a little, but it's all in your schedule."

"Thanks," Rowan said.

He stepped outside and pulled up the collar of his jacket.

He thought about walking home, but it was pouring again, and a hard wind was driving the rain straight into Rowan's face. He moved back under the awning above the doors to his office and shook the wet from his hair.

He watched as a young couple ran across the street beneath the almost entirely ceremonial cover of a newspaper and ducked into the coffee shop. Rowan smiled at the familiar scenario. He'd seen that scene played out countless times before. This was his neighborhood. This was where he felt safe and in control.

Rowan had leased the Pine Street office in Capitol Hill more than ten years ago, right out of college. It had taken all of his savings at the time, but he'd always believed in having a place for work that was separate from home. He thought this idea probably came from something his father had told him once, but Rowan had never been able to remember what that something was. His memories of his parents were opaque.

He could remember certain large signposts, and every once in a while he'd lean into an area that triggered an emotional response, but the actual events of his early life felt like half-remembered movies starring people he barely recognized. The stars of these movies looked exactly like his family, but something was off. They felt like strangers. Rowan had spoken with a few psychiatrists over the years, and they'd all assured him that this fading-memory issue was nothing to worry about, that it happened to a larger percentage of the population than Rowan might think.

The office was a medium-sized open industrial space on the ground floor of the Engine Three building, a gray concrete-and-glass three-story former candy factory. Rowan probably should have let the lease lapse ages ago, but for some reason he kept renewing it. He could afford a much nicer place—something newer in a more practical part of town—but he'd never been able to let it go. There was just something about the place that felt like home. More than the apartment he'd lived in for the past six years, or his parents' house in Bellingham, for Rowan, his office was a kind of spiritual sanctuary.

Rowan pulled out his phone to call an Uber, but he ended up

dialing Eliza's number instead. He'd only called her five or six times since her disappearance. He was torn between looking like some kind of crazy stalker and trying to figure out what had happened.

But none of that mattered anymore.

Eliza's number was out of service.

Rowan turned around and made his way back into the office.

"Hey, did you miss me?" Valentine said.

"Do you have a sec?"

"I work for you."

"This isn't exactly a work thing."

"What's up?"

"Do you talk to your ex these days?"

"Far too often. Why?"

"Do you think she might be interested in a job?"

"You looking to design a new website or app or something?"

"Not exactly."

"What would she be doing?"

Rowan didn't say anything.

"Is this a hacker thing?"

"Kind of. Is Lulu still allowed to use a computer?"

"As far as I know."

"Do you think she might be interested?"

"If there's money, she's interested. I'll text you her new number."

"Thanks."

"No problem."

What the hell was he doing? Was he seriously considering hiring a hacker to help him look into a woman he'd known for barely an hour? Were hackers still actually a thing?

He texted Lulu as soon as Valentine sent the number. She asked him for the name of the dating app and said she'd get back to him if she could find anything.

Lulu called a few hours later.

"There's no such person."

"What do you mean?" Rowan asked.

"A woman named Eliza Brand around the age you described

doesn't exist. At least, not in Washington, or any of the other forty-nine states."

"How can you be sure?"

"Well, I can't be one hundred percent certain—but if she does exist, she's never voted or paid state tax, and she has no governmental or social media footprint at all."

"Is that abnormal?"

"It's pretty much impossible."

"Do you think she may have given me a fake name?"

"I think for sure."

"What makes you say that?"

"That dating app you sent me, Find Your Person?"

"What about it?"

"I noticed something strange in the database architecture, so I asked a friend to look into it for me."

"And?"

"Eliza Brand's profile is fake."

"Oh. Okay." Rowan was surprised. He'd felt such a strong connection to Eliza. It didn't make sense. He couldn't believe she'd been lying.

"But that's not all."

"What else?"

"They're *all* fake."

"I'm not sure I quite understand what you're saying."

"I'm saying that every single profile on that app is fake except for one."

"Which one?"

"Yours."

8

TOMBSTONED

"WORRICKER'S MINIONS SAY there's no way." Valentine hung up the phone and turned to face Rowan's desk. "She's too busy this month."

"What does that mean, too busy?"

"I think it means you're not going to get an appointment with Helena Worricker anytime soon."

"Did you tell them she asked me to consult with them on an immersive escape room or something outside Las Vegas?"

"I did."

"And?"

"They said WorGames has nothing going on in Nevada."

That didn't make any sense. Helena had seemed extremely excited about getting Rowan involved.

"Did you try the dating app contact number again?" Rowan asked.

"Yep, and it's still just a recording."

"Are you sure you dialed it correctly?"

"I called the number listed in the app's terms of service and on their website. You want me to leave another message?"

"No, I think we've left enough."

"Yeah, seven is probably plenty. I have a call in to the company listed as the owner of the domain. I'll let you know if I hear back."

"Thanks," Rowan said as he slipped on his jacket.

"You headed out again?"

"Yeah. Unless there's something you need?"

"I'm waiting on a few things for you to sign, but there's nothing urgent."

"Thanks." Rowan closed the door and stepped out onto the sidewalk.

It had stopped raining. The air was cold, but it felt good against his cheeks. He took a deep breath and decided to leave his car and walk the fifteen minutes to his apartment.

He needed to clear his head.

If Lulu was right, Rowan's had been the only genuine profile on that dating app.

How the hell did that work? He'd swiped right and matched with a woman named Eliza Brand. They went out for dinner and hit it off. She looked just like her photographs. It was a perfect date right up to the point Eliza disappeared into the bathroom, never to return.

So much for clearing his head.

Rowan wasn't under the illusion that he was an amazing catch. He was perfectly presentable, he looked like his pictures, and he was polite, but he wasn't Chris Hemsworth. Getting ghosted by a beautiful stranger on a first date certainly fell within the realm of possibility. Two things gave him pause, however. The first was the fact that he and Eliza had been genuinely getting along. Sparks were flying, so to speak, and Rowan was certain that those sparks went both ways. The second thing was the nature of Eliza's disappearance. She hadn't left Rowan sitting in the restaurant while she'd escaped out some side door.

She'd vanished without a trace.

He turned away from his apartment and started walking in the opposite direction. He needed to figure out what the hell had happened.

Helena Worricker was the only person he could think of who might be able to provide an answer, but Rowan had been unable to get hold of her.

He clearly needed a different tactic.

Helena wasn't answering his calls, but she might find him harder to ignore if he was standing right in front of her.

On his way to the car, Rowan couldn't shake the feeling that he was being watched. He kept turning around to look behind him, but there was nobody there. The longer he walked, the more intense the feeling became. Every time he turned around to check, he expected to see someone there. The feeling eventually became so intense that Rowan had to resist the urge to run. He stopped in front of a hobby and electronics store to catch his breath and try to calm down.

He stared through the window at a vintage model train setup and waited for the feeling to pass. While he waited, he focused on the train, a burgundy passenger unit called the Rocky Mountaineer.

The diorama surrounding the train was extremely realistic and filled the entire front window of the store. There were rivers with actual running water, numerous tunnels, and high bridges. The track wound through intricately detailed scenes, including factory buildings that appeared to be inhabited, countless vehicles with working lights, and mining sets that featured motorized wheels and active construction equipment.

Rowan was momentarily hypnotized by the model train as it moved through the landscape. Without anyone manning the controls, the train would be unable to slow down or change course as it moved along its preordained path.

He thought for a moment about how freeing it would be if, like the model train, his path was already laid out before him. What if all he needed to do was keep going until he ran out of power? Would he simply keep living until his time was up? What if some part of the track eventually wore down and altered the train's path, suddenly placing the train, its crew, and any passengers in harm's way? Weren't there always going to be accidents? Random occurrences? Chaos? Nobody could control chaos.

But what if that wasn't the case? What if chaos itself was nothing more than a predetermined illusion, and we were just unable to see the order behind it?

Maybe, like the path of the train, everything that's going to happen has already been mapped out, and all anybody can do is just keep moving forward and hope for the best.

The feeling of being followed eventually dissipated, and Rowan finally made it to his car.

Rowan had been to WorGames a few times in the past—once for a symposium on artificial intelligence in augmented reality systems, again for a job interview straight out of college, and, finally, for a meeting related to a transmedia marketing blitz for a videogame property that he couldn't remember. The campus was huge, but Rowan figured Helena's office had to be located in The Tower, an enormous building that reminded Rowan of something you might find in the former Soviet Union. Cold and impassive, The Tower loomed over everything like a gigantic red-brick sentinel.

As he walked toward The Tower, Rowan once again considered the idea of free will versus determinism. Were human beings really able to alter the course of their lives, or were we simply clay in the hands of fate?

As he considered these things, he passed a giant ad for the up-coming rerelease of a videogame called Alienation Nation.

Released in 1999, the third-person alien invasion thriller was one of WorGames' biggest hits of the decade, an instant classic. Rowan had stayed up playing that game until four or five in the morning for an entire week when it was first released. It was one of the first third-person shooters to feature meaningful character interaction along with extremely cool (and extremely difficult) puzzles. The characters were fantastic, but it was the puzzles that kept Rowan coming back for more.

Ever since his mother had shown him crosswords for the first time, he'd loved solving puzzles. Before he'd even graduated high school, Rowan was completing the *New York Times* crossword in ink. In fact, he'd become so adept at figuring these things out that his mother hired him to improve her work.

"I'd like to speak with Helena Worricker, please." Rowan spoke slowly, the muscles in his jaw still thawing from the long, cold walk.

"Do you have an appointment?" the man at the desk replied, with just a subtle hint of irritation.

"No, but it's important that I speak with her."

"I'm sorry, but she isn't available at the moment."

"Would it be possible to make an appointment?"

"You'll have to speak with her executive assistant."

"If I could just have five minutes. Ms. Worricker was interested in hiring me to consult on something."

"What's your name?"

"Rowan Chess. I've left a few messages already."

The receptionist tilted his head, and Rowan had the feeling that he was listening to a voice in his Bluetooth headset. After a moment, he tapped a button on his keyboard and looked up at Rowan.

"Well?" Rowan asked.

A telephone beeped on a nearby desk.

"That's for you," the receptionist said.

Rowan picked it up. "Hello?"

"Rowan, it's Helena."

"Oh, hello."

"I'm so sorry I haven't been in touch. I've been unavoidably detained."

"No worries. I appreciate you taking the time to call."

"I'm afraid I don't have much time."

There was something different about the tone of her voice. At the escape room party Helena Worricker appeared confident and spoke in a cool, measured manner. This time she sounded frantic, almost panicky.

"I had a couple of questions about that app, Find Your Person?" Rowan asked.

There was a long pause before Helena spoke. "That app won't be going live, so I'm afraid you'll be unable to use it. They lost their funding."

"I actually went on a date. I met somebody."

"That's impossible. Those dating profiles were placeholders."

"Well, at least one of them was real, and now she's disappeared. I've been trying to track her down."

Another long pause.

"I need to see you right away," Helena said. "Would you be able to meet me later?"

"Um, sure."

"I'm coming from Vegas so it will take me a few hours. How's Goldfinch at ten?"

"I'll be there."

"Perfect." Helena hung up.

Rowan wasn't sure he was any closer to figuring out what had happened to his date, but at least he'd be able to ask Helena more about the app and the job opportunity in Las Vegas that she'd mentioned.

On his way home from WorGames, he received a call from Lulu.

"We have a problem," she said.

"What do you mean?"

"The Find Your Person app is gone."

"What?"

"Yeah—completely scrubbed, no website, no more access to the API or the proprietary link you sent, no nothing."

"How?"

"The *how* is the easy part. They just deleted some files. It's the *when* that's kind of freaking me out."

"How do you mean?"

"Well, about an hour ago I accessed their database and downloaded a number of files associated with your account ID."

"That sounds promising."

"It was, but when I tried to download the same information about your date, Miss Eliza Brand, the application was no longer there."

"Are you sure?"

"Yeah, check it out. There's no more Find Your Person. It's a tombstoned app."

Rowan checked his phone. She was right.

Find Your Person was gone.

"Were you able to dig up any other dating profiles?" Rowan asked.

"Nope. It looks like the whole thing kind of just . . . self-destructed."

"And you think it had something to do with what you did?"

"If it didn't, that's one hell of a coincidence, don't you think?"

"I suppose so."

Rowan didn't think it was a coincidence. His date had disappeared, the dating app was fake, and he couldn't shake the idea that somebody had been following him earlier.

Something strange was happening, perhaps something dangerous, and Rowan had the feeling that if he didn't figure out what it was—and soon—things were going to get much worse.

It turned out he was right.

Later that night, while Rowan was getting ready to go meet Helena, he received a text message from Valentine that included a link to a news article.

Rowan opened it up.

The story was about how an automated arm of a high-tech car wash went crazy and killed the driver of a car in Las Vegas. This article was only a few hours old.

The woman who'd been killed was Helena Worricker.

9

WRONG REINDEER

IT WAS JUST OVER THREE WEEKS into what was shaping up to be one of the hottest summers on record, and fourteen-year-old Emily Connors was in love with everything—from the mornings that smelled like dew and southern magnolias to the dusky evenings that seemed to go on forever. For Emily, summer was all about days spent riding bikes down to the water, and nights with her parents and their friends sitting around the fire on plastic lawn chairs in the backyard, drinking, laughing, and playing games.

Fourteen was a big year for Emily. She spent a few months pining after a much older camp counselor, French-kissed a rock star's son in the bathroom of a tour bus, and had fallen in what can only be described as "teen angst poetry love" with the twins who lived across the street. And yet, even with all of the heartache, blinding desire, and raw emotional confusion, Emily remembered that summer as the summer of parties.

As far back as she could remember, Emily's parents and their friends were always gathering to celebrate some holiday or anniversary or other arbitrary reason to get together and drink. Emily and Annie would listen at the heat vents in Emily's bedroom and giggle at the sounds of the alcohol-fueled excitement taking place in the living room below. Emily loved the vibrant sense of being alive that filled their house during their parents' parties—the random bursts of laughter, the old disco music, the constant opening and closing of screen doors, the seemingly endless sea of happy faces all smiling genuine smiles.

In the morning everything would be back to normal: her parents stern and focused on their work, and the girls heading out to enjoy their seemingly endless summer freedom. But for Emily, the best parts of summer were those warm dusky evenings when Emily's mom and dad and their friends filled the house with laughter and excitement.

It seemed to Emily, looking back, that those parties functioned as a kind of release valve for her parents and their friends—a way to let go of the intensity of the work that they were doing at the time.

That summer, Emily's family had been invited to a party at the biggest house Emily had ever seen. On a huge beachfront lot on Lake Washington, the house looked like something straight off the cover of *Architectural Digest*. From what Emily had heard, this was the Cofsky family's summer house; apparently they had an even bigger, far more ostentatious home in the city.

After a quick dip in the lake with some of the older kids, Emily made her way back to the house to check on her sister. Annie was two years younger than Emily and had a tendency to wander off whenever she got bored. Emily had heard there was a pinball machine somewhere in the house. Annie loved pinball, so Emily was pretty sure that's where she'd find her sister.

She was eventually able to track down the pinball machine, but there was no sign of Annie. One of the parents told Emily that he'd seen some of the younger kids playing out near a rack of kayaks by the water, so Emily went back outside to take a look.

There was nobody near the kayaks, but Emily had noticed an outbuilding of some kind while she was swimming in the lake. It had been barely visible from the water, but she could see a bit more of it now. It appeared to be a much smaller version of the main building, maybe a guest house or large storage shed of some kind.

Perhaps Annie and the other kids had wandered that way.

The building was located up the lake, about a quarter mile from the main house. Clearly designed by the same architect, this smaller structure featured the same rectangular mix of concrete, dark wood, and glass. But unlike the main house, which had been built on the open shore of the lake, this place was tucked away in a fairly dense section of forest.

As Emily approached the building, she heard the strains of eerie synthesizer music coming from an open window. She wasn't trying to be stealthy as she approached the place; she was simply going to knock and see if her sister was inside, but something caught her eye as she moved past the open window. Somebody was there, inside the room.

It was a man. He looked just like Emily's father, but it was hard to tell for certain due to the fact that he was blindfolded. What the hell would her father be doing blindfolded in a guest house deep in the woods?

The curtains were half closed, so Emily had to move closer to the window in order to get a proper view of the interior.

She was looking at an open living area. There was a small kitchen to the right, and a fireplace located in the middle of the wall opposite the window. The rest of the room was completely empty save for a few chairs and a small sofa that had been shoved into the far left corner, along with a Persian rug, which had been rolled up to reveal a polished concrete floor. Painted on the floor, running lengthwise from one end of the room to the other, was a thick red line that bisected the room almost perfectly. At one point, near the left-hand side of the room, a slightly smaller thin blue line had been painted across its thicker red counterpart, resulting in what looked like a large cross.

The man she'd noticed earlier was definitely her father. He and another blindfolded man Emily didn't recognize stood next to Emily's mother on the side of the red line closest to the window. Emily's mother wore a blindfold as well. Emily was careful not to make any noise as she positioned herself next to the window and peered inside.

Now she was being stealthy.

The synthesizer music Emily noticed earlier had evolved into something else—a kind of disseminated static ambiance. There were still familiar tones and harmonics in there, but it had become more abstract, and it felt like it was coming from everywhere all at once.

Emily had always been affected by music—not just emotionally but physically as well. Hearing a great song could cause goose-bumps, or shivers so intense that she felt like she wanted to scream. For Emily, hearing the right song at the right moment was almost like falling in love. But there was a flip side. There were certain types of music, like EDM—drum and bass in particular—that made Emily feel the opposite way. She'd become instantly irritable and scramble to turn it off.

In college, she got into a fight with a friend named Camilla on their way to a music festival in Glastonbury one year. Camilla put on some dance music, and Emily lunged forward and switched it off. Camilla was pissed, but Emily couldn't help it. It was instinctual. If she had heard so much as another minute, she would have thrown herself from the moving car.

That shit had to go.

But what she'd heard that summer day was different. Although the music coming through the window made Emily a bit fidgety, there was a weird hypnotic comfort to it.

Eventually, Emily didn't notice the music at all.

After a minute or so, she felt something change. A fourth figure began walking along the red line. It was a girl around Emily's age. She wore ripped light blue jeans, a New Kids on the Block T-shirt, and bright white Nike running shoes. The girl wasn't blindfolded, and Emily recognized her immediately. Her name was Natalie. She was the daughter of a man who worked with Emily's parents. A man named Edward Crawford, whom Emily would later come to know as Crow.

Emily could see Natalie clearly in her mind, but she didn't appear to be physically there in the room with Emily's parents and the other man.

Natalie was somewhere else.

Emily felt like she was looking into two seemingly identical parallel worlds, and felt a panic rising within her. She wanted to speak or clear her throat—anything to let her parents know that they were being watched—but something stopped her. She took another look at her parents. Why the blindfolds?

What the hell were they doing?

Emily was old enough to know that she definitely didn't want to witness any weird adult stuff, but she also understood that her parents were relatively normal people. She had no idea what was happening, but she was almost positive that this *wasn't* some kind of weird sex thing. She decided to keep her mouth shut until she figured out exactly what was going on.

Even though she couldn't actually see her physically, Emily could feel Natalie moving slowly along the red line. And, although she was standing outside the room, Emily could feel a palpable sense of anticipation coming from her parents and the other man.

Then, just as Emily sensed that Natalie had reached the point where the thick red line intersected the thinner blue one, something happened.

It felt like the moment right before an electrical storm. The lights dimmed and flickered, and Emily felt the atmosphere both inside and outside the room grow heavy.

"She's inside. She found the room!" the unknown blindfolded man called out.

"Something's wrong," Emily's father said.

And then, suddenly, Natalie was visible. She was standing exactly where Emily knew she would be, her face a mask of horrific pain, tears pouring down her cheeks.

Emily's stomach dropped like she'd been walking on rotted scaffolding, and she felt like she was slowly falling backward through space—her head light and tingly, her arms and legs distant and just barely connected.

"Is everybody wearing their blindfolds?" the unknown man asked.

"Yes," Emily's parents said in unison.

Emily could feel the pressure around her shift again. The world felt heavier.

Her father was right. Something was definitely wrong.

Everything had changed. The falling feeling had been replaced by something else. The ground beneath her feet, the light, the smell, the weight of the air itself. It was all . . . wrong.

Emily and Annie had a term for it. They called it "wrong reindeer."

Nobody in the family could remember who came up with it first, but it was something they all said. Whenever someone or something was slightly off in some frightening or incomprehensible way, that person or thing was a wrong reindeer.

Emily could see Natalie. She was clearly there, standing at the intersection of the two lines, but there was something wrong. Emily felt like Natalie was trapped somehow.

Suddenly, the whole world was a wrong reindeer.

Emily could feel her friend's pain, a bright white burning that felt like being ripped from the world. "Natalie?" she called.

Natalie spun around and looked at Emily.

"Someone is looking at the traveler!" the unknown man screamed.

Emily's father turned toward the window. "Emily?" His voice, muted by the thick glass window, a mix of surprise and fear.

"What's going on?" Emily demanded, her mind fighting against the reality of what she was seeing, working to come up with a scenario that made sense.

"Close your eyes," her father said.

"Daddy . . ."

"Close your eyes, Emmy. Right now!"

Emily shut her eyes as tight as she could.

"Don't open them again until you hear me say it's okay," her father continued.

Emily could hear rustling inside the room, and then a few seconds later she heard somebody walking through the grass toward her.

"You're okay," Emily's father said.

Emily opened her eyes. The dusky darkness and weird atmospheric pressure were gone. Everything appeared to be back to normal.

Her father led her into the room, where the carpet had been rolled back into place and the red and blue lines on the floor were no longer visible.

"My god," Emily's mother said, as she ran up and hugged her. "What are you doing here?"

"Looking for Annie," Emily replied. "What happened?" Natalie and the man who had been inside the room with her parents were nowhere to be seen. "Where's Natalie?"

Emily's mother and father shared a look.

"You saw Natalie?" her mother asked.

Emily nodded. She felt a wave of nausea move up through her head and shoulders. "I don't feel good," she said. And then she turned and vomited the contents of her stomach onto the carpet.

A little while later, the three of them were back at the main house, sitting together on the bed in one of the guest rooms. Emily's mother handed Emily a glass of water and some mouthwash from the bathroom.

"We were helping that magician practice an illusion," her father said. "Nobody is supposed to know about it. That's why we were out there in the guest house."

Emily was unconvinced. "That didn't look like any magic trick I've ever seen," she said.

Something had happened in that room, something that—even at fourteen—Emily understood wasn't normal.

Later that night, with Annie (who, it turned out, had been swimming with some of the other kids earlier) asleep in her room, Emily's parents sat her down and asked if Emily wouldn't mind answering a few questions while they recorded her using a small handheld machine.

Emily agreed.

"You called out for your friend Natalie," her father said. "Why?"

"Because she was there," Emily said.

"You could see her?"

"Not until the end. At first she was just . . ." Emily didn't want to say it out loud. She wanted to go back to regular life, where people didn't pop in and out of existence.

"What is it?" her mother asked, touching Emily's shoulder.

Emily looked down at her feet. "It's weird."

"Please, nothing is too weird. We promise," her father said, and smiled.

"I could *feel* her there, in that room."

"Could you see her?"

"Not with my eyes—not until she touched the blue line—but I still knew she was there."

"But you couldn't physically see her?"

"Not until she touched the blue line."

"But how did you know she was moving toward the blue line if you couldn't actually see her?" Emily's mother asked.

"I just knew. I could feel her," Emily said.

Her parents were clearly struck by her answers, but Emily couldn't tell if they were excited or terrified.

"Are you sure it wasn't just instinctual? Calling out for your friend because you were scared?" her father asked.

"It wasn't." Emily shook her head. "And I wouldn't call for Natalie. I mean, she's okay. But it's not like she's my best friend or anything."

Her parents shared a look.

"She was there," Emily said. "You saw her, right?"

Her parents didn't answer.

Emily could tell the interview was coming to an end and that she might only have one chance to ask the question she *really* wanted to ask.

"What happened to the light?" Emily said. "When Natalie stepped on the blue line, the whole room changed."

"The room changed?" her mother asked.

"It wasn't just the room," Emily replied. "*Everything* changed. The whole world. Even outside, it was darker and colder suddenly."

Emily noticed her parents share a quick look.

"I didn't notice anything like that," her father said.

Emily thought he was lying.

"Why did you make me close my eyes?" Emily asked.

"Because you weren't supposed to see the illusion," her father said.

"Is that why you and Mom and the other man—the magician—were blindfolded too?"

"Exactly," her father said, and Emily knew that he was lying again.

"Please, just tell me the truth," Emily said, doing her best to keep the frustration and anger from her voice. "Something happened at the end, when I was looking at Natalie. It was why you needed me to close my eyes."

"I sometimes forget that you're a lot smarter than I am."

"Smarter than both of us," her mother chimed in.

"Maybe too smart to let you trick me with nice words about how smart I am," Emily said, "no matter how true those words might be."

"Do you remember what I told you about the double-slit experiment?" her father asked. "How observation can change the outcome of the experiment?"

"You mean the dead cat in the box?"

He smiled. "Let's call it the observer's paradox."

"Sure," Emily said.

"Science would prefer to deal in absolutes," her father continued, "but right now, when it comes to quantum physics, all we really have are probabilities. Quantum objects live in a cloud of uncertainty known as quantum indeterminacy. Let's say an unknown cat in a box has a fifty percent chance of being alive or dead. When you lift the lid, you're forcing one probability into existence at the expense of the other. Essentially, you're changing the state of that object."

"You're killing the cat."

"Half the time."

"Did something happen when I was looking at Natalie?"

Emily's mother and father shared a look.

Emily's eyes widened. "Did I kill Natalie?"

"What? No," her mother said. "Natalie's fine."

"It was so weird," Emily said. "I could really feel her in that room. I knew that she was there. I didn't need to see her."

"That's extraordinary," Emily's father said. "That you could feel her."

"Where was she? What was that place?"

"We're looking for a special place, a room," her father said.

"With Natalie?" Emily asked.

Her mother nodded.

"Can *I* help you look for this special room?"

Emily caught her parents sharing another worried glance.

"What?" Emily asked.

"Nothing," her father said.

"Natalie wouldn't have been there if it was dangerous, right?"

"Right," her mother said, and Emily understood that she was lying too.

"There are some things we'll have to explain to you when you get a bit older," her father said. "So, for now, you just saw us helping a magician work on an illusion. And, in the very near future, we'll explain the rest. Agreed?"

"You're going to have to give me something," Emily said. "That shit was really weird."

"We don't say 'shit,'" Emily's mother replied.

"Sorry."

"We're not telling you the whole truth today," her father said. "But that's for your own good."

"Dad . . ." Emily protested.

"We were helping that man perform an experiment that might help a lot of people one day," her mother continued, "and we promise we'll explain more as soon as we can."

"Why did you bring up quantum mechanics and Schrödinger?" Emily asked.

Her mother smiled. Emily liked to surprise them with things that she learned or retained, and she knew that Schrödinger's cat would get a reaction.

"Imagine if quantum theory wasn't limited to just atoms and quarks," her father said. "What if it could be applied to the macro world as well?"

"I don't think that's good news for cats," Emily said.

Her parents both laughed, and Emily could tell they were relieved.

"We'll explain a whole lot more in the future," her mother said. "We promise."

"Fine," Emily said. She could tell that her mother meant it. "I accept your terms."

"We're so glad you're okay." Emily's mother hugged her.

Emily hugged her back as tight as she could.

The following night after dinner, while Emily was on her bed reading, her mother knocked on the door. "Is it okay if I come in?"

Emily nodded. "Of course."

Her mother reached for the book as she sat down. "*The Mathematical Principles of Quantum Mechanics,*" she said, "of all the books we have on the subject."

"It looked interesting," Emily said.

"You probably won't realize this for quite a while, but the fact that this particular book was the one that looked interesting makes *you* a whole lot more interesting."

"What is *that* supposed to mean?"

Her mother smiled. "It means I love you."

They sat there together for a long comfortable moment before Emily's mother spoke again. "What do you think about the word 'intuition'? What does that mean to you?"

"Trusting your gut?"

Her mother nodded. "Trusting your instincts is important, but certain instincts can be a bit more complicated."

"What do you mean?"

"Well, I'd like to try something, if you don't mind."

"Okay, you're kind of freaking me out."

Her mother laughed. "How would you feel about getting some ice cream?"

"It's eight o'clock at night."

"Exactly."

"Oreo Blizzard?"

"Absolutely. But this has to be our secret. You can't tell your father."

Emily nodded. "Okay."

The sun was low in the sky as they approached the Dairy Queen.

Emily's mother didn't even slow down.

"You passed it," Emily said.

"We're just going to make a quick stop first."

A few minutes later, her mother turned in to a parking lot and stopped the car.

"Umm," Emily said. "Why are we at the *park*?"

"I'll show you. Come on."

Although the sun was still above the horizon, it was getting late. Aside from a couple of people walking dogs in the distance, the park was empty.

Emily's mother led her past a set of rusty swings and down a small hill to a narrow dirt path that led into the woods. They walked along the path for about a minute before it eventually emptied into a wide clearing.

"Remember what I told you about intuition?" her mother asked as she stopped in the middle of the clearing.

"To trust it?"

"That there was more than one type."

"Right."

"Okay," Emily's mother said as she wrapped a fanny pack around Emily's waist, "we're going to try something."

"What's in here?" Emily shook the fanny pack.

"Colored sand. It's going to trickle out and mark where you walk."

"Why?"

Her mother ignored the question. "Trust me," she said. "I won't let anything bad happen."

"I trust you," Emily said. "I'm just kind of curious about what the heck we're doing out here."

"I want you to close your eyes and relax, focus inward, and really try to feel your surroundings."

"Okay," Emily said. "I feel like I'm standing in the park like an asshole."

"We don't say 'asshole.'"

"Sorry," Emily said.

"I want you to take a few deep breaths, then take two steps forward and stop."

Emily took three deep breaths and followed her mother's instructions.

"Now," her mother said, "this is important. Does anything feel different?"

Emily thought about it for a second. "I don't think so."

"Try to relax again. Take a few more deep breaths."

Emily took three more breaths and concentrated on relaxing her arms and legs.

"Focus on your intuition, wherever you feel that in your body," her mother said.

This time, Emily felt something. It was faint, thin, and far away, but she felt what she would describe later as a vibration. "I think I might feel something."

"Great," her mother said. "Now, with your eyes open this time, I want you to follow that feeling."

"Follow it how?"

"Just start walking, and concentrate on that feeling."

Emily did as she was told and walked around the park following her mother's instructions. It felt like she'd been walking around for fifteen minutes or so before a voice boomed out from behind them.

"What the hell is going on?"

It was Emily's father.

"Where's Annie?" her mother asked.

"Playing Nintendo in the car. Do you have any idea how dangerous this is?" he added, lowering his voice.

"I had to know if it was happening to Emily," her mother said, lowering her voice as well, although Emily could still make out what she was saying.

"And?"

"She walked the path and hit every single Radiant. She didn't step off, not even once."

"That's impossible," her father said.

"It happened."

Her father looked worried. "Are you sure?"

"We need to stop this, right now. We're leaving the program," her mother added in a tone that Emily was sure would lead to a fight.

She hated it when her parents fought. They were never aggressive or violent, but sometimes their arguments could last for days.

"Maybe you're right," her father said.

Emily was happy. It sounded like they weren't going to fight after all. "What program?" she asked, taking a step closer to her parents.

"It's something at work. It's not important," her father said.

Emily held her father's eyes for a long moment before finally turning her attention to her mother. "I have no idea what's really going on here, but there's no way you're getting out of Dairy Queen."

Her father smiled.

That was the only time they ever spoke about what had happened that night in the park.

10

OFF IS OFF

EMILY OPENED HER EYES and sat up in bed with a gasp.

She'd been having a dream, and in that dream she'd just woken up in a bed in Alan Scarpio's lakeside house, which was strange—because just now, when she woke up in real life, Emily was in an identical bed in Scarpio's lakeside house.

But it wasn't the bed from her dream, and it wasn't the same house.

Emily took a couple of really deep breaths and did her best to calm her racing mind. She knew this feeling. She'd been here before. She was still drifting, still feeling the effects of landing in this latest stream.

She remembered how K had once described the feeling of dimensional drift. *I feel like I can no longer trust my eyes. It doesn't matter how anything looks. What matters is how it feels, and off is off.*

The sense of waking in another world slowly began to fade, and Emily could feel her heartbeat slow as she gradually adjusted to her new surroundings.

She shook her head. Her mind was clear.

She was in the same dimensional stream she'd fallen asleep in.

She made her way to the bathroom, peeled off her clothing, and stepped into the shower.

As the warm water ran over her body, Emily began to feel more like herself, and by the time she'd shampooed her hair and scrubbed her face, she was ready to get out there and deal with the world—whatever form it took.

Over the years, Emily had learned to compartmentalize the sinking feeling of impending doom that had always followed slipping dimensional streams, but she'd never fully gotten used to it. There was no way to truly normalize the switch. Just like a bad hangover, time was the only thing that really helped.

At least she still remembered who she was. She'd heard stories of dimensional drift so bad that all memories of the previous iteration were lost, or pushed so deeply into the person's subconscious that there was no way to retrieve them without completely snapping that person's mind forever. This amnesiac effect was far more common with younger people. A young, unformed mind is more likely to lose its tether to reality when confronted with a slip between dimensional streams. Completely surrendering to the reality of the new stream and suppressing memories of the former dimensional reality is the mind's best defense mechanism against the drift.

Emily had never felt drift like she was experiencing now. She was really glad Scarpio was there. When dealing with wild interdimensional quantum chaos, it turns out a friendly face can make all the difference.

After she got dressed, Emily sat down on the bed and went over everything that had happened the night before in the restaurant. She and Scarpio had barely made it outside before four members of what appeared to be the Rabbits Police rushed in. But this time, it didn't look like they were there for Emily and Scarpio. If that was true, then why were they there?

Was somebody else looking into the game?

Emily entered the living room and made her way over to the large windows. She pressed her forehead against the glass and took a couple of deep breaths. As she stood there, she felt the pull of the waking city in the distance and wondered what it would be like to be part of the tapestry of regular lives that made up Seattle in the morning: the finance expert off to hit the gym before work, the nanny on a visa from Australia trying to start a new life, the students, the teachers, the sanitation workers. Were any of them concerned about waking up in a world that was slightly different from the one they'd fallen asleep in? Probably not. But who knew. Maybe there was no such thing as regular life. Maybe everybody had serious shit to deal with, multidimensional or not.

When Emily finally left the living room and went into the kitchen, she was surprised to discover Scarpio was already awake. He was sitting at the dining room table going over the video footage from the night before.

Emily sat down beside him.

"Check it out." Scarpio pressed the space bar and the video started to play.

The first thing on the screen was Emily's hand as she placed the camera and then rushed out of the room. Less than a minute later, four people dressed in black entered and moved past the camera toward the back of the restaurant. One of the four spoke briefly with a couple of the employees, who could be seen pointing to the bathroom area.

Emily pressed the space bar and the video stopped playing.

"They didn't even look at our table," Scarpio said.

"Shit." Emily said. "What if they weren't there for us?"

"That would explain why they arrived so quickly. But if they weren't there for us, then why the hell were they there?"

"I don't know, but I think we need to find out."

"Based on their movements, I think they were probably after somebody near the back of the room," he said, leaning back in his chair. "There's coffee. I made pour-over, like an asshole. You want one?"

"Thanks, but I like the machine."

Emily made herself a coffee using Scarpio's espresso machine and sat down beside him at the table. Scarpio restarted the video. "Do you think the Rabbits Police showing up had something to do with everybody in that restaurant getting a text message at exactly the same time?"

"That has to be part of it," Scarpio said.

Emily pulled out her phone and took a look at the spam text message she'd received in the restaurant: *Special Offer! Please Visit Agatha's Used Furniture for Big Saving!*

"What do we think about Agatha's Used Furniture?" she asked.

"I couldn't find any listing online."

He leaned back in his chair and pressed stop on the video. "They don't spend very much time searching the place. I wonder if they found whoever or whatever it was that they came for?"

"Can we get the restaurant's security camera feeds?"

"I tried that. No useable angles inside the building."

"Outside?"

"Two cameras. If they were operational at the time, we'll have that footage within the hour."

"What about him?"

"Where?"

"There." Emily pointed at a man wearing a dark jacket over a white Sub Pop T-shirt.

Scarpio leaned forward for a closer look.

"It was after the text alerts started going off, but before the Rabbits Police showed up. He was telling one of the wait staff that his date had disappeared. He looked pretty freaked out."

"Maybe his date just had enough and took off?"

Emily nodded. "Probably."

At that moment, Scarpio received an alert on his computer. "Neither of the restaurant's outdoor cameras was working, but I did get something from an ATM across the street."

"Wow." Emily shook her head.

"What?"

"Sometimes I can still be surprised by what money can buy."

"Hey, it's not just money. You still have to know who to pay."

"Uh huh." Emily nodded.

"You know I don't need this shit," Scarpio said, semiserious. "I could be in the South of France right now drinking four-thousand-dollar bottles of Burgundy."

"Settle down. I wasn't talking about you specifically."

Scarpio adjusted something on the monitor and scrolled through part of the restaurant footage again.

"Do people really spend that much money on wine?"

Scarpio ignored Emily's question and pointed to the monitor, where the man in the dark jacket could be seen stepping outside the restaurant. "Is that the guy?"

Emily nodded.

"He leaves just as the Rabbits Police are coming in."

"Can we see his car?"

"No, he exits the frame before the end of the block."

"Shit. How are we going to find him?"

Scarpio shook his head. "My contact said this was the only footage available that shows the doors of the restaurant. I'll ask him if he can find another camera with an angle on the street."

"You know who might be able to help us?" Emily asked.

"Who?"

"Fatman."

"Who's Fatman?"

"He's really skinny and he has a computer called Mother that he uses to watch and listen to Seattle."

"Sounds familiar now that you mention it." Scarpio shook his head. "I feel like I should remember, but I can't."

"I can't believe I didn't think of him sooner."

"Dimensional drift."

"Sinplay's about fifteen minutes from here."

"Sinplay?"

"It's where he works."

"Do you think we should call first?"

"Absolutely not."

Emily and Scarpio slowed as they approached the low brick building that housed the adult book and novelty shop. Easily identified by its bright pink neon sign, Sinplay was sandwiched between a bicycle repair shop and a dry cleaner.

Beneath the street-level storefronts was a basement section accessible only through a locked wrought iron gate. It was here, beneath Sinplay, that a really thin guy ironically known as Fatman operated a bespoke super-surveillance computer named Mother, featuring a highly illegal proprietary algorithm. Or, at least, that's how it had been the last time Emily had seen him, about three dimensional streams ago. Although he was almost always a raging misanthrope, if you knew where to find him, and he was playing the game, Fatman was one of the best resources an experienced Rabbits player had at their disposal. Emily was hoping that, if Fatman existed in this stream, he might be able to help them track down the mystery man from the restaurant.

"He really lives in a porn store basement?" Scarpio asked.

"I've heard he has an apartment somewhere, but he's almost always here."

"How do we get down there?"

Emily ran her hand along the top of the wrought iron gate. "There's normally a hidden buzzer, but there's nothing here."

Scarpio grabbed the top of the gate and started to hoist himself up.

"What are you doing?" Emily asked.

"I'm just going to climb over and knock."

"I'm not sure that's—"

"Fuck!" Scarpio yelled as he fell backward onto the sidewalk.

Emily rushed to his side. "What happened?"

"It's electric."

"Really?"

"That had to be at least two hundred volts."

"Just the standard one ten," said a voice from a speaker somewhere.

"Fatman?" Emily asked, standing up.

No response.

"We just want to ask you a couple of questions. We're not the police or anything."

"No shit," the voice replied.

"You can't just shock people," Scarpio said as he stood up and brushed himself off.

"What do you want?" said the voice.

"We need your help."

"Jesus Christ," the voice said, "did I just electrocute Alan Scarpio?"

"Yes," Scarpio said, "you fucking did."

"Just a sec," said the voice.

There was a rustling sound from the speaker, followed by a buzzing near the doorknob, and the wrought iron gate swung open with a slow creak.

Emily glanced over at Scarpio, who shrugged. The two of them walked down a half dozen small, steep concrete steps to a metal door that had been spray-painted matte black.

A few seconds later, the door opened and a tall skinny man wearing white Adidas track pants and a vintage WorGames T-shirt ushered them inside.

"Hurry," he said.

The space beneath the porn store was much larger than it appeared from the outside. The ceiling was low, and flickering fluorescent lights in a truly awful array of just-barely-off-white colors made the place feel like some kind of government records office at the end of time.

There were endless rows of high metal shelves filled with all kinds of media, including reel-to-reel audio recordings, cassette tapes, vinyl records, tons of books, and stacks upon stacks of magazines and newspapers.

A set of massive dark-red curtains, which looked like they'd been taken from the set of some gothic theatrical production, covered the entire back wall. The rest of the walls were filled with posters, almost all of them featuring the band Kiss.

"Nobody calls me Fatman anymore. It's frowned upon," Fatman said as he closed and locked the door behind them.

"What should we call you?" Scarpio asked.

"Neil."

"Seriously?"

"Fuck no. Call me Fatman."

"I'm pretty sure we've met before," Emily said.

"We haven't," Fatman said as he walked into the room.

Emily noticed that he had a slight limp and slowed her pace to match his. "No?" she asked. "You're sure you just don't remember?"

"I never forget a face—or anything else for that matter."

"Never?"

"Are you going to sue me?" Fatman asked Scarpio.

"Wasn't planning on it."

"I'm sorry about what happened with the gate. I don't like visitors."

"No shit," Scarpio replied.

"What do you want?"

"What's behind those curtains?" Emily pointed toward the back of the room. "Is it Mother?"

Fatman appeared confused. "Are you asking if I have my *mother* hidden in the back of my office?"

"No, I'm wondering if you have a citywide surveillance computer setup run by an algorithm you call Mother."

All expression left Fatman's face for a moment . . . then he burst out laughing. "Holy shit. That would be amazing. Can you imagine?"

"So what's actually back there?" Emily asked.

Fatman looked at Emily, then over to Scarpio. "You really are Alan Scarpio."

"It's true. I really am."

"One social post from you could change everything."

"I don't really do social media."

"Musk does it all the time. Remember Dogecoin? He drove that shit way up."

"What are you talking about?" Scarpio asked.

Fatman walked over to the red curtains and pushed a button. "Corinthium," he said as the curtains parted to reveal an enormous server farm sitting behind dozens of computer workstations and monitors.

"I'm sorry, what?" Emily said.

"It's crypto," Scarpio said. "It's been around for a while. It's supposed to be more anonymous."

"It's the *most* anonymous. Corinthium makes everything else look like PayPal. Do you have any?" Fatman asked, clearly excited by the prospect.

"Probably," Scarpio replied. "My people usually buy a bit of everything, just in case."

"It's going to reach five dollars by the end of the year," Fatman said.

"Congratulations, I suppose?" Scarpio said, then turned to Emily. "We should probably get going."

Scarpio was right. This version of Fatman clearly wasn't going to be able to help.

"Why did you come here?" Fatman asked.

"We thought you might be able to help us with something," Emily said. She thought about mentioning the game, but after what she and Scarpio had been through with the Rabbits Police, she decided it was too risky.

"What kind of help are you looking for?"

"We need to access some surveillance or security cameras," Scarpio said.

"Basically, we need to find somebody," Emily added.

"Do you have a location?"

Emily gave Fatman the address of the restaurant.

Scarpio nodded in the direction of Fatman's servers. "I thought your computers weren't connected to any citywide surveillance system?"

"Well . . ." Fatman replied, "what I actually said was that I don't own and operate a citywide surveillance super-system run by an algorithm. I didn't say I wasn't able to access certain cameras that may or may not help me keep my base of operations secure."

"So you *can* help us?" Emily asked.

"Seattle already has a citywide surveillance system. It's run by the NSA."

"And?"

"I may have advanced somebody a whole bunch of Corinthium in order to buy limited access to that network."

"How limited?"

"Seattle is covered by eight grid controllers. Your restaurant is close enough that it lands on the same grid as this place."

"So?"

"So maybe Mr. Scarpio tweets out a quick Corinthium mention and we take a look at that restaurant?"

"How about I just pay you?" Scarpio said.

Fatman thought for a moment. "That could work," he said finally.

It took Fatman about five minutes to access the relevant feeds and start scrolling through footage. A couple of minutes later, they had him.

"There." Emily pointed at the screen, where the man in the dark jacket and Sub Pop T-shirt was walking down the sidewalk. "That's the guy."

Fatman stopped the video and zoomed in. "You sure?"

"Positive."

"Okay." Fatman pressed a couple of buttons and a series of red dots appeared. They followed the man's head as he moved.

"What are those?" Emily asked.

"It's a connecting node. It tracks the subject between a series of linked cameras. They pick up the subject by matching data points."

"So you can follow him?"

"If any of my kinetic movement–matching algorithms or the system's extant facial recognition pick him up, we'll be able to follow his movements all over the grid." Fatman pressed a couple of buttons. "Or at least until he gets into his car."

"Where is this?"

"One block from the restaurant."

Emily watched as the man approached a black Volvo hatchback, got into the car, and drove away.

"Can you track his car?" Scarpio asked.

"Not for long. We're close to the edge of the grid, unfortunately. He'll be out of range by the next block."

And just like that, the black Volvo was gone.

"Can you rewind it?" Emily leaned forward.

"You're looking for the license plate?"

"Exactly."

Fatman rewound the footage and zoomed in on the license plate of the black Volvo. Emily took a picture of the screen with her phone.

"Thank you," Emily said. "This is really helpful. Any chance you could run the plate?"

"Sorry," Fatman replied, "I can't risk getting flagged if this guy's a criminal or high-profile individual."

"Do you think we might be able to set up a transfer of funds in an amount that makes running this guy's plate feel a little less challenging?" Scarpio asked.

"I think we could probably think of something."

Scarpio pulled out his phone, opened an application, and handed it to Fatman.

Fatman's eyes grew wide. "Yeah, I think this should cover it."

"Great." Scarpio smiled. "How long?"

"I should have something by tomorrow morning."

"You'll give us a call as soon as you find this guy?"

"You bet," he said, then Fatman got to work.

11

TRY NOT TO THINK
ABOUT A WHITE BEAR

ROWAN STEPPED INTO HIS OFFICE, tossed his umbrella into the bucket near the door, and shook the rain from his hair. Two nights earlier Eliza Brand had vanished from a restaurant bathroom. He'd known Eliza for less than an hour, but he couldn't stop thinking about her, no matter how hard he tried.

Valentine looked up when Rowan entered. She was holding a piece of paper up to her phone. Written on the paper was a message: *I lost The Game.*

She took a picture and then set her phone down on her desk and exhaled. She looked disappointed.

"What are you doing?" Rowan asked.

"It's kind of complicated."

"Okay," Rowan said as he sat down behind his desk and turned on his computer. Valentine was into some pretty out-there stuff. Rowan had learned to stop asking questions after she'd spent almost three hours detailing the nuanced differences between two groups of online treasure hunters looking into buried ceramic casques connected to a book called *The Secret* that had been published in 1982.

Valentine came over and leaned against Rowan's desk. "It's called The Game," she said.

"What is it?"

"It's based on the white bear problem."

Rowan stared.

"You don't know what that is, do you?" Valentine said.

"Nope."

"Okay, so, in simple terms, the point of The Game is to avoid thinking about The Game."

"Seems simple enough."

"Does it?"

"Sure."

"Try not thinking about a white bear."

Rowan nodded. Valentine was right, of course. A polar bear popped into his mind immediately. "I see," he said. "Dostoyevsky wrote something about a bear. I think he said set yourself the task not to think of a white bear, and the cursed thing comes to mind every minute."

She shrugged. "I don't know who that is."

"How does it work?"

"If you're playing The Game, you have to let everyone know when you lose."

"And you lose whenever you think about it?"

"Exactly."

"That doesn't seem like a great use of your free time."

"Nothing's free."

"I'm not sure what you mean," Rowan said.

"Exactly," she said—far too cryptically, Rowan thought.

"So how do you win?"

"I don't think you can. It's kind of like the whole world is playing The Game, even if they don't know it."

Rowan nodded. He enjoyed thought experiments like Schrödinger's cat or the ship of Theseus, but those felt rooted in quantum mechanics and the philosophy of identity. This game Valentine was talking about felt a bit gimmicky. But even so, Rowan kind of understood the allure.

When he was a kid, he used to play a game in his mind. Whenever he started feeling socially anxious or panicky, he told himself that if he could visualize the cover of his favorite album—Led Zeppelin's *Presence*—before he felt panicky again, then everything would be fine.

He was always able to picture the album cover in time.

Now Rowan understood, conceptually, that this was nothing but superstitious nonsense, but he'd felt himself doing it anyway. In fact, he still found himself doing it on occasion.

Some habits were hard to break.

"That's what you were doing with the sign? Letting people know you thought about The Game and lost?"

"Bingo," Valentine said as she returned to her desk. "Harriet from Disney is out sick for your twelve-thirty lunch, but I wanted to ask before I canceled the reservation."

"Where is it?"

"Fire & Sage. You'll have to drive if you want to make it in time."

Rowan checked his watch. He had fifteen minutes. "I'll make it." The thought of having to consider where and what to eat for lunch was too much for him at the moment. He just wanted to continue moving forward until he was no longer obsessing over the attractive and engaging woman who'd vanished at the restaurant.

"Cool," Valentine said, followed by, "Shit."

"You thought about your game again, didn't you?"

"Yep," she said as she lifted her *I lost The Game* sign and took another picture.

The restaurant was crowded. A tall friendly Black woman with an accent Rowan thought might be Portuguese led him to a long leather banquette made up of two-seat tables that ran the entire length of the back wall. She handed him a menu and told him his server would be along shortly. A few minutes later, a shortish twentysomething man in a graphic T-shirt and jeans arrived at Rowan's table. "Welcome to Fire and Sage. I'm Clayton. Can I get you something to drink?"

"Topo Chico, please."

"You got it. Lemon on the side?"

"That would be great, thank you."

"Awesome," he said, and just before he turned to go, Rowan noticed that the image on Clayton's T-shirt was familiar. It was part of a Coca-Cola ad campaign from the 1990s featuring a family of bears drinking Cokes. Polar bears.

White bears.

Rowan shook his head.

Talking about the white bear problem with Valentine, Rowan realized, was clearly having an effect on his state of mind.

Try not to think about a white bear.

When Clayton returned with Rowan's sparkling water, he ordered an ahi tower appetizer and the gnocchi special, then pulled out his phone, opened a dating app, and started swiping.

He wasn't feeling particularly confident about finding a match; it had simply become habit. Swiping left on somebody's picture felt good—not because Rowan felt powerful or superior, but because he felt productive, like he was somehow pruning away excess foliage surrounding the path to a potential future girlfriend. Swiping right was similar, but a bit more exciting due to the limited number of times Rowan actually did it. And, of course, getting a match always delivered an adrenaline burst.

A rat getting rewarded with cheese at the end of a maze.

Dating apps were games, and like a large part of the single population of Seattle, Rowan had become addicted to playing. But there was a bit more to it than that.

Rowan was still looking for Eliza Brand.

He thought maybe he'd discover her profile on another app.

A loud clanging caused Rowan to pause his swiping.

A couple of city workers were outside the restaurant in lift buckets, hanging promotional banners from the streetlights along 1st Avenue; the sound had come from one of them knocking a metal tool against the light pole.

He looked back down at his phone and was about to continue swiping for dates when his vision began to swim and the sound in the room became thin and tinny. It was as if all the bass had somehow been removed from the world.

What the hell was happening?

Rowan set his phone down and focused on the work crew outside. He looked up at the stylized white-on-dark-amber banner they were placing atop the light pole. The banners were being hung to promote a show at the Seattle Art Museum called *California: A*

Celebration of Art from the Golden Age of the Golden State. The graphic they were using to promote the new exhibit was a stylized modernization of the California state flag.

In this case, a white bear on a dark golden background.

Try not to think about a white bear.

It had to be a coincidence.

To calm himself, he turned his attention from the banner to the song that was playing on the restaurant's sound system. It was a shoegazer band from the early nineties and he knew the album had been released by Creation Records, but he couldn't remember the band's name or the title of the song.

He launched his audio fingerprint app, pressed the button called Listen and Identify, and a few seconds later, Rowan had the information he was looking for. It was a song by the English band Ride, from their debut album, *Nowhere.*

The song was called "Polar Bear."

Rowan took a couple of deep breaths and tried to relax, but he was dangerously close to hyperventilating. He needed fresh air, so he threw a couple of twenty-dollar bills onto the table, stood up, and hurried out of the restaurant.

Once outside, Rowan forced himself to picture the cover of Led Zeppelin's *Presence* album. As the familiar image of the oddly formal family surrounding the obelisk popped into his mind, he began to feel a little better, but there was no way he was going to be able to go back inside. There were just too many weird coincidences. He needed to get as far away from all of those white bears as fast as he possibly could, so Rowan started walking back to his car. As he walked, he glanced up at the banners hanging from the streetlamps.

The bears were leading him away from the restaurant.

Once again, Rowan had the feeling that he was being followed. He turned to check, but he couldn't see anyone. He hurried his pace, and when he finally reached his car, he turned around again.

There was nobody there.

He looked up and noticed that he'd reached the end of the bear banners. The last of them was hanging directly above Rowan's car.

Another coincidence.

Rowan noticed a pair of absolutely identical, brand-new shiny black Toyota Supras parked across the street, one behind the other. They were just idling, with no driver or passengers visible through the heavily tinted side windows. Rowan shivered. There was no way those cars could be connected to him, but he couldn't help but think there was something strange about the whole situation.

He exhaled and tried to focus on his breathing.

Slow and steady. In through the nose, out through the mouth.

There are all kinds of wild coincidences in life, he thought. *They happen all the time. They don't mean a thing. Those cars are probably just there to pick up Postmates orders and deliver them to stoned tech bros at Amazon.*

Valentine and Dostoyevsky's white bears had Rowan imagining things.

He got into his car and started driving down 1st Avenue toward the ocean. He put on Pink Floyd's *Animals* and opened the windows. *Animals* was one of Rowan's favorite albums. There were songs about pigs, dogs, and sheep—but most important, not one single track on that album featured a bear of any kind.

The combination of the music and the cool misty ocean air helped Rowan relax. People in Seattle were always complaining about the downtown traffic, but not Rowan.

He found it comforting.

He felt like he could get lost in it.

Rowan saw the first white bear about ten minutes after he'd left the restaurant.

It was sitting in the middle of the intersection of 1st and Bell, a child's stuffed animal. He kept driving. About thirty seconds later he saw another bear, and then another four. Pretty soon they were everywhere. Rowan could feel his heart pounding in his chest.

Try not to think about a white bear.

He stared straight ahead, demanding that his brain ignore the stuffed bears that suddenly littered the street. Instead, he tried his best to focus on the buildings he was passing and the traffic that surrounded him.

He'd finally stopped thinking about white bears when he glanced in the rearview mirror and noticed that the two black Toyota Supras he'd seen earlier were now behind him.

He wanted to speed up, but traffic had slowed to a crawl. As Rowan approached the next stoplight, he saw the reason why.

A large white delivery truck had rolled onto its side in the middle of the intersection, its back door was wide open, and there was an enormous pile of white bears both inside the truck and out on the street.

The truck had been delivering toys, which explained the bears.

Rowan felt a surge of relief and shook his head. He looked down at his hands, which were white from squeezing the steering wheel, and forced himself to relax.

Coincidences happen every single day. There was nothing to worry about.

Because the truck with the bears was blocking the entire back half of the intersection, police were directing all drivers to turn either left or right. Rowan made a right turn, happy to get away from those bears as fast as he possibly could. But shortly after making the turn, he drove over a deep pothole that shook him to attention with a loud bang. A few seconds later, he heard a familiar flapping sound.

Rowan had a flat tire. Two of them, actually.

He pulled over and parked in front of a restaurant he'd visited a few times called Shirokuma Sushi and got out to survey the damage.

Sure enough, both tires on the right side of his car were completely flat.

For the first time Rowan noticed that Shirokuma Sushi's mascot was a white bear.

He started to laugh. It was getting ridiculous.

"What the fuck is happening?" Rowan said to himself as he opened his trunk to look for a spare, which wouldn't really help considering the fact that two of his tires were flat.

"It's probably something called Rabbits," said a woman's voice from a few feet away.

Rowan jumped and then turned to face the woman who'd spoken—and, as he did that, two black Toyota Supras identical to the ones Rowan had noticed earlier turned onto the street behind him.

Those couldn't be the same two cars, could they?

The woman was around five foot six or seven with auburn hair and bright light brown eyes. She was wearing ripped blue jeans, Converse high-tops, and a black T-shirt with the number 90 on it. She reminded Rowan of somebody famous, but he couldn't place her.

Rowan felt the world begin to spin around him.

"If you don't want to end up drugged and imprisoned, you're going to want to come with me," she said. "Now."

He tried to speak, but he couldn't think of the right words.

Winona Ryder.

That's who it was. She reminded him of Winona Ryder in the movie *Celebrity*.

He took another look at the white bear sushi logo and then he noticed four people, dressed in black and wearing weird masks, step into the street behind the woman. He wasn't sure why, but he had the feeling that she might be telling him the truth, and that he might actually be in some kind of immediate danger.

"Rowan!" She grabbed Rowan's jacket and yanked him away from his car and into the flow of traffic.

He could have pulled himself away, but he didn't.

He left his car sitting in front of the restaurant and followed Winona across the street.

12

ENGINE THREE

Emily woke up and checked her phone. 4:44 a.m.

She couldn't get back to sleep, so she fell into sweatpants and a loose T-shirt that read KARMA POLICE and stepped into the hallway outside the bedroom.

Emily loved the way the heated hardwood floor warmed her feet as she moved down the hall toward the living room. Heated floors always reminded her of a cabin that she and K had stayed in during a trip to Iceland. It had been constructed almost entirely out of glass, in order to maximize the view of the northern lights, with a radiant-heated tile floor featuring beautifully intricate geometric floral patterns that reminded Emily of her grandmother's Formica dining room table.

That two-week trip was one of the happiest times in Emily's life.

When the sun set on the two of them in that tiny glass cabin, the sky became everything, and Emily felt like she was suddenly awake in another world. It was as if they'd become part of the tapestry of a distant planet and were looking down into a deep sea of stars awash in a bright blue-white fire.

Emily shook her head. The last thing she needed right now was to fall into some kind of self-pity nostalgia spiral. She needed to focus.

As she moved down the hall, the northern lights of Emily's memories became the distant sparkle of the city through the lake house's living room windows. The way the lights glittered and moved through the darkness made Emily feel like she was walking toward the viewing area of some kind of spacecraft.

Emily stared through the windows at the city slowly waking up. The headlights of cars snaking along distant boulevards, and the flashing of faraway streetlights created an impressionist tapestry of amber, green, and red. The windows on the far-right-hand side of the room, however, remained dark, filled with the distant quiet of the lake.

Emily took a moment to appreciate the stillness of the house and the accompanying sense of opportunity that came from being awake before the rest of the city—that feeling of freedom, like the pathways of the day had yet to be plotted, the labyrinth of exciting possibilities still to be drawn. She sat down at the dining room table and turned on Scarpio's computer.

Iceland always made Emily think of Sigur Rós, and a few clicks later, "Starálfur" started to play from the iMac's built-in speakers. Scarpio's bedroom was located at the far end of the house, but she lowered the volume just in case. Then she made some coffee and sat back down in front of the computer to search for any sign of Rabbits.

About half an hour later, Scarpio stepped into the kitchen and started rummaging around. "I just got off the phone with Fatman."

"He's up early."

"I don't think he's been to sleep. He said he'll have the restaurant guy's info by noon."

At twelve o'clock, as promised, Scarpio received a text message from Fatman.

"The car is registered to a man named Rowan Chess."

"Do we have an address?"

"Looks like he lives in Capitol Hill. His office is in the Engine Three building on Pine."

Emily performed an online search for Rowan Chess. The first result was an image of a man standing in front of a modern glass-and-concrete building in downtown Seattle. He was dressed in dark jeans and a navy blue sweater, and curly brown hair obscured one of his eyes as he stared into the distance. There was something absent-minded about the way he stood, like he was about to empty the contents of his pockets in search of a handkerchief or something equally anachronistic.

Rowan was an architect, and although he'd designed some residential buildings, it looked like his specialty was theme parks. There was an attraction at an amusement park in Texas that Emily had tried a couple of years earlier and absolutely loved: the Caves of Altamira. It was billed as a wholly unique experience: part haunted house, part adventure roller coaster, with a little bit of escape room thrown in. That thing was by far the best theme park ride Emily had ever experienced. For some reason Emily knew that when she searched for Rowan Chess and the Caves of Altamira, she would discover that he had designed it.

And she was right.

She felt a shiver run through her body.

In the midst of recovering from dimensional drift, those kinds of coincidences could be extremely unsettling. She took a screen capture of Rowan Chess.

"What do you think?" Scarpio asked. "Home or office?"

"The Engine Three building is closer."

"Well, then, let's go see if the man's at work."

"Any idea why it's called the Engine Three building?" Emily asked as she and Scarpio approached a three-story, concrete-and-glass building.

"It's named after the fire engine that saved it from burning down. It used to be a candy factory. A lot of neighborhood folks worked there, so its safety was important to the area's immigrant populations. Apparently, while the buildings on either side of it burned, the team of Engine Three—the oldest fire engine in the city, manned mostly by local residents—desperately fought to save it. Legend has it that liquid hard candy spilled from the doors out into the street, and in the days after the fire, the neighborhood kids were seen breaking up the candy and eating it."

"That sounds made up," Emily said.

"You're probably right, but it's a fun story. Here we are."

Carved into the building above four enormous windows that faced the street were a series of letters that spelled out: ENGINE THREE. Rowan's office was located directly below those letters. Stenciled onto a glass door next to one of the large windows was the name of his company, CHESS DESIGN & ARCHITECTURE.

There was a woman visible through the windows, leaning against a desk and talking on her phone. Her long blond hair had been pinned into a 1950s-style bun. She wore old-fashioned cat-eye glasses, a man's blue suede suit jacket, and a sky-blue poodle skirt. She barely glanced up when Emily and Scarpio stepped through the door and into the office.

"Is Rowan in?" Emily asked.

"He's out for lunch. I can leave him a message, if you'd like."

"What time do you expect him back?" Scarpio asked.

"You just missed him, so a couple of hours maybe?"

"Do you happen to know where he went? We'd really like to speak to him about a renovation project, part of the former Expo site in Montreal."

Emily figured that the possibility of a job would force her to take them a bit more seriously. But it turned out that wasn't going to be necessary.

"Holy shit, you're Alan Scarpio."

"Guilty."

"My name is Valentine. I'm a *huge* fan. Your tuition freeze initiative at the university made it possible for me and my sister to get advanced degrees."

Scarpio smiled. "Thank you."

"I took business management, and my sister got a degree in communications, which is funny because she's completely incapable of communicating with anybody."

"Rowan?" Emily asked.

"He's at Fire and Sage."

"On 1st Avenue?"

"Yeah."

"Thanks," Emily said.

"Are you going to ask him to design something?"

"Maybe," Scarpio replied.

"Cool." She nodded, then mumbled something under her breath while she took a photo of herself holding up a piece of paper that Scarpio and Emily couldn't see.

As they made their way back to Scarpio's SUV, Emily shivered and zipped up her hoodie. She could feel a slight breeze on her face, and a misty rain had just started to fall, but she knew that the weather wasn't the cause of the chill.

It was something else.

"I'll drive," Emily said as she opened the door and slid inside.

"We should hurry. If we're looking for this guy, the others won't be far behind."

Emily nodded, then pressed her foot down on the accelerator— and as she did, she felt a familiar feeling move through her body.

The chill she'd felt a few seconds earlier was replaced by something else.

It was something she hadn't felt for a long time.

Excitement.

Rabbits.

They passed by the front of the restaurant just as Rowan Chess was stepping outside. He looked stressed as he ran his hands through his hair and stared up at a crew of workers putting up promotional banners of some kind.

"There." Scarpio pointed. "He's walking away."

"Fuck, I can't turn around. Hang on." Emily sped up as she blasted through a yellow light. At the next intersection, she made an illegal U-turn and raced back in the direction Rowan Chess had been walking. After getting stuck at two interminable red lights, they finally tracked him down.

"Shit," Scarpio said.

"What?"

"He just pulled into traffic. Black Volvo."

"I see him." Emily changed lanes and maneuvered so she was directly behind Rowan's car.

"Stay close. We don't wanna lose him."

"I don't tell you how to do your billionaire shit. Don't tell me how to tail somebody."

"Fair enough," Scarpio said with a laugh.

They'd been driving for about ten minutes when Emily began noticing small stuffed animals scattered along the road. "What's with all the polar bears?" she asked.

"No idea," Scarpio said as he watched a pickup truck run over and completely destroy two of them. "But they're getting crushed out there."

About five minutes later, they reached the source of the stuffed bear apocalypse. A delivery truck had capsized in the middle of the street and hundreds of the small white bears had spilled from the truck and into the intersection.

"The police are directing people away." Scarpio pointed to the right where the black Volvo was disappearing around a corner. "You need to change lanes."

"Hang on," Emily said, and pulled across two lanes, cutting off an extremely angry woman in a hybrid Ford Escort.

"Looks like he might have a flat," Scarpio said as they turned and followed the black Volvo up a wide tree-lined street.

"That's perfect," Emily said as she drove by Rowan's car. A few seconds later, she stopped in the middle of the road and put the car in park.

"What are you doing?"

Emily opened her door and stepped into the street. "I'm going to check it out."

"We can't just stop here."

"There's a parking lot half a block up ahead."

Scarpio jumped into the driver's seat. "Don't do anything stupid," he called out, then shut the door and sped off up the street.

As she made her way back toward Rowan's car, Emily noticed two black Toyota Supras with extremely tinted (almost certainly illegal) windows pull into the street and start slowly moving toward Rowan's car.

"Shit," Emily said as she approached Rowan, who was staring into his trunk.

"What the fuck is happening?" Rowan asked.

"It's probably something called Rabbits," Emily said. "If you don't want to end up drugged and imprisoned, you're going to want to come with me. Now."

Rowan appeared dazed suddenly, his body swaying. Emily heard the thunk of car doors closing and turned to see four people dressed in black, wearing what looked like super-high-tech facial-recognition-blocking masks, step into the street behind her.

"Rowan!" Emily grabbed Rowan's jacket and yanked him away from his car and into the flow of traffic.

"What's going on?" Rowan asked as he blinked his eyes and tried to focus.

"Just a little something called saving your ass."

"Oh," Rowan said, groggily. "Okay."

Emily led Rowan through traffic as the people in super-high-tech masks stepped into the street behind them.

A few cars honked, and others stopped to watch the masked people in the black suits closing in on Rowan and Emily.

It was a scene right out of an action movie.

The masked people were closing in fast.

"What's happening?" Rowan asked, coming to his senses a little. "Who are you? Who are those people?"

"Those are the bad guys, Rowan," Emily said, scanning the street for any avenue of escape.

"Who are you?"

Emily ignored his question. She saw the familiar yellow of Seattle's most popular taxi company and yanked Rowan farther across the street toward a cab that was moving slowly through the intersection, the driver clearly doing his best to avoid the traffic jam that had been caused by the truck carrying the white teddy bears.

Emily ran in front of the cab, her right hand raised in the air, a confused and half-catatonic Rowan hanging from her left arm like a piece of human driftwood.

The cab stopped, and Emily shoved Rowan into the back seat.

"Drive!" she yelled.

As they moved through the intersection, Emily took a look out the rear window.

No sign of the black suits or their matching black cars.

"Where to?" the cabbie asked.

Emily handed him a fifty-dollar bill. "Please just drive. Fast."

The cabbie turned right and stepped on the accelerator.

A few minutes later, after Emily was fairly certain they weren't being followed, she gave the cabbie Scarpio's address, leaned back in the seat beside Rowan, and closed her eyes.

If the lake house had been compromised, Emily was pretty sure the Rabbits Police would have come for them much earlier. She knew it was risky, but she really had no place else to go. She also knew that Scarpio would head back there as soon as he possibly could.

"Where are we?" Rowan asked as the two of them stepped out of the elevator and into the house.

"Somewhere safe, I hope."

"You *hope*?"

"Don't make me repeat myself, Rowan. I'm having a shitty day."

"*You're* having a shitty day? I've just been kidnapped, my car is stuck in the middle of the street with two flat tires, and I have to get back to work."

"That's not a good idea."

"Why not?"

"Because they know who you are and they're looking for you."

"Who's looking for me?"

"The bad guys in the crazy masks. And I didn't kidnap you, you idiot. I *saved* you."

"Yeah." Rowan nodded. "Sure. I'm going to call a rideshare."

"What happened in the bathroom at that restaurant?" Emily asked.

Rowan turned very serious. "How do you know about that?"

"I was there."

"You saw her disappear?"

"Not exactly, but I believe the people in those black cars who were following you came to that restaurant looking for whoever was in that bathroom."

"Why would they be looking for Eliza?"

"Because I think she may have been playing a game."

"What game?"

"Rabbits."

"You mentioned that before. What the hell is Rabbits?"

"Get comfortable." Emily motioned for Rowan to sit. "I'm going to tell you one hell of a crazy story."

13

QUESTIONS AT THE END

ROWAN STARED ACROSS an enormous oak dining table at the woman who'd just taken him on a wild ride from one end of Seattle to the other with no regard for his opinion, comfort, or safety. And although he'd just abandoned his car and his head was swimming, Rowan wasn't upset. In fact, he felt alive in a way he hadn't since he was a kid. As strange as the whole situation was—and it was definitely off-the-charts nuts—Rowan was happy that someone other than himself was finally taking Eliza Brand's disappearance from that restaurant bathroom seriously.

Outside of telling him her name, Emily didn't speak much during the ride. Rowan was surprised when they turned onto Lake Washington Boulevard, and even more surprised by their final destination. He recognized the house immediately. He'd taken a mid-century architecture tour in college, and this place had been one of the stops.

Rowan thought it was the most beautiful house he'd ever seen.

Although his area of professional expertise was mainly large-scale architecture, Rowan had designed a handful of private homes over the years, and every one of those designs was inspired, at least in part, by this exact house.

What were the odds that he'd end up here?

"Can I get you something to drink?" Emily asked.

"This is the Orenbach House," Rowan said. "It's an impeccable example of original West Coast Modern post and beam. Arthur Erickson designed the expansion using the original Paul Thiry designs."

"I don't know what any of that means. You want a drink?"

"No, thank you. Do you live here?"

"Kind of," Emily said.

Rowan nodded. A drink didn't sound like a bad idea, actually, and Rowan wished he'd said yes, but there was something far more pressing on his mind. "Are you going to tell me what you know about Eliza Brand?" he asked.

"Who is that?"

"She was my date."

"Eliza Brand. That's the name of the person who disappeared in that restaurant?"

"Yes."

Emily wrote Eliza's name down on a piece of paper. "I don't know her—or at least I don't think I do—but I am going to tell you everything I know about the people I believe came into that restaurant looking for her right after you left."

Emily loaded a video file on Scarpio's iMac. She pressed the space bar, and the footage Emily and Scarpio had been watching earlier filled the screen.

Rowan watched as the scene played out.

Shortly after he left the restaurant, four people dressed in black rushed in and hurried toward the bathroom area.

Rowan had the feeling that he was floating as he watched the scene unfold. The whole situation was unreal. Rowan didn't live a life where people rushed into restaurants looking for his missing date. He didn't live a life where people rushed into restaurants at all.

"You think those people were looking for Eliza?" he asked, at last.

"I do, yes."

"Why?"

"I have no idea. I was hoping you might be able to tell me."

Emily replayed the footage from the camera she'd stuck on the fireplace.

"You really were in the restaurant that night," Rowan said as Emily briefly appeared on the screen.

"I really was. I was there with Alan Scarpio."

"Alan Scarpio? Really?"

Like Bill Gates and Elon Musk, Alan Scarpio was a famous billionaire. Rowan couldn't imagine a world in which he'd be crossing paths with him. Although Scarpio had become somewhat reclusive over the past few years, his name still popped up from time to time in relation to a brand-new environmentally conscious tech company or some altruistic social application.

"Yes," Emily said, "Alan Scarpio."

"You're serious."

"I am. He was with me in the car earlier. He should be here any minute. This is his house."

"Isn't this place owned by a trust called the Orenbach Appreciation and Preservation Society?"

Emily nodded. "I'm pretty sure Scarpio named the trust after the Kinks' 'The Village Green Preservation Society.' I think the fake person he has listed as controller is actually named Raymond Davies."

"You're telling me that you and *Alan Scarpio* were trying to save me from somebody?"

"Somebodies. Plural. Yes. The people in the black cars."

"How did you find me?"

"Your receptionist."

"Valentine?"

Of course Valentine would have told them where to find him. She was great at organization and extremely loyal, but discretion was definitely an area where she could use some improvement.

Emily pulled out her phone and started searching for something.

"What are you doing?"

"Trying to track Scarpio's phone," she said.

"I think I might take you up on that drink now, if you don't mind."

Rowan wasn't sure he believed what Emily was saying. Alan Scarpio had been looking for him? That sounded extremely unlikely. But then again, this entire day was feeling extremely un-likely.

Emily nodded in the direction of the fridge. "Could you grab me one as well? A Corona from the bottom drawer."

Rowan got up and made his way over to the fridge. "Do you think the message in the bathroom stall might have something to do with why those people were there?" he asked.

"What do you mean? What message?" Emily put down her phone and turned to face Rowan.

"There was something written on the back of the door in the final stall in the women's bathroom, in bright red lipstick," Rowan said as he pulled two beers from the fridge—a Corona for Emily and a Rolling Rock for himself.

"The door is open," Emily said.

Rowan spun around, almost dropping the two bottles. "How did you know that?"

Emily approached Rowan and grabbed the beer from his hand. "Are you sure that's what it said?"

Something about the expression on Emily's face had changed. It looked to Rowan like a light had been switched on someplace deep within her.

She knew something about what had happened.

She knew something about Eliza.

"What the hell is going on?" Rowan asked.

"So many things," Emily said, "and I'm going to tell you every-thing I can."

Rowan sat back down at the dining room table. "Okay," he said, and took a huge gulp of beer. "Please hurry."

"That phrase you found on the back of that bathroom stall door—The Door Is Open—is an important part of Rabbits," Emily said as she sat down next to Rowan at the table.

"You keep mentioning this thing called Rabbits. What is it?"

"That bit is kind of complicated, so I'm going to need you to save most of your questions for the end, if possible."

"I'll do my best."

"Okay, so, decades ago, a man named Kellan Meechum discov-

ered something that he compared to a pseudoscientific phenome-
non known as ley lines—alleged hidden veins of energy that exist
deep beneath the earth. His discovery would eventually become
known as the Meechum Radiants."

"Aren't ley lines connected to mythology from ancient Britain?"
Rowan asked.

"Questions for the end," Emily reminded him.

"Sorry." Rowan did his best to keep the irritation from his voice.
He needed information.

"Now, this is where things are going to sound kind of 'out there.'
I just need you to bear with me."

Rowan nodded, although he disagreed. To his thinking, things
had been kind of "out there" for a while already.

"We live in a multiverse," Emily said, "and there's something
going on beneath the surface of said multiverse—something that
you and I take for granted."

"Something like ley lines?"

Emily stared.

"You can't just throw around ley lines and multiverse theory and
expect me not to have a couple of questions," Rowan explained. "I
mean, that's not really fair . . . is it?"

Emily just continued to stare.

"Questions at the end. Fine."

"Back in 1945," Emily continued, "while Meechum was leading
an experiment related to strange attractors and the butterfly effect,
he discovered something surprising. By performing certain . . .
movements or patterns along certain pathways, and by following
connections and tracking coincidences, Meechum claimed he was
able to manipulate the butterfly effect. He could perform a series of
seemingly unconnected moves and, if his moves were enacted accurately, he would be able to facilitate an effect based on a completely unrelated cause."

"Wow, okay . . ."

"Meechum spent years mapping out a number of ostensibly random coincidences and anomalies in and around the city of Seattle,

and soon discovered that some of these things weren't as random as they initially appeared. He began noticing groups of highly improbable coincidences the closer he came to successfully engaging the pathways of energy he called Radiants. Meechum believed that his Radiants might be used to facilitate changes in the world. He often told a story about successfully manipulating a bank's interest rate by simply preventing a data analyst in an unrelated field from buying her morning coffee. In his later years, Meechum would suggest that by manipulating these Radiants, travel back and forth between universes was not only possible but probable."

Rowan exhaled and placed his hands on the table. "I'm sorry, but all of this sounds extremely . . . unlikely."

"You've never noticed anything strange? The world feels suddenly . . . different somehow?"

"Not really," Rowan said, but that was a lie. He knew exactly what she was talking about. He'd felt different for as long as he could remember.

"Has a small part of your reality ever just . . . changed?" Emily continued. "Maybe a company's logo looks different from the logo you remember as a kid, or perhaps a children's book no longer has the same name?"

"You're talking about the Mandela Effect? Berenstain Bears?"

"It's Berenstein, and that's part of it. But what I'm talking about is feeling like the world around you is slowly forgetting the world that you remember, one tiny piece at a time."

"I may have felt something like that," Rowan admitted.

He felt it all the time.

Emily nodded. "Me too."

"What does all of this have to do with my date disappearing from that restaurant and a game called Rabbits?"

Emily exhaled slowly, took a deep breath, and continued. "Okay, so, a few years after Kellan Meechum published his final paper on the Radiants, a computer scientist named Hawk Worricker discovered Meechum's work."

"WorGames' Hawk Worricker?" Rowan asked, surprised to hear

Worricker's name connected to whatever was going on after having so recently experienced something strange at the home of his daughter, Helena.

"Yes," Emily said. "Worricker eventually figured out that Meechum's Radiants were real—but not only that, he also discovered that they were decaying and would soon lose their efficacy."

"Their efficacy?"

"Worricker thought that what Meechum had discovered were more than simply invisible lines of manipulable energy. He believed that these Radiants existed for a reason, that they functioned as a kind of universal reset mechanism—a way to release a little steam, so to speak. Worricker became convinced that the Radiants were extremely important, that they were there to help maintain the integrity and health of the individual streams of the multiverse—a multiverse that Meechum realized was desperately in need of repair."

"I'm going to have to stop you there. This sounds absolutely—"

"Batshit, I know. But I'm almost finished," Emily continued. "Worricker needed to work out a way to fix what he believed was a decaying multiversal repair mechanism, and that's when he came up with Rabbits."

"A game?"

Emily nodded. "It began as an evolving artificial intelligence engine—a system capable of performing specific adjustments at specific times. Eventually, after over a decade of experimentation, Worricker figured out that the framework of a game was the most effective method of manipulating the Radiants. That was in 1959, which is when most of us believe that the modern version of the game began."

"A game acting as a multiverse repair mechanism?"

"Yes."

"And if that mechanism fails, what happens then?"

"We almost found out when a man called Crow put the multiverse at risk in an attempt to bring back his deceased daughter. This happened during the last iteration of the game."

"So the game is over?"

"I have no idea."

"Why not?"

"We haven't been able to find it."

"You can't find the game?"

Emily shook her head.

"Is that normal?"

"Well, it's possible that we're between iterations, but even if that's the case, there should be some indication that it exists, or existed at some point in the past."

"And there's nothing?"

"That's right."

"So what does that mean as far as multiverse repair goes?"

"That's what we're trying to find out."

"We? You mean you and Alan Scarpio?"

Emily nodded. "That phrase, The Door Is Open, is significant."

"How so?"

"You may have just discovered Rabbits."

"Me?"

Emily ignored his question, putting a finger to her lips.

Rowan heard voices coming from somewhere outside. It sounded like at least two people, maybe more.

"Is someone here?" Rowan whispered.

"Shit," Emily said as she jumped up and brushed her fingers across a tablet on the wall. It lit up with feeds from eight security cameras that appeared to be covering different angles of the exterior.

Rowan stood up and joined her.

The monitors showed three people walking toward the entrance of the elevator that led up to the main level.

"Who's that?" Rowan asked, pointing at a man wearing an expensive designer suit who'd just stepped into the elevator, flanked by a pair of men in navy blue uniforms who appeared to be either extremely muscular waiters or average-sized security guards.

"Looks like somebody found us," she said as she pulled the SIM card from her phone and slid it into the microwave.

"What are you doing?"

"Being careful."

Rowan slipped his hand into the back pocket of his jeans where he could feel his phone. "You don't want me to microwave *my* SIM card, do you?"

"Don't say anything. Just follow my lead." She pressed a button on the microwave and it started to cook her SIM card.

Rowan was beginning to think he'd fallen into something that was most likely insanely illegal. "We just broke into somebody's house, didn't we?"

Emily remained silent.

"Shit. You don't really know Alan Scarpio, do you?"

"Sshhh." Emily put her finger up to Rowan's lips to shut him up.

At that point, the elevator doors opened and Designer Suit stepped into the room followed by the two men—who, based on the way their matching uniforms bulged with what had to be hidden weaponry, were definitely not waiters.

Rowan watched Emily put her hands up and followed her example.

"Who the hell are you?" Emily asked.

"Sorry about this," Designer Suit said. "It's nothing personal."

"I hate it when people say that," Emily replied.

He smiled. "Oh really?"

"You're a person. I'm a person. When you do something, it's personal."

"Something like break into somebody's house?"

"We have permission to be here."

He just stood there, smiling.

"Who are you?" Emily asked.

"Private security."

"Can I see some identification?"

Rowan noticed that Emily hadn't mentioned Alan Scarpio, which meant she almost certainly didn't know him, which, in turn, meant that Rowan had just participated in breaking and entering.

This day just kept getting weirder.

"We're playing a game," Emily said.

"What does that mean?"

"It's an online scavenger hunt. We're supposed to take a photo of ourselves standing inside somebody's house. The trick is, we're not allowed to be invited in. We haven't taken anything, I promise. That's not what this is about."

Rowan thought the man was contemplating the possibility that Emily was telling the truth.

"Can we go?" Emily asked.

There was a long moment of silence before the man answered Emily's question.

"Of course. I apologize for any inconvenience."

Then the microwave beeped.

"Are you sure you're not playing another kind of game?" the man asked as he slowly walked over to the microwave.

Rowan got the idea that this man didn't seem all that concerned that they'd broken into Alan Scarpio's house.

The man opened the microwave and pulled out the SIM card. He took a second to look it over, then looked at Emily's phone sitting on the table. "Yours?"

Emily didn't reply.

Something about the situation felt off to Rowan. "Listen," he said. "I don't know what's happening here, but we're not criminals, and we'd really just appreciate it if you could either call the police or let us go on our way."

Emily glared at Rowan.

The man stared at the two of them for a moment, and then smiled. "We have no justification to hold you. I mean, you're just playing a game. Isn't that right?"

"Right," Rowan said, and then Emily started dragging him toward the elevator.

"Don't you need a photo before you go?" Designer Suit asked. "You know, for your game?"

"Maybe next time," Emily said as she pulled Rowan into the elevator.

"What the hell is going on?" Rowan asked as the doors closed and the elevator began to descend.

"Sshhh," Emily replied. "Get ready to run."

"What?"

But when the elevator doors opened again on the ground floor, Emily and Rowan were facing a group of six men and women, all dressed in black or dark gray clothing. They weren't brandishing any weapons, but it was pretty clear by the way they were standing that they had a whole bunch of them tucked away somewhere. Based on their similar wardrobe and the way they carried themselves, Rowan figured these people had to be working with Designer Suit.

"Emily Connors," said a tall woman with a Spanish accent, "we're going to need you and Mr. Chess to hand over your phones and come with us."

"If we say no?"

"Do you remember the headaches from the tranquilizer darts?"

Emily just glared.

But Rowan could tell by the expression on her face that Emily definitely remembered.

14

WE WANT THE FUTURE WE WERE PROMISED, NOT THE FUTURE WE DESERVE

EMILY STRUGGLED IN VAIN to keep her wrists apart as she and Rowan were zip-tied and led into a black cargo van.

She watched as one of the men in black closed the van's sliding door. She recognized him from an earlier encounter. She called him Elevator Shoes because he was clearly wearing lifts. She'd known who these people were as soon as she saw them.

Rabbits Police.

A few seconds later, the van started moving away from Scarpio's lake house toward wherever they were going. Emily could feel the zip ties against her wrists and ankles. Not tight enough to cause any pain or stop blood flow, but too snug to allow the torque required to break free.

These people were professionals.

"I thought you said you knew Alan Scarpio?" Rowan whispered.

"Sshhh," Emily said.

"Really? You're going to shush me again?"

Emily glared.

"Who are these people?" Rowan demanded.

Emily ignored Rowan as she examined the interior of the van.

They'd been placed side by side on a long bench seat, then carefully strapped in with seatbelts—a safety precaution Emily found interesting, although not all that reassuring. There were two people sitting up front—a man and a woman. Neither looked familiar.

"Are they going to kill us?" Rowan whispered.

"Can you please stop talking? I need to think."

Rowan opened his mouth to say something, but remained silent.

There were no windows in the back of the van, but Emily could see what appeared to be a two-lane road or highway through the driver's side-view mirror. Nothing but rain and trees. No significant clues to where they might be headed in the visible geography.

Emily was worried. She'd been kidnapped by these people before, but on each of those occasions, she'd eventually been able to convince them she had no knowledge of a game called Rabbits. She had a feeling that things were going to be different this time.

Probably very unpleasantly different.

Before they'd been taken, Rowan told Emily he'd seen the phrase "The Door Is Open" scrawled in lipstick on a bathroom stall door. If he was telling the truth, the appearance of that phrase might be evidence of the game.

Maybe Rabbits was alive and well.

Maybe the twelfth iteration had begun.

If either of those things was true, Emily might finally be able to figure out what the hell was going on with this dimensional stream, why the game had somehow remained hidden here, and what detrimental effect, if any, the fact that Rabbits was missing had on the health of this stream or perhaps even the multiverse itself. After what had happened in her last stream, Emily was understandably a little sensitive to certain types of interdimensional game-related anomalies. And there was something else. If she could find the game, she might be able to use it to slip into another stream, perhaps a stream where K remembered everything, a stream where Emily could get back to her real life.

She needed to know about the status of the game, but first, there was this unpleasant matter of getting captured to deal with.

They drove for about twenty minutes before the van started to slow down.

As they slowed, Emily noticed an identical black van behind

them in the side-view mirror. Based on what she'd been able to make out, they'd been traveling through cow country for two or three miles.

Why were they stopping?

Then she heard a familiar distant clanging. They were most likely approaching a railway crossing. It had to be a train.

The van eventually came to a complete stop, and a few seconds later, Emily heard the train. A phone rang somewhere, and the driver of the van and whoever was sitting in the passenger seat started arguing with whoever was on the other end of the line. Emily got the sense that the person on the phone was behind them in the matching black van, but she couldn't make out the details of their conversation over the noise of the van's engine, the passing train, and the incessant clanging of the rail crossing apparatus.

They'd been idling at the railway crossing for a few minutes when a loud smashing sound made both Emily and Rowan jump. Somebody had thrown a gray metal canister through the passenger-side window. It landed in the driver's lap and started to hiss.

It was some kind of smoke bomb.

The two people in the front thrashed in panic as they struggled to free themselves from their seatbelts in an attempt to avoid the thick white smoke flooding the interior of the van.

Emily tried to stand and move forward, but because her hands and feet were tied, she didn't quite make it. Instead, she fell face-first in between the front seats. She tried to take a deep breath and hold it, but she'd already inhaled too much of the smoke.

The world went black.

When Emily opened her eyes she had no idea what was happening.

There was a humming between her ears—an achy, ticklish buzz. She blinked a few times and tried to focus. She could tell that she was in a vehicle of some kind, probably on a freeway based on the sound of the wheels against the asphalt, but nothing in her immediate surroundings revealed exactly where she was or how long she'd been out.

She was staring at the immaculately clean black carpet of some type of SUV—foreign, maybe a Porsche. The carpet smelled brand-new. This was definitely not the vehicle she'd passed out in. Rowan was asleep in the seat beside her. He looked just about as comfortable as you could be sleeping in an SUV with your head bent awkwardly against the headrest.

Emily and Rowan were no longer zip-tied.

"Welcome back," said a green-eyed man with short-cropped dark blond hair. He was sitting directly across from Emily in one of two comfy-looking bucket seats. He appeared to be in his early thirties, and he spoke with a bit of an accent—maybe Greek or Italian. He wore shiny black shoes and a gray suit, obviously tailored.

He held out a bottle of water and two pills. "Your head is going to feel terrible."

Emily ignored the water and pills. "Where are we headed?" she asked as she clocked the exits of the SUV.

"You don't need to do that," he said.

"Do what?"

He smiled. "I'm a friend. You're not in any danger."

Emily stared at his face for a moment. She couldn't quite get a read on this guy.

She hated that.

"Are you the kind of friend who's going to tell me where we're going?" she asked. Her head was killing her. When she blinked, it felt like knives in her eye sockets.

"Someplace safe," he replied. Another smile.

Emily didn't much care for that smile either.

Rowan woke up and rubbed his eyes. "What happened?"

"This man says he's one of the good guys. Apparently he's taking us somewhere safe."

The man continued to smile. "It's nice to meet you, Mr. Chess." He offered Rowan the same bottle of water and pills that he'd offered Emily.

"How do you know my name?"

"Please, just try to relax. I'll fill you in on everything soon," he said. "I promise."

"What should we call you?" Emily asked.

"You can call me Hazel."

"Hazel?" Emily asked. "Really?"

"Is he one of them?" Rowan motioned to the man who called himself Hazel.

Hazel looked at Emily, who returned his gaze.

Emily stared at the man thoughtfully for a moment, then turned back to Rowan. "No," she said. "I have no idea what he is."

The man called Hazel smiled.

The SUV veered off the main road and entered what appeared to be a large industrial park. They eventually pulled over, and Emily and Rowan followed Hazel out of the vehicle.

After a very brief conversation between Hazel and the driver, the SUV pulled away and left the three of them standing in front of a group of old factories of some kind. There were seven or eight buildings on a large plot of land, all surrounded by a high metal fence with a security gate.

Hazel started walking toward the gate. Emily and Rowan followed.

"Your name's not really Hazel, is it?" Emily asked.

He ignored her and just kept walking.

Hazel, the alleged winner of the eighth iteration of the game, was the most famous Rabbits player of all time. It was possible that this was just some guy named Hazel, of course, but the glint in his eye said otherwise. Emily had no idea why this man was using Hazel's name, but it couldn't be a coincidence. The fact that he might actually be Hazel didn't cross her mind. Hazel was a legend. You don't just wake up in a strange motor vehicle with Hazel smiling in your face.

Unless, of course, she just did.

"Any chance you're going to fill us in on what's happening here?" Emily asked.

"Soon," Hazel said as he pushed aside some of the small bushes and trees that partially covered the gate to reveal a security panel.

"They say never allow yourself to be taken to a second location," Emily said.

He laughed. "You're free to go, if you'd like."

Emily stared at him for a moment, then shook her head.

He entered a code and the three of them passed through the open gate and into the industrial compound.

"What is this place?" Rowan asked.

"Operations center slash safe house," Hazel said as they approached the largest of the buildings: a low red-brick three-story affair. "We call it The Factory." He pulled out some keys and used one of them to unlock a set of light gray metal doors.

Inside, the building reminded Emily of a high school. The halls were extremely long, with wide linoleum floors and thickly painted yellow concrete walls. It was hard to tell what this place had been used for in the past. It appeared to be completely vacant now.

"Used to be a mannequin factory," Hazel said, as if reading Emily's mind.

As the double doors closed behind them, the reflected sunlight momentarily lit up the scuffed black tiles of the hallway. It looked to Emily like headlights moving over a dark street in the rain. She rubbed her temples and did her best to shake away the remnants of whatever drug had caused her to lose consciousness.

She needed to be sharp.

At the end of the hall they came to an extremely wide flight of stairs and made their way up to the second floor. Once upstairs, they continued down another long hallway toward yet another set of double doors.

Hazel pushed open the doors, and the three of them entered an enormous rectangular room.

What had once been a factory floor had been transformed into a beautiful modern live/work space straight out of a New York style magazine. A full chef-style kitchen took up most of the left side of the room, and the rest was a combination of living room, bedrooms, and office space. The wall opposite the kitchen to the right was almost completely filled with vintage leaded windows. On the far wall, directly ahead of them as they entered, was an enormous blurry poster of a dark-haired young woman screaming. Her mouth was open wide, her eyes were closed, and her hands were pressed against her ears. Written in translucent-white block letters in the middle of

the poster was the phrase: WE WANT THE FUTURE WE WERE PROM-
ISED, NOT THE FUTURE WE DESERVE. —HAZEL. Way back in the far-
left corner of the room was another set of double doors.

"You live here?" Emily asked.

"Sometimes," Hazel replied. "Make yourselves comfortable."
He pointed to a collection of chairs and sofas loosely arranged
around a glass coffee table shaped like a kidney bean, then walked
over to the kitchen and grabbed three bottles of water from an
enormous industrial-style refrigerator.

"What happened? Why did you bring us here?" Emily asked.

"We were looking for Alan Scarpio," he said, and tossed Emily
and Rowan each a bottle of water. "Do you know where we might
be able to find him?"

"No idea," Emily replied.

"That's unfortunate. We were counting on his help."

"Who's we?"

"Pardon me?"

"You said 'we were looking' for Scarpio, who is we?"

"I belong to a group of concerned citizens."

"Interesting," Emily said. "What is it that your group is concerned about?"

"The world."

Emily snorted a little. "So you wrote that message up there on
the wall? We want the future we were promised, not the future we
deserve? That was you?"

At that moment, two women entered the room. The first was tall
and full-figured, with shoulder-length straight light brown hair.
She wore a black bodysuit beneath a pair of denim overalls. The
second woman was almost a full foot shorter than the first, with
short-cropped black hair. She was wearing a red, white, and blue
Royal Air Force target T-shirt, ripped jeans, and black Doc Martens. Emily couldn't see if either of them had guns, but she had the
feeling they might.

The taller woman led the shorter one into the room and glared at
Hazel. "Who the fuck are they?" She motioned toward Emily and
Rowan.

This woman appeared to be the person in charge.

"You can talk to me. I am capable of speech," Emily said as she stood up from the sofa.

The woman ignored her.

"They were taken at the house owned by Alan Scarpio's holding company in Ireland," Hazel said.

"Where's Scarpio?"

"Unknown."

"Why did you bring them here? You know we don't interfere."

"His name is on the list, Hazel," their escort said, pointing to Rowan.

"That's impossible," the taller woman said.

"It's true."

"You called her Hazel," Rowan said, then turned to Emily. "He called her Hazel."

"What's up with that?" Emily asked, but she was less worried about who was actually named Hazel than she was about Alan Scarpio.

What if he'd been taken by the Rabbits Police?

No. She couldn't think that way. She had to believe that Scarpio would make it back to the lake house or was out there somewhere trying to find a way to get in touch. All she needed to do was make sure he'd be able to find her.

"We're all Hazel," said the taller woman.

"That must be confusing at Christmas," Emily said.

Tall Boss Lady Hazel walked forward until she was standing nose to nose with Emily.

Emily smiled and crossed her arms. She understood that she might be aggravating an already tense situation, but this kind of intrapersonal conflict was something Emily knew how to handle. She was happy for the opportunity to focus her attention on something other than Rabbits. She wanted to feel in control, even if just for a moment.

"I think we should sit down and have a civilized conversation," the first Hazel said, and motioned for everybody to take a seat.

"Why do you call one another Hazel?" Emily asked as she sat down next to Rowan.

Nobody answered.

"He's on the list," original Hazel said. "I think we can break the directive."

"Show me the list," Boss Lady Hazel said.

The first Hazel pulled out his phone, opened some kind of app, and showed it to her.

"What does that mean? What list?" Rowan asked.

Nobody answered. "You're Rowan Chess?" Boss Lady Hazel asked.

Rowan nodded.

"You can call me Datlow," the woman said. "He's Limerick," she continued, motioning to Hazel Number One. "And she's MayDay."

The shorter woman in the RAF T-shirt looked up from where she'd been furiously typing away on a sticker-covered laptop.

"So nobody's name is actually Hazel?" Rowan asked.

"We call one another Hazel in public. It provides an additional layer of protection or distance from those who might be looking for us."

"Who's looking for you?" Emily asked.

Datlow just stared.

"The people who picked you up at that house by the lake," Limerick said.

"What is all of this?" Rowan asked. He pointed at the quote on the wall. "Who the hell is Hazel?"

"You've never heard of Hazel?" Datlow asked.

"No," Rowan said. "Should I have?"

She turned to Emily. "What about you?"

Emily shook her head, but Datlow lingered on her face for a moment.

She doesn't believe me, Emily thought.

"I know that Hazel is a nut, and also a character in *Watership Down,*" Emily said, "but that's it."

Emily actually knew a lot more, including the fact that Hazel was the greatest Rabbits player that had ever lived—the player who had won, and then mysteriously forfeited, the eighth iteration of the game. But as far as Emily knew, Hazel was a puzzle-obsessed gamer, not some sociopolitical revolutionary.

"Somebody calling themselves Hazel started a movement a long time ago," Datlow said. "He or she began posting messages in private online forums, Discords, darknet meeting spaces, and barely moderated image boards. Hazel was asking us to take part in a revolution."

"What kind of revolution?" Rowan asked.

"The quiet but effective kind," Datlow said, leaning against the counter.

"A bunch of us interested in taking from the one percent and giving to the ninety-nine began working together to spread Hazel's message," Limerick said.

"I'm guessing Scarpio represents the one percent? What were you going to do, kidnap him? Kill him?"

"Jesus," Limerick said, "nothing like that. We'd like his help with some corporate environmental concerns. He's the world's only carbon-neutral billionaire. At least he's trying. No, Scarpio's not a target."

"We want the future we were promised, not the future we deserve?" Rowan said. "That's the message?"

"Exactly," Limerick said.

"What does that mean? What future were we promised?" Rowan asked.

"We've been sold a bill of goods. Work hard, play fair, and the American dream can be yours. What we were never told is that we're simply coal for the rich to shovel into stoves in order to make themselves richer," Datlow said.

"Great metaphor, but don't you think that might be a bit reductive?" Emily asked. "I mean, there are all kinds of rags to riches stories. Do you think Selena Gomez or Snoop Dogg would tell you that the American dream is dead?"

"A few success stories don't change the facts," Limerick said. "Things need to change."

"And how does that work?" Emily asked. "What have you changed?"

"Hazel sent us hacked banking information from the worst offenders—environmental polluters, drug dealers, actual pirates and kidnappers, slumlords, and the rest. They lied to us, cheated us, spied on us, so we did the same to them."

"What did you do, exactly?"

"An eye for an eye," Datlow replied.

"What the hell does that mean?"

"Those who didn't hurt anybody didn't get hurt. Those who did, did."

"And? Did it help?"

"At first we felt like we were making a difference—but, in the end, it was nothing but slow, tiny drops of good falling into a seemingly endless bucket of shit," Limerick replied.

"But shortly before he or she disappeared, Hazel started talking about another way," Datlow said. "Something he or she had discovered that was going to change the world."

"What was it? What happened?"

"We received the list."

"What list?"

"This one." Limerick pulled something up on his phone and showed them from across the coffee table. It was a website. "Hazel's final message told us that the people on this list were the key to a new way of changing the world—a way to set everything right."

"What do you mean, Hazel's final message?"

"Immediately after sending the list, Hazel stopped posting. He or she just disappeared."

"When was this?"

"Sometime around 2006," Limerick said.

"And ever since then you've been—"

"Working to spread Hazel's message," Limerick said. "Hazel inspired us to change. We have a responsibility."

"It's been almost twenty years, does anybody still remember Hazel?"

"Those of us who believe in the message continue to do everything we can to spread the word."

"How do you know Hazel's a real person?" Emily asked.

"It doesn't matter. The question of whether or not there actually was a Hazel, or if Hazel was actually a group of people, is irrelevant. The message remains."

"And that's the message?" Emily asked, pointing at the giant sign on the wall. "We want the future we were promised, not the future we deserve?"

"That's the most popular phrase attributed to Hazel, but there's so much more to it than just a simple catchphrase."

"What else is there?"

"There's balance, a sharing of resources, a different and better way to live."

"I'm sorry, but that all sounds a bit Pollyanna to me," Rowan said.

Limerick and Datlow turned to face Rowan.

"Human nature is greed and self-preservation," Rowan continued. "Our most abundant resource is rampant stupidity. Do you honestly believe that the balance of power is going to substantially shift before humanity destroys itself over its inability to escape bigotry, racism, and the malignant ignorance of organized religion?"

Emily looked over at Rowan and raised her eyebrows. Maybe there was more to this guy than she'd initially thought.

"The war between the haves and the have-nots is a struggle as old as time," Rowan continued. "Many have tried to even the playing field. I genuinely hope you succeed, but I wouldn't bet on it."

"What can you tell us about this list?" Emily asked.

Limerick looked over at Datlow, who nodded.

"When Hazel first sent us the list," Limerick said, "there were thousands of names on it. The morning after Hazel's disappearance, half of the names were gone. Within a week, there were only about fifty."

"Who's in charge of this list?"

"No idea. It's entirely decentralized."

"How does it work?" Rowan asked.

"As far as we can tell, the list uses a type of blockchain technology. Every participant or participating link in the chain has an unalterable record of that information. Every new iteration of the list is secure. It's pretty much impossible to hack or cheat."

"So you don't know who's been adding or removing names from the list?"

"No."

"Did you try to track any of them down?"

Limerick glanced over at Datlow.

"What?" Emily asked.

"We tried."

"And?"

"They were all either very recently deceased, using impossible to trace pseudonyms, or they simply didn't exist," Limerick said.

"All of them?" Emily asked.

Limerick nodded. "They either died and dropped off the list, or . . ."

"Or what?" Emily asked.

"Maybe it's the other way around."

"What do you mean?" Rowan asked.

"Maybe they're knocked off the list and *then* they die."

Rowan turned to Emily. "Is this really happening?"

"Are new names ever added to this thing?" Emily asked, ignoring Rowan's question.

"Just once."

"When?"

"A few days ago, a new name appeared on the list for the first time."

"Just one?" Emily asked.

"Yes."

"How many names are on the list right now?" Emily asked.

Limerick looked over at Datlow, who once again nodded her approval.

"Just one."

"The name that was added?" Emily asked.

"That's right," Limerick said.

"Can we take a look?" Emily asked.

Datlow nodded, and Limerick handed Emily his phone.

There, on the screen, was one name.

Rowan Chess.

"I don't understand," Rowan said, looking over Emily's shoulder. "What's *my* name doing on there?"

Emily returned Limerick's phone.

"You've seen the list before, haven't you?" Datlow asked Emily.

"No," Emily said, which was a lie. She had seen the list before—or one just like it.

It was something called The Index.

The Index was, allegedly, a list of all the people currently playing Rabbits. It was reportedly impossible to find, hidden in programs running deep beneath the traditional Internet. The Index was a legendary automated artifact, something that existed at or very near the heart of Rabbits.

Emily leaned back in her chair and exhaled. She'd finally found hard evidence that the game existed in this stream, but for Rabbits to function as it should, there should be tens of thousands of names on that list—players from all over the world manipulating the Meechum Radiants and stabilizing the multiverse.

If that really was The Index, the multiverse was in serious trouble.

15

HOME SWEET HOME

ROWAN SAT NEXT TO EMILY on the Hazels' sofa, and listened as Datlow and Limerick shared information about the group of people who'd abducted them at Scarpio's lake house. The Hazels believed that those people showing up was somehow related to the list.

"You have no idea what they want or how they're connected to this list?" Rowan asked.

Datlow shook her head and turned to Emily. "How about you?"

"What about me?"

"Do you know who those people are?"

"I have no idea. Maybe they were there to rob Scarpio?"

"How well do you know Alan Scarpio?"

"Not that well," Emily said. "We have a couple of mutual friends."

"Why do I feel like you're not telling us the truth?"

Emily stared at Datlow for a long moment, then turned to Rowan. "I'm hungry. I think we should probably get going."

"You can't go out there," Limerick said. "They'll be looking for you."

"Because of the list?" Rowan asked.

Limerick nodded.

Rowan wanted to ask more questions about those people in the black van, but something about the situation told him that he should let Emily take the lead with the Hazels. She clearly knew a whole lot more about whatever the hell was going on, and Rowan didn't want to say anything to mess up whatever story she was feeding them. He'd ask her more about everything as soon as the two of them were alone. "I could eat," he said.

"Great." Emily stood up.

"You know, the next time you're taken by those people, we're not going to be there to save you," Datlow said.

Emily nodded. "Thank you for the hospitality."

"We can't just let them walk out there like everything is normal," Limerick said, then turned to Datlow. "You know what's going to happen."

"It's up to them."

"But his name is on the list." Limerick pointed at Rowan. "Can we at least give them a phone?"

Datlow stared at Emily for a long moment, then finally nodded. The woman called MayDay pulled a burner phone from one of the kitchen cupboards and handed it to Emily. "Ours is the only number stored."

"So, what, we just ask for Hazel?" she said.

Rowan looked over at Datlow, who just shook her head and walked away.

Limerick insisted on driving them from The Factory. Rowan suggested they go back to his place. He wanted to grab some of his things, a change of clothing, and a shower, but Emily wouldn't allow it. She made Limerick take them to an ATM, where she withdrew as much money as she could, and then asked him to drop them off at a Target across the street from a cluster of motels way out on the edge of the city, five miles away.

Rowan followed Emily as she powered through Target, pushing her shopping cart with purpose. He had a lot of questions.

"What do you know about the Hazels?"

"Where I came from there's only one Hazel, and Hazel was just somebody who played the game, not some fortune cookie revolutionary."

"You don't think we should have stayed with them, at least until we have a better idea about what the hell is going on?"

"No. I don't."

"Why not?"

"Because I'm not sure they're careful enough to avoid attracting unwanted attention, and I don't think they can help us."

"Help us do what?"

"Stay alive."

"You know, I'm going to have to go home at some point," Rowan said.

"Terribly suicidal idea," Emily said as she took a sharp right turn into the women's clothing section, "but I won't try to stop you."

As they moved through the various sections and aisles, Emily tossed a bunch of items into the cart: a small suitcase, clothes, snacks, and water. When they reached the toiletries section, Emily stopped the cart and turned to Rowan.

"Well?" Emily asked.

"You really think they'll be waiting for me at home?"

"For sure."

"What about Alan Scarpio's lake house?"

"They're most likely still watching it as well."

Rowan imagined getting taken by those people again, this time without Emily. He shuddered. It wasn't that he was frightened; he wasn't easily shaken. It was more the sense of unknowing that freaked him out. His name was on that list, whatever that meant. Rowan needed information, and Emily appeared to be the only person who understood what the hell was going on.

"If you decide to stick with me for a while, you're probably going to need a few things," Emily said, as if she'd been reading his mind.

Rowan went over the events of the past few days in his head as he watched Emily load the cart with deodorant, toothpaste, a twin pack of toothbrushes, and some mouthwash. He'd lost his date in a restaurant, had a strange encounter with Helena Worricker, discovered that his was the only working profile on a mysterious dating app, and he'd been kidnapped—twice.

Emily tossed a few things into the cart and then turned to face Rowan. "Well?" she asked.

Rowan had the feeling this was an important moment, a turning point of some kind. Was he going to stick with Emily or return to whatever his life looked like post-abduction? If he decided to go home, would he be taken and thrown into a black van again? Why was Rowan's name on that list and what did it mean? If he had to spend some time on the run, as far as travel companions went, he could do a whole lot worse than Emily Connors. She was bright, completely bullshit-free, and although Rowan found her energy and focus a little over-the-top, it was also extremely attractive.

Rowan's mind was racing, filled with uncertainty about what was to come. Would he ever be able to go back to the way things were before?

Did he actually want to?

Although his life had become a total shit show from the moment he'd met Emily Connors, he'd been feeling far more connected to the world, and something about her made him feel safer than he'd felt in a long time.

"What's it going to be?" Emily asked.

"Are you really friends with Alan Scarpio?"

"Yes. I really am."

"How do I know you're not lying to me?"

"I don't care."

Rowan had the feeling she was telling the truth. Maybe she knew Alan Scarpio, or maybe she didn't, but she definitely didn't give a shit whether Rowan believed her or not.

Rowan tossed some deodorant into the cart. "Can we share toothpaste?"

Emily rolled her eyes and pushed on toward the next aisle.

They filled the cart with everything two people might need to survive a few days on the run, including another phone, two remote cameras, and a cheap laptop.

Rowan offered his credit card, but Emily told him they were "cash only" moving forward.

"I'm sorry," Emily said, "we lost everything when they stole our car."

The clerk behind the desk of the two-star motel frowned as he pushed his wire-rimmed glasses up the bridge of his nose and then scratched his cheek. "Driver's license?"

"No," Emily said, "sorry."

"I'm afraid we're unable to rent a room without ID."

"I understand," Emily said. "We did manage to get some cash from a friend. We're trustworthy people, I promise."

Rowan watched the clerk's expression soften, just a little.

"You don't have *anything*? Nothing with your names on it?"

Emily bit her lip, and Rowan could see tears welling up in her eyes.

The clerk looked over at Rowan, who did his best to appear as nonthreatening and friendly as possible, and, after one more quick glance at Emily, he finally produced a small smile. "How many keys?"

"Thank you *so* much," Emily replied. "One key should be fine."

Getting chased and kidnapped and hiding out in a motel on the edge of town should have been a terrifying life experience, but all Rowan could do was smile.

This was by far the most exciting thing that had ever happened to him.

While he watched the clerk prepare the paperwork, Rowan suddenly realized that they were renting one room, and Emily had told the clerk they were married. There was a pretty good chance there might only be one bed.

Rowan's entire world had changed in the space of a few hours, and here he was thinking about the number of beds in an old roadside motel.

He couldn't decide if he was hoping for one bed or two.

"Home sweet home," Emily said as she closed the door behind them.

Rowan took a look around. It was a decent-sized room with a small fridge, a large television, and two queen-sized beds. The place was almost entirely beige except for a large bluish-orange painting of horses running along a stormy beach at sunset that hung above the beds. The shades on the bedside lamps were burned in a few places, and the entire room smelled like an ashtray dipped in a bowl of Febreze.

As Rowan checked out the faux wood walls and marveled at the seventies rec room–style décor, he wasn't thinking about the fact that there were two beds. He'd forgotten all about the sleeping situation. He was wondering if the people who'd kidnapped them from Alan Scarpio's house were going to show up and try again.

He took a look out the window. The parking lot was empty.

Rowan turned at the sound of popping springs. Emily had hopped up onto one of the beds. She was going through the bags from their shopping spree. As he watched her stuff a flashlight and some rolled-up underwear into a bright yellow My Little Pony backpack, Rowan realized that he didn't care if those people showed up again. Whatever was going to happen next, he was going to stick with Emily. Other than Eliza Brand—and, to a lesser extent, Helena Worricker—Rowan couldn't remember feeling this comfortable around anyone for a very long time, and he had no desire to lose that sense of comfort anytime soon.

He sat down on the bed and helped Emily organize their haul.

16

CRAZY BANGS, ANGRY SWEATER, AND COURTNEY THORNE-SMITH

AFTER SHE AND ROWAN had unpacked all of the toiletries and clothing, Emily took the longest shower in the world. Although the motel itself clearly hadn't been remodeled since the seventies, the bathroom wasn't bad. The lighting was bright, the fixtures worked, and the water pressure was strong.

While she showered, Emily went over everything that had happened since she'd woken up in Alan Scarpio's guest bedroom. She thought about the people they referred to as the Rabbits Police, their hired-security-meets-NSA vibe, and their propensity for asking weird and often extremely personal questions related to a game that didn't appear to actually exist in any meaningful way.

But if there was no Rabbits, how to explain the man named Rowan Chess?

If Rowan was telling the truth, he'd uncovered the phrase "The Door Is Open" written on the back of a bathroom stall door shortly after his date had vanished from that very same bathroom. The fact that Rowan's was the only name on The Index led Emily to believe he was telling the truth about the message. Rowan might be the key to uncovering something important, but, outside of providing circumstantial evidence that the game might actually exist, Emily had no idea what the hell that something might be.

"What are you watching?" Emily stepped out of the bathroom

wearing some of the clothes she'd picked out at Target—plain black leggings and a gray tank top, her hair wrapped in a well-used white towel.

"No idea. It looks like a Lifetime movie."

"Great," Emily said as she towel-dried her hair. She was stuck in a motel with a man who watched Lifetime movies.

Rowan was just about to change the channel when a middle-aged blond woman entered the scene with an over-the-top emotional flourish.

Emily leaned forward a little. "Whoa, is that Courtney Thorne-Smith?"

"Sure is."

"She looks amazing." Emily sat down on the bed.

Maybe a Lifetime movie was just the thing to momentarily free her mind from the hurricane of panic and bullshit swirling around up there. Emily didn't smoke pot very often, but she suddenly wished she had a joint more than anything in the world.

"The movie just started," Rowan said. "The blond woman with the insane bangs is the guy in the angry sweater's wife." He pointed at the screen. "The husband's best friend is a generic agent or lawyer or something, which will probably come into play later. Crazy Bangs and Angry Sweater are in marriage counseling with Dr. Courtney, who just discovered that the couple has been secretly recording their sessions. I'm pretty sure Angry Sweater is actually sleeping with Courtney. I think that's the story so far."

Emily nodded as she yanked the price tags from her leggings and tank top. "Sounds like a classic."

"I can change the channel."

"Are you kidding? I have to see what happens now."

Rowan laughed, opened a bag of generic popcorn, and offered some to Emily.

Emily looked at Rowan, sitting across from her on an identical bed, and wondered how the hell she'd ended up in a shitty motel room, actually excited to start watching a terrible movie. She smiled and leaned back against the headboard.

She was too fucking exhausted to think.

She grabbed a handful of popcorn, ready to absorb whatever lesson in abject domestic terror was going to be visited upon poor Courtney Thorne-Smith over the next eighty minutes.

Twenty or so minutes later, Rowan sat up with a start. "Holy shit," he said. "That's her."

"Her who?"

"That woman in the baseball cap."

"I think she's supposed to be Courtney Thorne-Smith's daughter, the roller derby champion," Emily said, "but I'm not sure. The plot of this movie is kind of all over the place."

"That's Eliza Brand," Rowan said as he stood up and moved closer to the television.

"The woman who disappeared?"

"Yes. That's her."

"Are you sure?"

"I'm positive."

Emily reached down beside the bed and grabbed the new laptop.

She unwrapped it, plugged it in, and after a few updates, it was ready. She connected to the motel's free Wi-Fi and performed a search for the cast of the movie. The role of Courtney Thorne-Smith's daughter, Melissa Marshall, was played by somebody named Julie Furuno. Emily flipped the computer around and showed it to Rowan.

"Is this her?" she asked.

"Yes."

"Are you sure?"

"Positive."

"It says her name is Julie Furuno, not Eliza Brand."

"Maybe she was using a fake name? Or maybe Julie Furuno is a stage name? Can we look her up?"

Emily nodded and entered Julie Furuno's name into a search engine. A whole bunch of sites came up. Julie wasn't a star by any means, but she appeared to be fairly active on social media. She had just over fifteen thousand combined followers. Her filmography comprised almost entirely small television roles, but she'd played the lead in one critically successful independent feature, a murderous undead nun out for revenge. Her biography said that she was born in Sacramento but that she lived and worked in Seattle. There was no stage name mentioned anywhere.

"You're sure this is her?" Emily asked as she pulled up Julie Furuno's Instagram account. A smiling Julie, holding an ice cream sandwich, filled the screen.

"Her hair looks a bit different. But yeah, that's definitely Eliza."

"Julie," Emily said.

"Right. Julie. How recent is that picture?"

"Looks like she posted it yesterday from a concert in Tacoma."

"Shit," Rowan said. "I guess she didn't vanish from the face of the Earth. I should probably call the police."

"Let's put a pin in calling the police, for now."

"I really think we should let them know she's okay," Rowan said as he reached for the burner phone the Hazels had provided.

Emily beat him to the phone, grabbed it, and set it on the nightstand farthest from Rowan's bed. "Now might be a good time for a bit more background on Rabbits."

"You don't think I need to tell somebody about Eliza, or Julie or whatever?"

"How about you give me a few minutes, and if you still feel you need to call after that, I'll dial the number for you."

"Fine," Rowan said as he leaned back against the headboard.

"So," Emily began, "first of all, Rabbits is not always active. That phrase, 'The door is open,' is associated with the beginning of a new iteration of the game."

"How is that phrase connected to Eliza's disappearance?"

"I'm not sure it is connected, but there is another key element of the game at work here."

"What is that?"

"Coincidence—or, rather, extreme coincidence. Like seeing the woman who disappeared from that bathroom in a Lifetime movie."

"What does that have to do with anything?"

"Finding patterns and identifying coincidences are central to the game."

"Patterns?"

"Once a player finds their way into Rabbits," Emily continued, "either by discovering certain patterns, joining with other players, or uncovering the phrase 'The door is open,' they're in. At that point, the game takes notice, and that's when things get really interesting."

"What does that mean, the game takes notice?"

"The game appears to know who is playing."

"So there's somebody in charge?"

"There are rumors of a group known as the Wardens who control the game, or at least manage certain aspects of it, but there are a number of players who believe that Rabbits is entirely automated."

"Okay . . ." Rowan nodded.

Emily could tell she was losing him. She felt like she needed to offer something a bit more concrete. "You remember that encrypted blockchain list containing your name?"

"What about it?"

"I didn't mention anything when we were with the Hazels, but I've seen that list before. It's something Rabbits players call The Index. It's an active list of all the people currently playing the game—a leaderboard of sorts. It's a way of authenticating the players. Some people believe that you're not officially playing until your name is on The Index. It's normally filled with tens of thousands of names."

"Why is mine the only name on that list?"

"It looks like you might be the only person officially playing the game."

"Me?"

"Yes. There's something strange going on in this dimensional stream. The game appears to be . . . hiding. Either that, or somebody is working pretty damn hard to keep it hidden."

"Those people who picked us up at Scarpio's house?"

"Maybe, but I suspect they're more like low-level security."

"Low-level security that's probably going to show up again at some point, right?"

"Probably."

"So what do we do?"

"I think we should try to speak with Julie Furuno."

"How? Just DM her and say, Hey, remember me? The guy you abandoned in a restaurant?"

Emily thought for a moment. "No, I think we need to surprise her."

"Why?"

"In case she's involved."

"How do you propose we do that?" he asked.

"An audition."

"For what?"

"For a fake movie."

"You really think that's going to work?" Rowan didn't appear convinced.

"One hundred percent. Most of those Lifetime movies are shot in Vancouver. Seattle isn't really a hotbed of audition activity. If we put something compelling enough in front of Julie, I'm positive she'll show up."

"I don't like lying to her like this," Rowan said.

"You could try sliding into her DMs, but I really don't think that's a good idea. There's a chance that things might get a little . . . weird. And when that happens, I find that face-to-face conversation is always preferable."

"What do you mean, things might get weird?"

"She might not remember you, in which case it will get awkward pretty quickly. Or maybe she does remember you. Is it possible that she might not be happy to see you? I mean, isn't it within the realm of possibility that she actually did ditch you in that restaurant?"

"I don't think so," Rowan said.

"Neither do I, but it is a possibility."

"Right." Rowan nodded. "I suppose it is."

"So," Emily said as she typed something on the laptop, "what kind of cinematic opportunity are we going to use to bait Julie Furuno into responding to our ad?"

"Are you sure this is a good idea?"

"I think it could work."

"I remember a Japanese movie where a couple of men did something similar. I don't think it went all that well for them."

Emily laughed. "That movie is called *Audition,* and it's completely different. Those men created a fake movie in order to get laid. We're trying to figure out if there's something terminally wrong with this dimensional stream."

"Seriously?"

"Yep."

"That's what we're doing?"

Emily ignored his question. "I'll make it something good enough to apply for, but not great enough to make her care if she doesn't get it."

"Like a Lifetime movie."

"Actors actually love those things; so many tears. No, this will be more like a cattle call for a generic horror movie."

"You really think she'll show up?"

"Definitely. We're going to send her a message that includes an audition date and time at a reputable casting studio."

"How the hell are we going to do that?"

"We rent a room at the studio, email her agent, book a time, and wait for her to show. When she gets there, we ask her a couple of questions and move on with our day."

"You really think this is going to work?" Rowan asked.

"Absolutely." Emily smiled. "What could possibly go wrong?"

17

WE NEED TO TALK
ABOUT RABBITS

ROWAN WAS NERVOUS, but he wasn't sure why. He barely knew the woman who'd called herself Eliza Brand. In fact, you could say he didn't know her at all. But he had felt a deep and genuine connection, and it had been a very long time since he'd felt that way about another person. Meeting Eliza had been electric, and Rowan desperately wanted to feel that again.

The agent got back to them early the next morning with Julie Furuno's schedule. Emily was right. Julie was available anytime. Emily told the agent that they were holding general auditions for a supporting role, and that the actors should prepare a dramatic monologue to read. He tried to sell them on seeing a couple of his other clients, but Emily made it clear that they were only interested in Julie. They'd seen her on the website, and they just really dug her look. Rowan went out to pick up some breakfast while Emily booked the casting studio. She set everything up for noon.

While he was waiting for their breakfast to be prepared, Rowan thought about what Emily had told him the night before. She said that extreme coincidences were a part of Rabbits, and that at least part of the way you participated in the game involved following signs and patterns.

Try not to think about a white bear.

Rowan went back over everything that had happened to him from the moment Valentine had mentioned the white bear problem. Could the string of incredible coincidences that had followed his conversation with Valentine somehow be part of Emily's game?

He decided he'd hold off on sharing his experience with the white bears until he had a better grasp of the situation. Besides, he had something more important to think about. He needed to focus his attention on figuring out what was going on with Eliza Brand.

The studio was located in a strip mall a couple of miles from the motel. The room was very small—maybe ten or twelve feet square—but it came with shared access to a good-sized lobby and a sign-in desk to keep track of the actors.

There was a camera, a long table, and four chairs.

"How do you know what one of these sessions is supposed to look like?" Rowan asked as he took off his jacket and hung it on the back of a chair.

"My friend from college is a casting director in L.A. I helped her read scripts with actors for a few weeks when her assistant was away on vacation."

Rowan helped Emily arrange some water bottles next to a sign-in sheet, and then the two of them sat down side by side at the long table to wait.

When Julie Furuno showed up a few minutes early, they were ready.

They'd agreed that Emily would meet Julie in the lobby, then lead her into the audition studio where Rowan would be able to determine whether she recognized him or not.

"Hi," Julie said as Emily stepped from the studio into the waiting area to greet her. "Do you need a headshot and résumé?"

"We have everything online," Emily said. "Thank you so much for coming. My name is Emily."

"Nice to meet you. I'm Julie."

Emily smiled and led Julie into the small casting room.

Eliza/Julie looked slightly different than Rowan remembered. Could she be a bit taller, maybe? That was impossible. It was probably her shoes.

"This is my associate, Rowan," Emily said.

"I'm Julie," she replied. "It's nice to meet you."

Rowan nodded with a smile, doing his best to appear calm and professional.

If Julie Furuno recognized him, she didn't say anything, and there was nothing immediately apparent in her eyes that Rowan felt revealed any sense of familiarity.

Emily closed the studio door.

"Do you need me to slate for the recording?" Julie asked.

Rowan kept staring at Julie's face, which had been Eliza's face.

He was waiting for her to remember.

"A slate would be great," Emily said. "Name and agency, please. We just need to start the camera." She looked over at Rowan with eyes that told him to stop acting weird and press Record.

"Sorry," Rowan said. He stood up and pressed a button on the camera. "We're recording," he said, which he hoped was true. He and Emily had discussed recording the session, but they hadn't gone over the details. He had no idea if there was any type of recording media in the camera.

"Whenever you're ready," Emily said.

"Hi, my name is Julie Furuno and I'm with Aspect Talent." A few seconds later, Julie, or Eliza or whoever she was, began to speak again—and in that moment, she became another person altogether.

"You remember this room, don't you? This is where it all began, where he passed into the next world, if you believe in that kind of thing. I wanted to talk here, because I thought maybe this was the kind of place where boundaries might be erased and the truth might eventually be revealed. But first, before we open the door and step inside, there's something I just can't seem to wrap my head around. Whenever I talk to you about anything good in my life, you get fidgety, uncomfortable, miserable, even. You shut down completely. And yet, when I'm feeling down, questioning my life choices, my dire financial situation, or my taste in women, your eyes betray a sudden hunger. You're ravenous for details, hanging on every word. Now, I want to like you—I mean, you're my best friend, for fuck's sake—but every single time the two of us speak—

and I mean every single fucking time—I look into your eyes and all I can see is your desperate need. You're practically vibrating with it. And, the thing is, even now, I know you're not listening to a thing I'm saying. You're just standing there, waiting for your turn to talk. Well, you win. I'm fucking exhausted. Now that we've both made it here, to this place, and, finally, to this room, I think it's time to open the door and step inside. I'd like to hear what you have to say about what happened. I'd like to hear what you have to say about my sister."

Julie Furuno lowered her head for a moment and then looked up. "Would you like me to do it again? Do you have any notes?"

Emily looked over at Rowan, then turned back to Julie.

"That was great. Really great," Emily said.

Rowan agreed. Whatever magical property a human being needed to electrify an audience—that thing people meant when they used the phrase "star quality"—Julie had it.

"What's that monologue from?" Emily asked.

"It's from a play by a Belgian playwright named Olivia Dubois. It's called *The Quiet Room*."

Emily grabbed a pen and started writing on a scrap of paper. "Did you say Olivia Dubois?"

Julie nodded.

"That was amazing," Rowan said. "Really terrific."

"Thank you."

"I hope this doesn't sound weird," Rowan said, doing his best to sound as unthreatening and casual as possible, "but you look very familiar. Do you recognize me at all?"

"No, I don't. Sorry. Have we met?" Julie smiled, but her smile quickly changed to a frown. "Shit," she said, "I haven't auditioned for this already, have I?"

"No," Rowan said. "It's nothing like that. I think maybe it's just that you look an awful lot like somebody I know. Her name is Eliza Brand."

Did a flash of recognition pass over her face? Rowan thought maybe—just for a second—but he couldn't be sure.

"That's everything we need," Emily said as she walked over and opened the door to the studio. "Thank you so much for coming in today."

"You're welcome." Julie smiled. "If you do need anything, you have my agent's info."

"We sure do," Emily said. "Thanks again."

Emily closed the door and walked back to meet Rowan behind the long table. "Well?"

"I don't know," Rowan said. "I thought maybe there was a brief flash of something when I mentioned the name Eliza Brand."

"Play it back," Emily said. "Let's take a look."

"I'm not sure there's anything in the camera. I just pressed Record."

"I put an SD card in here earlier," Emily said as she popped out the card.

Rowan took the card and slipped it into the laptop. A few seconds later, they were watching Julie's audition. Rowan fast-forwarded to the end.

"There," Emily said. "When you mention Eliza Brand, she definitely has some kind of reaction."

Rowan nodded. It did look like she'd recognized that name.

But if that were true, why would she pretend she didn't know him? Was it possible that he was mistaken about their connection?

"Listen," Emily said, "have you ever heard of that play she mentioned? *The Quiet Room*?"

"No. Why?"

There was a knock at the door.

Rowan looked at Emily. She shrugged, then walked over to the door and opened it.

Julie was standing there. "I don't want to be a bother, but since none of the other actors are here yet"—she motioned to the empty waiting area—"would it be okay if I asked you guys a quick question?"

Emily looked at Rowan, then turned back to Julie. "No problem. Come on in."

"I can stay out here. It'll just take a second."

"Oh," Emily said. "Okay."

"What I'm wondering is . . . well, this is going to sound strange but I'm just going to ask before I change my mind." She paused. "That name you mentioned? Eliza Brand?"

"Yes?" Rowan stood up. This was the moment. She was going to come clean about everything.

"How do you know that name?" Julie continued.

"She was somebody I went on a date with recently," Rowan said.

"You recognize that name," Emily said. "Don't you?"

Julie nodded. "Like I said, this is going to sound really weird, so I'm just going to say it."

Rowan nodded.

"Eliza Brand is me," Julie said.

Rowan nodded. "I knew it," he said.

"I mean, not really me, but kind of an imaginary me."

"I . . . don't understand," Rowan said.

"Well, it was a long time ago. I was having some trouble making friends in middle school and my mother told me to come up with an alter ego, somebody I could pretend to be—somebody fun and outgoing, completely the opposite of myself. So I came up with Eliza Brand. Eliza because my mother and I loved *My Fair Lady,* and Brand because that was my grandmother's last name. She was incredibly strong and beautiful."

Rowan and Emily shared a look.

"So," Julie continued, "you can see how hearing you mistake me for Eliza Brand would startle me just a little."

"You really don't recognize me at all?" Rowan asked.

Julie shook her head. "Sorry."

"Thank you so much for coming in," Emily said.

Julie stood there for a moment, as if considering something. "You're not really auditioning for a movie, are you?" she asked, finally.

"Of course we are," Emily said.

"How come there are no other actors?"

Rowan looked at Emily, then back to Julie.

At that moment, the main lobby doors opened and a woman stepped inside. "It's raining like a bastard out there," she said, shaking her umbrella and setting it down in the stand. "Sorry I'm late."

"Okay," Julie said. "Thank you for seeing me."

Rowan and Emily watched as Julie Furuno walked away. When she was out of sight, they turned their attention to the woman who'd just entered the room.

It was MayDay from the Hazel Factory.

"What the hell are you doing here?" Emily asked.

"We need to talk about Rabbits," she said.

18

MAYDAY

EMILY AND ROWAN LED MAYDAY into the small casting room and shut the door.

"How did you find us?" Rowan asked.

MayDay lifted her finger to her lips and pulled an electronic device about the size of a standard cellphone from her pocket. The device emitted a low staticky growl as MayDay methodically waved it around the room. When she reached Rowan's jacket, which was hanging on the back of a chair, the device started to beep. MayDay reached into Rowan's jacket pocket and pulled out the burner phone she had given them at The Factory. MayDay removed a thin black sticker from the bottom of the phone, checked something on her scanning device, then put it away.

"All clear," she said.

"What the hell is going on?" Emily asked.

"Settle down. I just want to ask you a few questions and I'll be on my way."

"They put a tracking device on the burner phone." Emily shook her head. "I can't believe I didn't check it."

"*I* put the device on the phone, not the Hazels," MayDay said.

"Aren't you one of them?" Rowan asked.

"No," MayDay said. "I found them while I was looking for someone else."

"Who?" Emily asked.

MayDay ignored Emily's question.

"What do you know about Rabbits?" Emily asked.

"I thought I was the one asking the questions," MayDay replied.

"Whatever gave you that idea?" Emily took a step toward May-Day. This woman was getting on Emily's nerves.

"How about we just take a few minutes to talk?" Rowan said. "Both of you clearly know a lot about this Rabbits thing, and I'd like to learn as much as possible before a whole bunch of other crazy shit starts happening."

Emily and MayDay continued to glare at each other.

"Please?" Rowan asked.

"You want me to start?" MayDay asked, finally.

"Fine," Emily said.

"Okay," MayDay said, "I'll spare you most of the hard-luck story, but some brief highlights include a truly terrible boyfriend, some really good drugs, and said boyfriend's decision to break into my parents' house and steal my father's coin collection, which re-sulted in two people dying—neither of which was my terrible boy-friend, sadly. The pot of gold at the end of the rainbow? Me living on the street trying to claw my way back into the world and forget what I did to my family."

"That sounds terrible," Emily said, "but what the hell does that have to do with Rabbits?"

"I'm getting there," MayDay said, and turned to Rowan. "Is she always this impatient?"

Rowan didn't answer.

"I discovered the game while I was living in a makeshift tent city in Northeast Los Angeles," MayDay continued. "One of the women in charge of a shower truck that showed up occasionally wanted to know if I could help her solve some kind of puzzle. It was a series of geometric patterns on the bottom of an industrial cookie tin. She claimed that the patterns on the bottom of the tin didn't match the patterns on the cookies she remembered from her youth. She said that she thought there was a message hidden in the design. When I asked her why she thought that, she told me she was looking for a game. When I asked her for more details, she told me she wasn't allowed to say."

"She was looking for Rabbits?" Emily asked.

"You really know how to interrupt the flow of a story."
Emily glared.

"So, anyway," MayDay continued, "I've always been really good at puzzles and stuff like that, and I found the solution the woman was looking for almost immediately. That pattern revealed a message that led the woman to a haunted-castle ride at an amusement park in nearby Pasadena. A few days later, she tracked me down and asked me to accompany her to the park. She said she'd been there twice, but wasn't able to find anything. I told her thanks but no thanks. I was living on the street, but I wasn't starving, and I had no desire for a new best friend. It was at that point, when I turned down her little field trip, that she finally told me about the game."

"Rabbits," Emily said.

MayDay nodded. "She told me it was a special game, that only a select few even knew it existed, and that, if you were good enough at following the clues, you could win millions, maybe even billions of dollars."

"So you started helping her play?" Rowan asked.

"Exactly—but only until I'd learned enough to start playing on my own. Shortly after that, I discovered a group of like-minded people who became my close friends. They introduced me to key aspects of the game like The Circle and The Index. I got deep into it, probably too deep if I'm being honest, but I couldn't stop. I was positive that I was going to win, but shortly after I started playing the tenth iteration of the game, something changed."

"What happened?" Rowan asked.

"Things were slightly different. A building wasn't where it was supposed to be, a song's lyrics weren't quite the way I remembered them."

"That sounds unlikely," Rowan said.

"Sure—and if I wasn't absolutely certain, I would have chalked it all up to my mishearing or misremembering, but I knew that wasn't the case. My world had actually changed. I could feel it."

MayDay took a deep breath before continuing.

"And that's when something else happened," she said. "Suddenly, the game just disappeared."

Emily noticed Rowan leaning forward a little, clearly engaged in MayDay's story.

"You mentioned something called The Circle and The Index," Rowan said. "I understand The Index is a list of players currently playing the game, but what's The Circle?"

MayDay turned to Emily. "You wanna take this, or should I?"

"The Circle is a list of the winners of each iteration of the game," Emily said. "When The Circle starts popping up more frequently, there's a pretty good chance that a new iteration of Rabbits is running."

"Very good," MayDay said. "Now I have to ask the two of you a question."

"What?" Rowan asked.

"How long have you been playing the game?"

"We're not playing anything," Rowan said.

Emily looked over at Rowan and then turned back to MayDay. "A few days," she replied.

"What?" Rowan asked.

"I told you," Emily said, "that phrase, 'The door is open,' it's connected to Rabbits."

"You actually saw The Phrase?" MayDay replied, surprised.

Emily pointed at Rowan.

"Where?"

Rowan looked over at Emily. She nodded her approval.

"It was written in lipstick on the wall of a bathroom stall in a restaurant," he said.

"Do you have any idea how long I've been waiting to hear somebody say those words?" MayDay asked.

"What?" Emily asked. "Bathroom stall?"

MayDay ignored Emily's dig and pointed to Rowan. "He's playing."

"Maybe," Emily said. "Maybe not."

"The Index doesn't lie. For whatever reason, it looks like the game has found him, and that means the bad guys are not going to be far behind."

"What makes you think they'll be able to find us?" Rowan asked.

"Because those fuckers are relentless," MayDay replied as she handed Emily a phone. "I'm going to call you in a few hours. There's somebody I think you'll want to meet."

"Who?" Emily asked.

"Just answer the phone. I'm the only person with the number," MayDay replied.

Emily and Rowan had Thai food for lunch and then made their way back to the motel to regroup. While Rowan had a shower, Emily hopped onto her bed and did her best to let the stress of the day leave her body. She had been lying there for about ten minutes when she noticed something.

The television was tilted at an angle.

Had it been like that earlier? Had housekeeping moved it?

As she stood up to take a look around, she heard a muted click coming from the direction of the door.

"What's going on?" Rowan asked as he stepped out of the bathroom.

Emily shushed Rowan as she moved slowly over toward the window.

Just as Emily was pulling back the curtains to take a look, four people wearing gray metal masks burst into the room brandishing handguns that had been fitted with long silencers.

"They're going to gas us," Emily said.

"Why the hell would you say that?" Rowan asked.

"Because of this," Emily said—and then started screaming as loud as she could.

19

YOU MIGHT WANNA GET READY FOR A WHOLE LOTTA NOT MAKING SENSE

Emily woke up in a twin-sized bed. Her mouth was dry and she had one hell of a headache. She could hear the soft hum of what sounded like the building's ventilation system and the movement of water through distant pipes.

Next to the bed was a Persian rug on a polished concrete floor. A dresser, desk, and lamp lined the opposite wall of what appeared to be a narrow bedroom. Then she saw the mesh of extremely strong thin metal bars at the far end of the space.

It wasn't a bedroom. It was some kind of holding cell.

Directly to Emily's left, on the wall opposite the bars, a door led to a small bathroom. The bathroom contained a sink and shower, and was fully stocked with high-end personal grooming products. Just like the main room, the bathroom's fixtures were modern and the room was spotlessly clean. As far as prison cells that you might wake up in after getting drugged went, this one wasn't terrible.

After she'd thoroughly checked the bathroom for any avenue of escape, Emily made her way over to the bars. They were woven together so tightly that the only body parts Emily could fit through the thick, superstrong metal mesh were her fingers.

The room was secure.

There was no way she was getting out.

There was a bottle of water on the ground next to the bars. Emily downed the entire thing, took a deep breath, and started screaming.

After a few minutes, Emily stopped screaming and sat down on the bed. Her throat was sore and all the blood had gone to her head.

"You're not going to get anywhere yelling like that," said a man's voice.

"Hello?" Emily rushed toward the bars. It sounded like the voice had come from the hallway. There was somebody nearby—most likely in a room next to Emily's, based on the sound of his voice.

"Rowan?" Emily asked, although she was pretty sure it wasn't him.

"Nope," said the voice.

She felt like she recognized the voice from somewhere, but she couldn't quite place it. "Who are you?"

"Just another guest at the hotel," said the man. "Who are you?"

"The same, I suppose." Emily tried pushing and pulling on the metal mesh. Nothing moved.

"I did all of that already," said the man.

"How many of us are there?"

"Just you and me, as far as I can tell."

"Shit," Emily said.

"You weren't alone when they took you?"

"I was with a friend," Emily said as she looked through the bars. She couldn't see anything except the hallway. "How about you?"

"It was just me."

"How long have you been here?"

"I think I arrived sometime before you, but the passage of time is a concept I've had difficulty grasping lately."

"Hey!" Emily yelled into the hallway outside of her cell. "I wanna talk to whoever's in charge!"

"I tried that as well," her companion said.

"And?"

"Nothing."

"Are they watching and listening?"

"Definitely. There are at least two cameras, and something that looks like a small parabolic microphone mounted on the ceiling."

Whenever the man spoke, Emily heard a tapping that sounded like it was coming from the room next door. She didn't think anything of it at first, but there was something familiar about the rhythm. It sounded like Morse code.

But Emily thought it might be something else.

"When do you think our jailors might pay one of us a visit?" Emily asked—but while she was asking that question, she was secretly asking another.

Rabbits players need to be familiar with all kinds of codes, patterns, symbols, and pop culture detritus in order to move forward in the game. Things like Morse code and encrypted GPS coordinates are fairly common in Rabbits, but if you really want to advance, you need to dig deeper.

Smitty code—also called a tap code or knock code—was something that prisoners of war used to communicate in Vietnam. It was based on a five-by-five numerical grid called a Polybius square that allowed every letter in the alphabet (save for C and K, which shared a space) to be indicated by two numbers. For example, the letter A, located in the top-left corner of the numbered grid would be represented by one and one. The tapping version of the letter A would be one tap, pause, one tap. The letter B, still in the first row but located in the second column, would be represented by one tap, pause, two taps. And so on.

Emily discovered Smitty code in an old Boy Scouts handbook and had used it to uncover a clue connected to the ninth iteration of Rabbits. Clues are everything when it comes to Rabbits, and that particular clue helped her almost win the game.

She was using that code to send another message now.

"No idea," the man said. "It varies, but I suspect they'll want to talk to you soon."

"Well, speaking with me hasn't gotten them anywhere in the past," Emily replied, "so I wouldn't be so sure."

While she spoke, she knocked out two words against the wall adjacent to the other prisoner's cell.

Smitty code?

The other prisoner tapped out a one-word reply as he spoke. *Yes.*

"You've been their guest in the past, have you?" he asked.

"I sure have," Emily said. "A few times."

Escape? Emily tapped.

"Interesting," he replied. "So are you playing this game they asked me about?"

Then he tapped: *No way out.*

What if this man was one of the bad guys trying to get information out of Emily? What if Smitty code tapping was part of it?

"No offense," Emily said, "but I'm pretty sure you're one of their agents or whatever, placed here to try to get information from me."

"I'm working under the assumption you're a secret spy as well," he said.

"Naturally," Emily replied, but she decided she'd had enough. She didn't care if this guy was a spy. She was in custody already. What the hell did it matter? *R U Playing?* she tapped.

"You didn't answer my question about playing their game," the man said while tapping his response: *No Rabbits.*

"I don't suppose it really matters at this point, but no, I'm not playing any game," Emily replied.

"I wonder what kind of game it is," he said, and as he spoke he tapped: *He wants the Quiet Room.*

"Whatever this game is, it must be important," Emily said.

She tapped. *Who?*

Nothing.

She tapped again: *Quiet Room?*

"Emily," he said as he tapped a word Emily wasn't able to recognize.

"How do you know my name?" she asked.

"I played a game once."

"Who are you?"

"Once I started playing, I very quickly learned that the game takes everything."

More tapping. Another series of letters Emily couldn't decipher.

"Who are you?"

"And it doesn't matter who you are or what you do. The less you have to give, the more the game will take," he continued.

"Do I know you?"

No answer.

Emily started screaming and kicking the front door of her cell. After a few seconds, she started to feel woozy. She swayed back and forth as all of the blood in her body rushed into her head in thick pulsing waves.

Then she realized where she'd heard the man's voice before.

Wake.

It was her father.

Up.

And Emily woke up.

She got to her feet, head still filled with the fog of sleep, and walked over to the mesh of metal bars. She knew that she'd been sleeping, but had no idea how much time had passed.

"Dad?" she called out.

No answer.

Emily knew that her father was dead, but it *had* been his voice. She was sure of it. "Dad!" she yelled.

Nothing.

Then Emily started banging and screaming again.

After a few minutes, she heard movement coming from somewhere down the hall.

"Hello?" Emily called out.

"Jesus Christ. Keep it down," a woman's voice whispered from the hallway—another voice Emily recognized.

"MayDay?"

"Sshhh," MayDay replied as she opened the door to Emily's cell and took her hand. "Follow me and be really fucking quiet," May-Day whispered.

"What about the man next door?" Emily whispered. "We have to bring him with us."

"What man?" MayDay asked.

Emily let go of MayDay's hand and ran over to the other cell.

But there was no other cell.

There was nothing but a small storage closet.

"Hello?" Emily whispered, but apart from some mops and other cleaning supplies, the closet was completely empty.

"What are you doing?" MayDay asked.

"There's nobody there," Emily whispered.

"No shit. It's a closet."

"What about Rowan? They took the two of us together."

"We think they may have taken him to one of their other buildings."

"Are you sure?"

"No, but I am sure that you're the only person here, and if you want to make it out, you're going to have to stop fucking around."

"You said 'we'—who's we this time?"

MayDay yanked Emily toward a door at the end of the hall. "Just follow me and stay quiet."

They moved carefully through a maze of corridors until they finally reached a maintenance door a few floors below the level that contained Emily's cell. MayDay opened the door and the two of them stepped out of the building into complete darkness. The sound of dopplering crickets filled the air, and Emily heard what sounded like freeway traffic coming from somewhere far off in the distance.

MayDay led them along a narrow sidewalk, constantly checking to see if they were being followed. After a few minutes, she switched on a small flashlight and pulled Emily toward a dirt path that led into the woods.

They'd been walking in silence through a lightly forested area for about ten minutes when MayDay finally stopped in front of a large tree stump. "My car's not far."

"What time is it?" Emily asked. Maybe it was the fact that she'd been imprisoned inside a windowless room, but it felt to Emily like there was a strange quality to the darkness—a timelessness she found unsettling.

"Two in the morning," MayDay said. "We should hurry. We need to be clear of this place before they find out you're missing."

"How did you know where to find me?"

"A little less talking and a bit more walking would be helpful right now."

Emily stopped walking. "I'm sorry, but I need some answers."

MayDay turned back and put her hand over Emily's mouth. "You need to be quiet," she whispered. "There might be guards patrolling this part of the forest, and if they hear us, we're fucked."

Emily glared.

"Please nod if you understand," MayDay said.

Emily wanted to punch her in the face, but she had no desire to end up back in that cell. She eventually nodded.

"Great," MayDay said, and then she pulled her hand away from Emily's mouth and continued walking.

Emily would do her best to try to keep quiet for now, but she had a whole bunch of questions and there was no way she was going to be able to keep her mouth shut for very long.

That really wasn't her style.

They eventually stepped out of the woods into a small parking lot where MayDay led Emily to a dark gray four-door Audi sedan, lifted a key fob from its hiding place atop the driver's-side front tire, and unlocked the doors.

"Where are you taking me?" Emily asked.

"Somewhere safe," MayDay said as she slid into the driver's seat and started the car.

"Do you have any idea how many times I've heard that exact sentence lately?"

"Sorry, we don't have time to play trivia games. Get in."

Emily glared.

"Please hurry," MayDay said. "They'll be here any second."

Emily decided MayDay was the lesser of two evils and slipped into the passenger seat.

"Seatbelt," MayDay said as she put the car in gear and sped out of the parking lot onto a narrow two-lane road.

"Seriously?" Emily asked.

"Yeah. Seriously. If I hear that annoying 'scatbelt' beeping, I'm going to shoot you."

"Are you for real?"

The seatbelt alarm started to beep.

MayDay glared. "You don't think I have a gun?"

Emily rolled her eyes and fastened her seatbelt.

"Thank you," MayDay said.

"No problem," Emily said as she reclined her seat and closed her eyes.

At some point MayDay put on some music. Phoebe Bridgers was singing about an old abandoned subway station. Emily thought she knew the title of the song, but she was unable to come up with it.

Emily woke up as MayDay pulled the car over to the side of a two-lane country road.

"Welcome back." MayDay opened the door and stepped out of the car.

Emily rubbed her eyes as she sat up and took a look around.

They were parked along a rural highway of some kind. There was dense forest on either side of the road. Emily had no idea how long they'd been driving. She couldn't remember falling asleep.

MayDay banged on Emily's side of the car.

Emily jumped at the sound, then rolled down the window.

"A little help?" MayDay asked.

Emily stepped out of the car and followed MayDay toward a low barbed-wire fence that ran parallel to the road. The ground was fairly even, but the thick thorny brambles made walking without tripping a bit tricky.

The night was clear, and the full moon, which was visible shining directly above them between the trees, cast a strange blue light over the narrow highway. It felt like they'd stepped into the alien abduction scene from a Hollywood movie, or some kind of dusky photographic art project.

Other than the occasional distant crying-nocturnal-animal sound and whatever insects clicked and buzzed among the fir and birch trees, it was completely still and quiet.

Emily stopped walking, closed her eyes for a moment and just listened.

It was peaceful.

She wondered what it might be like to live there, in that moment—to constantly feel that sense of freedom and stillness— and then MayDay's voice shattered the fantasy.

"We just need to clear enough of these brambles to get at the gate," MayDay said as she walked along the barbed-wire fence.

"What gate?" Emily asked. There were trees and fence and a whole lot of prickly bushes, but no sign of a gate.

"Here." MayDay pointed toward a patch of thick dark green brambles that covered an eight- or ten-foot section of the fence.

Emily leaned in for a closer look. The vegetation MayDay was referring to had been hooked onto various sections of the fence using wires and twine.

It was a gate, but it looked like it hadn't been opened in ages.

"What is this place?" Emily asked.

"Secret road," MayDay replied.

It wasn't visible from the main road, but the gate opened onto a hidden dirt-and-grass pathway just wide enough for a car.

It took the two of them a few minutes, but they were eventually able to pull back enough of the brambles to open the gate.

MayDay drove down the road far enough to make sure that the car wouldn't be visible to anybody passing by, and then the two of them went back and re-covered everything.

The narrow road wound through the forest for ten minutes or so before eventually ending in a medium-sized clearing. At the back of the clearing, against a wall of tall birch trees, was a large silver Airstream. In front of the trailer, surrounding a well-used firepit, were a couple of beat-up green-and-white aluminum lawn chairs.

"What the hell is this place?" Emily asked as MayDay stepped out of the car. "Another secret Hazel hideout?"

"It's just a trailer in the woods," MayDay said.

Emily got out of the car and followed MayDay to the front door of the Airstream.

At first glance, it looked like the type of off-the-grid situation you might find deep in the forests of Oregon or Florida, but Emily knew that particular trailer cost more than a hundred thousand dollars, and the satellite array up on the roof looked a lot more like a cutting-edge deep space antenna than a regular TV dish.

"It's me," MayDay called as she gently knocked on the door.

"Come in," said a woman's voice.

MayDay opened the door and Emily entered behind her.

The trailer was sparsely furnished, clean and modern, with that cool mid-century-meets-rocket-science vibe Airstream is famous for.

As they stepped inside, the woman who'd invited them in appeared from behind a curtain near the back of the trailer and smiled. "Emily Connors," she said.

Emily recognized the woman's face and voice at the same time. She caught her breath.

"Pepper Prince?" Emily said. "What the hell?"

Pepper smiled, and then she and Emily embraced.

Pepper was older, but Emily thought she looked even more beautiful than she had the day she walked into Emily's record store all those years ago.

"What are you doing here?" Emily asked.

"Most recently, I've been looking for you," Pepper replied.

"For me? That doesn't make any sense."

"Yeah, well," Pepper said, "you might wanna get ready for a whole lotta not making sense."

20

PEPPER

A MONTH AFTER PEPPER PRINCE had walked into the record store looking for a Scott Walker album that didn't exist, she and Emily were dating. Six months later, Emily moved everything she owned into Pepper's apartment.

They had the same taste in music, furniture, and movies, and both of them were completely obsessed with games. Emily loved role-playing games like Might and Magic and Baldur's Gate, while Pepper was into first-person shooters exclusively. But when it came to the only game that really mattered, they were absolutely simpatico.

Rabbits was everything.

And they both desperately wanted to win.

Emily had discovered Rabbits via her parents many years earlier, but she'd stopped looking into it immediately after her sister's death. Pepper came to the game later, but unlike Emily, Pepper never stopped trying to play.

It was Pepper who reignited Emily's desire to follow the patterns and find the discrepancies that led players to the game, and it was Pepper who played Emily her first audio clips from *The Prescott Competition Manifesto*.

When they discovered the eighth iteration of the game, things between the two of them were amazing. It was the happiest Emily had ever been. They went for headphone-sharing romantic walks every evening, started saving for a trip to Greece, and were in very serious last-stage negotiations with Pepper's landlord for permission to get a dog.

Then, out of nowhere, one freezing cold November morning, Pepper rushed into the apartment, packed a small suitcase, and disappeared.

Emily asked why she was leaving, and if it had anything to do with Rabbits, but Pepper didn't respond. She just hopped into a waiting car and vanished into the night.

Emily, convinced that Pepper would eventually return, ended up hanging on to the apartment for six months longer than she was able to afford, but, in the end, it didn't matter.

Pepper never came back.

Emily was crushed.

She looked up Pepper online every once in a while. There was nothing.

But Emily would see Pepper Prince once more before she walked into that Airstream trailer with MayDay many years later.

It was more than five years after Pepper had disappeared.

Emily and K had just gotten married and were on their honeymoon (in Greece of all places), when Emily ran into Pepper at a farmer's market on Mykonos.

They both reached for the same container of kalamata olives.

"Fuck," Pepper said, "I'm sorry. You take it."

"No." Emily turned. "You can have it."

"But it's the last one."

They smiled in unison.

"Well, holy shit, if it isn't Pepper Prince," Emily said.

Pepper laughed, and the two of them embraced.

Pepper's scent brought Emily back to rainy early-morning Seattle, drinking ridiculously strong Turkish coffee while doing crossword puzzles in bed. Emily felt her body warming, and her head was suddenly light and spacey. Pepper had taken off without any explanation or warning, but Emily couldn't find it within herself to get angry. She couldn't stop smiling.

"What the hell are you doing in Greece?" Pepper asked, finally breaking the spell.

"I'm on my honeymoon," Emily replied.

"Wow," Pepper said. "Really?"

"Yeah. What the hell are you doing in Greece?"

"It's kind of complicated," Pepper said.

"Oh, okay." Emily nodded, shifting her weight to her back foot. She was finding a little bit of anger now. "I'm guessing it was also pretty complicated when you took off and left me in our apartment?"

"I'm sorry. I can only imagine how that felt. I know there's nothing I can say to fix what happened, but I want you to know that there was a lot more going on at the time. It wasn't what it looked like."

Emily nodded, and shifted her weight back to her other foot.

"Do you want to get a drink or something?" Pepper asked.

"I have to get back to the hotel," Emily said.

"Right," Pepper said. "It's your honeymoon."

"Yes, there is that."

Pepper smiled for a moment, sad, and then grabbed Emily's hand. "I'm so sorry about what happened in Seattle, but I need you to know that something happened, and I wasn't able to get home."

"You could explain it now?" Emily offered.

"I wanted to come back for you, desperately, but . . . I didn't make it in time."

"What the hell is that supposed to mean? You left."

Pepper shook her head. "It's a really long story, and it's not going to make a difference."

Emily nodded as she let go of Pepper's hand. "Fine."

"I'm so sorry, Em."

The two of them just stood there in silence for a moment before Pepper grabbed Emily's hand again.

"Are you happy?" Pepper asked, finally.

Emily thought about it for a moment, then smiled. "I am so fucking happy."

Pepper nodded. "Good."

They embraced again.

"Okay, well. You still look amazing," Pepper said.

"Thanks. You too." But if Emily had been honest, Pepper looked tired. It was probably nothing that a few nights' sleep wouldn't fix, but still, Pepper was clearly worn out and stressed.

"Hey," Pepper said, "looks like we made it to Greece after all."

"Yeah," said Emily, "looks like we did."

Pepper took off without her olives.

Emily watched as Pepper disappeared into the crowd, and then, after purchasing the container of olives, went back to her hotel and her honeymoon.

But Emily hadn't been completely honest. She was on her honeymoon, that part was true. But she and K were doing something besides seeing the sights of Greece.

They were playing Rabbits, or to be more clear, they were looking for a sign that the ninth iteration of the game had begun. There were rumors that Nine was about to start, and the first major clues that the game was coming back had allegedly been found in the Greek islands.

That had to be why Pepper Prince was there as well. And if Pepper was there, there was something happening with the game.

Emily smiled as she hurried back to tell K.

They were on the right path.

If Emily had had any idea where that path was going to lead, however, she would have stopped playing the game immediately.

21

THE FUCKING END OF
EVERYONE AND ALL THINGS

MayDay opened three bottles of beer, handed one to Pepper and
another to Emily.

"When MayDay told me that somebody named Emily Connors
had been captured by those assholes, I had to see if it was really
you," Pepper said, clinking her bottle against Emily's.

"It's me," Emily said.

Pepper smiled.

"I'm sorry. It's really great to see you, but I'm not sure I understand exactly what's going on," Emily continued. "Why are you
here?"

"You should sit down." Pepper nodded in the direction of a two-
seat bench in front of the table. "Some of what I'm about to tell you
might sound a bit . . . out there."

Emily started to laugh, which actually made her feel a little bit
better.

"What?" Pepper asked.

"It's just that I'm normally on the other side of this conversation," Emily replied.

Pepper grinned, and then continued. "Okay, so then you'll forgive me if some of my questions sound a bit odd."

"You're going to ask me about Rabbits?"

"Exactly, yes. And there's a chance you're already up to speed
with everything I'm about to say, but I'd like to know where you're
at, if you don't mind."

"Of course." Emily nodded. "Ask away."

"Do you remember when I told you that we live in a multiverse filled with a very large number of dimensional streams, that those streams are managed by an elaborate system of what Kellan Meechum referred to as Radiants, and that Hawk Worricker created a complex artificial intelligence engine that eventually became Rabbits as a way to help maintain the health of that elaborate system, and by proxy maintain the health of our multiverse and its numerous dimensional streams?"

"Yes," Emily replied. "Of course I remember all of that, but I didn't hear about those particular aspects of the game from you. I learned that stuff from somebody else."

"Interesting," Pepper said.

"What do you mean?"

"I remember it differently."

"What do you remember?"

"I remember the two of us talking about it in Greece."

"What?"

"You were there with a couple of girlfriends. We ended up spending a week in Santorini looking for signs that the ninth iteration of the game had begun. I told you way too many things I wasn't supposed to."

"What kind of things?"

"Things about the game, the Meechum Radiants. We spoke about the fact that you believed I left you in Seattle."

"That conversation never happened, at least not like that, and you did leave me in Seattle."

"You don't remember?" Pepper asked.

"Oh no, I remember very clearly. I was on my honeymoon in Greece. I saw you for a grand total of five minutes."

"Oh," Pepper said.

"You had a different experience?"

"Oh, yes," Pepper said. "Definitely, yes."

"How so?"

"Well, for one thing, there was a whole bunch of getting to know each other again."

"I think I'd remember something like that," Emily said.

"You definitely would have. It was . . . Let's just say . . . I'll never forget it."

Emily felt blood warming her face and she shifted in place, trying to hide her sudden blush from Pepper.

Pepper smiled.

"Different streams," Emily said.

"Different streams." Pepper nodded.

"Jesus Christ, you guys," MayDay said, "get to the important bit."

"Okay, so this dimensional stream is severely fucked-up," Pepper said.

Emily shook her head and exhaled. "Out of the interdimensional frying pan and into the multidimensional fire."

Pepper and MayDay shared a look.

"My previous stream was in a similar state," Emily told them.

"What happened?" Pepper asked.

"I think it mostly worked out, in the end," Emily said.

"Mostly?"

Emily nodded, and did her best to push the thoughts of everything and everyone she'd lost in the previous stream from her mind. It would be pretty easy to fall into a despair spiral if she started thinking about what had happened with K, but Emily could tell by the expression on Pepper's face that something had her extremely worried. Emily knew she would need to focus her attention on whatever that was at some point, but there was something she wanted to talk about first.

"Do you remember what we did the day before you left?" Emily asked.

Pepper smiled.

"We bought bookshelves and had lunch at Ikea," Emily continued.

Pepper's eyes started to well up with tears.

"It was a nothing day," Emily said, "and yet, it's one of the happiest moments I can remember."

"I remember," Pepper said, wiping the tears from her eyes. "We got ice cream."

"Yeah," Emily said. "Ice cream and a shitty little bookshelf."

After Pepper left, Emily was emotionally adrift for a long time. It wasn't because she was alone. Emily valued time spent by herself more than anything. And it wasn't as if she needed somebody else to complete her in some codependent way; it was just that something within her felt slightly fragmented and incomplete. Even years later, when Emily reconnected and fell deeply in love with her childhood friend K, there was still something that felt unfinished about the part of her life she'd spent with Pepper.

Emily eventually married K, and when she brought up what had happened with Pepper, K suggested that Emily think about her life with Pepper as a point in the center of a spiral. As the spiral grows, you end up looking at the center from farther and farther away; with each successive turn you're another layer removed. That thing in the middle of the spiral will never disappear completely, but each additional layer will act as a kind of insulation, and it will eventually become much harder to see and feel the thing that you put in the middle of the spiral the way you did in the beginning.

K was right. Emily's pain surrounding what had happened did eventually fade, but with Pepper standing in front of her, it all came flooding back.

"Why did you leave?" Emily asked. "What did you have to do that was so much better?"

"This stuff can be difficult," Pepper replied, "especially when it comes to personal relationships."

"What was so difficult that you needed to take off and leave me alone in our apartment?"

"It's a bit more complicated than that, Em."

"How so?"

"It was . . ."

Emily watched as Pepper wiped some more tears from her eyes.

She was clearly in pain. Emily had to resist the urge to run over and hug her.

"It wasn't me," Pepper finally said.

"What?"

"I mean, it was me at Ikea, but . . . do you remember later that evening, I met some friends from work for a drink?"

"Kind of," Emily said.

"Well, on my way home, I started to notice some very bizarre coincidences. I thought it might be a trailhead, the beginning of the ninth iteration of the game. I followed, and something happened."

"Something Rabbits-related?"

"Yes."

"Why didn't you say something? We could have followed the clues together."

"I couldn't say anything."

"Why not?"

"Because I'd temporarily slipped. The two of us were no longer living in the same dimensional stream."

"What?"

"It had something to do with the Meechum Radiants. I temporarily slipped into a stream where the ninth iteration of the game was already running."

"So that means . . ."

"The person who abandoned you wasn't me, or, at least, wasn't the iteration of me who took you to Ikea for ice cream."

Emily could no longer control her breathing. She could feel herself about to hyperventilate.

"I explained all of this to you in Greece," Pepper continued, "but the Emily I met in Mykonos must have come from yet another dimensional stream."

Emily felt sick; her arms hung loose at her sides.

"I'm sorry," Pepper said. "I know it's a lot."

"What the fuck am I supposed to do with this information, Pepper?"

Pepper moved forward and hugged Emily.

"I could hang around and watch this beautiful reunion all day,"

MayDay said, "but we have a more pressing concern to deal with, remember?"

Emily pulled away from Pepper and turned to MayDay. "What are you talking about?"

"She's right," Pepper said. "Things are a little tense at the moment."

"A little tense?" MayDay said. "Getting blinked out of existence isn't something you refer to as 'a little tense,' Pepper. It's something you refer to as 'the fucking end of everyone and all things.'"

"Okay," Emily said, "I'm going to need one of you to start making sense."

"Like I mentioned earlier," Pepper said, "I have no way of knowing how much this version of you knows about the game, so stop me if I'm going over familiar territory."

"Okay," Emily replied.

"Worricker's game is capable of protecting itself, so if Rabbits—and by extension the multiverse—is threatened, the game works to make sure the Meechum Radiants are manipulated in a certain way, resulting in a kind of multidimensional self-repair. It's normally as simple as shifting a little, a discrepancy here or a pathway change there, but the game did something a little while ago that it's never done before."

"What happened?"

"It chopped off this stream like a rotten limb before any of us had a chance to manipulate the Radiants and facilitate a slip back to our primary streams."

"That sounds counterintuitive and extreme," Emily said. "Why the hell would the game do something like that?"

"That's what we're trying to figure out," MayDay replied.

"Who's we?"

"I was sent here to look for somebody," Pepper said.

"*We* were sent here," MayDay interjected.

"You were a stowaway," Pepper said.

"Semantics."

"Who sent you, and why would they send you to a chopped-off stream?" Emily asked.

"One of the Wardens sent me, and this stream was intact at the time. We had no idea it was about to be severed from the rest of the multiverse."

"Wardens are real?"

"Yes," Pepper said.

"Who are they? Are they human?"

"I don't know. I've never physically met one of them. They communicate through the game."

"Have you communicated with a lot of Wardens?"

"Just the one," Pepper said, "as far as I know."

Emily felt light-headed. She had a million questions. "How does a stream get chopped off or whatever?"

"Worricker's AI, and eventually Rabbits, were created to manipulate Meechum's Radiants and maintain multidimensional stability," Pepper said. "We've heard rumors of orphaned dimensional streams in the past, but those were naturally occurring—the underlying pre-Rabbits multiverse repair system doing some housekeeping, so to speak."

"But something was different this time?"

"Yes. This is the first time Rabbits orphaned a dimensional stream on its own."

"So the game chopping off a stream like a rotten limb isn't normal?"

"No, it certainly isn't."

"You referenced something called a primary stream. What does that mean?"

"Each of us is anchored to the stream of our birth consciousness. Most people live their entire lives without ever leaving their primary dimensional stream, and if they do end up leaving, it's only for a very brief period of time, and then they shift right back."

Emily wondered how many dimensions she'd visited in her life, and how long she'd been away from her primary stream. She was still feeling some residual dimensional drift, and she knew that it would be a while before she'd feel anchored again. But if what Pepper was telling her was true, none of that mattered anymore.

"So what happened?" Emily asked. "Why was this stream cut off from the rest?"

"Apparently, at some point, somebody playing Rabbits triggered an alert of some kind. The system behind the game had determined that this individual was a threat to the entire multiverse. It took a long time, but this person was eventually identified and trapped in one particular dimensional stream."

"This stream?" Emily asked.

Pepper nodded.

"You're sure about all of this?" Emily asked.

"Yes. I was sent here to look into it. It was just shortly after we arrived that this stream was cut off," Pepper replied.

"What does that mean exactly?"

"It means we're fucked," MayDay said.

Pepper glared at MayDay. "What she's trying to say is that this stream is going to disappear, and all of us along with it."

"How long?"

"We're not sure, but it'll be soon," Pepper said.

"What makes you say that?"

"Any dimensional stream left long enough without Radiant manipulation will very quickly succumb to entropy and die."

"The way I understand it, our individual consciousness is part of an interdimensional pool," Emily said. "So won't we just be assimilated with the other versions of ourselves?"

"Things work differently with an orphaned stream. In this case, any person not native to the cutoff dimension—meaning people like the three of us who somehow slipped here from another stream—are now trapped outside of that interdimensional pool of consciousness."

"And?"

"And once this dimension disappears, we will no longer exist. Our unique memories, consciousnesses, and experiences will be snuffed out like a candle."

"Which makes it the most efficient and effective method for the game to permanently eliminate a multidimensional threat," May-Day added.

"All this is happening because the game wants to destroy one person?" Emily asked.

"Yes," MayDay said.

"What individual is so bad that they have to be permanently erased from existence?"

"Somebody called the Engineer," Pepper said.

"Who is that?"

"We have no idea," Pepper replied, "but he's extremely dangerous."

"What about Gatewick?" Emily asked. "In my previous stream, experiments by the Institute allowed some affected children of Gatewick parents to influence the Radiants due to their physiology."

"Your parents were Gatewick?" MayDay asked.

Emily nodded. "Under the right circumstances, some of us have been able to create a kind of temporary slip, and in certain situations, even switch streams permanently."

"Well, no matter how you do it, you can only slip streams if they're next to each other," Pepper said. "Sadly, that option doesn't exist with an orphaned stream. In this case, there are no longer dimensions next door to slip into."

"So, can you call the Wardens for help?"

"It doesn't work like that," Pepper said. "Wardens get in touch with you, not the other way around. I'm afraid we're on our own."

"So what's the plan?" Emily asked. "We can't just sit here and wait to get blinked out of existence."

Pepper and MayDay shared a look, but didn't speak.

"We have to do something." Emily raised her voice. "I'm not going to just fucking vanish without a fight."

"There is one thing," Pepper said, "but it's definitely a long shot."

"What is it?"

"We think maybe, if we can find a way to play the game," MayDay said, "we might be able to trigger the Radiants and maybe facilitate a dimensional reset."

"But in order to play the game, we have to find the game," Pepper said, "and the only person who's been able to find it so far is Rowan Chess."

"His name might be on The Index, but Rowan isn't actually playing Rabbits. When we met, he'd never even heard of it."

"Well," Pepper said, "he doesn't need to know how to play. He just needs to work with those of us who do."

"I don't know," Emily said. "That sounds like kind of a shit plan."

Pepper smiled. "We do Rabbits things the way we always do Rabbits things, one step at a time. All we need to do is take the first step. After that, we do what comes next."

"How the hell are we going to find Rowan Chess?" Emily asked.

"Shit," MayDay said.

"What?" Pepper asked.

"You're gonna be mad."

Pepper put her hands on her hips. "What did you do?"

"I may have left her in the trunk," MayDay said.

"What?" Emily asked. "Her who?"

"Jesus Christ, MayDay," Pepper said.

"I'm sorry. We just got to talking, and it was all so exciting," MayDay said as she jumped up and rushed outside.

Pepper and Emily stepped out of the trailer and watched as May-Day dragged an angry woman from the trunk of her car.

The woman was zip-tied and there was duct tape across her mouth, but Emily recognized her immediately. She was a tester. The woman who'd shown Emily a photo of a Brittany spaniel.

"You stole a member of the Rabbits Police?" Emily asked as MayDay gently led the grumbling woman toward the Airstream.

"Is that what you call them?" Pepper asked.

Emily nodded.

"Wow, that's different than what we call them."

"What do you call them?"

"The assholes," MayDay replied, then turned to the tester. "No offense."

The tester's eyes went huge.

Pepper smiled and placed her hand on the tester's shoulder. "Sorry about all this," Pepper said, her voice calm and reassuring. "I promise it won't take long."

The tester struggled and tried to scream through the duct tape, her eyes wild, pupils darting around, looking for any avenue of escape.

Emily blinked. What the hell was happening?

"Can you please stop staring and help me carry her into the trailer?" MayDay asked. "And be careful with her head. I kind of bumped it a bit earlier."

"Can we at least take off the duct tape?" Emily asked as Pepper and MayDay carried the tester toward the Airstream.

"She's going to scream," MayDay said.

"There's nobody around for miles in any direction," Emily said, and she removed the duct tape from the tester's face. "She's not going to scream."

MayDay shook her head.

"See?" Emily said. "She's fine."

And then the tester opened her mouth and started screaming.

22

THE HOPPER

ROWAN WOKE UP shouting something incoherent, his body covered in sweat, his limbs tense and wired. He felt like he'd been running or fighting for hours. He must have been having some kind of nightmare, but outside of a fading, deep, staticky hum, his mind was completely blank.

He sat up and took a look around the room. He was lying in a king-sized bed with a thick oak headboard. There was a dark brown armoire directly in front of him, which Rowan was certain would contain a large, old-school tube-style television. To his right, a medium-sized set of curtains covered a window he knew would be fake, and to the left, a pair of matching dark wooden bookshelves filled with a wide variety of novels, comics, games, and puzzles covered most of the wall. Hanging opposite the bookshelves next to the fake window was a print of the Edward Hopper painting titled *Gas*.

It looked just like the room he'd fallen asleep in last night, but Rowan had woken up in rooms that appeared identical in the past.

He leaned back and stretched, and while he did, he felt behind the large headboard. His fingers found an indentation—a small letter X that Rowan had carved into the wood using his fingernail.

He was in the room he'd come to think of as his primary prison.

He called it The Hopper.

The Hopper wasn't the first room he'd woken up in. That was The Kitchen Sink—a much larger room, furnished in a wild, anachronistic style that reminded Rowan of a church basement thrift store. Then there was The Aquarium—a smaller room with sand-colored walls and a beach-style décor that included a wooden ship's steering wheel, a sextant, and a whole bunch of Pottery Barn–style crab-and-seashell pillows. Rowan figured he'd woken up in at least nine different rooms in all.

His handler told Rowan that the reason they switched up his living space was because one of the higher-ups read a study that indicated a change of scenery was good for their guests' mental health.

They always referred to Rowan as a guest.

He was a prisoner.

He had no idea exactly how long he'd been imprisoned. The windows were always fake. Behind the thick curtains was nothing but bricks under double-paned glass.

When Rowan asked how long they were going to keep him, his handler always delivered the same response: "You'll be going home soon." There was something about the way his handler spoke that reminded Rowan of a smiling cult leader reassuring a virgin about to be tossed into a volcano as a sacrifice to an ancient god.

To Rowan, it sounded like "going home" meant dying.

There was a knock, and a few seconds later two hands slipped a tray filled with food and beverages through a narrow slot that had suddenly appeared along the bottom of the wall next to the door.

He knew what would be on the tray without looking. Coffee, orange juice, pancakes, hash browns, and two over-easy eggs—exactly what Rowan had written on the order slip before he went to sleep. He also knew that when he finished eating, whoever came to pick up his plate and utensils would deliver a cardboard box. That box would contain a copy of *Wired* magazine, a yoga mat, and a Nintendo Switch loaded with Zelda—the three things he'd written on a different order slip the day before.

They brought Rowan almost everything he asked for.

Of course he'd tried asking for materials he might use to escape or communicate with the outside world. Those requests were ignored, but pretty much everything else was on the menu, from obscure books, jigsaw puzzles, and vinyl records to imported candy bars, Jamaican Blue Mountain coffee, and anything else he could think of. The only things missing were companionship, sunlight, and freedom.

Rowan had been missing those things an awful lot lately.

"How did you sleep?" his handler asked as he took a seat next to Rowan on the bed. The man was thin, clean-shaven, with light brown eyes and long dark hair that was always pulled up into a ponytail, topknot, or bun. He reminded Rowan of somebody you might find trying to sell meditation or deep stretching sessions to bored housewives in a shopping mall somewhere.

"As well as can be expected under the circumstances," Rowan said.

"Would you like some medication?"

"What I'd like is for you to let me out of here." Rowan wanted to scream, to punch him in the face, to run out the door and down the long hallway he knew was waiting on the other side, but he'd tried all of those things before. More than once.

They never worked.

"Do you have any idea when I might be able to return home?" Rowan asked.

"When my superiors are certain you're not playing the game."

"But you know that I'm not playing any games. You're watching me."

"Listen," his handler said, "I have to ask you something, and I need you to be completely honest with me."

"Okay," Rowan said.

"What can you tell me about The Hall of Incredible Possibilities?"

Rowan's mouth went dry and he forgot how to breathe. "I've never heard of it."

"You're lying."

He was right. Rowan was lying, but that was only because he was in shock. The Hall of Incredible Possibilities existed in only two places on Earth: in Rowan's mind and in a three-ring notebook in Rowan's biometrically protected safe deposit box, along with his father's Patek Philippe watch and his mother's jewelry collection.

The Hall of Incredible Possibilities was Rowan's life's work.

Ever since he was a kid, Rowan had closed his eyes and visualized buildings. He'd stay up far too late at night, lying in bed, walking through imaginary rooms, opening doors, and climbing staircases. Inevitably, at some point during his wandering, the rooms and hallways would become a labyrinth and Rowan would finally fall asleep, lost inside an endless maze of possibilities. Most people would feel stressed or uneasy by the relentless rooms and hallways, but not Rowan. He felt at home. The limitless possibilities made him feel safe.

It took him surprisingly little time to come up with the idea for The Hall of Incredible Possibilities, but it would take decades for Rowan to fully realize his vision. In the end, the entertainment structure Rowan had designed was a fully immersive game experience like nothing else, so blindingly perfect that he didn't trust it. How could he have imagined something so . . . incredible? It didn't seem possible.

So, Rowan wrote it all down and locked it away in a safe. He figured he'd give it a few months and then take another look. Hopefully that distance would give him some perspective.

That was two years ago.

Rowan told himself that he still needed more time, that he wasn't ready to go back because the project had taken so much out of him, but that wasn't exactly true. The real reason Rowan was afraid to dig back into The Hall of Incredible Possibilities was because he was worried that it might not be as incredible as he remembered.

How could his handler know about The Hall?

There was no way somebody could have stolen his plans. It had to be a coincidence. Somebody must have created something using the same name. But if that was the case, why was Rowan's heart suddenly beating through his chest, and his arms tingling like they'd fallen asleep and were just waking up?

"What can you tell *me* about this Hall of Incredible Possibilities? Maybe some details will jog my memory," Rowan asked, doing his best to keep his voice calm and even.

"Where is it?" his handler asked.

"What makes you think that I know anything about it?" Rowan asked.

"Did you hire Victor Garland?"

Rowan knew the name. Garland was a developer from Las Vegas whom Rowan had worked with on a theme park project in Dubai that never made it off the ground.

"Why are you asking me about this?" Rowan asked.

But before his handler could answer, a series of loud popping and banging noises and what sounded like dozens of voices yelling filled the hallway outside Rowan's room.

"Stay here," his handler said as he opened the door and poked his head out into the hallway.

The banging, which was louder now that the door was open, continued, followed by another series of sharp popping sounds, and Rowan watched as his handler fell away from the doorframe and into the hall in a blur of pink mist and limbs.

And then, silence.

In any other circumstance, stepping out into whatever chaos was waiting for him in that hallway would have been far less appealing than staying put, but this wasn't any other circumstance.

He'd been imprisoned for weeks.

He was leaving.

Rowan carefully stepped out of his room and took a look around.

He was standing in the middle of a long hall with the type of black-and-white harlequin-tiled floor you'd find in an old office building or a hotel. Based on the construction style and materials, this building had been built in the Art Deco style; Rowan put its year of construction somewhere around 1935.

Rowan wanted to continue thinking about the architecture of the building, but he was very quickly forced to focus on something else: the mess of bloody broken bodies that covered the floor directly in front of him. He tried to look away, but he was too late. The blood yanked him right back to the day that body had landed on the sidewalk while he'd been walking home from band practice.

He could feel his heart speed up, and he felt like he could no longer get enough air into his lungs. If he didn't calm down, he thought he might pass out. He leaned against the door and tried to slow his breathing.

"Do you mind helping me up?"

Rowan heard the muted sound of a woman's voice coming from beneath the body of his handler, which was lying twisted and broken on the floor.

"Hello?" Rowan asked.

"Down here."

Rowan shoved the body of his handler aside to reveal an Asian woman with shoulder-length black hair. She was wearing dark jeans and a sheer beige shirt over a white bra. She appeared to be in her late thirties. A dark red stain was slowly seeping through her shirt and expanding across her abdomen.

"Is that yours?" he said, nodding toward the stain.

She looked down at her stomach. "Fuck," she said, and winced as she stood up, using what looked like a thin metal cane to try to steady herself.

But it wasn't a cane.

"Is that a *sword*?" Rowan asked.

"Wow," she said. "Are you a detective?"

Rowan shook his head, too shocked to realize she was fucking with him. "I was being held against my will," he offered, as if that was somehow important information.

"Have you seen this man?" She handed Rowan a four-by-six-inch photograph of three people standing in front of a red-brick office building, a professional couple in their late twenties or early thirties and an older gray-haired man, maybe seventy years old. The older man's face had been circled in red marker. At first Rowan thought the man looked like his father, but a closer look ruled that out. This man was taller with slightly sharper features.

"No," Rowan said, "sorry."

"You should run," she said, nodding toward the hall behind her. "You have five minutes before the others arrive."

"What others?"

"I heard a bunch more of them on the stairs."

Rowan just stared.

"Suit yourself, but stay the fuck out of my way." She grabbed a gun from one of the dead suits and started walking up the hall away from Rowan.

Rowan wanted to ask a whole bunch of questions, but he also desperately wanted to escape this place alive. He silently wished the woman good luck, and then took off running down the hall in the opposite direction.

He eventually made it to a door that led to a steep set of concrete stairs. Taking the stairs two at a time, Rowan reached the ground floor in a matter of seconds, where he slammed into the push bar of a wide metal door and stumbled out of the building into a dimly lit narrow alley. He ran through the alley until he eventually reached the street, where he turned to see if anyone was following him.

He was alone.

Rowan looked up into the sky. It was overcast and a light rain had started to fall. Based on the quality of light, he thought it had to be sometime in the late afternoon. He thought briefly about going back to check on the woman with the sword, but whatever the hell was going on in that building had nothing to do with him.

So he turned and started running up the street.

There was no way they were going to catch him again.

Rowan Chess was free and he was damn well going to stay that way.

23

JUST A COG IN THE MACHINE

PEPPER AND MAYDAY LED the tester into the Airstream and shut the door.

"Please don't kill her," Emily said.

The tester's eyes went huge as she looked back and forth from Emily to Pepper.

"Jesus Christ, Em. We're not going to kill her," Pepper said. "What the hell do you think we're doing here?"

Emily exhaled, relieved. "I don't know. Some of this stuff has been a little . . . scary."

"Not that scary," Pepper said as she cut the zip ties from the tester's hands using a small jackknife.

"I am so sorry for the inconvenience," MayDay said as she grabbed the knife from Pepper and used it to free the woman's ankles.

"I know her," Emily said. "She's one of them. She gave me a test."

"We grabbed her leaving a building where we knew some people had been tested earlier," Pepper said.

Emily nodded. So these two women had been able to do what Emily and Scarpio couldn't. They'd managed to capture a member of the Rabbits Police.

"Her name is Millicent Hanley," Pepper said.

"Millie," the tester said, rubbing her wrists.

"She speaks," MayDay replied.

"Please don't hurt me," Millie said. "I don't know anything."

"But you must know why we picked you up," Pepper said.

"Because I asked the questions?"

"Yes."

"Sorry about that. It's nothing personal. It's just my job."

"Who do you work for?"

"The Company."

"What company is that?"

"I have no idea. We just call it The Company. My paychecks come from a numbered corporation."

"Where?"

"I don't know, exactly. I think The Company is registered in Delaware."

"What is it that you do for a living?"

"Well, I used to work for the LAPD running the polygraph unit, but for the past few years, I've been working for this corporation. I'm tasked with administering a number of questions in an interview format and then analyzing the subject's responses."

"Who do you interview?"

"The subjects I'm presented with."

"And then what happens?"

"I upload the results of those interviews and my analysis to an anonymous server."

"That's it?"

"That's it."

"How did you get the job?"

"I applied online."

"Who hired you?"

"I was contacted by the corporation."

"I mean, physically, who interviewed you, trained you, and the rest?"

"Nobody."

"What do you mean?"

"Everything is online—through an app-based text exchange or email. The few real-life interactions I've had on the administration side have all been very low-level. I've never spoken with anyone in charge of anything."

"Never?"

She shook her head. "The only people I've met connected to my job are the security personnel at the interview locations. I get paid via direct deposit, my flights are booked online, and all of my training is handled remotely."

"Did you know that the subjects of your interviews are taken by force in order to submit to them?" Emily asked.

The tester's face dropped. "We're not allowed to ask questions related to the subjects or the testing process."

"She's just a cog in the machine," MayDay said. "She doesn't know shit."

"I've never hurt anybody," Millie said.

"We've interviewed dozens of them," Pepper said, ignoring Millie. "They're all hired online. Nobody has spoken with a human being at The Company who actually knows anything."

"What are you saying?" Emily asked. "She can't help us?"

"I can help," Millie said. "I might know something."

"I sincerely doubt that," Pepper said.

"I was flown here to interview her," Millie said, pointing at Emily. "They're not letting me go home until they get whatever it is they want."

"I thought you said you didn't know anything," MayDay said, leaning forward as she spoke.

"I suppose it depends on what you want to know," Millie said.

"We're looking for somebody, a man," Emily said, and held up her phone to show Millie the photograph of Rowan Chess from his website. "We were taken together, but were separated at some point."

"We never take two subjects to the same location," Millie said as she leaned forward to take a look. "Yeah, I recognize that guy. I asked him a packet of questions."

"When?"

"A couple of weeks ago, I think."

"You think?"

"I'm sorry. I ask a lot of people questions."

"Where?"

Millie looked around at her captors. "Are you going to let me go?"

"Of course," MayDay said.

"You'll have to forgive me, but that doesn't sound very reassuring."

"How about you tell us where to find the guy we're looking for and we'll drop you off wherever you want?" Pepper said.

Millie took a long look at Pepper, then turned her attention back to MayDay. "That doesn't work for me."

"What?" MayDay asked.

"You let me go first. I'll tell you the last place I saw him," Millie said.

"That doesn't work for us," MayDay said.

"How about this," Emily said. "Take us to the last place you saw him, and we'll let you go when we get there."

"I don't know . . ." Millie said.

"That's the best offer you're going to get," Pepper said.

Millie took a long look at Emily and then rolled her eyes. "Fine," she said.

Millie led them to a four-story stone apartment building set on half an acre of deep green woods at the very top of Capitol Hill. Long-time Seattle residents referred to it as the Bunker.

From what Emily could remember, the neoclassical gray concrete structure had been built by a railroad baron's ex-wife sometime around the beginning of the twentieth century. It was semi-famous in Seattle because, at one point, there had been a small amateur observatory located on the roof. The rotating dome was still up there, but Emily had heard that it was no longer functional.

"The last time I saw Rowan Chess was here in this building," Millie said.

"Which room?"

"Four hundred." Millie shuffled in place. "Can I go now?"

"When you deliver Rowan Chess, you can go," MayDay said.

"Fine." Millie shook her head, exasperated. "You guys ready?"

"Is there a number we need to buzz?" MayDay asked as they

walked up the wide set of concrete stairs that led to the front door of the building.

"Six, seven, eight, nine, followed by the pound sign," Millie said.

MayDay pressed the buttons, and a few seconds later there was a loud click, followed by a buzzing sound.

Pepper opened the door and the three of them entered the building.

The first thing Emily thought, when confronted by the building's lobby, was that there was a surprising amount of blue. From the cerulean walls to the turquoise-and-navy nautical symbols that littered the old mosaic tile beneath their feet, walking into the building kind of felt like stepping underwater. Directly in front of them, a wide set of royal blue carpeted stairs led up to the second floor.

"No elevator?" MayDay asked as the door closed behind them with a deep clang that reverberated through the room.

"I think there's a wooden freight elevator somewhere in the back, but I'm not sure it's operational," Millie said as she led the three of them up the carpeted stairs.

The way Millie had spoken made Emily wonder. It wasn't that she thought Millie was lying about the freight elevator; it was something else. Playing Rabbits meant keeping track of intricate details, including the way people spoke. Millie's detail about the freight elevator sounded a bit too specific.

As Millie and MayDay turned a corner and continued walking up to the fourth floor, Emily pulled Pepper aside and led her back down to the second-floor landing. The hall stretched away from them, a checkerboard of black and white tiles.

"We should be careful," Emily said.

"What is it?"

"I don't know. Something doesn't feel right."

Pepper nodded. "Okay. I'll see if I can find the freight elevator or a second staircase on the other side, in case things go bad."

Emily watched Pepper jog down the second-floor hallway, and then turned and hurried to catch up with the others.

She found them standing in front of the door to room number 400.

"Where's the boss lady?" Millie asked.

"She was right behind me," Emily said.

"What makes you think *she's* the boss?" MayDay said. "What if I'm the boss?"

Millie forced a smile and then raised her hand to knock on the door.

But before Millie was able to knock, Emily grabbed her hand.

"You knew his name was Rowan Chess," Emily said.

"What?" Millie asked, seemingly confused.

"We asked you about an unnamed man in a photograph, and a few minutes later you said, 'The last time I saw Rowan Chess was here in this building.'"

"So?" Millie said. "I remembered his name. Who cares?"

Millie may have been a polygraph expert, but she was a terrible liar.

"Something's wrong," Emily said.

And that's when Millie winked at Emily.

"It's a trap," Emily said.

Millie just smiled.

"Fuck!" MayDay said as she grabbed Emily's hand and yanked her down the hallway, toward the opposite end of the building.

A second later, the door to room 400 burst open and the Rabbits Police poured out.

"What about Pepper?" Emily asked MayDay as the two of them reached the end of the long hallway.

"Just keep moving," MayDay replied as she led Emily around the corner and into a staircase that was almost identical to the one on the other side of the building. The only difference was that this staircase didn't end at the fourth floor. There were stairs leading both up and down.

MayDay had already started heading downstairs when Emily grabbed her arm and pointed to two people rushing up from the ground level.

"Shit," MayDay said as she changed direction and followed Emily up the stairs.

"Don't worry," MayDay said. "Pepper can take care of herself."

They took the stairs two at a time.

Emily shoved open the metal door at the top of the final set of stairs and the two of them stumbled out onto the roof.

The top of the building was littered with metal vents, pipes, and ducts, but Emily's eyes were immediately drawn to the feature that made this building unique: the gray dome and white shutters of the building's rooftop observatory.

Emily pointed toward the set of narrow gray metal stairs that led up to the observatory, and the two of them ran in that direction.

The door was unlocked.

Emily and MayDay burst into the observatory and shut the door behind them.

It was pitch-black.

"I think there's a light switch near the door, a foot or so to the right." Emily jumped at the sound of a woman's voice coming from somewhere near the back of the room.

"Who's there?" MayDay said.

Emily felt around and eventually discovered a switch along the wall. She flipped it up and the space was flooded with warm yellow light.

They were standing in a perfectly circular chamber. Above their heads, where a ceiling would normally be, was a large geodesic dome. In the center of the room was a large rotating green metal telescope. It looked like it had been manufactured sometime around the end of the nineteenth century. The metal around the switches and levers appeared worn, but not overly so. Emily wouldn't have been surprised if the telescope remained functional.

The dome itself was made of some type of galvanized steel that had been painted white. The observatory walls were covered with built-in shelves, and there was a low three-foot-wide counter that ran the circumference of the room. Lying on the floor directly across from Emily and MayDay, beneath part of the counter, was the woman who'd spoken. She was Asian, late thirties, with shiny black hair that had been cut into a perfect A-line bob. She was wearing a white bra and dark jeans. She held a blood-soaked beige shirt or scarf tight against her abdomen.

"Who are you?" MayDay asked. "What happened?"

"You got a lotta questions," the woman said, her voice thin and strained. She struggled to stand, but ended up sitting back down on the ground.

MayDay grabbed a metal chair and jammed it against the handle of the door. "Do you think this actually works?" she asked nobody in particular.

Emily finally got a clear look at the face of the woman who'd spoken.

"Swan?" Emily asked.

"Emily Connors?" Swan replied. "What the fuck are you doing here?"

In another world, Swan had advised Emily not to send the person she loved more than anything in the world into an adjacent dimensional stream to try to stop a man named Crow from potentially destroying the multiverse. And—although it would almost certainly mean risking life, the universe, and everything—if it were possible, Emily would have gone back in time and heeded Swan's warning.

"Don't try to get up." Emily rushed to Swan's side.

"What the hell, Em," Swan said, her voice barely more than a whisper. "You shouldn't be here."

"I couldn't agree more," Emily said.

"You two know each other?" MayDay asked.

"We go way back," Swan said.

Emily took a closer look at the blood-soaked shirt that Swan held against her abdomen. She appeared to be seriously wounded.

"What happened?" Emily asked.

"Fuckers lured me into a trap with some false information. I took care of most of them, but one of them nicked me on his way out."

"We have to get you to a hospital."

"No," Swan said. "I'm fine."

"Maybe, but you're not going to stay that way unless we get you to a doctor."

"Where's K?"

Emily shook her head.

"Doesn't seem fair that you ended up stuck here after everything you two did, but I suppose fairness has never been part of it."

"You remember what happened with Crow?"

"I do," Swan replied.

"Are you the same . . . you?"

"I am."

"How do you know?"

"You just do."

Emily nodded. Swan was right. Emily recognized something about her friend. It had been the same with Pepper. When Emily stepped into that Airstream trailer, she knew she was looking into the eyes of the Pepper who took her to Ikea for ice cream.

"Nobody's tried the door yet," MayDay said. "Do you think they know where we are?"

"They know," Swan said.

"So what happens now?" Emily asked. "Are they going to kill us?"

"No. Maybe. I don't think so, but it doesn't matter anyway. It's over. This stream is going to vanish soon."

"How soon?" MayDay asked.

But Swan didn't respond. She'd started slipping in and out of consciousness.

"Is she okay?" MayDay asked.

"I think she probably needs blood," Emily said.

There was a loud banging. Whoever was on the other side was trying to get in. The small metal chair that MayDay had jammed beneath the knob shook, but held.

"What do you know? The chair thing actually works," MayDay said.

"MayDay!" a woman's voice yelled from outside the door.

"It's Pepper," MayDay said.

"What if it's a trap?" Emily asked.

"No way," MayDay replied. "Pepper would take a bullet before she'd set us up."

"Emily, are you in there?" It was a man's voice this time.

"Open the door," Emily said as she stood up.

MayDay pulled the chair free from where she'd jammed it beneath the doorknob, and Pepper Prince and Alan Scarpio stepped into the room, followed by two military-looking dudes with guns who nodded at Scarpio and positioned themselves at the door.

"You're alive," Scarpio said as he ran forward to embrace Emily.

"We need to get her to a hospital," Emily said as she turned back to where Swan was lying injured on the floor.

"No hospital," Swan said.

"Swan?" Pepper asked.

"You know this woman too?" MayDay asked.

"Yes," Pepper said. "She's a friend."

"Just our luck to end up stranded in a fucking terminal stub," Swan said, then winced as she tried to laugh.

"What are you doing here?" Pepper asked, sitting down beside her.

"Got stuck looking for some guy," Swan said, her voice barely a raspy gasp. "The game trapped him here." Swan handed Pepper a photograph. "That's him on the right," Swan said. "He's called the Engineer."

"I was sent here to track down the Engineer as well," Pepper said, "but I didn't get a picture."

Emily kneeled next to Pepper to take a look. There were three people in the photograph—a couple who appeared to be in their early thirties and an older man in his late sixties or early seventies. The Engineer didn't look familiar, but the couple standing next to him sure did.

"Shit," Emily said, pointing at the couple on the left. "Those are my parents."

"You don't recognize the older man on the right?" Swan asked.

"No," Emily said, "sorry."

"Listen," Swan said, then winced in pain as she tried to stand again.

"I really think we need to get you to the hospital," Emily said.

"We don't have time," Swan said.

"Either way," Scarpio replied, "we need to get you out of here."

"The higher-ups at Gatewick . . . they found a place," Swan said.

"Save your strength," Emily said as she gently pushed Swan's hair away from her eyes.

Swan smiled, then pulled Emily in close. "It's real," she said, and then her eyes slowly rolled back in her head.

"What's real?" Emily asked.

But Swan was out.

"Swan?" Pepper leaned down and gently touched Swan's head.

"Pepper?" Swan replied, blinking back into consciousness. "You shouldn't be here."

"Just try to stay awake, okay?" Pepper asked.

"The Quiet Room," Swan whispered. "It's the way home."

"What did you say?" Emily asked.

"Sshhh," Pepper said, setting her finger gently against Swan's lips. "We can talk about it later." She turned to Scarpio. "Do you have a doctor you could call? Off the books?"

Scarpio nodded.

"You have to find it," Swan continued. "Use it to escape."

"What's the Quiet Room?" Emily asked. Julie Furuno had recited a monologue from a play with that title, and the man from her dream or vision or whatever it was had mentioned it as well.

He wants the Quiet Room.

The man had sounded like Emily's father.

"Save your strength," Pepper said. "We're taking you to see a doctor."

"If we can find it before this stream collapses, we can . . ." But Swan appeared to lose her train of thought as she closed her eyes.

"We'll figure it out," Emily said. "Just hang on."

One of the military-looking guys stepped away from the door and approached Scarpio. "We've cleared the building, but they might send another team. We should get moving."

Scarpio nodded and turned to Emily. "Help me get her up. The car is waiting outside."

Swan groaned as Scarpio, Emily, and Pepper helped her stand.

"Just a few more minutes," Pepper said. "You have to stay awake."

"Hang in there," Emily said, squeezing Swan's hand. "You're going to be okay."

But Emily could tell by the expression on Pepper's face that Swan might not be okay. Which, in the grand scheme of things probably didn't matter much at all. If the dimensional stream they currently inhabited had been severed from the multiverse, none of them was going to be okay ever again.

24

SO MUCH FOR ROCK STAR DEBAUCHERY

ROWAN RAN UNTIL a fire was burning in his chest, and then he ran some more. He ran until tiny points of starry lights began to fill his peripheral vision, at which point he stumbled and fell forward onto a patch of wet grass. As he lay there, clawing up at the sky, gasping for air, he wondered if this was the place he was going to die.

He'd been kidnapped by some weird corporate or shadow government operatives, inadvertently rescued by a woman during some kind of violent attack, and questioned about something called The Hall of Incredible Possibilities—an enormous, comprehensive game park experience that existed only in Rowan's mind and his safe deposit box. In that moment, the idea of his life ending in some strange quiet pocket of suburbia didn't sound like the worst thing Rowan had ever heard.

But he wasn't ready to die, not yet.

When he'd calmed down enough to breathe normally again, Rowan sat up and took a look around. He'd fallen onto somebody's front yard in a cul-de-sac in a nice upper-middle-class neighborhood. It was raining pretty hard now, and the cars all had Washington plates, so he was pretty sure he was still in Seattle. But he had no idea where.

Rowan had no phone, which felt terrifying and oddly comforting at the same time. He had no way of calling for help or reporting his abduction to the police, but, on the other hand, he felt untraceable. He felt like he could very easily disappear and never come back.

He scrambled over to a large willow tree in the middle of the lawn to escape the rain and leaned back against the solid trunk.

But Rowan didn't want to disappear.

He wanted to keep going, to figure out what was going on. But how the hell was he supposed to do that?

He needed to come up with a plan.

First, he would find something warm to eat and some dry clothing.

His apartment contained both of those things, but he was pretty sure whoever had imprisoned him earlier would have somebody watching his home and his office.

He had no immediate family left and no friends close enough to put up with an unannounced drop-in, which left him with only one choice.

"What the hell happened to you?" Valentine asked as she stepped aside and let a completely rain-soaked Rowan into her condo.

"I'm sorry," Rowan said. "I didn't know where else to go."

"I'm surprised you remembered where I live."

"I've actually been here a couple of times before," Rowan said. "Your housewarming and then your birthday."

"That was seven years ago," Valentine said as she handed Rowan a large bath towel.

"Thanks," Rowan said as he started towel drying his hair. "It's a pretty easy location to remember. You're right across the street from my favorite record store."

Valentine led Rowan into the living room. "So what's going on? I was kind of pissed off I didn't get to go to Montreal with you. You know I love Canada."

"Montreal?" Rowan asked.

"Did you hit your head or something?"

"Sorry, I haven't been sleeping much."

"In your last message, you said that you were going to Montreal to work on the Cirque du Soleil addition with that Jane's Addiction guy."

Was it possible that one of the people who'd kidnapped him had sent Valentine a message using Rowan's phone number or email address?

Rowan nodded. "That's right; sorry," he lied. "It was all pretty last-minute."

Valentine tilted her head a little, clearly confused.

"They moved it to Toronto in the end, and it was no fun. You would have hated it," he said.

"I don't know about that. I love the Canadians."

"I got back a few hours ago to find my apartment had been broken into," Rowan continued, "and three masked intruders were still inside." Rowan figured if he was going to lie, he might as well go big.

"Jesus." Valentine's eyes widened. "Are you okay?"

Rowan nodded. "They took my wallet and my phone and eventually let me go."

"Thank god," she said.

"I came straight here after talking to the police. I didn't feel like going back to my place. I can leave if you'd rather be alone. It's no problem."

"It's okay," Valentine said. "Are you hungry? I can make you some canned soup or something."

"Canned soup would be amazing," Rowan said, and he meant it.

In less than ten minutes, Rowan was bundled up in front of Valentine's fireplace with a bowl of Campbell's alphabet soup, a stack of Ritz crackers, and a steaming cup of Earl Grey tea.

"I know how it feels to have somebody break in," Valentine said. "It's an unforgivable invasion of your private life. It feels so horribly personal."

Rowan nodded, and felt even worse for lying to Valentine. "How is everything going with you?" he asked, in an attempt to change the subject.

"Oh, you know, about the same—although I did meet somebody. He's part of my new book club."

"What's his name?"

"Marlon. He's actually . . ."

"What?"

"Well, we're supposed to be going out for a drink."

"I'm so sorry," Rowan said. "What time?"

Valentine shook her head. "It's okay. I can cancel."

Rowan showing up at Valentine's door was keeping her from a date she'd been clearly looking forward to. He was her boss, so of course she was going to help him. He felt terrible.

"I won't hear of it," Rowan said. "I've been fed, dried, and provided with hot tea. You have gone above and beyond."

"I'm not supposed to meet him for another hour . . ."

"I'm almost finished," Rowan said. "But I do have a rather embarrassing favor to ask."

"What is it?"

"Do you have any cash?" Rowan was going to need some money. He'd pay her back, of course, along with a bonus.

"How much do you need?"

"How much do you have?"

"I know it's none of my business, but are you in some kind of trouble?" she asked.

"Not at all," Rowan said, doing his best to keep a smile on his face. "It's just that I'd like to stay in a hotel for a couple of nights until I feel a bit better about going home."

"Of course," she said as she lifted a large gray ceramic shark from the counter. "I have some emergency cash I can loan you in the cookie jar. Is five hundred enough?"

"That would be perfect. I'll get it back to you in a day or two at the most."

"No worries," she said. "I know you're good for it."

"There's one more thing," Rowan said.

"What?"

"Could I borrow your corporate credit card?"

"Of course. I never use this thing anyway."

"You do use it for gas and car insurance, though, right? I don't want you paying out of pocket for those things."

"I do," she said, handing Rowan the card.

"Thanks again," Rowan said. "You're the best."

Valentine smiled. "I really am, aren't I?"

Shortly after he left Valentine's apartment, Rowan checked into room 270 at The Edgewater Hotel.

As a huge music fan, Rowan had always wanted to book a room in the infamous hotel. Most of the music-obsessed were interested in booking the room next door to Rowan's—room 272, where the Beatles had stayed in 1964—but Rowan was thinking only about his favorite band, Led Zeppelin, throwing TVs out of the windows and getting up to god-knows-what level of shocking rock star debauchery. Rowan had read every biography available on Led Zeppelin, but was unable to find out exactly which of the hotel's rooms the band had trashed.

Rowan had lived in Seattle most of his adult life, but had never set foot inside The Edgewater.

The room was nice enough. There was a fireplace and a king-sized bed, and a large painting of a shark in motion filled the wall behind the bed. The room also came with a small stuffed teddy bear—thankfully not white—that smiled at Rowan from between two large pillows on the bed. The sharks didn't feel out of place, but the teddy bear definitely didn't mesh with the images of The Edgewater from Rowan's imagination.

So much for rock star debauchery.

Rowan lay back on the bed and closed his eyes. He'd only planned on resting for a moment, but when he opened his eyes again, it was dark outside.

He checked the clock next to the bed. Eight o'clock. He'd slept for two hours.

He stood up and stretched. All he'd had to eat was Valentine's bowl of soup. He'd need something more substantial eventually, but he had more important things on his mind at the moment.

Rowan felt like he'd reached a kind of crossroads. At this point, he could either go back home and hope that whoever had imprisoned him was no longer interested, or he could do something else.

But what?

That's when an idea popped into his head.

He stepped into the lobby of the hotel, which was an explosion of Pacific Northwest–ness. Everywhere you looked there were potted plants, vines, and trees, and in between all of that vibrant greenery, Haida artwork glimmered with trademark shiny black, red, and gold lines.

When he was checking in, Rowan had noticed a computer and printer set up in a small business center just off the main lobby. As he approached, he could see that it was empty—though he would have been shocked to find somebody actually using it. Everybody had a phone, and these days most documents were signed and scanned via email. Rowan found the fact that hotels continued to provide office equipment surprising, but he was sure glad they did.

He had no idea how much he actually depended on his phone until it was gone.

He logged in to the email account he and Emily had used to set up the fake casting call, navigated to the message he was looking for, wrote down a phone number, and went back up to his room.

He thought about ordering room service, but he couldn't stop thinking about the phone number from his email. The number belonged to Julie Furuno, the actor Rowan had originally met as Eliza Brand, the woman who'd auditioned for a film project that didn't exist. He winced at the thought of betraying her like that. But it had worked.

Rowan dialed.

A woman answered in the middle of the second ring.

"Hello?"

"Hi," Rowan said. "Is that Julie?"

Nothing.

"Hello?" Rowan asked.

"Why are you calling me?"

He thought there was something off about her voice.

"I'm sorry. My name is Rowan Chess."

"Are you alone?"

"Yes."

"Where?"

"I'm at a hotel."

"Which one?"

"The Edgewater."

"Room?"

Her sudden change of attitude seemed suspicious, and Rowan thought about hanging up, but for some reason he couldn't bring himself to do it. He had no idea what was going on, but he was tired of being alone. "Two seventy," he said.

She hung up.

He called back, but there was no answer.

Rowan made himself a drink from the minibar—something he'd never done before in his entire life, but ever since Emily Connors burst into his world and started talking about a game called Rabbits, nothing had felt the same. Everything that had happened, everyone he'd met, all of it lacked a sense of permanence, and Rowan found himself torn between a constant uneasy, anxious feeling and the terrifying sense that he was slowly disappearing, losing himself little by little. He almost felt like he was being erased. So if he wanted to have a couple of twenty-dollar highballs on the way out, then so fucking be it.

Rowan was on his second gin and tonic when there was a knock at the door.

He ran into the bathroom and struggled to remove the hard plastic wrap from a small container of pale blue mouthwash. By the time he managed to peel it off, he'd cut his thumb and spilled half the bottle onto his leg.

"Fuck," he said, trying to brush the liquid from his pants.

Another knock.

"I'm coming," he said as he rubbed one of the thick white towels across his black pants, leaving a trail of light fuzzy bits behind with every wipe. He finally made his way over to the door. "Who is it?"

No answer.

But he knew who it was. Who it had to be.

Rowan used the peephole.

Standing in the hallway was the actor named Julie Furuno.

"It's Eliza Brand," she said. "May I come in?"

25

I CAN LOSE, BUT I ALWAYS WIN

IT WAS 2008. The Large Hadron Collider had just been inaugurated in Geneva, Spotify and Android were introduced to the world, Satoshi Nakamoto published "Bitcoin: A Peer-to-Peer Electronic Cash System," and Pepper Prince had run off to wherever the fuck she went, leaving Emily to deal with the emotional carnage of being alone and suddenly single in Seattle.

But rather than sit around obsessing over what might have been with Pepper, Emily began obsessing about something else.

Rabbits.

Emily spent the next year doing nothing but digging into the game. She logged countless hours researching the history of Rabbits, pored over every bit of online speculation she could find about the previous winners and the handful of other well-known players she'd heard of, like Murmur, Lachman Seed, and—of course—Hazel. But in the end, she focused most of her attention on figuring out what she would need to do to win. That was when Emily finally began to suspect that Rabbits was much deeper and more wide-reaching than she'd ever imagined.

Rabbits was everywhere.

Emily received confirmation of the global nature of the game while in Paris.

She'd agreed to attend a wedding with a friend of a friend—who just happened to be the singer in a very high-profile rock band. It was Emily's first time on a private jet. The singer himself was actually piloting the aircraft, which kind of freaked Emily out at first, but she figured, what the hell, if nothing else, it should make for a pretty good story.

They were meant to fly in and out for the wedding, but Emily had never been to France, so she decided she'd stay behind for a little while to check out some of the sights. She'd seen the movie *Amélie* at least a dozen times, which had led to her studying French in order to fulfill her second language requirement in college.

She'd been looking forward to speaking French in Paris for a long time.

She booked a hotel near the Eiffel Tower—she didn't particularly like the Eiffel Tower, it was just a really nice room for a good price—and a return flight for a week later.

She loved the city—the museums and Versailles in particular—but Emily didn't last long as a tourist. After a couple of days, she was back at the hotel room sitting in front of her computer digging into Rabbits.

She'd always known that people outside of the United States played the game. In fact, she'd spoken with a number of them online. But Emily's understanding of most everything surrounding Rabbits remained Seattle-centric. It would be a couple of years before she fully understood the global scope of the game, but the seeds of Emily's eventual understanding were planted right there, in Paris.

At first, Emily wasn't able to find anything related to Rabbits, but she eventually discovered something in an unlikely place—a Minitel terminal in a café across the street from her hotel.

Minitel was a communication viewdata service accessible through telephone lines, and was the world's most successful online provider before the World Wide Web would eventually deliver a global decentralized Internet. At one time, Minitel was the bulletin board for the entire country of France, but the rising popularity of the Web would finally force it to go dark in June of 2012. Before it was shut down, Minitel still had about ten million active users.

It was the breakfast rush in the café, and the place was packed.

The only available table was right next to a desk featuring the café's Minitel terminal. It looked like an old CRT-style desktop computer from the early to mid-nineties.

Emily sat down, ordered la tartine (a fresh-from-the-oven baguette with salted butter and jam) and coffee. When the server arrived, there wasn't quite enough room on the tiny table, so Emily moved her enormous coffee—in France, breakfast coffee comes in a bowl—over to the desk next to the terminal. She was surprised to see that it was switched on and appeared to be active.

There was a menu on the screen, a list of numbers on the left and a series of corresponding options on the right. Emily loved the retro look and style of the blocky color graphics. It reminded her of text-based videogames from the early 1980s.

While she ate, she played around with the menu.

She understood enough French to get the general idea: white pages; weather; tickets and showtimes for movies, theater, and sporting events; and, of course, there was a version of email. But the thing that immediately grabbed Emily's attention was an option titled "Les Babillards" (BBS). She'd always loved trolling through BBS graveyards online, and this felt like the perfect opportunity to see how the French online obsessives lived.

She didn't find anything all that interesting on the first couple of pages, but on page four, Emily found a link to follow—a bulletin board titled "Les Jeux" (Games). That link led to a submenu featuring a number of specific types of games, including board games, role-playing games, sports games, and, finally, something called "jeu en réalité intégrée" or "JRI," which Emily understood was French for alternate reality game, or ARG. Emily clicked that link. The menu loaded, and Emily was looking at a list of user postings.

There were archived questions and discussions about Perplex City, I Love Bees, Year Zero, and a few others, as well as some lively discussion surrounding more recent ARGs like This Is My Milwaukee and Commander Video, but the thing that really grabbed Emily's attention was the last entry on the second page. Posted a week earlier, it was nothing more than a very brief question: *R U Playing?*

Emily couldn't believe it.

She'd stumbled onto a discussion about Rabbits.

She clicked on the entry, expecting to find something exciting, perhaps news that the new iteration of the game had begun, but the message itself appeared to be blank. It was just a title. It had been posted by somebody calling themselves Cowslip6878.

There were four replies to the message. The first appeared to be nothing more than a simple grammar question: *Lapins or Lapines? Rabbits masculin ou féminin?* This person was wondering if the game's name was masculine or feminine in the French language. Emily couldn't possibly imagine why anyone might care. She leaned back and continued looking through the rest of the replies.

Somebody who had clearly never heard of the game had replied to the grammar question with a straight and obvious answer: *The noun "rabbit" is masculine, a female rabbit may be referred to as a "lapine."* The next reply, which was addressing the original *R U Playing?* question, read simply: *Tu joues, tu ne dis jamais,* a phrase Emily knew well in English, because it was the first and only rule about the game. It meant "You play, you never tell." The final post on the page was a reply from Cowslip6878 to their original post. It was written entirely in English and read as follows: *Hazel in trouble. Please advise.*

Most of the replies had been posted by users who no longer had valid accounts, but one of the participants on the message board remained listed as active.

It was the user calling themselves Cowslip6878.

Emily created an account. Cowslip was the name of a rabbit in Richard Adams's seminal novel *Watership Down,* so Emily chose another Watership Down rabbit for her own username: Dandelion. Emily sent a private message to Cowslip6878—a brief question: *Is the door open?* Then she finished her breakfast and made her way back over to her hotel.

In the lobby, Emily noticed a bunch of posters being put up promoting an upcoming series of films at the Cinémathèque Française. There were three films on the poster: *La Règle du Jeu (The Rules of the Game), L'Année Dernière à Marienbad (Last Year at Marienbad),* and *Masculin Féminin (Masculine Feminine).* Emily had seen all three in college. *Last Year at Marienbad* was her favorite of the bunch, but it was the two other films on the poster that immediately drew her attention. Jean-Luc Godard's *Masculine Feminine,* because of the question one of the users had asked in the Minitel forum concerning the gender of Rabbits, and *The Rules of the Game,* because the poster for the film was a minimalist graphic of people sitting around a large dinner table, and in the center of the table was a large live rabbit, its leg bleeding, caught in a snare.

Emily had seen *The Rules of the Game* and recognized that the snared rabbit was simply part of the film's plot, but still, for those who play the game, any mention or image of a rabbit is always worth exploring. So Emily took a photograph of the poster and went up to her room to check it out.

She examined the poster from every possible angle, but she was unable to find anything outside of the large rabbit in the middle of the poster that stood out as potentially related to the game. She sat back on the bed and thought about what she might do next. She could take a walk along the River Seine, ride the tram up to Sacré-Cœur, but Emily had always wanted to see a film in the Cinémathèque.

She checked the time.

The first of the three films was starting in less than an hour.

The Cinémathèque Française was housed in a large, iconic post-modern building designed by Frank Gehry. Inside was a museum dedicated to world cinema, and, of course, almost constant film screenings.

Emily bought a day pass and went to the movies.

In between films, she ate at the Cinémathèque's restaurant, Le 51. She loved it. For the first time since she'd landed in Paris, Emily felt immersed in the romantic world she'd always imagined the City of Light would deliver.

Last Year at Marienbad was the final film of the night. It was the film Emily was the most familiar with, so she thought about skipping it, but she'd started drinking wine with dinner, and the soft, fuzzy afterglow from the perfectly poached salmon and the Bordeaux had Emily feeling exactly like sitting down and experiencing the glorious strangeness that is Marienbad.

Emily was happy she'd decided to stay.

She loved watching the film again, and in Paris of all places. It was heaven.

So far, her Cinémathèque Française experience was everything she'd imagined it might be. The only French film she adored as much as *Last Year at Marienbad* was Jean-Luc Godard's *Le Mépris*, which she'd actually just missed by a week.

The plot of *Last Year at Marienbad* is a bit difficult to explain. It revolves around two men and a woman. They are unnamed in the film, but in the script (which Emily studied in college), the screenwriter refers to the characters using letters:

The woman is called A.

A man who may (or may not) be the woman's former lover is X.

Another man who may (or may not) be the woman's husband is M.

X tells A that the two of them met the year before and had an intense romance. He claims that he'd asked her to run away with him, but she told him to wait a year and ask again.

Now, a year later, A insists that she's never met X. He does everything he can to remind her of their shared experience, but she claims to remember things differently. In between scenes with A and X, a second man, M, who is most likely A's husband, repeatedly beats X at a mysterious mathematical game called Nim.

Emily felt a profound sense of comfort watching the familiar images flickering up there on the screen at twenty-four frames per second. Seeing the film again after so many years, she was reminded of why she loved it so much. The contradictory pasts of the couple at the center of the story lent the film an overwhelming air of uncertainty—and, of course, there's the fact that the characters on the screen are constantly playing games. At one point, while playing Nim, X asks M if he can ever lose. M tells him: "I can lose, but I always win," which he proceeds to do. Watching *Last Year at Marienbad* felt to Emily like a reminder to question your own reality every once in a while—and, at the same time, perhaps even question the very nature of reality itself.

Watching *Last Year at Marienbad* felt like playing Rabbits.

At the end of the film, the man called X descends an enormous winding staircase and meets the woman called A in a baroque hotel's massive lobby. The bell of a clock rings twelve times, the woman leaves with X, and M descends the stairs and watches them go. As the film concludes, we remain uncertain as to whether or not X and A have actually met before. Emily thought this was the brilliance of the film.

Except that wasn't what happened as she watched now.

Emily sat up in her chair, and the sense of comfort she'd been experiencing began to unravel.

In *Last Year at Marienbad,* the two leading men look very similar from a distance (which Emily had always assumed was by design), so it took a moment for her to realize that something had changed.

The woman called A was leaving with the man called M, not X.

What was going on?

Emily assumed it had to be an alternate ending, but nothing in the advertisements had mentioned that they were screening a different cut of the film. Emily's French wasn't great, so she thought she'd probably missed something.

By the time Emily and the dozen or so other late-night cinema fans stepped out of the theater, it was well after midnight. After the longest pee in the world, Emily went to the ticket counter to ask about the version of the movie she had just watched, but there was nobody there. While she was looking around for a member of the Cinémathèque staff, she noticed a narrow red door. Stamped on the door was the graphic of a film projector. Emily had visited projection booths before as part of a film studies course. If anyone could tell her about an alternate ending to a famous French film, Emily figured a projectionist at the Cinémathèque Française was a pretty strong choice.

Emily opened the door, walked up a narrow wooden staircase, and stepped through an opening into a small dark room.

It took a moment for her eyes to adjust, but as soon as they did, Emily realized she wasn't alone. There was a woman sitting on the floor examining a pile of huge metal canisters.

"Bonjour," Emily said.

"Bonsoir," the woman replied, glancing up at Emily.

"I'm sorry?"

"It's night. Bonsoir."

"Oh, right."

She was in her early twenties, Asian, with long, straight black hair. She was wearing a denim jacket, a Blondie T-shirt, and black-and-red-striped leggings. "Did you see the movie?" she asked.

"You speak English?" Emily said.

"You're American. I figured it was faster."

"How did you know I was American?"

The woman ignored Emily's question. "When you came in, I thought you might have been the projectionist."

"Oh."

"What?"

"I was actually hoping *you* were the projectionist," Emily said.

"Are you familiar with this movie? *Last Year at Marienbad*?"

"Yes."

The woman set the film canisters she'd been examining to the side and looked up at Emily. "How familiar?"

"Pretty familiar," Emily said. "That's why I came up here."

"Did you notice something off about the movie?"

"How did you know?"

At that point, a young man wearing a black-and-white usher's uniform entered the room. "Qu'est-ce que vous faites?" he asked, more curious than concerned.

The woman took two quick photos of the film canisters, using a small portable camera, then stood up. "I was just leaving."

The young man just stared.

"Sortie," said the woman, as she shoved past the young man and started walking toward the exit.

Just as the woman was about to step out of the projection booth, Emily said, "The door is open."

The woman stopped and turned around. "What did you say?"

"La porte est ouverte?" Emily repeated.

The woman hurried back, grabbed Emily's arm, and dragged her out of the room. Once they were back in the lobby, she turned to face Emily.

"What's your name?"

"Emily."

"You can call me Swan," she said. "And if you're playing Rabbits, you're going to want to follow me."

"Why is that?" Emily asked.

"Because I think the ninth iteration of the game is about to start. And I'm going to win it," Swan said as she turned and started walking toward the front doors of the Cinémathèque.

Emily did end up following Swan—not only out the doors of the Cinémathèque, but also deeper into the world of the game. And although Swan was wrong, it would be quite a while before the ninth iteration began, and neither one of them would end up winning, Emily and Swan kept in touch.

They crossed paths quite a bit over the next few years. They bumped into each other in the spa at a luxury hotel in Cairo, met twice at the same ramen restaurant in Hokkaido (three years apart), and the two of them took part in a kind of Rabbits Running of the Bulls in Pamplona. (There were no actual bulls, just an entire block converted to an escape room experience with a huge monetary prize.) Swan won. Emily came in fourth. A few months later, Swan attended Emily's wedding to K, and shortly after that, while searching for the graphic of a rabbit allegedly hidden in a wax museum in London, Emily ended up convincing one of the greatest Rabbits players in the world that he was looking in the wrong place, which gave both Emily and Swan head starts as they tried to track down the next iteration of the game.

The last time Emily had seen Swan was at the end of the eleventh iteration, when Swan saved Emily's life by shooting and killing a deranged man in a high glass tower.

But that's another story.

26

THE CONCORDE

EMILY HELPED MAYDAY load Swan into the back of a dark gray Audi SUV that Scarpio had somehow summoned with his phone, and tried to imagine how the hell Swan had ended up bleeding profusely in an observatory atop an old building in Seattle.

"Where are we headed?" MayDay asked.

"Someplace safe," Scarpio said as he guided the SUV up the street and away from the building.

"No hospital," Swan mumbled, her head bouncing against Pepper's shoulder as she spoke.

"Do you need me to enter anything into the GPS?" Emily asked from the passenger seat as she activated the car's touch screen.

Scarpio shook his head. "I know the way."

"What the hell happened?" Emily said. "The last time I saw you, you were going to look for parking."

"The lot was full, and when I tried to leave, the police stopped me. They claimed that somebody had called in a threat related to a black SUV. They kept me for more than twenty minutes. I tried to call you, but my phone had been bricked."

"Rabbits Police hacked your phone?"

"Definitely."

"Shit."

"I had to shake two tails on my way home, and when I finally made it back there, you were gone."

"How the hell did you find me?"

"Fatman," Scarpio said.

"Shit," Emily said again. "I hope you didn't have to promise him too much."

"Just a couple of social posts about his sketchy crypto," Scarpio said as he jammed his foot down on the gas pedal in order to make it through a yellow light. "It was tough. You were out there for a long time."

Emily nodded. "I don't suppose any of that matters much now," she said.

"What do you mean?"

"Apparently this dimensional stream has been cut off from the rest of the multiverse and we're all going to blink out of existence."

Scarpio nodded. "I can't wait to hear more about that."

Swan burst out laughing from the back seat. Soon Emily, Scarpio, and everybody else was laughing as well, and for just a moment, Emily felt like it didn't matter that the world was ending.

"She'll be okay," Scarpio said, after everyone had finally stopped laughing. "I have a doctor waiting for us."

"I'm fine," Swan said, doing her best to sit up.

"Oh, yeah," Emily said. "You look totally fine."

Swan gave her the finger from the back seat, which Emily thought was a really good sign.

Scarpio turned to Emily. "I'm glad you're okay."

Emily nodded. "I'm glad you're okay too."

"So," Scarpio said with a glance in the rearview mirror, "where did you pick up the new friends?"

Emily thought she heard MayDay snort from the back seat.

Scarpio parked in the alley behind a posh waterfront restaurant that Emily had visited a few times in the past, and the four of them helped Swan out of the SUV and through an open door that led to the restaurant's kitchen.

With Scarpio in the lead, they guided Swan past wary sous chefs and dishwashers toward a beat-up elevator in the far-right corner of the kitchen.

The elevator brought them to the building's mezzanine, where they transferred to a second elevator that took them up to the forti-eth floor.

A few seconds after they stepped off the elevator, two people wearing blue hospital scrubs rushed out and grabbed Swan.

"Where are they taking her?" Pepper asked.

"Everything is set up in one of the guest bedrooms," Scarpio said.

Pepper turned and started to follow the medical team.

"Please," Scarpio said, "let them do their jobs."

Pepper stopped walking and turned back around.

"It's sterile," Scarpio said. "They've asked that nobody else enters the room until they've had a chance to examine her."

"Show me," Pepper said.

Scarpio took a step closer to Pepper. "No offense, but I don't know you. I'm not going to risk somebody's life because you have trust issues."

"*I* have trust issues?" Pepper said, taking a step toward Scarpio, bringing the two of them less than a foot apart.

"It's okay," Emily said, gently grabbing Pepper's arm. "Scarpio's my friend. I trust him with my life."

Pepper stared at Scarpio for a moment, then eventually nodded.

"She has one of the best physicians in the country with her right now, I promise," Scarpio said.

"I suppose you can afford it," Pepper said.

"I can," Scarpio said. "So, please, get something to eat and drink. I asked them for a wide range of food. If you have any dietary re-strictions, everything should be clearly marked."

"We have no idea what's coming," Emily said. "Everybody needs to eat."

"I don't know about you guys," MayDay said, eventually break-ing the silence, "but I could fucking murder an old-fashioned right now."

The first thing Emily noticed as she moved closer to the kitchen was the smell. The combination of savory scents was incredible. Emily was reminded of the roast beef and Yorkshire pudding her mom used to make, and as she followed the smell farther into the kitchen, additional scents were added to the mélange: a hint of salty brine, the warm waft of buttery baked bread, freshly chopped basil and arugula, and, of course, plenty of sizzling garlic.

Emily relaxed and let the stress of the past few hours fall away, and as she did so, she realized that she was really fucking hungry.

There were cheese and charcuterie plates, oyster stations, and countless bottles of wine and beer sticking out of ice-filled buckets. Some kind of slow jazz that sounded like it was coming from everywhere at once was playing at the perfect volume. Emily was positive that the person singing and playing the trumpet was Chet Baker, but she had no idea how she knew that. As far as she could remember, she didn't know any Chet Baker songs.

"What happened back there?" Emily asked Pepper as the two of them loaded their plates with lobster rolls and caprese salad.

"I ran into Alan fucking Scarpio, of all people, while I was going to get help," Pepper replied. "He and his security team were on their way up."

MayDay arrived with a tray of highballs and the three of them clinked glasses and drank.

"Swan said something earlier," Emily said. "Something about the Quiet Room being the way home?"

"She was pretty out of it, Em," Pepper said.

"Did you recognize that guy in the picture, the Engineer?"

"No."

"You said that you were sent here to find him as well."

"I was."

"By who?"

"A Warden, I think."

"You think?"

"It was complicated."

"What do you know about this Engineer?"

"Not much. Just that he was a scientist and that he was supposed to be in Seattle. I was waiting for more information when this stream was cut off."

"What about the Quiet Room?"

"I've heard rumors."

"What is it?" Emily asked.

"It's just a story," Pepper replied.

"Swan seemed to think it was important," Emily said as the three of them sat down at a large oak dining table. Emily left out the fact that Julie Furuno's monologue had been taken from a play called *The Quiet Room,* as well as the dream or auditory hallucination she'd experienced earlier, when a fellow prisoner—who sounded remarkably like Emily's father—had mentioned the Quiet Room via Smitty code.

"The Quiet Room is a myth," Pepper replied. "It doesn't exist."

"Swan said the Gatewick Institute had been looking into it. Maybe there's something we can dig up there?"

"Gatewick was nothing more than a blip in this stream. The offices in Seattle and San Francisco were abandoned in 2008. There's nothing left."

Emily nodded. She'd looked into Gatewick herself when she'd first arrived in this stream in order to try to find info on her parents. Pepper was right. There wasn't much of anything there. "So what's the Quiet Room myth?"

Pepper took a moment to swallow an oyster. "Oh my god. That's fucking wonderful."

"The Quiet Room?" Emily reminded her.

"Right, well, as the legend goes," Pepper continued, "there's a place where a whole bunch of powerful prime Meechum Radiants meet—a point of special convergence—and in that place there's a room. I'm not sure about the details, but apparently if you somehow manage to find your way inside this room, you'll have access to every single stream or thread in the entire multiverse. Those who believe in this stuff claim that the Quiet Room exists outside of the multiverse proper, and therefore isn't governed by the same physical laws."

"Wow," Emily said.

"I told you. It's nonsense."

"Do you think Swan actually believes this stuff?" Emily asked.

"Maybe," Pepper said. "I don't know. She was pretty banged up."

"You're saying there are people who believe the Quiet Room is capable of facilitating travel between dimensional streams?"

Pepper nodded.

"Even from an orphan dimension like this one?" Emily asked.

"Theoretically," Pepper replied, "yes."

"This sounds like a whole lot of bullshit," MayDay said.

"I agree," Pepper replied. "It's a fairy tale, but it doesn't matter. Because even if the Quiet Room did exist, we'll never be able to find it."

"Why not?" Emily asked.

"It would be too difficult to activate the proper Radiants without actually playing the game," Scarpio said as he stepped into the room.

"Exactly." Pepper pointed at Scarpio.

"So we need to find a way to play Rabbits," Emily said.

"Which brings us right back to Rowan Chess," MayDay added. "He's the only person listed in The Index, which means he's the only person actually playing the game."

"Maybe we can change that," Emily said.

"What do you mean?" MayDay asked.

"Look at us," Emily said. "We have the winner of the sixth iteration of the game, two relentless psychopathic Rabbits experts, and I think I may have helped save at least part of the multiverse by helping reset a fucked-up dimensional stream. If the four of us can't find Rabbits, nobody can."

"You really believe I won the sixth iteration of the game?" Scarpio asked with a grin.

"What?" MayDay said. "You're Californiac? You won Six?"

Scarpio looked like he was about to answer her when the doctor stepped into the room and nodded in Emily's direction. "The patient's awake. She's asking to speak with you."

"Me?" Emily asked.

The doctor nodded. "I'm not sure how much time we have, so you should hurry."

"What do you mean?" Pepper asked, but Emily could tell exactly what he meant by the expression on his face.

Swan was dying.

The guest bedroom had been turned into a small hospital. There were more than a dozen quietly beeping machines, and bags of fluids—including blood, saline, and whatever other medication they'd administered—hung from a small forest of metal stands.

Swan was lying on her back in a slightly elevated bed. She opened her eyes and smiled as Emily entered. "Hey."

"Hey, yourself." Emily approached and took Swan's hand as she sat down beside her in a small wooden chair.

"You look good," Swan said.

"You too."

Swan smiled. "You've always been a fucking terrible liar."

"How do you feel?"

"Fine. I mean, I'm on a shit ton of morphine, so, you know . . ."

"Yeah," Emily said, doing her best to keep the implications of Swan taking morphine from entering her thoughts. "So, what's the big deal here? Rabbits is fucked and the multiverse is dying? Nothing I haven't seen before."

"This time it's just us, I'm afraid."

"That makes it a bit better, I suppose."

"And the game isn't fucked, exactly. It's more like it's . . . hiding."

"Hiding? What does that mean?"

"I'm not sure, but I know that it has something to do with a man called the Engineer."

"Pepper says she was sent here to find him as well. Who the hell is this Engineer?"

"From what I was told, the Engineer is different from the rest of us. His mental and emotional makeup are entirely unique. Most of us spend our entire existence in our primary dimensional stream, our consciousness set, anchored, and strong."

"Most of us?"

"Yes. Unlike those of us here in this room, and certain others who play Rabbits at the highest level, most human beings never become aware that they've slipped into another dimensional stream.

This is because our psyches are equipped with certain defense mechanisms, including dimensional drift and extreme compartmentalization. These things allow our brains time to adjust to the transfer, blend, or exchange of dual-stream consciousness, whichever nomenclature you prefer. The Engineer, however, is different."

"How so?" Emily asked.

"Okay, so our minds—yours and mine—are tethered to a primary stream, and we only very briefly dip into our pool of multidimensional consciousnesses when we slip. In certain cases, parts of us may merge with other instances of ourselves, but we will always be experiencing the multiverse through one active consciousness."

"Right."

"But imagine somebody born untethered to any primary stream—a person who, upon entering puberty, experiences an expansion from one consciousness to a seemingly unlimited number of instances of their self. With no separation between dimensional minds, it's amazing that the Engineer survived at all—and certainly not surprising that he turned out the way he did."

"How did he turn out?" Emily asked.

"Mostly insane."

"Just mostly?"

"Apparently, the Engineer's intelligence is so far off the scale that he's capable of marvelous complexities that the rest of us can barely begin to imagine. It was a terrible tragedy somebody like that discovered the game."

"How so?"

"Can you imagine what a person with a limitless destructive imagination and absolutely zero capacity for empathy might do with a mechanism like Worricker's game?"

"Yeah. I feel like I just dealt with somebody like that," Emily said.

Swan smiled. "This guy has way more destructive potential than Crow."

"And that's why this stream was cut off, to trap the Engineer?"

"In his quest to understand the multiverse, the Engineer discovered Rabbits and started to play, but while he was playing, he very quickly realized that Rabbits was more than just a game. At that point, the Engineer decided it wasn't going to be enough to win. He wanted more—and in order to get it, he was going to have to challenge the force behind everything."

"Who is that?"

"Not who," Swan replied, "what."

"Are we still talking about Rabbits?"

"Yes, but we're also talking about so much more," Swan continued. "Rabbits is run by the most advanced artificial intelligence engine in the history of the world, operating on the most sophisticated quantum computing network, capable of machine learning so complex that it could bump us up from a type zero civilization to a type one in less than seventy years. But Worricker's game only scratches the surface."

"Type one civilization?"

"It's a Kardashev scale measurement," Swan said. "Type ones can harness all planetary power, including the Sun, interplanetary spaceflight is possible, that kind of stuff."

"Okay," Emily said. "But how does this get us to the Engineer needing to be completely removed from the multiverse?"

"Worricker's game is an incredible invention, but Rabbits is simply a repair patch placed atop a far more complex and powerful system."

"The Meechum Radiants," Emily said.

Swan nodded. "Exactly. The Engineer was trying to get past the game in order to discover the power behind the Meechum Radiants—the secret at the heart of the entire multiverse."

"And did he succeed?" Emily asked.

"No. Fortunately for us, Hawk Worricker's game is a lot more formidable than that."

"Okay, so what happened? Where is the Engineer now?"

"I'm getting to that," Swan replied. "So, by the time the Engineer discovered Worricker's game, it had become incredibly advanced. Rabbits was now capable of reading extremely intricate signs and patterns, and predicting certain systems' movements with alarming accuracy."

"What kind of systems?"

"All of them—from the weather to the stock market and everything in between. But it wasn't only complex systems that the game was able to predict. It was also capable of tracking historical movements and contemporary patterns within human behavior, and then using those patterns to map and predict the future. It was while modeling a number of our most likely future outcomes that the AI discovered a threat."

"The Engineer," Emily said.

"Exactly," Swan replied. "He'd discovered Rabbits, and had begun using the game to manipulate the multiverse, but he had no idea that Rabbits was looking right back at him and had determined he was on a path that could permanently and irrevocably destroy everything, including the game itself. So, the AI did what it had to do and took defensive action."

"How does that work?" Emily asked.

"The game, like any highly intelligent complex system, is a kind of organism. And the goal of every organism is self-preservation. Find the threat and eliminate it. So, near the end of the eighth iteration of the game, Rabbits began working to set things right. Some players believe this is at least part of the reason there's such a large gap between the eighth and ninth iterations of the game, but, either way, by the end of the tenth iteration, the last remaining versions of the Engineer populated only a dozen or so streams. And finally, at the end of Eleven, the Engineer existed in one dimension alone—this one—which has now been severed from the whole and is currently speeding toward oblivion. When this stream dies, he dies with it, but you don't have to."

Swan paused and took a moment to collect herself and catch her breath.

"We should stop," Emily said. "You need to rest."

"We can't stop," Swan said. "Besides, I feel great. The morphine is incredible."

"I'll come back in an hour or so . . ."

"I'm not sure we have an hour, Emily."

Emily did her best to keep the tears from her eyes.

Swan squeezed Emily's hand and pulled her closer. "It's too late to worry about the Engineer now. You have to find the Quiet Room. It's your only chance to escape this stream."

"*Our* only chance, Swan. Don't fuck with me."

Swan smiled. "Right, sorry. *Our* only chance."

"Pepper told me about the Quiet Room."

"She doesn't believe it's real," Swan said, "but the Quiet Room exists."

"If we can find it, do you think we can use it to escape this dying stream?" Emily asked. "Find our way back home?"

"Yes," Swan said. "Don't think of this stub as a box, think of it as a maze. There's a way out, but . . . you're going to need a map. And there's something else."

"What?"

"The Quiet Room is a powerful way station, but it wasn't built for us. It's something entirely . . . other." Swan nodded in the direction of her clothing. "My jeans."

Emily grabbed Swan's jeans from a nearby chair and handed them to her.

Swan removed a small electronic device from her pocket and passed it to Emily. It was the size of a credit card and about twice as thick. One side was clearly a digital display or touch screen, but it didn't appear to be turned on.

"What's this?" Emily asked.

"It's a timer. You have to keep it safe."

"What's it for?" Emily felt around for buttons, but there was nothing.

"When this dimensional stream starts to really fall apart, a count-down clock will appear on that screen."

"A countdown clock? What's it counting down to?" But Emily knew what Swan was going to say.

"To the end."

Emily nodded. "Of course."

Swan smiled. "Sorry."

"How much warning are we going to get?"

"I'm not sure. The last time I had a timer activate, we had thirty-six hours."

"The last time? Was I there? Was that during Eleven?"

"Yes."

"Do dimensional streams collapse often?"

"Not if we can help it," Swan said.

"We?"

"I've been working for some people who have been charged with maintaining the integrity of the mechanism behind the game."

"The Wardens?"

Swan nodded.

Emily slipped the countdown timer into her jacket pocket. She had a million questions about the Wardens, but she stopped herself from asking any of them. She could tell that Swan was fading.

"Take this as well," Swan said, and handed Emily the photograph of Emily's parents and the Engineer that Swan had shown her earlier.

"This guy actually worked with my parents at Gatewick?"

"For quite a while."

"He looks kind of familiar."

"He's incredibly dangerous, Emily. If you see him, you run."

"He'd be at least ninety years old now. How can this guy be so dangerous that the mechanism behind Rabbits trapped him and then cut him off from the rest of the multiverse?"

"Those questions are above my pay grade, I'm afraid."

"What if the game is wrong? What if this isn't the guy?"

"The game is never wrong."

"How can you be sure?"

"Moral certainty isn't my department either. I'm just here as a kind of insurance policy."

"So, how the hell are we supposed to find this room?"

"A few years ago, I met a Warden in Constantinople who told me that somebody called the Concorde has a map to the Quiet Room."

"Constantinople? You mean Istanbul?"

"Right, sorry. That stream was different."

"Who the hell is the Concorde?"

"He's an old friend. I was on my way to see him when I received a tip that the Engineer was hiding in the building where you found me. I stopped to check it out. That's when I got this." She winced as she reached for her injured abdomen.

"Was he there? The Engineer?"

"No. There was nobody there matching his description. It was an ambush. They were waiting for me. There were just so many of them . . ."

"What do you think we should do now?" Emily asked.

But Swan's eyes were closed.

"Swan?"

Once again, she'd slipped out of consciousness.

27

BOOBS AND SWORDS

Julie Furuno entered Rowan's hotel room and took a look around. "I think rock stars threw TVs out the windows of this place in the seventies."

"I've heard the same thing," Rowan said.

"Do you have anything to drink?"

"Yeah." Rowan nodded in the direction of the minibar. "What would you like?"

"Vodka or gin?"

Rowan walked over and grabbed a prefab Moscow Mule in a can from the tiny fridge, poured some into a glass, and handed it to Julie.

"You know," she said as she took a seat at a small table next to the window. "I've been feeling kind of strange ever since I left that audition."

"How so?"

"For one thing, I can't stop thinking that I know you from somewhere."

Rowan sat down across from her. "Are you sure you don't remember having dinner with me?"

"I'm sure."

"You really don't recall asking me to come up with some way you could tell me apart from my evil twin, then going to the bathroom and never coming out?"

"Never coming out? Are you saying I died?"

"No, you disappeared."

"I don't remember anything like that."

"I'm sorry about the fake audition. It wasn't my idea."

"I knew something was off." She slapped her thigh as she spoke. "But then that other actor showed up."

"She wasn't an actor."

"Who was she?"

"I'm not actually sure."

Julie finished her drink, and Rowan poured the remainder of the can into her glass.

"When you knocked on the door just now, you called yourself Eliza Brand."

"Yeah," Julie said. "That's another thing. Ever since I left that audition, I've been . . ."

"What is it?"

"It's just . . . I've been feeling a lot more Eliza than Julie. It's really weird."

Rowan nodded. He wasn't sure what to think. He wondered if she was feeling okay, or if she might be experiencing some kind of identity crisis. If there was something Rowan could understand, it was an identity crisis. He'd felt out of place for as long as he could remember.

Julie took a big sip of her drink. "I'm sorry. I have no idea what I'm doing here."

"Do you remember using a dating app called Find Your Person?"

"I don't remember, but it's possible. I did sign up for a few of those apps a couple of years ago. I wanted to try online dating, but I chickened out."

"Did you sign up as Julie or Eliza?"

"I might have used Eliza, but I'm not sure. It was a long time ago."

"Right." Rowan nodded.

"I do know that I definitely never went on any dates."

"Do you have any of those apps on your phone now?"

Julie shook her head. "I deleted all of them shortly after I created my profiles. I actually met somebody in real life—at Trader Joe's, of all places."

"Oh," Rowan said, shifting away from her slightly.

"No, I'm not seeing anybody now," she said. "Turns out Trader Joe's Guy was kind of a psychopath."

"Oh," Rowan said. "I'm sorry to hear that. Not the bit about you being single, I mean. The psychopath part."

Julie nodded. "I got what you meant."

"Of course," Rowan said.

They sat at the table in silence for a moment before Julie stood up. "I haven't been completely honest with you about something," she said.

"What is it?" Rowan was sure she was about to come clean and admit that she remembered their date.

"I think I've had dreams about you."

"You think?" Rowan asked.

Julie nodded. "I know."

"How many?"

"Let's just say a lot more than one."

Rowan was surprised. "There can't have been that many. The audition wasn't that long ago."

"The dreams started well before that."

"You didn't let on that you recognized me in the audition room . . ."

"I'm a really good actress."

Rowan smiled and nodded. He couldn't argue with that.

"Also, seeing your face out of context, I wasn't a hundred percent sure it was you."

"But now you think it was me?"

"It was definitely you."

He was surprised. He'd spent a lot of time obsessing over what had happened, both in the restaurant and that audition room, and had finally reached a place where he was ready to let Eliza Brand go. Now here she was, in his hotel room, telling Rowan she'd been having dreams about him.

"Fuck," she said, pacing. "I shouldn't have told you."

Rowan watched as she walked over to the window, and then

went over to raid the minibar for another drink. He grabbed a pre-fab gin and tonic and sat down on the bed. "What kind of dreams? If you don't mind my asking."

"Mostly the extremely boring kind. Picking up the mail, trolling thrift stores for vintage magazines, eating Vietnamese food."

"What magazines?" Rowan asked.

"I was collecting old issues of *Vogue,* and you were into some boobs-and-swords magazine called *Heavy Metal*."

"Boobs and swords." Rowan nodded. "That's a perfect way to put it."

She smiled and then took a sip of her drink.

"I love Vietnamese food," Rowan said, doing his best to hide his surprise. He'd only ever seriously collected one magazine in his life-time, and that was *Heavy Metal*. His searching thrift stores for his favorite magazine in Julie's dreams had to be a coincidence, but it was hard for Rowan not to take that detail as a sign that he and Julie were connected somehow.

"Wait," she said, suddenly very serious.

"What is it?"

"You didn't actually collect that magazine in real life, did you?"

"Not really," he lied. "Although I did have a few issues lying around as a kid." He could tell she was a bit freaked out and he didn't want to do or say anything that might push her away again.

"Speaking of Vietnamese food," she said, "are you hungry?"

Rowan had been planning on ordering room service, going to bed, and then getting up early to visit the bank, check on his safe deposit box, and look into The Hall of Incredible Possibilities. But that was before Julie Furuno reentered the picture. "Sure," he said. "The seafood restaurant in the hotel is pretty good, but I'm happy to go anywhere at all."

Julie took the last sip of her drink and set her glass down on the coffee table. "How about let's walk for a bit and stop when we see something we like?"

"Works for me," Rowan said.

The two of them stepped out of the hotel onto a wide gray

wooden walkway that ran parallel to the water. The sounds of the ocean sloshing and the cries of the last seabirds filled the bracing, briny night air as they started walking along the seawall.

After a few minutes, they passed a busy restaurant. Everybody appeared to be having a good time, laughing and drinking inside the large, dimly lit dining room. Rowan made certain he paused a little as they approached the place. Julie had mentioned she was hungry, and Rowan wanted to let her know that stopping at the first restaurant they passed was okay by him.

But she just kept walking.

A few minutes later, without discussion, she stepped off the wooden walkway and started leading Rowan away from the water and deeper into the city.

After they'd walked a few blocks, Julie stopped in front of a small gray stone building. "What do you think?" she asked.

The entrance to the place was set back a few feet from the sidewalk. Inside it was French bistro 101: black-and-white-checkered floor and pristine white tablecloths. A soft yellow glow from a fireplace somewhere flickered against the worn red bricks of the interior.

Rowan thought it looked absolutely perfect.

"Well?" Julie asked.

"What made you choose this place?" Rowan asked.

Julie shrugged. "Just felt right, I guess. What do you think?"

"Looks good to me," he said. He couldn't see a sign anywhere, but there was a small brass plaque stuck onto the old red bricks. On that plaque was the name of the restaurant and a small graphic.

The place was called Le Lièvre de Mars.

The graphic on the plaque was, of course, a rabbit.

28

DE STILLE KAMER

"How's Swan?" Pepper asked as Emily entered the living room.

"Not good," Emily said. "The doctor's checking on her now."

"Did she tell you what happened?" Scarpio asked.

"She said that she was sent here to find the same person Pepper was looking for, somebody called the Engineer."

"Who the hell is that?" Scarpio asked.

"Apparently Rabbits believes the Engineer is going to destroy the multiverse, so it trapped him here, in this decaying stub, and now we're stuck right along with him."

"It sounds like maybe Swan was a little out of it?" Scarpio suggested.

"Actually, she was extremely lucid, all things considered. She gave me this." Emily pulled out the timer.

"What is it?" Scarpio said.

"Fuck," Pepper said when she saw what Emily was holding. "It's a countdown timer."

"Countdown to what?" Scarpio asked.

"To the moment this dimensional stream dies."

"I'm sorry I asked."

Emily laughed.

"Did she say anything else?" Pepper asked.

"Apparently she was ambushed on her way to meet somebody called the Concorde. She said this Concorde has a map to the Quiet Room."

"What the hell is the Quiet Room?" Scarpio asked.

"Long story," Emily said.

"It's a myth," Pepper said. "A magical place outside of space and time where all dimensional streams meet."

"I'm not sure it's a myth," Emily said. "Swan is convinced it's real."

"It's not real," Pepper said. She clearly wasn't buying it.

"I think it's at least worth looking into," Emily said. "Swan isn't the type of person who believes in fairy tales."

"I thought we were trying to figure out how to find the game," MayDay said. "Now we're supposed to go looking for this Quiet Room? We need to pick a lane."

"MayDay's right," Pepper said. "It's a waste of time."

"Maybe not," Emily said. "What if it's all the same thing?"

"What do you mean?" MayDay asked.

"The Quiet Room. What if that's the game?"

"That's interesting," Pepper said, leaning forward. "What makes you say that?"

"Rowan Chess and I went searching for a woman who disappeared from a restaurant while she and Rowan were on a first date. She told him that her name was Eliza Brand, but we were unable to find her anywhere. After a remarkable coincidence, we tracked down a woman Rowan swore was Eliza Brand, but it turns out that she's actually an actor named Julie Furuno. She claimed to have no memory of ever meeting Rowan Chess."

"That's strange, but what does that have to do with anything?" MayDay asked.

"I'm getting there," Emily replied. "We held an audition for a fake project in order to meet Julie Furuno and ask her about Rowan."

"Like you do," MayDay added.

"During that audition," Emily continued, "Julie performed a monologue she claimed had been taken from a play by a Belgian playwright named Olivia Dubois. That play was called *The Quiet Room*."

"That can't be a coincidence," Scarpio said.

"Shit," Pepper said.

"What is it?" Emily replied.

"Well," Pepper continued, "I haven't mentioned this before, because I didn't believe looking into imaginary shit like the Quiet Room was an effective use of time and resources, but now I'm not so sure."

"What are you talking about?" MayDay asked.

"A few weeks before Limerick led Emily to the warehouse filled with Hazels, I met a man in a bar. I'd been looking for something connected to an airport that was allegedly missing a number of runways, and I discovered another person I thought had been researching the same thing. It turns out this guy was looking for something else, however—something he was hoping to find in the airport's lost and found."

"What was it?" MayDay asked.

"A set of thirty-five millimeter film canisters containing a movie."

"What movie?"

"A Dutch film called *De Stille Kamer*."

"Why do I think 'stille' means quiet and 'kamer' means room?" Emily asked.

"Yeah, in Dutch."

"Did he find the movie?"

"I have no idea," Pepper said. "I took off once I'd discovered that the airport had the requisite number of runways. But the Quiet Room reference can't be a coincidence."

"No way," MayDay said.

"Are you sure Swan said the Concorde had a map to the Quiet Room?" Pepper asked.

"Yes," Emily replied.

Pepper shook her head. "That's not great."

"Why not?"

"The last time I saw the Concorde, he threw me out of a three-story window."

"Jesus," Emily said. "What happened?"

"We were out for dinner, and I tried to stop him ripping a baby grand piano apart with a tire iron."

"What?"

"He was convinced that there was a message hidden somewhere in the strings of the piano. I tried to stop him."

"And he threw you out the window?"

"Yeah. Thankfully I hit an awning on the way down."

"We need to talk to this guy," Emily said, putting her arm around Pepper. "Do you know where to find him?"

Pepper took a moment, and then exhaled. "Yes. But I want to go on the record that I believe this is a terrible idea."

"Noted," Emily said. "Where is he?"

"The Northgate Station Mall. He lives there, or he did," Pepper said.

"He lives in a mall?" Emily asked.

"How the hell do you live in a mall?" MayDay asked.

"When we get there, you can ask him."

"How far is it?"

"Not far, but we'll have to wait until it opens tomorrow morning."

The following morning, Scarpio took them down to a private parking garage that contained four cars: the black prototype electric SUV, a dark green mid-seventies Corvette, a forest green Range Rover, and a white Aston Martin Vantage.

MayDay walked directly over to the Aston Martin.

"We're not all going to fit in that one," Scarpio said as he held up a key fob and unlocked the door of the Range Rover.

"Is this a twelve cylinder?" MayDay asked.

"I think so. I've never actually driven it," Scarpio replied. "I'm not sure it's street legal, to be honest."

MayDay snorted. "Fucking rich people."

"Do you mind if I drive?" Pepper asked. "It helps me think."

"Knock yourself out," Scarpio replied, and smiled as he climbed into the back seat next to MayDay, who rolled her eyes.

"What about Swan?" Pepper asked while scrolling through a list of satellite radio stations. When Emily had checked on her in the morning, she was still holding on, but unconscious.

"Her doctor is head of surgery at the University of Washington Med Center," Scarpio said. "He'll get in touch if there's any change in her condition."

"So," Emily asked as she slipped into the passenger seat next to Pepper, "everybody ready?"

"Not remotely," Pepper said as she turned up AC/DC's "Gone Shootin'," and guided the Range Rover out of the parking garage and into traffic. "I just hope we're able to get a few words in before he tries to throw one of us out of a fucking window."

29

BED BATH & BEYOND

IT TOOK THEM just under an hour to track down the Concorde.

They found him reclining in a chair in a Barnes & Noble reading *Swann's Way*. He was tall and thin, with wavy dark hair and slightly hawkish features. The way he'd folded himself into the chair reminded Emily of a sailor sprawled over an Adirondack chair on the deck of an ancient ocean liner adrift somewhere in the Atlantic.

He didn't look up from his book, but started reading aloud as soon as they arrived.

"I feel something start within me," he said, his voice low and rough, like wheels on roadside gravel, "something that leaves its resting-place and attempts to rise, something that has been embedded like an anchor at a great depth; I do not know yet what it is, but I can feel it mounting slowly; I can measure the resistance, I can hear the echo of great spaces traversed."

He set the book down on a small table and smiled at Pepper. "Have you read Marcel Proust?"

"I tried once in college," Pepper said, "but it just ended up on the shelf beside *Gravity's Rainbow* and *Ulysses*."

"Proust understood dimensional drift on a molecular level, even though he himself had most likely never experienced it. I remember you." He nodded at Pepper. "Who are your friends?"

"He's Alan Scarpio," Pepper said, "she's MayDay, and—"

Emily held out her hand. "Emily Connors."

"They call me the Concorde," the man said, shaking Emily's hand.

"I'm sorry about the last time we met," he said, turning his attention back to Pepper. "I was going through a bit of a rough patch."

"Sure," Pepper said, "a rough patch."

"You've come looking for a map to the Quiet Room," he said.

"Yes," Emily said. "How did you know?"

"Because the end is near, and the end is the time people go looking for anything they believe might help them survive."

"What can you tell us about the Quiet Room?" Emily asked. "And please hurry." She was very quickly running out of patience for speechmaking and self-indulgent ambiguity.

"Not here," the Concorde said. "Meet me at the towels in Bed Bath & Beyond."

"Seriously?" Emily asked, but the Concorde was already up and on his way out.

"What did I tell you?" Pepper said.

Bed Bath & Beyond was fairly quiet, with maybe half a dozen people shopping for sheets, coffee makers, those weird metal-pronged head-massager things, and whatever else people bought at BB&B. Pepper led Emily and the others to the towel section, located in the far corner of the store.

There was nobody there.

"Anybody else feel like this Concorde dude is fucking with us?" MayDay asked as she held up a beach towel featuring a large rabbit wearing sunglasses.

Emily was checking out an eight-foot-tall shelf filled with bath towels when she heard something click behind her. She spun around, then watched as one of the display cases on the wall popped out to reveal a set of concrete stairs leading down into darkness.

"Hurry up," the Concorde said as his head popped into view. "You have six seconds before the door closes automatically."

Emily looked over at Pepper and the others, who were staring at the hidden staircase, and mouthed *What the fuck?*

"Six . . . five . . ." the Concorde counted.

"Are we really doing this?" Emily whispered as the Concorde disappeared down the stairs, his countdown still audible.

"Four . . . three . . ."

"Seriously?" Emily said as Pepper grabbed her arm and led her down the stairs. Scarpio and MayDay followed close behind.

The display case slid back into place with a muted click, and the four of them were left in total darkness. A few seconds later, the Concorde switched on the lights.

They were standing at the base of the staircase in a narrow concrete hallway. The floor was covered in mismatched Turkish rugs. At the far end of the hall was a door.

"Please remove your shoes," the Concorde said, looking down at his own feet, which were bare.

"Socks?" MayDay asked.

"Optional," he said. "But we must be quiet, you understand."

"Of course," MayDay said with a smirk as she slipped off her shoes. Emily glanced over at Pepper, who had already removed her shoes. "Have you done this before?"

"No," Pepper said. "This is definitely new."

Footwear in hand, they followed the Concorde to the end of the hall, where he opened another door and led them into a room that looked like a studio apartment in a large high-tech city like Tokyo, Hong Kong, or San Francisco.

Emily imagined that whoever designed the place must have been given the instructions West Elm meets *Blade Runner*. Against the wall across from the door was a queen-sized bed. Directly above the bed hung a large rectangular illustration by the French artist Jean Giraud (also known as Moebius), featuring a woman in motion chasing a very large bright blue dragonfly toward a futuristic space station. Based on the location and the circumstances, Emily figured it had to be a print, but there was something about the texture and quality of the work that led her to believe it might be an original. On the right-hand side of the room was an array of vintage computer and radio equipment, a refrigerator, and a sink. On the left, an Eames lounge chair and ottoman sat beneath a huge flat-screen monitor that was playing what appeared to be a looped video of the view from a very high floor of an apartment building in downtown Seattle.

"Jesus," Pepper said, pointing in the direction of the video monitor. "That's unsettling."

"The view initially feels a little uncanny," the Concorde said, "but you get used to it. You'd be surprised how much the illusion of a window helps."

"What is this place?" Emily asked.

"It's amazing, isn't it?" the Concorde asked.

"It's something," MayDay replied.

"I heard about it in a private Discord," the Concorde said. "The group is called HHSP, which stands for Hidden Homes Secret Places. Four university students described how they'd been living in a hidden room in a Bed Bath & Beyond for a year. They wrote about it in detail—how they installed the fridge, the sink, and toilet, how they tapped into the water, sewer, and electrical systems."

"Wow," MayDay said. "That's actually really cool."

"Most of the people posting in that Discord were dumpster divers or zero-waste advocates," the Concorde continued, "committed to things like living carbon free or eating nothing but trash for a set period of time, and there were a few others who came looking for alternative housing, either because they were struggling financially or seeking a major lifestyle change. The people who created this particular space, however, were a group of curious minds interested in conducting a kind of social experiment."

Pepper had mentioned that the Concorde was mentally unbalanced, but as far as Emily could tell, he seemed perfectly fine—except for the part about him living in a hidden room underneath a Bed Bath & Beyond in a suburb of Seattle.

"How long have you been staying here?" Emily asked as she watched Pepper swipe at a fly that had somehow made its way into the room.

"Just about a year."

"How the hell does it work?" MayDay asked.

"It's a lot easier than you'd think."

"You don't feel trapped?" MayDay continued. "What happens if the display case up there in the towel section fails?"

"There's another entrance, through a hidden door there." He

pointed toward a tall wooden bookshelf. "It leads directly to the mall's parking structure."

"So you just park there and come in that way?" Emily asked.

The Concorde shook his head. "Oh no. I don't leave the mall."

"Seriously?"

"I haven't been outside for months."

"Why not?" Scarpio asked.

"Because this universe is collapsing, and the darkness is out there, waiting."

"You're aware of the fact that this stream is collapsing?" Pepper asked.

He nodded. "Of course."

"Why stay here, in this place?" Emily asked. "It seems like a lot of work."

"This room is located right at the beginning of one of Kellan Meechum's Radiants, something called the Lifeson Radiant," he said, "which is a very important pathway. And also, Bed Bath & Beyond is a very significant place. It soothes me."

Emily nodded. So maybe the Concorde wasn't quite as well-adjusted as he'd initially appeared. "What can you tell us about the Quiet Room?" she asked.

The Concorde ignored Emily's question. He opened the fridge, pulled out five cans of grapefruit LaCroix, and brought them, along with four clear plastic cups, over to the small dining room table beneath the television screen.

"I'm sorry, but I don't think I have a map to the Quiet Room," he said as he set four cans and the cups down on the table and opened his own can of LaCroix with a fizzy crack.

"You don't?" Emily asked.

"I don't think so, and you should thank whatever gods you believe in for that."

"Why?" Emily asked.

"Because those who go looking for the Quiet Room never return."

"That's dramatic," Pepper said as she swiped at the fly, now buzzing around her can of LaCroix.

"Some believe it's possible to access the Quiet Room by playing the game, or by otherwise manipulating the Radiants," the Concorde said, "but that's impossible. No human being can survive the journey."

"Why not?" Pepper asked.

The Concorde lowered his voice to a whisper. "Because the path is darkness. The Quiet Room exists in another realm."

"Are we still talking about Rabbits?" Emily asked.

"Oh yes," the Concorde said, "but there's so much more."

"So, you believe the Quiet Room is real?" Emily asked as Pepper held up her empty can of LaCroix, which was suddenly buzzing. The fly had flown inside.

"The Quiet Room is all over ancient human history and mythology," the Concorde continued, "if you know where to look. It moves around. The Tibetans placed it in the city of Shambhala, and in another age it was in a small hidden chamber in a pyramid at Giza. It exists, I'm certain of it, but it's too dangerous for humankind to enter."

"How so?" Emily asked.

"The Quiet Room is populated by the light that kills."

"What the hell are you talking about?" Pepper asked.

"They say, in order to find the path, you need to play the game, but you must beware the light."

"Who says that?" MayDay asked.

The Concorde ignored her question.

"So it is possible to play the game here in this stream?" Emily asked.

"Of course," said the Concorde. "If you can find it. You see, in a healthy dimensional stream, the game is active. It guides the players, becomes aware of them, and leads them to the Radiants required for whatever dimensional stream mechanics the game is working to correct. But here, in this stream, the game appears to be doing the opposite."

"What do you mean?" MayDay asked.

"In this stream, I believe that Rabbits is actively working not only to avoid being discovered by potential players, but to confuse and distract those players who have been lucky or persistent enough to actually discover the game."

Emily nodded. Datlow and her group of Hazels had described something similar.

"But even if you do manage to figure out a way to play the game, finding your way to the Quiet Room will require something else," the Concorde continued.

"What?" Emily asked.

"A map—which is why you came to me."

"But you don't have the map," Pepper said.

"I didn't say that," the Concorde replied. "I said I don't *think* I have a map. Big difference."

"What the fuck are you talking about?" Pepper said, clearly losing patience.

"There has to be something we can try," Emily said.

"Well, lucky for you, there is," the Concorde said as he made his way over to his desk and pulled a large three-ring binder from an old leather case. "And this is the second-to-last thing I tell you before I no longer know what I'm going to say."

"What?" MayDay asked.

The Concorde opened the three-ring binder filled with pages that had clearly been typed on a manual typewriter. On the last few pages was a transcript of their conversation with the Concorde. It was all there, from the very first lines the Concorde had spoken about Proust in the bookstore until right now.

"The map is trapped," the Concorde said, and then smiled.

Emily said, "What the hell?" before she saw that exact line was typed after her name, near the end of the page. And after that, on the very last line, Pepper said . . .

"What is this?" Pepper leaned forward. "This is impossible."

THE CONCORDE: In this stream, I believe that
Rabbits is actively working not only to avoid being
discovered by potential players, but to confuse
and distract those players who have been lucky or

persistent enough to actually discover the game.
But even if you do manage to figure out a way to
play the game, finding your way to the Quiet Room
will require something else.
EMILY CONNORS: What?
THE CONCORDE: A map—which is why you came to me.
PEPPER PRINCE: But you don't have the map.
THE CONCORDE: I didn't say that. I said I don't
think I have a map. Big difference.
PEPPER PRINCE: What the fuck are you talking about?
EMILY CONNORS: There has to be something we can
try.
THE CONCORDE: Well, lucky for you, there is. And
this is the second-to-last thing I tell you before
I no longer know what I'm going to say.
MAYDAY: What?
THE CONCORDE: The map is trapped.
EMILY CONNORS: What the hell?
PEPPER PRINCE: What is this? This is impossible.

—END TRANSCRIPT—

"How did you do that?" Pepper asked. "Is this some kind of magic trick?"

"It's no trick," the Concorde said, "I assure you. This is real."

"Where did you get these pages?" Emily said.

"Does it matter?"

"This is a record of our conversation," Scarpio said. "A conversation we just had."

The Concorde nodded. "Yes."

"What the hell is going on?" Pepper asked. "How far back does this go?"

"As far as I can tell, the conversations contained in this document began six months ago," the Concorde said. "But aside from a brief conversation about a botched colonoscopy and a slightly erotic encounter with a shoplifter in a Foot Locker bathroom, nothing exciting happens until you four approach me in the bookstore."

"Where did you get this?" Pepper asked as she flipped through the pages.

"I found this document in the bottom drawer of a filing cabinet in a thrift store in Montreal while playing the eighth iteration of the game."

"Eight ended in 2005," Emily said. "How could a conversation that wouldn't actually take place until eighteen years in the future end up typed onto the pages of this manuscript? It's impossible."

The Concorde smiled. "It's pretty wild, isn't it?"

Emily opened her mouth to tell the Concorde that it wasn't wild, it was impossible—a trick that he must have somehow planned and executed using some type of microphone and hidden printer setup—but there was no way he could have typed the last part of their conversation without an elaborate and perfectly silent printing system hidden somewhere.

They checked everywhere. There was no hidden printer, and there was nobody in the room except for the five of them.

It looked like the transcript of the conversation they'd just had with the Concorde—a conversation recorded word for word in the pages of that manuscript—had somehow been typed more than eighteen years before those words would actually be spoken.

"Do you have any idea what the fuck is going on?" Emily asked as she stared over Pepper's shoulder at the transcript.

"I do not," Pepper replied.

There was a bit of text and a symbol stamped onto the first page of the document. The text read: PROPERTY OF THE GATEWICK INSTITUTE. The symbol was a moon floating above a pyramid.

"This came from the Gatewick Institute?" Emily asked.

The Concorde nodded. "Have you heard of it?"

"I think I may have heard that name somewhere before, but I can't remember exactly where," Emily lied.

Pepper flipped back to the last page.

"It's a trip, isn't it?" the Concorde said. "I've been waiting for today for a long time. I feel like I'm finally free."

"You knew what we were going to say?" Scarpio asked.

"Yes."

"Why didn't you say something? Warn us somehow?"

"I had to follow the script," the Concorde said.

"Had to or chose to?" Emily asked.

"Is there a difference?"

"Definitely," Pepper said.

"Maybe I had no choice, or maybe I just wanted to know if what you were going to say would match the transcript," he said.

"Well, it looks like it did."

The Concorde just smiled.

"Why did you say this?" MayDay pointed to the last line of the transcript attributed to the Concorde: *The map is trapped.*

"I have no idea," he replied.

"You told us that we needed a map," Emily said.

"It's my understanding that the Quiet Room is impossible to find without a map."

"How do you know that?" Pepper asked.

"A Russian woman told me," he replied.

"Seriously?" MayDay asked.

The Concorde nodded. "She was very serious. In fact, she's the person who sold me the contents of the filing cabinet that contained that document," the Concorde added. "Among other things."

"The map is trapped? What do you suppose that means?" Emily asked.

"I have no idea," the Concorde replied. "But it must be connected to you four."

"How so?" Pepper asked.

"You came here looking for the Quiet Room, which allegedly requires a map, and the transcript only mentions a map *after* you arrive here, in this room."

Emily looked around. "You really think the map is connected to us?"

"That would make the most sense," he replied, "but you need to remember, although Meechum's Radiants may be triggered, and a possible path to the Quiet Room revealed, the game is still going to be working against you."

"It feels like everything is working against us," Emily said as she took another look around the room. There was nothing that looked like a map. "You said that the map is trapped," Emily repeated. "That has to be significant somehow."

"Agreed," said the Concorde. "That's the one part of the conversation that feels like it exists outside of what I might naturally say under the circumstances."

"Right," Emily said. "That's a clue."

Pepper stood up and started examining the artwork hanging above the bed. "Shit," she said. "This is an original, isn't it?"

The Concorde nodded. "Moebius gave it to me shortly before he died."

Emily shook her head. Her instinct had been right. There was an original Moebius illustration hanging on the wall in a hidden room under a Bed Bath & Beyond.

This was getting stranger by the second.

"It's called *Empath,*" the Concorde said, pointing at the illustration. "Last year, I figured out that 'empath' is an anagram for 'the map'—but, similar to the transcript, I haven't been able to find anything hidden in the image that suggests a map or a clue to the location of a map."

He pulled the illustration off the wall and flipped it around.

"There's this," he said, pointing to some writing in pencil on the back of the illustration.

Reality is a blanket, comfortable, but a lie. There's always a loose thread, even if you can't see it, and all you have to do is pull, just a little, and things will start to unravel. Will you find the answers that you seek? Or will you end up freezing to death beside a pile of thread?

"Any idea what it means?" Emily asked.

"I've looked it up," he replied. "There's nothing."

"There has to be something we're missing," Scarpio said.

"I've been over every inch of the place," the Concorde said. "There is no map."

———

After an hour spent staring at the Moebius illustration, and another hour digging through magazines, books, and other printed material, Emily sat back down at the dining room table and took a sip of her LaCroix. As she did so, she noticed a buzzing sound coming from Pepper's empty can.

Emily picked up the can and turned it upside down. The fly landed on the table. It was moving very slowly, as if trying to fight through thick invisible molasses. The poor thing appeared to be nearing the end of its life.

Emily could relate.

The map is trapped.

She leaned forward and took a closer look at the fly.

Its body was bright blue, and its wings were larger than normal— Emily thought that she had never seen an insect like this one in her life.

"Hey, guys?" Emily said as she took a look at the blue dragonfly in the Moebius illustration.

Pepper and the Concorde turned their attention to Emily.

"I'm going to need you to come over here and take a look at something."

The fly had definitely been trapped.

But how the hell could a fly be a map?

30

ALPHA LEPORIS

ROWAN WOKE UP feeling the way he felt whenever he was on an airplane, like he wasn't actually living or dead, but rather floating in a kind of in-between place, a disconnected holding-pattern limbo. He rubbed his eyes and sat up. He wasn't on an airplane. He was lying on a large bed in the middle of a dim, loft-style apartment.

"Good morning, sleepyhead." Julie Furuno smiled at him from where she sat across the room, dangling in a wicker chair that was suspended from the ceiling in what appeared to be the loft's main living area.

"Where are we?"

"My apartment."

"How?"

"How can I afford such a magnificent living space, or how did we get here?"

"The last thing I remember, we were walking into a restaurant."

"Seriously?"

Rowan nodded.

Julie shook her head. "Wow. Things are worse than I thought."

The floating fuzzy feeling was slowly starting to leave Rowan's head, but he still had no memory of anything that had happened after they decided to eat at Le Lièvre de Mars.

"Is it really morning?" Rowan asked.

"Kind of. It's two thirty."

"What happened?"

"When?"

"Did we eat?"

"Wow, okay. You are really starting to freak me out here."

"I'm sorry," Rowan said. He could tell that Julie was worried. "I must have just blacked out or something. I'm sure everything will come back to me."

Julie nodded. "Okay, well, we did eat. You had a squid ink seafood pasta you said that you loved because it was light on squid ink, which I thought was funny. I had the bouillabaisse, which was amazing."

"And after dinner?"

"You said you needed to buy a phone." Julie nodded to a cellphone currently charging on the nightstand.

"And then?"

"Long romantic walk along the water. I told you about my dreams. You told me almost nothing at all about your life. You walked me back here like a gentleman, and I invited you up for a drink like a modern woman with questionable morals. You said you shouldn't, that it was getting late. I said fuck you, it's one drink."

Rowan laughed in spite of the fact that she was narrating part of his life he had no memory of living.

"Then you said you weren't feeling well," Julie continued, "so I suggested you lie down on the bed for a bit. That was two hours ago. I checked your breathing and heartbeat a few times to make sure you were still alive. I was just about to walk over there and yell in your ear when you sat up."

Rowan was starting to feel more like himself, but a sense of something unfinished continued to hang over the whole situation. It felt a bit like he was living in a simulation, like nothing existed outside the walls of Julie's apartment unless Rowan decided to look, at which point the world within his field of view would be assembled by whoever or whatever was in charge. It was disconcerting— but not as disconcerting as the fact that he was missing two or three hours of his life.

"Anything else happen last night that I should be aware of?" he asked, finally.

"Well, there was the dinner, the romantic bunny hunt, and then we ended up here." She put her finger to her lips as if trying to remember. "I think that's everything, you know, outside of the ferocious lovemaking."

"What?"

"I'm fucking with you."

He nodded, distracted. "Did you say . . . bunny hunt?"

"You really don't remember?"

"No."

"None of it?"

"Sorry, no, but I'm sure it will come back eventually."

Julie blinked. She didn't appear convinced.

"Do you mind telling me exactly what happened after we finished eating?" Rowan asked. "My brain is a bit foggy at the moment."

"Okay, well, I paid the bill and then we left."

"Thank you," Rowan said.

"You really don't remember?"

"I really don't."

"I lied. You were sneaky. You paid the check while I was in the restroom. Shortly after we left the restaurant, I suggested we go for a long walk along the water. That's when you got excited."

"How so?"

"Sorry, no. That's not right. You got excited before that, when you snuck off to pay the bill. When you saw the picture."

"What picture?"

"The picture in the restaurant. It was an old *Playboy* magazine cover behind glass, of a girl licking a stamp."

"I got excited when I saw a *Playboy* magazine in the restaurant?"

"Yeah, and you got even more excited when you saw something else *Playboy*-related on our walk."

"I don't understand. Why would I care about *Playboy*?"

"Maybe you really love tits?"

"What?"

"I'm kidding. You said it was facing the wrong way."

"The magazine?"

"The rabbit. You said the rabbit's profile normally faces left."

Rowan nodded. "That sounds right."

"But these rabbits were facing right."

"It should be left."

"That's what you said when you saw the *Playboy* bunny again on a necklace and T-shirt in the window of Nordstrom's. You got so excited, I thought you were going to pass out."

"I did?"

She nodded.

"What happened next?"

"You wanted to go looking for more."

Rowan was shocked. He had no memory of anything she was describing. Could she be lying? If so, why?

"Why are you so obsessed with these things?" Julie said.

"I'm not," Rowan said.

"Well, you sure seemed obsessed last night. You almost ripped my arm off dragging us in search of more bunnies."

"I don't understand," he said. "I have no idea why I would do something like that. I have no interest in *Playboy* magazine or its logo."

Rowan wanted to change the subject, to say something that might make Julie forget about his strange behavior, but he really needed to know what the hell was going on.

He was worried.

He hadn't experienced a blackout like this since he was fifteen years old.

It was the summer between ninth and tenth grade. Rowan had been spending his days at the mall hanging out with his friends, sneaking into three movies for the price of one, and generally just killing time until school started up again.

There was a bowling alley in the mall that had a bunch of old videogames next to the snack bar. They had Donkey Kong, Double Dragon, Gauntlet, and Rowan's favorite, Silver Swords—a side-scrolling hack-and-slasher that involved slaying dragons, collecting treasure, and saving a princess from evil.

Rowan spent hundreds of hours (and dollars) playing Silver

Swords. Those afternoons spent guiding the tiny blond knight through enchanted forests and haunted dungeons were some of the happiest in Rowan's life. He loved memorizing all of the intricate patterns of movement required to collect the gold coins that added life force to the main character and extended the game.

For as long as he could remember, Rowan had trouble falling asleep. The one thing he found that helped was running over Silver Swords patterns in his mind.

At the end of the summer, he managed to convince his mother to let him go to New Hampshire to visit his uncle Allen. He loved his uncle, but Rowan was actually going on that trip in order to compete in a contest at an arcade called Funspot. Rowan had beat the world record Silver Swords high score a few times at the bowling alley, but in order to enter arcade game history, he would need to reproduce that feat in front of the crowds at Funspot. But a week before Rowan was supposed to leave for New Hampshire, something happened.

Silver Swords disappeared from the bowling alley.

Rowan had been sick for a couple of days around the time it happened. It wasn't the flu or a cold; it was more like a general sense of malaise. He just wasn't feeling like himself. Although he weighed the same as always, his body felt heavier, and his mind seemed to be operating at a reduced capacity, like he was thinking through a thick, cloudy gauze.

But Rowan didn't have time to be sick. The contest at Funspot was coming up in a week, and he needed to practice. He asked the manager of the bowling alley what had happened to the machine and when it would be back. The manager told Rowan she'd never heard of Silver Swords and that the bowling alley's arcade had never featured any such game.

What the hell was happening? Had the whole world gone crazy? He asked his friends if they knew where he could find another Silver Swords machine, but they claimed to have never heard of the game either.

Were his friends in on it? Were they playing some kind of prank?

By the time he made it back home, it was getting late, and Rowan wanted to make sure he had time to do his laundry before he left for his uncle's place in New Hampshire.

While he was upstairs packing, his mother came in and asked him what he was doing. When Rowan told her he was packing for his trip to visit his uncle, his mother laughed.

"You think you're ready for another week with Uncle Allen?"

"What are you talking about?"

"You were just there, sweetheart, and as much as your uncle loves you, I'm pretty sure he's not going to be able to handle another week with a teenager."

Rowan was shocked. What the hell was his mother talking about? Rowan felt the room start to spin. He sat down on his bed and his mother told him to lie down and rest and that she'd bring up some soup in a few minutes.

While he was resting, Rowan opened up a photo album that he knew contained pictures of all three times he'd beaten the high score on Silver Swords at the bowling alley. He was going to prove to everybody that the game existed.

But the photographs weren't there.

Rowan was just about to go downstairs and ask his mother what was going on, when he saw a picture in the album that he didn't recognize. It was Rowan and Uncle Allen. They were standing in front of Funspot. Rowan was wearing an Atari T-shirt that he'd just purchased a few days ago.

This photograph was impossible.

There were other strange photos in the album as well, including pictures of Rowan on an airplane to New Hampshire. He couldn't remember any of them being taken.

He dug up an old videogame magazine from his closet and started flipping through the pages. He was looking for an article he'd read the previous year that featured a photo of a Silver Swords cabinet.

The article was no longer there.

Rowan curled up in a ball on his bed and shut his eyes. He would go to sleep, and when he woke up everything would be back to normal. He'd feel like himself again, and Silver Swords would be back in the bowling alley where it belonged.

But that's not what happened.

When Rowan woke up, he still didn't feel like himself, and Silver Swords wasn't back in the bowling alley or anywhere else. It was gone, and he couldn't find anybody else who'd even heard of it.

Rowan never mentioned that game again, or the fact that he couldn't remember eight days of his life spent with his uncle in New Hampshire.

Until he met Eliza Brand decades later, playing Silver Swords in the bowling alley was the last time Rowan could remember truly feeling like he belonged in the world.

"Did you notice which way the bunny was facing in the picture at the restaurant?" Rowan asked. Maybe he'd been mistaken about the anomaly? He had no idea why the hell he'd become so interested in *Playboy* bunnies all of a sudden, but he felt like he needed to find out.

"Left," Julie said.

Rowan nodded. So it had been facing the proper way.

"Sorry," Julie continued. "I think it was facing right, maybe."

"Are you sure?"

"Fuck. No. I can't remember."

Rowan stood up. "I should probably get going."

"Wow," Julie said. "This isn't the way it usually happens in romantic comedies."

"I'm so sorry," Rowan said, "it's nothing like that. I really want to see you again. It's just I'm feeling a bit off." He did desperately want to see her again, but he was pretty sure losing his memory and rambling about weird Internet conspiracies wasn't going to help him land another date.

"What if something happens?" Julie asked.

And Rowan was right back in the restaurant the night Eliza Brand had asked him to think of some way she could tell him apart from his identical evil twin.

This woman was the same person. She had to be.

"What do you mean?" he asked.

Julie slipped out of the hanging chair, made her way over to a nearby teak desk, and pulled out a small dark wooden box. "Well, let's say you leave my place at three in the morning after passing out and acting weird, and then something bad happens to you. How do you think that's going to make me feel?"

She had a point.

Rowan was still feeling a little out of it, and not particularly confident in his ability to make rational decisions. He needed to check with his bank to make sure nobody had accessed his safe deposit box without his knowledge, but the bank wouldn't be open for at least another six hours.

"Relax," Julie said as she pulled a joint from the wooden box, lit it, and then plopped herself down on the sofa. "I'm going to stay up for another hour playing videogames and killing bosses. If you wanna hang and sleep over, it's up to you. Or you can head home; that's cool, too. My number's in your phone."

Rowan thought about stepping out into the cold world at three in the morning to wait for an Uber, and then glanced over at Julie Furuno sitting there warm and cozy in her T-shirt, snuggled under a blanket on the sofa. "Do you have another controller?" he asked as he sat down next to her.

"I knew you'd come around," Julie said as she tossed him a controller. "Try to keep up. I'm really good at this shit."

31

I'M NEVER GOING TO TRUST
ANOTHER BOOKSHELF AGAIN

"I'M PRETTY SURE IT'S DEAD," MayDay said.

"I think you're right," Emily replied. The fly hadn't moved for quite some time.

Emily and the others stood around the table staring at the fly that had been trapped in Pepper's empty can.

"I've never seen an insect quite like this one," the Concorde said. "That blue color is so vivid, and the wings are long—almost like a tiny dragonfly."

"What do you think?" Emily asked. "I mean, it was trapped, right?"

"This is a bit of a stretch, Em," Pepper said.

"That Moebius picture features a woman chasing a strange blue dragonfly," Emily said, "plus it's called *Empath,* which is an anagram for 'the map.' It doesn't feel all that stretchy to me."

"That is very interesting," the Concorde said as he walked over to a bookshelf next to his desk and pulled a rectangular box from a high shelf.

"What is that?"

"Optical microscope," he said as he opened the box and removed a small high-school-science-lab-type microscope with a cellphone-sized screen attached to the front.

"You just happen to have an optical microscope on hand?" May-Day asked.

"It was here when I found the place," he said as he set the microscope down on the desk and plugged it into the wall. Then he walked over to the dining room table, picked up the fly, and carried it back to the desk.

Emily and Pepper shared a look before hurrying over to join him.

"You really think this has something to do with the fly?" Pepper asked.

The Concorde ignored her. He was on a mission. His face betrayed an enthusiasm that Emily recognized immediately. It was the kind of excitement that came over her when she was playing the game.

He slipped the fly under the microscope and zoomed in.

There was no hidden message written on its body, but no species of fly that they could find online matched the shape and coloration of the insect under the microscope. "I'm not sure this is strictly organic material," the Concorde said.

"A miniature drone or something?" Pepper asked.

He nodded. "Maybe."

"That's impossible," Emily said.

"Nanotech is light-years ahead of where people believe it is," Scarpio said, leaning forward, "but I've never seen anything quite this small."

The Concorde went over the tiny thing again, zooming in on one of the wings, then the other. After a few seconds, he took a step back. "I have a theory," he said.

"Do you mind sharing?" Pepper asked.

The Concorde smiled. "Why would I do that when it's so much more fun to test it dramatically?"

"Of course," Pepper said. "Why indeed."

The Concorde pulled out his phone and took a photograph of the screen that contained the magnified image of the fly's wing.

"What are you doing?"

"Emailing myself a copy of the image."

"What for?" Emily asked.

"Patience, Emily Connors. I'm about to show you," he said, and then opened the image using a photo editing app on his computer.

He spent about a minute or so adjusting the contrast and opacity of the image before he opened another tab and loaded some kind of software.

"What is that?" Scarpio asked.

"Facial recognition software."

"It looks advanced," Scarpio added.

"It's an NSA prototype."

"That makes sense."

"What does facial recognition have to do with the fly?"

"It's not just faces. This software can identify patterns of all kinds—and it's capable of searching every type of file imaginable, including images and pdfs."

"That sounds impossible," MayDay said.

"Not at all," the Concorde replied. "It's just expensive."

A few seconds later, an image filled the screen.

It was a map of northern Washington State.

"I don't get it," Emily said.

"Watch," the Concorde said, and pressed a key.

Suddenly, the image of the fly's wing and the map were side by side on the screen.

Then, the Concorde pulled the image of the map over the image of the wing, and the software snapped the two images in place.

They were a match.

The veins of the fly's wings lined up perfectly with the freeways and main roads in and around northern Washington.

"No way," Pepper said.

"Shit." Emily leaned forward. "The map *was* trapped."

"What are all these symbols?" MayDay said, pointing to a number of geometric shapes arranged around the map.

"One of the points marked by a symbol is probably what you're looking for," the Concorde said as he zoomed in on the images.

Emily noticed a tiny green triangle in the lower part of the fly's wing. Just above that triangle was a small pink dot. It was the symbol stamped on the first page of the transcript contained in the Concorde's binder. The dot was hovering right over Lakewood, Washington.

"It's The Moonrise," Emily said, pointing to the circle above the triangle.

"What's The Moonrise?" MayDay asked.

"It's the Gatewick Institute logo," Pepper said.

"A circle floating above a triangle or pyramid," Emily added.

"If The Moonrise marks the spot," Pepper continued, "then whatever it is we're looking for is located somewhere around Lakewood, Washington."

"What the hell could possibly be in Lakewood?" MayDay asked.

"Lakewood is actually quite significant," the Concorde said. "There's a Radiant there—"

Suddenly a loud beeping filled the room.

"What's that?" Emily asked.

"Put on your shoes," the Concorde said.

"Why?"

"Someone's here."

He pressed a few keys and the feed from a security camera filled the screen. There were four people standing around the towel section of Bed Bath & Beyond—two women and two men. The two men were holding what appeared to be large metal detectors.

"They can't know we're down here, can they?" Emily asked, just as one of the women began shaking the display cabinet that hid the staircase to the Concorde's secret chamber.

"Shit," Emily said.

A few seconds later, they had the door open and were moving down the stairs.

"It's time to go," the Concorde said as he picked up the fly, popped the hard drive from his computer, grabbed a small leather bag from a nearby cabinet, then slid a tall bookshelf aside to reveal a gray metal door.

Emily shook her head as she slipped on her shoes. "I'm never going to trust another bookshelf again."

"Come on," Pepper said as she grabbed Emily's hand and pulled her toward the door.

The sounds of banging were muted as the Concorde pulled the bookshelf back into place using a small wooden ball on a string.

He led them through a series of hallways to another metal door, and, finally, out into a narrow concrete walkway that emptied into a five-level parking structure.

"They'll find the hidden door in about eight seconds," the Concorde said. "You should get moving."

"You're not coming with us?" Pepper asked.

He shook his head, then looked back in the direction they'd just come from and yelled, "Run!"

The four of them took off as fast as they could into the parking garage, running between the cars as they made their way toward a pair of elevators located straight ahead of them, just to the left of a wide set of concrete stairs.

Emily was already halfway down the first flight of stairs when Pepper called after her.

"We should take the elevator," Pepper said.

"The stairs are faster," Emily said.

"The elevator's here," Pepper said. "Come on."

Just as Emily started walking back up the stairs, the elevator doors opened, and three people dressed in black stepped out.

Emily watched MayDay, Scarpio, and Pepper sprint away in opposite directions, and then she turned and ran down the stairs as fast as she could.

She was out of the parking structure in less than twenty seconds.

Emily took a look around. Straight ahead and to the left and right were moderately busy city streets. Behind her was the door to the parking structure. Next to that door was another entrance to the shopping mall.

Her first instinct was to run to the left, but she thought that was exactly what they'd expect her to do. So instead she turned and ran back into the mall.

She figured she'd have a much better shot at losing them there.

It turned out, she was right.

She bought a burner phone at the first cellular place she found, then ran into Macy's, where she purchased a Seahawks baseball hat and a change of clothes. After that, she slipped into a movie theater where she sat through about ten minutes of a pointless superhero film, then another ten minutes of an almost funny action comedy starring a comedian she recognized from *Saturday Night Live*. When she snuck out of the theater and left the mall an hour or so later, there were no signs of any Rabbits Police.

Emily had escaped.

She opened the burner phone and called Alan Scarpio. No answer. She tried to remember Pepper's number, but she could only recall the first few digits.

She would eventually return to Scarpio's apartment to rendezvous with the others, but she wanted to check something first. The Concorde had zoomed in on the Gatewick symbol that had been hovering just above Lakewood, Washington, like a pink UFO.

MayDay had asked, *What the hell could possibly be in Lakewood?*

Emily didn't say anything at the time, but she had an idea.

They hadn't been able to find much of anything on the Gatewick Institute in this dimensional stream, but there was one place nobody would have bothered to check.

Emily's family home was located in Lakewood, right around the area the Concorde had zoomed in on on that half-insect, half-Google map.

Emily Connors was going home.

32

YOU WANNA GET
AN ICE CREAM?

IT TOOK AN HOUR AND A HALF to get to Lakewood by train. Emily had considered taking an Uber, but spending that much money on a rideshare felt morally wrong.

She had no idea what she was going to say to whoever was currently living in the house she'd grown up in. She'd have to come up with something when she got there.

But when Emily finally stepped up to the door and knocked, her mind was a complete blank.

Thankfully, there was no answer.

She took a look around the outside of the house. There was nobody visible through any of the windows, and there were no cars in the garage. It was midafternoon, so Emily figured that whoever lived there was most likely at work. The trees and hedges surrounding the place grew high and thick, so, unless there were hidden cameras in the trees, it looked like Emily was going to be able to attempt her breaking and entering without being seen.

When Emily lived there, the sliding door that led into the kitchen had been super janky. All you had to do was pull it really hard and it opened every time. Emily gave it a try, but it was securely locked. She took a closer look and saw that it had been replaced with a much newer (and far more secure) type of door.

Looking down at the replacement door, Emily felt a momentary tinge of loss. That sliding door, with its weather-worn wooden handle and glaringly obvious security shortcomings, had been a part of her life. Emily's sister's most embarrassing moment had been smashing into that sliding door while carrying a tray of hot dogs, right in front of Reggie Marsh at one of their parents' many back-yard parties.

Emily missed her little sister, and the love that had filled their family home, but she didn't have time for a melancholy trip down memory lane.

There had to be another way into the house.

The old wooden windows had been replaced by double-paned, energy-efficient plastic models, and all the doors had been securely dead-bolted. What Emily needed was a doggie door, or a ladder to access the busted-up attic window that appeared to be unchanged from when she'd lived there.

Or she could just break a window and hope that there was no alarm.

Before she broke any glass, Emily decided to try all of the win-dows, just to see if any of them were unlocked. Her father had told her something when she was about twelve years old. They'd been locked out of their house because he'd lost his keys down a storm drain. It was pouring rain and they needed to get inside. As he pulled open the window to his office, he winked and told Emily that "people forget to lock the windows they use most often."

The third window Emily tried was located in the kitchen, di-rectly above the sink. She carefully removed the screen and pulled at the white plastic.

It slid open effortlessly.

Emily tripped as she crawled over the sink and tumbled hard onto the familiar Spanish-tiled floor. "Fuck," she said as a sharp pain radi-ated up her arm from where she'd smashed her elbow on the counter.

She'd have a bruise. But she was in.

She didn't waste time looking around at what had changed since she'd lived there last. She went straight down into the basement.

She was on a mission.

The tiki bar her parents had built was still there, although it looked like the current owners were using it as a storage area.

Emily had no idea if her parents had maintained a secret office in this dimension or not, but that pyramid symbol's location on the map hidden in that fly's wing was far too coincidental to ignore.

She lifted the tile and pulled the lever.

The hidden door popped open.

It looked exactly as it had the last time she'd seen it, and based on the smell and the layer of dust that covered everything, the hidden office hadn't been disturbed since Emily's family had lived there at the turn of the century.

She could have spent months going over everything in that office, but if what Swan had told them was accurate, this stream was going to vanish soon, and Emily's time would be better spent looking for some way out, not reliving her parents' prior life as weird secret-office-hiding Gatewick Institute operatives.

Swan said the Quiet Room was the key to finding a way home, and that the Gatewick Institute believed it existed, so the first thing Emily did was look for anything and everything related to Gatewick or the Quiet Room.

It took her about forty-five minutes of combing through a packed three-drawer filing cabinet, but she eventually found a file folder that contained information on both.

It was pretty clear, based on everything Emily discovered in the secret office, that her parents had been borrowing documents from the Gatewick Institute, quite possibly without permission. The Quiet Room was mentioned in just one document in a folder labeled MEECHUM RADIANT TRAVEL. That document was titled "Convergence in Betweenspace."

CONVERGENCE IN BETWEENSPACE

DATE: ██████

ACTIVATION PERIOD: Seventh Iteration

RABBITS ACTIVE: Yes

SUBJECTS INVOLVED: ████████, ████████

After collecting the available data from 1939 to 1996, the advisory council made up of senior members ████████, ████████, ████████ have concluded the following:

1. Although there is strong anecdotal evidence supporting its existence(s), none of those interviewed were able to provide any tangible methods of accessing the "Convergence Area" described by ▮▮▮▮▮▮▮ for study. Therefore, it must be assumed that the proposed "Convergence Area" is either: a) currently beyond our ability to access, b) discoverable only via some ritual related to manipulation of the Radiants themselves, or c) accessible by express permission from some (as of this date) unknown sentinels or other controlling entity or ▮▮▮▮▮▮▮.

2. ▮▮▮▮▮▮ believes that the "Convergence Area" is most likely synonymous with what ▮▮▮▮▮▮ and ▮▮▮▮▮▮ referred to as the "Quiet Room."

3. All of the subjects* interviewed between 1939 and 1996 seem to agree on the following facts: A. The Quiet Room exists. B. The Quiet Room exists outside of regular space/matter in some kind of neutral-space/matter or state of temporal and/or physical stasis known as Betweenspace.** C. The Quiet Room allows access between a very high number of dimensional streams. (Potentially all of them?)

*None of the subjects interviewed had firsthand experience with the Quiet Room. All of the information collected in these interviews should be considered anecdotal and has been included here strictly in response to Enlightened Truth Enterprises' request for information (per: the Clooney/Hamilton interviews, unknown).

**The term "Betweenspace," initially coined by Dr. Gabriel Bennington and Edward Crawford, has been used to describe the energy field involved in transitional stream mechanics (per: Bennington & Crawford, *Radiant Mechanics Revisited* 3rd edition, G.I./San Francisco, 1998).

There was a Post-it note atop the second page featuring two words written in Emily's mother's handwriting: *Quiet Room/Map?* Below the Post-it, stuck to the page using packing tape, was a small bluish brass key with the name DEXTER stamped into the front. It looked like the kind of key that might fit an old safe deposit box or a locker. Emily slipped the "Convergence in Betweenspace" document and the key into her pocket, and then sealed up the office.

As she moved back upstairs, Emily considered what she'd just discovered.

The Quiet Room? Betweenspace? If these things actually existed, surely the scientific community would have some knowledge of them? Why weren't they looking into this stuff using the Large Hadron Collider?

Was somebody or something working behind the scenes to keep everything hidden?

When Emily had started thinking about this stuff, she was walking toward the front door, but somehow she'd ended up on the second floor, standing in the doorway of her old bedroom.

The room's current occupant appeared to be a high school girl, based on the clothing on the floor (bras, leggings, tank tops) and the posters that filled the walls (Harry Styles, *Cheerleader Death Squad, Midsommar*). And, although the walls had been painted a terrible blue and the carpet replaced with fake hardwood veneer, the room looked eerily similar to the way it had been way back when it was Emily's. The bed and other furniture—including two mismatched side tables and a desk—were precisely where Emily would have put them. The geography of the space was the same, and the air inside the room felt familiar. She knew it was impossible, of course, but Emily had the distinct feeling that the room remembered her.

As she stepped inside, she felt a wave of warm comfort. It wasn't nostalgia exactly, more like slipping into another, happier life. To Emily it felt like pulling the covers over her head when she was a child, knowing that her parents were downstairs and that everything was going to be okay.

But this time, Emily knew that everything wasn't going to be okay.

When Emily woke up, she was staring into the eyes of a teenage girl.

"Why are you sleeping in my bed?" the girl demanded.

Emily jumped up. "Shit."

"It's fine."

Emily must have fallen asleep at some point, but she couldn't even remember lying down. "I'm sorry," she said. "I think I dozed off."

"Are you okay?"

Emily took a close look at the girl. She appeared to be about sixteen, with bright green eyes and blond pixie-cut hair. She was wearing a black leather jacket over a cropped black cardigan and low-rise jeans with rips across both knees. On her feet she wore faded black Doc Marten boots. Emily could hear the rain falling outside the bedroom window. If the girl's parents had been home, Emily figured the Doc Martens would have been left behind at the front door.

Emily checked the time. She'd been asleep for an hour.

"My name is Emily," she said. "I'm not going to hurt you."

The girl smiled. "I'm Brix. Why the hell are you in my room?"

"I grew up in this house," Emily said.

Brix nodded, then bit her lip for a moment. "That tracks," she said, then she pulled a small aluminum baseball bat from behind her back.

"Shit," Emily said. "Was that for me?"

"You can't be too careful these days," Brix said as she tossed the bat onto the bed.

"I love your hair," Emily said.

"Thanks, I just did it."

Emily stood up, and as she did so, she noticed the distant sound of circus music coming from somewhere outside the house.

"Are you a drug addict or something?" Brix asked.

"No," Emily replied. "It's nothing like that."

"Shit. I was hoping you had some weed."

Emily laughed.

"You wanna get an ice cream?" Brix asked.

Emily looked out the window and saw the familiar shape of an ice cream truck driving slowly up the street. But the tinny circus music suddenly sounded muddy, as if there were two speakers playing two distinctly different melodies.

"Come on," Brix said. "They never turn down our street. We should get something."

Emily followed her outside, where the two of them were greeted by a surprising sight.

"What the fuck?" Brix said, her eyes wide.

"I'm guessing this isn't normal," Emily said.

"No way," Brix replied. "This shit is turbo weird."

Instead of the single ice cream truck they'd been expecting, there were six different trucks, all playing familiar jingly-jangly circus music, all pulling into the cul-de-sac at roughly the same time.

Emily could tell by the expressions on the ice cream truck drivers' faces that they were just as surprised as Brix and Emily by the fact that six of them had somehow ended up at the same place at the same time.

"I've gotta go," Emily said.

"Okay," Brix replied.

Just before Emily started to walk away, however, Brix grabbed her by the arm.

"Should I be scared?" she asked.

Emily smiled and shook her head. "There's nothing to be afraid of."

She hated lying to someone who'd shown her nothing but kindness, but Emily couldn't think of a way to explain to Brix that the dimensional stream they both currently inhabited was going to be permanently severed from the multiverse without potentially freaking the poor girl out even further.

On her way out of the cul-de-sac, Emily asked two of the ice cream truck drivers if they'd gathered there for a reason. They both told her that it was just a wild coincidence—which is exactly what she'd known they were going to say.

It was a wild coincidence, but it was so much more than that.

It was Rabbits.

Emily could feel it.

She ran her fingers over the small key in the front pocket of her jeans. It had been stamped with the name Dexter. Emily knew it had to mean something, but she had no idea what that something might be. She needed another set of eyes.

She started walking in the direction of the train station.

She tried Scarpio's phone again as she walked. No answer.

Going back to Scarpio's penthouse apartment without speaking to him first was risky, but Emily needed help—and more important, she needed to know if Pepper and the others had somehow managed to escape those people in the elevator.

Emily had lost pretty much everybody who'd ever mattered to her.

There was no way she was losing Pepper or Scarpio again without a fight.

33

DEXTER

"I'm so happy you're alive," Pepper said, after the longest hug in the world.

"Me too," Emily said. "About you, I mean."

Emily had barely managed to open the door to Scarpio's suite before Pepper rushed over and embraced her.

After they finished their hug, Emily turned and ran to the room where Swan had been recovering from her injuries.

It was empty.

"She's gone," Pepper said. "They were cleaning out the room when I got here."

Emily was struck, but she wasn't surprised. Once they'd started the morphine, she was pretty sure Swan wasn't going to make it.

"What happened?"

"The doctor said she succumbed to her injuries shortly after we left."

Emily nodded, doing her best to fight the tears forming in her eyes. "Scarpio and MayDay?"

Pepper shook her head. "Haven't seen them since we split up back at the mall."

"What happened to you?"

Pepper explained how she lost one of the bad guys in a crowd of people lined up to purchase some limited edition sneakers. As soon as she was sure nobody was following her, she came straight to Scarpio's place and had been there ever since.

"Do you have a number for MayDay?" Emily asked.

"Goes straight to voicemail."

"Same with Scarpio."

"You hungry?" Pepper asked. "I was just about to make some food."

"I'm ravenous."

"What the hell happened to you?" Pepper asked as she rummaged through the kitchen drawers.

"What are you looking for?"

"Corkscrew," Pepper said.

"Thank god," Emily said as she moved into the kitchen to help.

Pepper picked out a bottle of sauvignon blanc from one of the apartment's two fully stocked wine fridges and started boiling some water.

Emily eventually found a corkscrew and poured them each a glass of wine.

"Santé," Pepper said, and then, after sharing a brief half smile that said everything they didn't have the energy to verbalize, the two women clinked glasses.

After a few fairly large sips of wine, Emily explained everything that had happened to her since they'd split up. When she was finished, she handed Pepper the document and key that she'd discovered in her parents' hidden office.

"The Quiet Room again," Pepper said.

"Have you ever heard of this thing they call Betweenspace?"

Pepper nodded. "The Quiet Room sounds like a fantasy, but I don't know . . . I've experienced things that lead me to believe that Betweenspace might be real."

"What kind of things?"

"Okay, well, once—after traveling along a series of Radiants connected to the final movement of a confirmed game element in a specific order—I activated what's known as the Southern Terminal Radiant."

"That's here in Seattle?"

Pepper nodded. "It's one of Meechum's big ones."

"And what happened?"

"Something I described at the time as . . . transitional."

"Okay . . ."

"At first I thought I'd slipped into another stream, but that wasn't the case."

"What do you mean?"

"I'd entered a physical space almost identical to my pre-transition stream of origin, but something was different, off somehow. The temperature was just slightly cooler, and I experienced a dusky-filtered optical anomaly, like a gauzy haze over everything. Another time, while I was walking home from a party during the ninth iteration, there was suddenly far less foot traffic than normal, and the sound of the world was different. It had taken on a strange sonic quality, like the bass had been turned up and the treble down. I don't think there were any insects, which was odd. And it was hazy then, too. It's kind of difficult to explain exactly how it felt."

"You don't have to explain it. I've been there," Emily said.

"What do you mean?"

"I mean I've experienced something very similar."

"When?"

"A couple of times," Emily said, "most recently when K and I slipped streams at the end of the last iteration of the game. It felt like we'd entered a kind of 'shadow world.' There were far fewer people around, and there was this weird dark haze covering everything. And then, another time with my parents, they were playing a game and something happened, the room changed. It felt like I was looking at the same thing, suddenly I was seeing the world through a kind of unfinished gauzy blur."

"That sounds the same," Pepper said.

"Yeah."

"I found something a long time ago," Pepper continued, "a website dedicated to the mystery of Rabbits. It's not around anymore, but one of the posters—somebody calling themselves Neuromancer—uploaded a recording. He claimed the voices on the recording belonged to two Gatewick Institute research scientists. They were arguing about getting stuck in what they referred to as 'Between-space,' and lamenting their inability to return to what they called the real world. Neuromancer claimed that this recording had been found on the body of one of the two research team members, and that both of them had been dead for over a month when they were finally discovered in the basement of a boarding house, two thousand miles away from their last reported position. Apparently, they'd frozen to death in Southern California during one of the hottest July Fourth weekends in modern history."

"That sounds highly improbable," Emily replied.

"Maybe, but it definitely sounds like Rabbits."

Emily nodded. "Yeah. Shit."

"I've heard a few whispers through the years," Pepper continued, "reported claims of travel through, or encounters with, Between-space, but it's really just a lot of rumor and speculation. Beyond some infrequent anecdotal descriptions, all we really have is that recording of those two researchers, a few scattered references to something similar in the Vatican Council Files, and the theoretical Radiant Travel Field suggested by Kellan Meechum in his final paper on the mechanics of the Modern Mechanism."

"I've never seen that paper. What's it about?"

"Although Meechum was never able to prove it, he'd always believed that traveling between dimensions was possible by manipulating his Radiants in deliberate ways."

"Right." Emily nodded.

"Well, in that final paper, Meechum mentions something he called a Radiant Travel Field—a theoretical place where a large number of Radiants met. Meechum believed that it was possible that this place existed outside of space and time."

"Someplace like the Quiet Room?"

"I'm not sure I'm ready to go there, but you know that transcript of our conversation that the Concorde pulled out?"

"That was insane," Emily said. "He must have been recording us somehow."

"Maybe, but what if it was something else?"

"Something like what?"

"You know how I just said that Meechum believed that his hypothetical Radiant Travel Field might exist outside of space and time?"

"Yes."

"Well, once in a while, some of those experienced or lucky enough to manipulate Meechum's Radiants to facilitate a slip between dimensional streams end up experiencing very strange things related to the passage of time."

"What do you mean?"

"Either time moves differently between dimensional streams, or different dimensional streams are running on different units of time."

"Whoa. That's a bit . . . out there, even for Rabbits."

"It sounds complicated, but it's really not. The end result is the same."

"Which is what?"

"Temporal anomalies."

"How does that work?"

"It's what happened to me when you thought I'd disappeared. I slipped into another dimension for a couple of days. Imagine my surprise when I came back to discover that years had passed and you'd gotten married to somebody else."

Emily nodded. But she wasn't ready to think about that shit. Not now.

"What does any of this have to do with the Concorde's transcript?"

"What if that transcript came from a dimensional stream operating under a different space/time dynamic than this one?"

"Are you saying that whoever created that transcript existed in a dimensional stream that was operating eighteen years ahead of this one somehow?" Emily asked.

"Maybe."

"You really believe that's possible?"

"I don't know."

The two of them sat there for a long moment until Emily finally broke the silence. "Maybe we should start by looking into the name Dexter," she said as she pulled out the key that she'd discovered in her parents' secret office.

"Good idea," Pepper said, "but first some food."

They opened a second bottle of wine and shared a huge plate of spaghetti aglio e olio, which was a dish the two of them used to eat a lot back when they lived together. Emily loved the way Pepper made it. She said that using enough salt was the key, that the water had to taste like the ocean by the time the noodles were cooked, but Emily could never bring herself to add that much salt. As a result, her pasta was never quite as good as Pepper's.

After dinner, they moved to the living room.

"Let's start with the Dexter key," Pepper said as she sat down on the sofa next to Emily, with laptop, pad, and pen in hand.

"Where did you get the computer?"

"It was in the closet along with a bunch of phones and tablets."

"When a billionaire plays Rabbits, he gets all the toys."

Pepper laughed, but Emily immediately regretted making her little joke. Scarpio was out there somewhere, and he might be in trouble. "Shit," she said. "Do you think they're okay?"

"I do," Pepper replied. "There's no way those people took May-Day. They'll be back." Pepper angled the laptop a bit more in Emily's direction. "Can you see?"

"I think so."

"Snuggle up."

Emily moved closer, and as she did, she noticed a familiar scent, like sandy vanilla. She recognized that smell, but she couldn't remember if it was Pepper's body lotion or shampoo or something else. "Obviously Dexter is a serial killer from the TV show," Emily offered, forcing her attention away from Pepper's scent, and the way her ex-girlfriend's body was currently pressed against her own. "And it means 'right' in Latin, which is the opposite of left, or sinister."

"Good," Pepper said. "What else?"

"Looks like a company that makes car axles?"

"In Seattle?"

"Ummm . . ." Emily checked. "Negative."

"Okay. I'll write it down anyway, but if we're activating Radiants, my understanding is that the activation sites will be relatively close together, geographically speaking."

"Good point," Emily said. "There's a town called Dexter in Maine. I'm sure that's not relevant, but maybe make a note, just in case?"

Pepper nodded, and Emily performed another search.

"How about an apartment complex called The Dexter on Dexter Avenue in Seattle?" Emily asked, leaning back and bumping against Pepper, who'd started leaning forward at the same time. They shared a laugh.

"Dexter apartments, that's good," Pepper said as she rested her arm on Emily's shoulder. "Where is it?"

"Near the Aurora Bridge."

"I think that's our best bet so far. Maybe there's a mailbox or locker or something that the key fits?" Pepper asked.

Emily nodded.

They spent the next twenty minutes going over anything and everything Dexter, but Pepper was right. Nothing else in the search results was nearly as promising as The Dexter apartments. Emily took a sip of wine, and bit her lip. She couldn't stop thinking about Scarpio and MayDay.

"You really think they're okay out there?" Emily asked.

"I'm sure they're fine."

"Yeah?"

"Yeah." Pepper nodded. "MayDay is tough, and Scarpio most likely won the sixth iteration of the game. You have to believe those two are gonna be able to handle some shit."

Emily laughed. "You're probably right."

"I'm definitely right."

Emily smiled, and then she suddenly remembered Rowan Chess. With all of the drama surrounding Swan and what had happened with the Concorde, she'd forgotten all about Rowan.

"Do we have any way to access The Index?"

"I haven't been able to find a link," Pepper replied. "Why?"

"To see if Rowan's name is still on there, or if anybody else has been able to find the game." Emily looked down at the small brass key on the table. Her parents had taped it to that page for some reason. It had to mean something. Emily had played enough Rabbits to recognize a trailhead. That key was a clue. She'd stumbled onto some kind of path. Now all they needed to do was keep following that path and see where it took them.

When Pepper finally started kissing her neck, Emily leaned back and closed her eyes, grateful to be thinking about something other than the game for the first time in as long as she could remember.

34

WATER CONSERVATION SITUATION

WHEN ROWAN OPENED HIS EYES, the sun was shining directly onto his face.

He sat up and rubbed the sleep from his eyes. He was back on the bed in Julie Furuno's loft. He appeared to be alone. "Hello?" he called out. "Julie?"

No answer.

He stood up and made his way into the dining room area, where he discovered a note sitting in the middle of a modern oak-and-hammered-metal picnic table.

at work. call later. coffee is ready. xo

Rowan poured himself a coffee from a beat-up old Mr. Coffee machine and sat down on the sofa. He still couldn't remember anything that had happened between the moment they'd approached the restaurant and when he'd woken up in the middle of the night, but, thankfully, he didn't think he'd forgotten anything new.

He remembered playing videogames with Julie for an hour or so, then there was teeth-brushing and face-washing, and finally they slid into bed together, kissed for a minute or two, and promptly fell asleep.

They'd kissed.

And it had felt comfortable—not stressful like most other first kisses Rowan could remember. It was just his lips on hers, a perfect fit.

He smiled, because he knew that he was going to see her again.

Rowan took a sip of coffee, pulled out his phone, and took another look at the *Playboy* bunny logo. He was having a hard time imagining why he'd been obsessed with it.

It would have been strange if the bunny had been facing the wrong way in the photograph of the magazine cover and the officially licensed *Playboy* gear in that store window, but it was strange in such a minor way. Why had Rowan found that fact interesting enough to mention to Julie? The *Playboy* logo on that cover could have been a random mistake, and as far as the gear went, maybe they were mirror-image knockoffs?

Who could possibly care?

He took another sip of coffee. It was a coincidence, nothing more.

But the *Playboy* bunny was also a rabbit.

He performed another search for *Playboy bunny logo* and looked through dozens of pages featuring various bunnies, but none of them was facing right. Another search led him to the cover Julie had mentioned featuring the close-up of a woman licking a stamp. It was the April 1973 issue. It didn't appear to be extremely rare or anything. There were a lot of copies out there. And, of course, all of the bunnies on all of the stamps were facing the usual way.

Just as Rowan was about to put down his phone, he clicked through an eBay listing for a lot of twenty-five 1970s *Playboy* magazines and something caught his eye.

There, at the bottom of the listing, was a thumbnail of the April 1973 issue.

The rabbit on the stamp was facing right.

It was backward.

The auction listing had ended a few days earlier. The magazines hadn't sold.

The seller's eBay ID was GiantNYCMouse. Rowan looked them up. Whoever this person was, they were selling a whole bunch of vintage toys and magazines. Based on the quality of the presentation and the sheer amount of stuff, Rowan figured they were most likely representing a used bookstore or thrift shop. The shipping section of the listing indicated they were based in Seattle. He sent them a message asking if they still had that lot of magazines and if there was a physical location he might be able to visit to check them out. Then, he took a shower.

He was in there for five or six minutes when there was a light knock on the door.

"Um . . . hello?"

The door opened and Julie stepped into the bathroom. "Hey," she said.

"Hey," Rowan said, initially unsure about the situation. The glass on the shower door was a bit fogged up and he was covered in soapy water, but he was still absolutely naked.

"So, I was halfway to my audition when I realized that I forgot to take a shower this morning," Julie continued as she slowly started to unbutton her fly.

"That sounds like a terrible oversight," Rowan said.

"It really was. I'm super dirty."

"Well, then, it's a good thing you came back."

"I thought about waiting until you were finished, but there was the potential water conservation situation to consider," Julie said as she slipped out of her jeans.

"It makes me happy to hear you say that," Rowan replied.

"Does it?" she asked as she pulled off her T-shirt, followed by a cream-colored faux-lace bralette.

"Absolutely," Rowan said, completely serious. "Water conservation is an incredibly important part of—"

And then her body was pressed against his.

And then they were kissing.

After their shower, Julie sat down on the bed to go through some auditions her agent had sent over, and Rowan stepped into the living area to call the bank.

After he'd answered all of her security questions, the woman on the phone assured Rowan that nobody had accessed his safe deposit box since Rowan himself two years earlier.

He hung up and called the office.

"Chess Design & Architecture," Valentine answered, "this is Val."

"It's me."

"Oh, hey, boss."

"I just wanted to check in and make sure everything is okay."

"You need to call the World Talent Agency people. You had a meeting scheduled at their offices this morning."

"Shit," he said. He'd completely forgotten. "Can you apologize and let them know we'll have to reschedule?"

"Already did."

"Great. Thanks."

"Are you okay?"

Rowan just remembered that the last time he'd spoken with Valentine was when he'd shown up at her place in a panic, where she'd generously provided comfort, food, and money.

"I'm good. Thank you, and thanks again for helping me out, and feeding me soup."

"Anytime. Are you sure you're okay?"

"Yes, sorry. I'm fine. I'm just a bit tired. Listen, while I have you on the line, could you dig up Victor Garland's cell number?"

"Sure, just a sec."

Rowan wrote down the number and then told Valentine to take a couple of days off. He was still a bit shaken from recent events and he had no idea when he'd be able to focus on work. There was also the possibility that the people who had kidnapped him might come back, and the last thing he wanted was for Valentine to get caught up in anything dangerous. He hung up, sent her the money she'd lent him—plus a little extra—and then dialed Victor Garland.

"It's nice to hear from you," Victor said. "It's been a minute."

"It sure has," Rowan replied. "I saw the installation you did in New York. It was fantastic, the lighted glass bridge was a really nice touch."

"Thanks. Coming from you that means a lot," he said. "Did you notice the koi pond?"

"I did."

"That was a nod to the moat you designed for the Wizard's Library in Oslo."

"You did it better."

"That's bullshit, but thank you for saying it."

"Listen." Rowan took a moment to consider the best way to bring it up. "I'm going to ask you a kind of crazy question."

"Go ahead."

"Have you ever heard of something called The Hall of Incredible Possibilities?"

Victor was silent.

"Are you still there?" Rowan asked.

"Where did you hear that name?"

Rowan wasn't sure what to say. If he told Victor Garland that he'd designed a building with the exact same name, that it was his life's work, and that it essentially only existed in his mind, Victor might start asking a whole lot of questions Rowan wasn't prepared to answer. So Rowan went with a partial truth. "Somebody asked me if I'd ever heard of an escape room called The Hall of Incredible Possibilities. They suggested you may have been involved. They said it was supposed to be next-level stuff. I thought it sounded interesting."

"It's not an escape room," Victor replied. "This thing is . . . well, it's something else."

"I'd love to check it out," Rowan said.

Victor was silent.

"Victor?"

"I'm afraid that's not possible."

"Oh, that's too bad. Is it not operational?"

"It's not that, it's just that I've been sworn to secrecy."

"That sounds serious."

"You know how these people get."

Part of Rowan wanted to ask for details, anything that might confirm what he believed had to be true: that this was nothing more than an extremely unlikely coincidence and that this Hall of Incredible Possibilities had nothing to do with the building by the same name that Rowan had spent most of his adult life conceiving and designing. But another part of Rowan was worried about something far more terrifying.

What if it was the same?

"I understand completely," Rowan said. "It's too bad. It sounds really cool."

"It's like nothing else. Frankly, I'm not sure how a lot of it actually works, and I'm the one who built it."

"I almost feel like I have to see it now," Rowan said.

Victor was silent on the other end of the line, and Rowan tried to come up with some way to keep the conversation going.

"There might be a way," Victor said, finally, "if you're really interested."

"I am," Rowan replied, perhaps a bit too quickly.

"I do have full control over employee clearance. I could hire you as a consultant for a dollar. That would technically satisfy my NDA, but you'd have to travel."

"I'm fine with that. Where is it located?"

"It's here, in Vegas."

"I've been planning a Las Vegas visit for a while," Rowan lied. "Is this week okay?"

"Anytime," Victor said. "I'll text you the details. Just let me know when you're coming."

"Great," Rowan said, and then hung up.

"Do you know how long it takes to get to Las Vegas?" Rowan asked as Julie stepped into the living room wearing nothing but an old Soundgarden baseball shirt.

"I usually drive it in two nine-hour chunks."

"You drive to Vegas?"

"What can I say? I love road trips."

"By air?"

"Two and a half hours or so."

"I need to book a flight."

"You're going to Las Vegas?"

"It looks like it."

Julie nodded. "Okay."

"What would you say if I asked you to come with me?"

"I wouldn't say anything. I'd just do this." She jumped up, arms around Rowan's neck, and wrapped her legs around his waist. They kissed and then she jumped down and ran over to the closet. "I'm gonna need a couple of dresses."

"At least a couple," Rowan said.

Julie smiled, then hurried back and gave Rowan another long kiss.

"What was that for?"

"Just because," she said as she returned to her closet, where she grabbed a small suitcase and tossed it onto the bed.

Rowan smiled.

"Do you need to go home and pack?" she asked as she opened the top drawer of her dresser and threw a handful of socks and underwear into her suitcase.

"I think I'll just grab whatever I need when we get there."

"I like your style," she said. "Do you think we'll be swimming?"

"I don't know. Maybe?"

"I'll bring a bikini or two just in case."

"Ummm . . . There's something I feel like I should tell you."

"What?"

"I was recently kidnapped and kept as a hostage."

She stopped packing and turned to face Rowan. "How recently?"

"I escaped yesterday."

"Are you serious?"

He nodded.

"Fuck." She rushed over and hugged him. "Why didn't you tell me?"

"It's been kind of a whirlwind."

"That's probably why you can't remember last night." She pulled away and looked him in the eye. "Do you think you might have PTSD?"

"I don't think so. It wasn't a violent situation—at least, not at first. It was actually kind of weird."

"Shit," she said, "do you think they might still be after you?"

Rowan wasn't sure, but something about the sparkle in Julie's eyes as she spoke gave him the impression that she was more than a little bit excited by the idea.

"I don't know," he said, and it was true. He hadn't thought about anything other than Julie since she'd knocked on his hotel room door. "I suppose they could be out there somewhere."

"Do you think you should be flying off to Vegas with a stranger?"

"I don't feel like you're a stranger."

She smiled. "Me either. I feel like I'm in a movie. I dream about this interesting guy, and he suddenly shows up in real life. It's kind of amazing."

He smiled. It really was kind of amazing.

"I need to go," Rowan said, "and I'll be much happier if you're with me."

"What are you going to do in Vegas?"

"I need to speak with an acquaintance of mine about something called The Hall of Incredible Possibilities."

"Wow. That sounds intense."

Rowan nodded. "Yeah, I guess it kind of does."

Julie tossed a bikini into her suitcase with a flourish and then threw her hands into the air. "Vegas, baby!"

Rowan's cheeks were starting to hurt from smiling.

He knew that he should be worried about the people who'd kidnapped him, the possibility that he might be going to visit a building that couldn't possibly exist, and recent events connected to the mysterious game known as Rabbits. But he didn't feel worried at all.

In fact, Rowan couldn't remember feeling this happy in his entire life.

35

TWO OF THE SIX

EMILY WAS WALKING DOWN the hallway on her way to the bathroom when she saw a light flickering. It appeared to be coming from the living room. She thought her parents must have fallen asleep in front of the television or something, so she decided to skip the bathroom for the moment and check it out.

When she stepped into the living room, Emily saw her sister kneeling on the brown shag carpet. Static from the television flickered like digital snow across Annie's face as she lifted a black VHS tape from her lap.

"What's the video?" Emily asked.

"I know it sounds weird," Annie replied, "but I think this tape might contain something important."

Emily looked at the clock on the wall. She couldn't read the numbers, but for some reason she knew that it was after midnight. What the hell was Annie doing up so late?

"Something important like what?" Emily asked.

Annie shrugged. "I don't know."

Emily smiled. Her younger sister looked different somehow, more subdued maybe, but when she spoke, Emily could see the familiar bright sparkle behind her wide, curious eyes.

"You wanna find out?" Annie asked.

Emily had the sudden feeling that whatever was on that tape was dangerous. "I'm not sure," she said. "Maybe we shouldn't."

"Too late," Annie said as she slipped the tape into a VCR located beneath the TV.

"Annie . . ." Emily warned.

"It's okay," Annie said as she pressed a button on the remote.

Emily felt a wave of terror wash over her as a video began to play.

On the screen, a hooded man and a stern professional woman sat across from each other at a small metal table in an approximately ten-by-ten-foot room. Located on the wall directly behind the woman was a red door.

The woman spoke first. She sounded like a lawyer. "Do you know why you're here?"

"No."

"You've been selected. It is a great honor."

"Let's just get this over with, shall we?"

The woman smiled. "Fine," she said, then leaned over and removed the man's hood.

Emily gasped.

The man was Emily's father.

"Is the room behind there?" he asked with a nod toward the red door.

"It is."

"How do you know this is the place we've been searching for?"

"We don't."

"So, what?" he said. "I just walk in?"

The woman nodded.

Emily's father stood up and slowly approached the door. As he did, Emily saw something move across her father's face—something she couldn't remember ever seeing before.

Fear.

Her father was frightened of whatever was waiting beyond that door.

Emily wanted to reach out, to help him, but she knew that he wasn't really there. He was just an image on a television screen.

He took another step forward, put his hand on the doorknob, and slowly turned it.

Behind the door was nothing but darkness.

Once the door was open, her father just stood there, staring into the darkness for a long moment, and then, after one last pensive glance back at the woman, he stepped forward and disappeared. After a second or two, the red door slowly shut behind him.

At that point, the woman turned to face the camera and smiled, a wide twisted smile from a mouth filled with far too many teeth. Then, Emily heard her father screaming—deep, heartrending wails of terror, from somewhere behind the door.

It was horrible.

Emily tried to cover her ears, but that did nothing. She turned away from the screen and begged Annie to turn it off, but Annie was no longer there.

Annie was suddenly up on the screen with the woman.

The woman turned away from the camera and pointed toward the red door.

"No," Emily cried, but Annie had already started walking.

Annie opened the red door, and the woman pushed her into the darkness.

Annie screamed, and that's when the woman turned and looked directly into the camera and smiled.

The woman was Emily.

Emily woke up to the sound of a door slamming.

She glanced at the clock on the bedside table. Just after one A.M.

She'd been having a nightmare.

She shook Pepper's shoulder.

"What?" Pepper said as she leaned up on one elbow, barely awake.

"Sshhh." Emily put her finger to her lips and whispered, "I think somebody's here."

"Fuck," Pepper whispered back, fully alert now. She unplugged the bedside lamp, tested its weight, then quietly moved over to the door, ready to smash whoever was out there in the head.

"Maybe it's them?" Emily whispered, getting out of bed. She really wanted Scarpio to be okay. They'd been through a lot together.

Emily and Pepper stood there, side by side in the dark, watching as lights were switched on in the hall outside the bedroom and shadows moved across the bottom of the door.

Emily looked over at Pepper.

Pepper raised the lamp.

Then there was a quiet knock on the door.

"Emily?"

It was Scarpio.

"Yeah," Emily said. "We're in here."

Pepper put the lamp down on the bed and switched on the bedroom light. Scarpio and MayDay entered the room. Emily ran over and embraced Scarpio.

"I heard the news about Swan," he said. "I'm sorry."

"Thanks," Emily said.

"You wanna hug too?" MayDay asked, nodding in Pepper's direction.

Pepper just smiled and gave MayDay the finger.

"What happened?" Emily asked.

"I was just going to ask you the same thing," MayDay said.

"We can get caught up in the morning, if you two want to go back to sleep," Scarpio said.

"Or whatever it was you were doing," MayDay added with a smirk.

Emily had been so excited to see Scarpio alive that she didn't notice she was wearing nothing but a thin tank top and bikini briefs. Pepper was wearing even less.

"I'm going to make some tea," Scarpio said.

There was no way Emily was going to be able to get back to sleep, so she pulled on some leggings and followed him and MayDay into the kitchen.

"Everything okay?" Scarpio asked as Emily entered the kitchen. "All things considered?"

Emily nodded. "All things considered I'm good. What happened to you guys?" she asked as Scarpio dug through his cupboards for tea.

"The Concorde saved us," MayDay said.

"What?" Pepper asked as she sat down next to MayDay at the table.

"The Rabbits Police had us surrounded in a park just outside the mall," Scarpio said as he pulled out a kettle and started filling it with water. "They were just about to grab us when the Concorde pulled us into a garden. He said we could follow him as long as we threw our phones into a nearby fountain, or we could stick around and take our chances with the Rabbits Police."

"Dramatic," Pepper said.

"Then he took us through a sewer grate into an abandoned tunnel system," MayDay continued. "We walked for about half an hour until the tunnel he'd chosen eventually ended in front of a huge vault door."

"This guy really loves his secret passageways," Emily said.

"What kind of tunnel?" Pepper asked.

"Flood prevention," Scarpio said. "That's what took us so long to get back here."

"Why? Was there a flood?" Pepper asked.

"No," Scarpio said, "but there was a time lock. Once we went into the vault area, we had to wait until midnight for the door on the other side to open."

"Thankfully, we didn't run out of air," MayDay added.

"What the hell?" Pepper asked. "You two were stuck in some underground sewer room for most of a day?"

"It was more like a huge office," Scarpio said.

"It was fully furnished. He had an espresso machine," MayDay said. "I actually had a nice nap."

"Yeah," Scarpio agreed. "It wasn't bad at all."

"Except for the part where we were cut off from the world," MayDay added.

"How many secret lairs does this guy have?" Pepper asked.

"I know, right?" MayDay replied.

"He gave us something he thought might help," Scarpio added as he picked up a dark green backpack from beneath the table. He pulled out a file folder.

"What is it?" Emily asked.

"The Concorde told us about a woman who'd shown up at the vault shortly before he moved into the Bed Bath & Beyond. Apparently, she was playing the game. He said that she stayed for a couple of days, and then went out for breakfast one day and never came back. She left a few things behind." Scarpio set the file folder down in the middle of the table. "Including this."

Emily picked up the folder and removed two thick blue rubber bands that had been wrapped around it to prevent it from falling apart. The first page was a table of contents, and right there at the top was a familiar symbol: a circle floating above a triangle.

"Shit," Emily said. "This stuff is from the Gatewick Institute?"

Scarpio nodded. "I read through everything. There's not much in there that appears to be relevant outside of some intake instructions and guidelines for sleep-research subject treatment. There are some pictures in there as well, although a couple of them are stuck together." He pulled out a stack of photographs and handed them to Emily.

They were pictures of research subjects in what appeared to be some kind of sleep therapy situation. The subjects wore caps on their heads or had wires stuck to their chests. Everything was plugged into large machines that reminded Emily of synthesizers from the 1970s. She pulled at one of the photographs that had been stuck to the back of another, but it started to rip.

"Bad idea," MayDay said. "You have to soak them in water."

"Really?" Emily asked.

"Yeah," MayDay said. "I had to unstick a whole shoebox full of my mom's old pictures. It took me an entire weekend."

When Emily lifted up the last of the photographs that wasn't stuck to one of the others, she gasped a little. "Shit."

"What?"

"It's my parents."

Sitting on either side of what appeared to be a sleep study participant were Emily's mom and dad. She barely recognized them at first. They were so young. And they were both smiling, which was something Emily didn't remember them doing all that often.

Across the bottom of the photograph, in black marker, somebody had written the following question:

Two of The Six? The Somnologist and the Neuroscientist?

"Two of The Six?" Emily asked. "What the hell does that mean?"

Scarpio and the others leaned in to take a closer look at the photo. "Your parents were scientists, weren't they?"

Emily nodded—and although they both had numerous advanced degrees, the descriptions of Somnologist and Neuroscientist fit. Mom covered sleep research and Dad handled brain stuff.

"The San Francisco address listed on the first two sets of documents was torn down ages ago," Scarpio continued, "but there are three other facilities or offices." He flipped through the pages until he found what he was looking for. "Here."

"Mexico City, Los Angeles, and Seattle," Emily said.

Emily looked up the addresses.

The Mexico City site had been demolished a decade ago and was currently a football stadium parking lot. The Los Angeles address was now an indie rock concert venue. But the Seattle office was located in a building that was only five miles away.

MayDay ran a couple of searches and pulled up the latest information on the building's owner. It belonged to a holding company from San Francisco called Enlightened Truth Enterprises.

"Wait," Emily said. "I've seen that name before." She dug up the "Convergence in Betweenspace" document and the key that she'd found at her family home and brought them over to the table.

"Where did you get this stuff?" Scarpio asked as he leaned forward to get a closer look.

Emily explained how the Concorde's map had led her to her childhood home, where she found the papers and the key.

"The Quiet Room just keeps popping up," he said. "What's Betweenspace?"

"Apparently it's a kind of limbo between dimensions or something," Emily said. "Pepper's heard of it."

"And the key?" Scarpio picked it up.

"We think it might be connected to The Dexter, an apartment complex here in Seattle," Pepper said. "We're planning to check it out first thing in the morning."

MayDay pointed to a footnote at the bottom of the page.

*None of the subjects interviewed had firsthand experience with the Quiet Room. All of the information collected in these interviews should be considered anecdotal, and has been included here strictly in response to Enlightened Truth Enterprises' request for information (per: the Clooney/Hamilton interviews, unknown).

"Shit," Pepper said, "everything is coming up Gatewick."

"It's been a hell of a couple days," Scarpio said. "Maybe we should try to get some sleep and tackle this thing in the morning?"

"Good idea," MayDay said. "I'm fucking exhausted."

As the others stood up and stretched, Emily sat and stared at the photograph of her parents, smiling on either side of a stranger in what was clearly some kind of weird research facility. She missed the two of them so much.

But what the hell were they doing at the Gatewick Institute?

She didn't think there was any way she'd be able to get back to sleep, but she was out a few seconds after her head hit the pillow.

36

SOMETHING FOR EVERYONE

THE DEXTER APARTMENTS and the Gatewick building were in opposite directions, so the four of them decided to split up. Emily and
Pepper would visit The Dexter, while Scarpio and MayDay checked
out the Gatewick address.

They agreed to meet for lunch at the pier in a few hours to com-
pare notes.

Emily and Pepper took Scarpio's SUV and parked a block away
from The Dexter apartments—a small four-floor red-brick complex that had gone through a terrible stucco-and-aluminum-panel
face-lift in the eighties or nineties.

It did not look promising.

Emily had called ahead and made an appointment with the building's manager—a portly fiftysomething woman named Jasmine
with a wide, beautiful smile and an awful yellowish perm. She took
a look at the key and shook her head. "Nothing around here takes
one like that, I'm afraid, unless . . ."

"What?" Emily asked.

"We used mailboxes before we had the mail slots installed. Maybe
the boxes took one like yours," she said. "Hang on, I've got my old
key around here somewhere."

But the old mailbox key wasn't a match, and Jasmine assured
them that there were no storage lockers or anything else that might
fit the bill.

They were out of luck.

They thanked Jasmine for her time, then made their way back to the car.

"I thought for sure that place was going to give us something," Pepper said.

"Me too," Emily replied as she opened the passenger door. "What if the Concorde was right, and the game is working to stay hidden?"

"It definitely feels like that's the case," Emily said.

Pepper started the car and was pulling away from the curb when Emily grabbed her arm.

"Holy shit," Emily said as she pulled off her seatbelt and opened the door. "Come on."

"What the hell?" Pepper said as she hit the brakes. "We're moving."

"It's Agatha's Used Furniture," Emily said as she ran toward a low red-brick building.

"So what?" Pepper called after her, but Emily was already halfway across the street.

Drilled into the brick, directly above a large rectangular window caked with decades of dust and dirt, were dark gray metal letters that spelled out AGATHA'S USED FURNITURE. Beneath those letters was what appeared to be the store's motto: THERE'S SOMETHING FOR EVERYONE!

Stepping into Agatha's Used Furniture was like going back in time. It was a combination of high-end antiques store and junky knickknack emporium. French dressers sat beside old pinball machines that were barely visible beneath stacks of old magazines and baskets stuffed full of children's toys from the 1950s. Against the back wall was a bank of old washing machines from a laundromat, a Zoltar fortune teller, an ancient coin-operated claw game, and two Skee-Ball machines. If you were looking for a way to inspect or reconstruct the past, there was no better place to start than an old thrift store.

A thirtysomething red-haired woman with a ponytail looked up as Emily approached the long glass counter that ran along the left side of the store. "Welcome," she said. "I'm Agatha. If you have any questions, let me know."

"I actually do have a couple of questions," Emily said, "if you don't mind."

"Shoot," Agatha said as Pepper opened the door and stepped inside.

"A friend looked online, but couldn't find Agatha's Used Furniture listed anywhere," Emily said.

"Yeah," Agatha replied. "The store is officially still listed everywhere as The Thrift Attic. I've never bothered to have it changed."

"That can't be great for business."

"We're more of a word-of-mouth kind of place." She smiled at Pepper, who approached the counter and put her arm around Emily.

"Sure, I get it," Emily said, "but I received a text recently promoting your store."

Agatha nodded. "That was probably my nephew, Michael. He's always trying to get me to push this place, but I'm already swamped keeping up with the film and television prop rentals. The last thing I need is more customers—no offense."

"None taken." Emily smiled. "Do you mind if we take a look around?"

"Knock yourselves out. Like the sign says, there's something for everyone."

Emily smiled. She liked people who seemed to be exactly where they belonged. She hated the idea that Agatha would disappear forever when their dimensional stream was destroyed. She hoped there was another version of her out there somewhere in the multiverse, subtly not giving a shit about anything at all.

"Why are we here?" Pepper said.

"The night Rowan Chess's date disappeared, everyone in the restaurant received a spam text at roughly the same time," Emily said, "a message promoting Agatha's Used Furniture."

"Well, then, we should definitely take a look around," Pepper said. "Anything in particular we should be looking for?"

"Rabbits shit?"

"Great." Pepper gave Emily the finger.

They split up and began wading through the sea of physical and cultural detritus, looking for anything that might be related to the game. There were ancient Barbie and Blythe dolls, Polaroid and Kodak cameras, Sony and JVC tape recorders, and a seemingly endless number of toys and electronics from Hasbro, Kenner, Fisher-Price, and Mattel. One shelf was filled from top to bottom with what appeared to be every single Braun product ever made.

But nothing obviously Rabbits-related.

The Concorde said that it would be difficult to find the game, to activate the Radiants, but this was ridiculous. There were far too many possibilities to consider. Emily rubbed her eyes and examined a Chinese checkers set from 1939 that featured the graphic of a rabbit and a velvet bag full of marbles. How were they supposed to find any kind of connection here? Count the marbles in the bag? Look up the manufacturing company to see where that led?

Emily thought back to something Pepper had told her the first time they played the game together. She'd said that it was easy to get distracted if you tried to see everything all at once. What you needed to do was focus on something small, something right in front of your eyes, and it was only once you could see that small thing clearly that you'd be able to pull back and see the bigger picture.

Emily took a look around and exhaled. There were so many little things.

"There's way too much shit in this place," Pepper said, as if reading Emily's mind. "Maybe it's not the right Agatha's Used Furniture?"

After combing through the place for more than an hour, Pepper and Emily met up near the Skee-Ball machines at the back of the store.

"You can play 'em if you want," Agatha yelled out from the counter, "but it'll cost ya a quarter a shot. Change machine's in the corner."

Emily looked at the Skee-Ball machines. Maybe if they won, the machine would print a ticket with some kind of clue, or maybe the Zoltar machine would deliver a fortune?

There had to be something.

"Do you have a quarter?" Emily asked Pepper.

"No. But I have a couple of singles."

They got some quarters from the change machine and started walking back toward the Skee-Ball games. Then Emily noticed something and stopped in front of the wall of washing machines that looked like they'd been pulled out of a laundromat sometime in the 1960s. Pepper went straight over to the Zoltar machine and slipped a quarter into the slot.

"Those washing machines have been in some important movies," Agatha yelled from the counter. "P. T. Anderson's production designer just put them on hold."

"Cool," Emily said.

"Or maybe it was Wes Anderson. I know it was one of the Andersons."

"Hey," Emily said.

"What?" Pepper replied. "I'm waiting for Zoltar to deliver our fortune."

But then she saw what Emily was looking at.

"Fuck me," Pepper said as she left Zoltar and hurried over to Emily, who was standing in front of the washing machines. Emily was pointing at their logo. They'd been manufactured by a company called Dexter.

"This has to be something," Pepper said, excited.

Beneath each of the three washing machines' coin slots was a locked box.

Emily pulled the key from her pocket and walked over to the first machine. Even though she had been playing the game for a long time, moments like this still made her feel alive in a way very few other things did.

Her hands were shaking as she slipped the key into the first slot.

Emily looked over at Pepper, who looked just as excited as Emily felt, and then she turned the key. The lock opened with a low, grinding click, and Emily pulled out the metal box.

Empty.

She put the box back in place, moved to the next machine, and handed Pepper the key. "Your turn."

Pepper tried the key in the second machine.

Empty as well.

Emily took the key from Pepper and approached the third machine. She slipped the key into the lock, turned it with the now familiar grind and click, and slowly opened the box.

There was something inside.

Emily pulled it out. It was a small promotional pamphlet that had been folded up to fit into the washing machine's coin slot.

Emily looked over at Pepper, who stared back at Emily wide-eyed.

"What are you guys up to?" Emily and Pepper both jumped at the sound of Agatha's voice from behind them. "And how the hell did you manage to open my machines?"

"We have a key." Emily handed Agatha the lockbox and the key.

"Well, would you look at that," Agatha said. "It fits."

"We're sorry for opening the boxes without permission," Emily said.

"We had no idea the key would fit these machines," Pepper added.

"Does it work in all three?" Agatha asked.

Emily nodded.

"Cool," Agatha said. "They didn't come with a key."

"It's yours," Emily said.

"What's that?" Agatha nodded toward the folded pages in Emily's hand.

Emily looked over at Pepper, who was shaking her head.

"It was in one of the boxes," Emily said. "We've been looking for something for a very long time. We think this might help us find it."

"What is it?" Agatha asked.

Emily unfolded the pages.

It was a pamphlet titled "Museo del Futuro." On the cover was a space-age-looking building that made Emily think of Ridley Scott's

Blade Runner. Below the image was the name of the architect and the publication date. Antonio Sant'Elia. 1957.

When the pamphlet was unfolded, it became a blueprint or schematic for three floors of what appeared to be both office and living space. There were a lot of rooms—at least a hundred or more. The building would require a great deal of space—at least a contemporary city block. On top of the schematic, in black ink, somebody had drawn a long meandering path through the complex maze of hallways and rooms. It went from one end of the building all the way to the other.

"You really think this thing might help you find what you're looking for?" Agatha asked, unconvinced.

"I do," Emily said.

"You guys mind telling me how you ended up with a key to my machines?" Agatha asked, clearly more curious than angry.

"It's a kind of scavenger hunt," Emily half lied as she held up the map they pulled out of the old machine. "Do you mind if we keep this?"

"Is it some kind of collectable?"

"Not that we know of," Emily replied.

Agatha nodded. "It's all yours."

"Thanks," Emily said. "And thank you for your time."

Agatha smiled. "Happy to help."

Emily and Pepper made their way back to the store's entrance, but just as they were about to open the door and step outside, they heard Agatha calling from the back of the room.

"What is it?" Pepper said as Agatha approached the front door.

"You're forgetting something important," Agatha said, and handed Pepper a small rectangular yellow card.

"What's this?" Pepper asked.

"It's your fortune," Agatha replied, "from Zoltar. I hope it's everything you wanted it to be," she added, before she smiled and made her way back behind the counter. They thanked Agatha again, then stepped outside so Pepper could take a closer look at their fortune.

"What is it?" Emily asked. "Am I going to meet a mysterious blond Libra?"

Pepper handed Emily the card.

"Is this for real?" Emily asked.

Pepper shrugged.

At the top of the small yellow card were the words YOUR FORTUNE, along with a tiny graphic of Zoltar himself. Below that image, where the text of the fortune would normally have been located, was something else. The graphic of a partially opened door.

"Um . . ." Emily said, "that's an open door."

"Yeah," Pepper said as she flipped the card over to reveal the other side.

> I: MICKIE MOUTH
> II: THE CONDOR
> III: ALISON CAT
> IV: RADIO KNIFE
> V: CARBON THING
> VI: CALIFORNIAC
> VII: NOVA TRAIL
> VIII:
> IX: BISCUITHAMMER85
> X: CONTROLG
> XI: K

It was The Circle.

"K won Eleven?" Pepper asked.

"Sure looks like it."

All of a sudden Emily's stomach dropped. She felt like she was on a roller coaster. Could this version of The Circle be legit? Did K really win? How did that work if K didn't exist in this stream? Maybe Scarpio was wrong? Maybe K was out there somewhere? What if it was yet another version of K that had no idea they'd been married? "I guess this means that the game is active," Emily said, finally.

"Maybe, but there's no way to know for sure without confirmation from at least one other player."

"Rowan Chess saw The Phrase written on the back of a bathroom stall, and his name was in The Index."

Pepper nodded. "I'm not sure any of that matters."

"Why not?" Emily asked.

"Even if we did just find the game, and even if we somehow manage to win Rabbits in record time, there's a pretty good chance that this dimensional stream is finished."

"Weren't you the one who said we should try to find Rabbits and play?"

"I was trying to think positive."

"Well, keep it up," Emily said. "If we just found the game, maybe we can find the Quiet Room." She held up the pamphlet they'd just pulled out of the washing machine. "We have a map."

"Do we?" Pepper asked, clearly not convinced.

Emily felt something cool on her cheek as she turned and started walking in the direction of the car. "It's raining. We should head back."

Pepper was just about to follow, when Emily grabbed her arm and yanked her back.

"What the fuck?" Pepper asked.

"There," Emily whispered, pointing toward the car.

A black Toyota Supra was double-parked beside Scarpio's SUV, and two extremely tall women wearing black hoodies were staring into the windows on either side of the car.

"How the hell did they find us?" Pepper asked.

"Doesn't matter," Emily said. "Let's see if Agatha's has a back door."

Agatha pointed them toward a door at the back of the store. "It says it's alarmed, but that hasn't worked for fifteen years."

"Thanks," Emily said.

Pepper and Emily stepped through the store's emergency exit into a wide back alley.

"What now?" Pepper asked.

"I think we should meet up with the others, then try to find the Quiet Room and get the hell out of this cursed stream before the two of us permanently blink out of existence."

"Sounds like a plan," Pepper said as she started walking up the alley and away from Agatha's Used Furniture.

Emily was doing her best to stay positive, but she didn't think what she'd said sounded like a plan at all. Those words coming out of her mouth felt more like lines from a movie than something a person would actually say, which led her to wonder about the transcript that the Concorde had in his office.

What if everything they did and said was preordained, just waiting to be discovered and written down in another transcript? Did anything the two of them did matter? And if not, then why do anything at all? There was no such thing as the wrong choice in a deterministic world.

But Emily wasn't prepared to give up on free will just yet—and, of course, if they were living in a deterministic world, it didn't matter.

Either way, however, whatever was going to happen was going to happen soon.

She could feel it.

And then, Pepper was hit by a car.

37

THE HALL OF
INCREDIBLE POSSIBILITIES

Rowan was strapped into his seat, hunched forward and looking for his headphones, as the airplane banked through a canopy of dense clouds and began its bumpy descent into Las Vegas. Julie Furuno squeezed his hand and smiled. Then, without warning, the enormous aircraft lurched down and to the right. Rowan felt a screaming in his ears and closed his eyes against a blinding flash of light.

And then he was somewhere else.

Julie was still holding his hand, but the airplane was flying perfectly calm and steady. There was no sound outside of regular passenger cabin airflow and engine noise, and absolutely no turbulence at all.

But something was very different.

It wasn't the same plane.

They were no longer on a JetBlue flight to Las Vegas. They were on a wide-body aircraft—a 777, if Rowan had to guess. Their seats, which were now covered in a thick blue leaf-print upholstery, were larger than they'd been just a moment earlier. There were no longer any video monitors built into the seats in front of them, but there were screens on the walls displaying information in a language that looked like Arabic. Rowan couldn't make out anything beyond the time and their destination. It looked like they were headed for Beijing, and they were scheduled to arrive at six thirty in the morning. Based on the image of the flight tracker, they'd been flying for just over half an hour. It was one twenty in the morning.

They had five hours to go.

Rowan shivered as a chill passed over him—a kind of worrying cold that felt like it came from somewhere deep inside his body.

This wasn't right.

He experienced a deep sense of foreboding. He was in the wrong place. He looked around at the faces of the other passengers. Something was going to happen very soon. Something scary.

His stomach dropped as the airplane lurched again to the right, sped up, and then banked sharply to the left. He tried to sit up, but it felt like there was an invisible anvil or something similar on his chest, sinking into him, pressing him back farther and farther into his seat.

And then he felt like he was falling. No. That wasn't right. He wasn't falling.

He was fading.

He was slowly being blended or folded into a thick darkness, a terrifying void that Rowan understood was going to erase him from the world forever. He tried to squeeze Julie's hand to get her attention, but he couldn't move. He was completely frozen in place.

Then something passed into his field of vision and he was looking up into a pair of familiar eyes.

Somewhere far away, a hand gently squeezed his own, and a voice that sounded like it was coming from the other side of forever said, "It's okay. It's me. It's Eliza."

But Rowan just kept falling backward, deeper into the endless abyss.

Just before he was about to disappear forever, Rowan woke up.

"Welcome back," Julie said, her mouth full of ice as she finished off the last of a cocktail or soda of some kind.

Rowan straightened up and looked around. The plane was still moving, but they were on the ground.

"What do you think it means when planes taxi? Why that verb?" Julie asked.

Rowan rubbed his eyes. "I have no idea. How long was I asleep?"

"An hour or so. You fell asleep during *Zoolander*—which I consider a crime, by the way."

"We're in Las Vegas, right?"

"Wow," she said. "Are you okay?"

"Sorry. Bad dream."

"Was I in it?"

Rowan nodded. "We were on a plane, actually."

"Oh," she said, the tone of her voice suddenly strained. "This plane?"

Rowan shook his head. "No, a different one, bigger. We were heading to Beijing."

"What color were the seats?" Julie asked.

"Blue," he said. "With little trees or something on them."

She nodded.

"It was kind of terrifying, actually."

Rowan noticed the color slowly draining from Julie's face. "What is it?" he asked. "Are you okay?"

"I don't wanna talk about it."

"Oh, I'm sorry. I didn't mean to drag you into my shit . . ."

"It's not that," she said. "It's the dream."

"What about it?"

"I hate that one."

"What are you talking about?" Rowan asked.

But Julie just shook her head, and Rowan understood that it was time to stop talking. He grabbed her hand. "Is everything okay?"

She nodded. "I'm fine. I just want to get the hell off this plane and into a fucking air-conditioned casino where I can order two white Russians at a time and slowly lose all my money playing cards."

Rowan forced the nightmare from his mind and smiled. He was in Las Vegas with the woman of his dreams. No bad guys, no weird games, just good old-fashioned American cultural decay and overblown opulent decadence.

"I think we can make that happen," he said.

———

They checked in to the Mirage, took their second shower of the day together, and got ready for dinner. Julie suggested they hit the tasting counter at Momofuku and then drink and gamble until they passed out.

That sounded just about perfect to Rowan.

"Looks like we have a message." Julie nodded in the direction of the telephone, where a red light was blinking on and off.

"It's probably the person I came here to meet." Rowan had texted Victor Garland just before they got on the plane.

Rowan pressed a couple of keys and accessed the voicemail.

"Hey, Rowan, it's Victor. A car will pick you and your friend up at eight P.M. Dress however you want. Looking forward."

"Good news?" Julie asked.

"Apparently he's taking the two of us to dinner."

Julie smiled. "I have the perfect dress."

"Rowan Chess." Victor stood and smiled as Rowan and Julie approached an intimate, purple-upholstered booth in a baroque French restaurant located just off the MGM Grand casino floor. The restaurant appeared to be expensive, but everything in Las Vegas looked that way to Rowan.

"I told them to bring us the chef's tasting menu," Victor said, "then we'll head over to the warehouse and you can have a look at everything they've managed to pull together so far."

"The *warehouse*?"

"We're not supposed to refer to it using the title you mentioned on the phone, so we just call it the warehouse."

"What is it?" Julie asked.

"You haven't told her?" Victor asked.

Rowan shook his head.

But he had told her a little. He'd told her that he was going to meet an acquaintance about something called The Hall of Incredible Possibilities. He asked her not to mention any of that to Victor.

Victor turned to Julie. "The employment and nondisclosure agreement is fairly extensive, but if you're interested in taking a look at the place yourself . . ." He pulled a small tablet from his pocket. "This is the same agreement Rowan signed earlier. Just change the name and Venmo address and sign with your finger at the bottom."

Rowan hadn't considered the possibility that Julie would end up meeting Victor. He thought she'd be out exploring the city while he took care of his imaginary building business in private.

"I don't think she's interested in—"

But Julie had already scrolled down to the bottom and signed. "I'd kill for a glass of wine," she said, handing the tablet back to Victor.

As if on cue, the first course arrived. It was a summer squash carpaccio with salt-broiled shrimp. Julie was excited. It came paired with a half bottle of deliciously oaky Chardonnay.

Rowan's concern about both the meeting and The Hall of Incredible Possibilities faded. Having Julie there made everything better. The food was amazing (as was the wine), and by the time the second course arrived, the three of them were laughing, eating, and drinking like old friends.

"So," Julie said, "what's the deal with this building? What makes it so special?"

"To be honest with you," Victor said, "The Hall of Incredible Possibilities has been the strangest thing that's ever happened to me in my professional life."

Julie leaned forward. "Tell me everything."

Victor laughed and then ordered an additional bottle of wine for the table. Once it arrived, Victor poured them each a glass, and told them how he ended up building an incredible hall in the desert.

"It started with an email. Somebody wanted to know if I was interested in taking on a project with an enormous budget and very little in the way of limitations, an immersive experience similar to an escape room but far more complex and interesting."

"I'm guessing you said yes right away?" Julie asked.

"No way," he said. "I deleted the email. I thought it was a scam. But a week later I received a call from an attorney in Delaware. He assured me that the project was absolutely real, and asked if I'd be willing to sign an NDA in order to see the plans. I agreed and a few minutes later I received an email that included a pdf. As the name implied, The Hall of Incredible Possibilities was incredible, but, to me, actually building it felt impossible. The cost would be astronomical, and certain technological elements of the design that didn't currently exist would need to be created."

"That sounds expensive," Julie said.

"It was. In fact, the number I quoted them was so high that I was convinced there was no possible way I'd receive a reply."

Rowan was having a hard time coming to terms with where this conversation appeared to be headed. He suddenly wanted to be anywhere else.

"After an environmentally damaging amount of paperwork that included far too many NDA contracts and exclusivity addendums," Victor continued, "I was finally invited to meet somebody in real life. That meeting took place in Toronto at a really cool mussels-and-beer joint below street level. The man I was meeting must have paid off the owner, because we were the only two people there and the food was amazing."

As if on cue, their next course arrived. Mussels and mushroom risotto.

"He told me that they wanted me to build an immersive experience unlike any other," Victor said, his mouth half-full of mussels.

"An escape room?" Julie asked.

"He said that it would be a physical space where a unique experience happens or begins. It's utterly original, and he told me that I'd have unlimited resources including access to the most sophisticated computer systems both on the planet and in orbit around it. I asked him for a few more concrete details about the budget and he told me that I was to set the price. When I asked him why he contacted me, he said that my name kept coming up. Now, the biggest question for me was—"

"How soon do you need it," Rowan interrupted.

Victor smiled. "That was exactly what I said, and do you know what he told me? He said, 'Whenever you feel like it's ready.' Now I was suspicious. When something sounds too good to be true, it's cause for concern. But when I voiced these concerns, he told me that he disagreed completely. He said that he believed his offer came with an extraordinary amount of risk and pressure."

"How so?" Julie asked.

"He told me that, although I would be given detailed plans, I was being tasked with creating something where nothing exists, with very little in the way of obstructions or limitations. And, to add even more pressure, this thing that I was going to build needed to be a uniquely transcendent experience. 'Now,' he said, 'that sounds like a hell of a challenge to me—and then there's the added pressure of your own compensation as contractor, which I expect will be significant.'"

Rowan nodded. Victor had a point. Taking a large amount of money for something unknown would come with a great deal of creative anxiety. Whoever had hired Victor was smart. He knew exactly what he was doing. The more money Victor asked for, the more committed he would be to delivering something truly special.

"So," Julie said, "what happened next?"

"Well, imagine my surprise when I was sent login and password information for a bank account with a significant nine-figure balance."

"A hundred million dollars?" Julie replied.

"It didn't start with a one."

"Holy shit," Julie said with a laugh.

Victor laughed as well, and Rowan couldn't help but smile.

"But this is where things get really weird."

"How so?" Rowan asked.

"I received the plans and the budget via secure encrypted mail, spent the next two years hiring the team and building the thing, and haven't heard a word from the buyer since."

"That is strange," Julie said.

"It sure is. And now this thing is just sitting out there in the middle of the desert."

Rowan shifted in his seat and felt a low tickly hum rising from the back of his neck.

Victor smiled. "Would you like to see it?"

"You're goddamn right we would," Julie said.

Rowan didn't actually share Julie's enthusiasm, but he had no choice. He needed to see it. He knew that Victor Garland's building couldn't possibly have much, if anything, in common with Rowan's design for his own Hall of Incredible Possibilities. But there was only one way to make sure.

After dessert, Victor led them through the restaurant and out onto Las Vegas Boulevard where an SUV was waiting.

As they pulled away from the hotel, with Julie snuggled up next to Rowan in the back seat, he reflected on the meal they'd just experienced. It had been exhilarating. Rowan had always assumed that Michelin stars were kind of a racket, and that all really high-end dining experiences were roughly the same, but now he wasn't so sure.

Maybe it was being there with Julie, or the effects of the two bottles of wine, but as they drove along a crowded Las Vegas Boulevard, Rowan's concerns about Victor's building gave way to thoughts about Julie and what they might do once the meeting with Victor was over and the two of them were left alone.

"How far is it to the warehouse?" Rowan asked, as the SUV finally turned off Las Vegas Boulevard onto a side street. Rowan couldn't bring himself to utter the name of The Hall of Incredible Possibilities, as if saying it out loud would reveal Rowan's secret.

"It's not too far," Victor said. "It will be worth it, I promise."

They drove for about forty minutes—ten minutes to reach the city limits, and another thirty to get to the warehouse. The driver eventually pulled into an empty parking area in front of an enormous polished metal, concrete, and glass structure. Visible behind it, way off in the distance, were four of the largest buildings Rowan had ever seen in his life. They were semicylindrical, like Quonsets, and they appeared to be at least as large as football stadiums, possibly bigger, but it was hard to tell due to the distance.

"Whoa," Julie said as they approached. "What is this place?"

"Welcome to The Hall of Incredible Possibilities," said Victor.

There were three disks of increasing size sitting atop the building, giving it a kind of mid-century Olympic venue meets Italian neorealist film meets Star Trek vibe. It looked more like a modern museum in Brazil than something you'd find in the middle of the desert outside of Las Vegas.

"This sure as hell doesn't look like a warehouse," Julie said as they stepped out of the SUV.

Victor smiled at Julie and then turned to Rowan. "What do you think?"

But Rowan couldn't speak. He was in shock. He was standing in front of something that, until that moment, had existed only in his imagination.

It was Rowan's design. It was Rowan's building. It had never been built.

But here he was, staring at The Hall of Incredible Possibilities.

"What are those buildings out there?" Rowan pointed to the four enormous semicylindrical structures in the distance.

"I'm not sure," Victor replied. "Rumor has it they're owned by a Hollywood studio or Amazon or Apple. There's a lot of security. I don't know anyone who's ever been inside."

"Are we going in, or what?" Julie asked, nodding in the direction of Victor's building.

"There's a lot that I won't be able to power up without a couple of days' notice," Victor said, "but there's one thing I really think you should see."

"Cool," Julie said.

"Okay," Rowan replied, his mouth suddenly dry, his hands cool and clammy. He wanted to ask about the plans for the building, who had sent them to Victor, but Rowan couldn't find the words.

"Are you okay?" Julie whispered.

Rowan nodded. "Yeah." But he could tell by the way Julie squeezed his hand that she wasn't buying it.

Victor led them into the foyer, which had been designed to mimic the lobby of a hotel in Paris. It was perfect. From the Eurofase chandeliers to the design and placement of the furniture, everything was exactly how Rowan had envisioned it. Even the color and type of marble they'd used to construct the floor was exactly as Rowan had described it in his notebook.

How was this happening?

There was no way anyone could have stolen Rowan's notebook. The bank had assured him that nobody had accessed his safe deposit box, and Rowan had never told another soul about his plans for this building. And yet, here it was.

What the hell was going on?

"The attraction I want to show you is located just past the first checkpoint," Victor said as he led them down a hallway toward a series of metal detectors.

As they walked through the hall, images floated across the walls, ceiling, and floor, and they were suddenly moving through a hallway deep underwater. The air pressure felt different, and there was a slight hint of brine and moisture in the air.

Large bluish-gray fish swam deep beneath their feet.

"Where are the fish coming from?" Julie asked. "I can't see a projector anywhere."

But Rowan knew that the images on the floor weren't coming from a projector. The floor, ceiling, and walls were actually video screens that were both touch and sound sensitive. The whole room felt immersive in precisely the way Rowan had conceived it. Although, when he'd described it in his plans, he was pretty sure this technology didn't exist.

"This place is insane," Julie said, to nobody in particular.

They stepped through a couple of wide metal doors and entered what appeared to be some kind of waiting area, the kind of space you might find in a DMV or some other random civic office. A NOW SERVING NUMBER ___ sign hung overhead.

One side of the room was nothing but a whole lot of red molded-plastic-and-metal chairs, and the other side was filled with a dozen metal doors numbered from one to twelve. There were plastic dust covers on most of the chairs and a line of red masking tape ran the entire length of the space from the chairs to the doors. It had the appearance of a room that had recently been completed and was just waiting for a final polish before it could be cleared for public appreciation. Unlike a government office, however, there were no counters or desks for any future agents to serve those who might be waiting.

"What is this place?" Julie asked.

"It's the Liminal Space Exhibit," Rowan replied, barely able to constrain his sense of amazement at seeing a room he'd so recently created in his imagination come to life.

"It certainly is," Victor said. "How the hell did you know that?"

Rowan forced a smile and nodded in the direction of a sign on the wall that displayed the name. But Rowan had known where they were headed as soon as they'd stepped into the hallway with the fish.

"What the hell is liminal space?" Julie asked.

The Liminal Space Exhibit was the last aspect of The Hall of Incredible Possibilities that Rowan had created. In the world of architecture, liminal spaces were defined as the physical areas between one destination and the next—places like hallways, airports, streets, and other connective or in-between regions.

"The word 'liminal' is Latin," Rowan explained. "It means 'threshold.' Think of liminal spaces as crossing-over points, or spaces where you've left something behind. You've come from one place, and yet are not fully somewhere else. Horror films often use liminal space to increase the audience's discomfort when moving through a scene."

"Like a hallway?"

"Exactly, yes. A hallway is one of the most common forms of physical liminal space."

"So it has to be physical?"

"Normally yes, but not necessarily. A significant aspect of liminality is perception."

"I'm not sure I get it," Julie said.

"Okay," Rowan said, "the same physical space might be liminal at one time and yet not liminal in another. And other places will feel liminal regardless of when you encounter them. Sometimes visiting a space outside of normal operating hours can feel unsettling. That's liminality at work."

"And that unsettling feeling is why I wanted to bring you here," Victor said.

"What do you mean?"

"I have to come clean about something."

"What is it?"

Rowan was certain that Victor was about to admit somehow stealing or purchasing Rowan's designs, but that wasn't the case.

"When you called, I was actually just about to reach out to you," he said.

"What for?"

"I'm a builder. I can build anything you can show me how to build. But I'm not an architect, and I'm certainly not a scientist. When I first received the plans for this building I thought they were like nothing I'd ever seen, but then I realized that wasn't exactly true. I had seen something similar in the past."

Rowan began feeling strange, as if he were hovering outside and above himself. He tried to take a deep breath, but stopped when he felt like he might pass out.

"Oh?" Rowan asked, doing his best to keep the rising panic from his voice.

"Something about the plans always felt kind of familiar," Victor said.

"How so?" Rowan asked.

"It reminds me of a cross between Zaha Hadid and Arthur Erickson, with a number of unique interior elements that I've only seen once before."

"Where?" Rowan asked, but he knew what Victor was about to say.

"In your designs for the theme park we were working on in Dubai."

Rowan felt the sound of the room change. Suddenly, it was as if the outside world had moved inside Rowan's head, buzzing and humming between his ears in a series of uneven waves. He felt like he was about to throw up. He looked down and noticed that his hands were shaking. "Oh, that's interesting," he said, in a voice that sounded like it was coming from someone else's body.

Julie, perhaps sensing that something was wrong, squeezed his hand and Rowan felt the world slowly return to normal.

"I do see some similarities with that project," Rowan said.

"I thought so," Victor said.

Rowan felt better, as if Julie holding his hand had grounded him somehow.

"But I am curious about something," Rowan said, feeling more like himself with each passing second.

"What is it?" Victor replied.

"Why did you angle the building away from the access road the way you did?"

"What do you mean?"

"I would have thought parallel, which would mirror the lines of the mountains in the distance."

Victor nodded. "I thought the same thing, but along with the plans I received were a set of specific instructions. I was to construct this building in a very particular way, along one intricate geographic line."

"Did they tell you why?"

"They did not."

Rowan was confused. Based on the geography of the nearby infrastructure and the shape of the lot in relation to the local countryside, the way the building had been angled just didn't make sense.

"Are you ready to experience something incredible?" Victor asked, clearly unable to contain his excitement about the exhibit.

"Absolutely," Julie said.

Rowan forced a smile. "Of course."

"Okay, so, like I mentioned earlier, one of the central attractions in this place is the Liminal Space Exhibit. It's designed to enhance the strange feeling of moving through liminal space. Per the instructions, only one person is allowed into the exhibit at a time."

The Liminal Space Exhibit was one of the most technically challenging attractions that Rowan had ever designed. He created each hallway in order to provide a unique experience based on the occupants' sensory reaction to the design of the carpet, the smell, and myriad other factors.

These similarities to his plans couldn't possibly be coincidental, but Rowan could tell that Victor had no idea this design was actually Rowan's. Whoever hired Victor must have seen Rowan's plans. He was going to have to ask Victor Garland some questions, but first, he had to experience the Liminal Space Exhibit.

"Before we continue," Victor said, "I should tell you that two of my contractors experienced something strange while testing the exhibit."

"Experienced what, exactly?" Rowan asked.

"I think it'll be more fun if you experience it yourself."

Julie smiled. "Sounds exciting."

"It only works if you begin seated in one of these three chairs." He pointed to a line of chairs sitting atop a long strip of red masking tape on the floor.

"What's the red tape for?" Julie asked.

"That's the path you need to follow," Victor replied.

"How does it work?"

"You're supposed to take a number and then wait until you hear your number called. Then you'll be assigned a door," Victor said.

This entire room, from the chairs to the doors to the number system, was exactly what Rowan had designed. The only thing he hadn't included was a line of tape on the floor.

"Once you're assigned a door, you step through it into the liminal space of your chosen hallway and, whenever you're ready, you walk through that hallway until you reach another door. On the other side of that door you'll find a waiting room identical to the one you just left. Then you take another number and return through the assigned hallway to this room."

"That's it? You spend time in a hallway and then another waiting room?" Julie asked.

Victor nodded. "I think you'll find there's slightly more to it than that."

"I wanna try," Julie said.

Rowan had no reason to believe that there was anything dangerous about the Liminal Space Exhibit. There certainly wasn't anything harmful about the experience that Rowan had imagined. He'd designed the exhibit to amplify the inherent strangeness of liminal spaces, the disconnectedness so many people feel while experiencing the "spaces in between spaces." It was harmless, nothing more than some physical illusions and advanced kinetic special effects designed to illicit an emotional response.

But something about this place felt different, charged somehow.

"I'd like to go first," Rowan said. "If you don't mind?"

"Great," Victor said.

Rowan walked up to the dispenser and picked a number. Fourteen.

"Oh," Victor added, "when the voice calls your number, no matter which door it sends you to, just go to door number twelve."

Rowan looked across the room at the doors. The red masking tape on the floor led directly to door number twelve.

"We put the tape there to make it easy," Victor said.

"What's so special about door number twelve?" Julie asked.

Victor smiled. "You'll see."

Then a woman's voice, emanating from a number of speakers located around the room, called a number. "Fourteen. Could the participant who has chosen number fourteen please proceed to door number twelve?"

"Well, that's certainly fortuitous," Victor said.

Rowan nodded, but he wasn't sure. It didn't feel fortuitous. It felt ominous.

He stood up.

"Make sure you follow the red line on both sides of the hall," Victor said, pointing to the masking tape on the floor. "Otherwise it might not work."

"What might not work?" Julie asked.

Rowan was thinking the exact same thing. There was nothing in his plans for the Liminal Space Exhibit that was dependent on specific doors or numbers. He had a sinking feeling in his stomach. As far as he could tell, everything about the building had been constructed to Rowan's exact specifications, so why did it feel so other-worldly and strange?

Victor just smiled and turned to Rowan. "Ready?"

Rowan walked over to door number twelve, making sure he followed the line of red masking tape on the floor. When he got to the door, he turned and smiled at Julie. She gave him a little wave.

And then Rowan moved through the door into pitch-darkness.

When the door finally closed behind him with a muted click, the hallway was illuminated.

The first thing he noticed was the carpet. It was orange, red, and brown—an exact replica of the David Hicks hexagonal carpet from the Overlook Hotel in *The Shining*. This was Rowan's favorite of his twelve hallway designs. The others were a mixed bag that was supposed to include: a long staircase that actually only went up a few feet, an airplane passenger-loading corridor on wheels, a narrow concrete hallway from the basement of a shopping mall, a seemingly endless conveyer belt, and a handful more. The hallway Rowan had stepped into was about a hundred feet long. There were prints of Native American art on the walls. At the end of the hall was another door.

As Rowan moved through the hall, he felt his legs grow heavy. This was most likely caused by this hallway's illusion. Rowan's plans included weaving complex illusory detail and design into each hallway. This particular hall actually grew in width and height as you moved from one end to the other. The change was too subtle to notice consciously, but subconsciously, it was disarming. Rowan had designed some of the other hallways to include trick mirrors, slight temperature changes, very subtle scents, and a number of other alterations in the nature of the floors and wall surfaces.

Rowan walked quickly toward the door at the far end of the hall. Part of him was interested in taking his time and experiencing the liminal exhibit the way he'd intended, but he was worried about Julie. It wasn't just that he felt bad about leaving her behind, it was the feeling of foreboding that had been with him ever since they'd arrived in Las Vegas.

It was the same thing he'd felt on that airplane in the dream with Julie.

Something bad was going to happen.

He opened the door at the end of the hall and stepped into a waiting room that was the mirror image of the room he'd just left. Then he followed another line of red masking tape over to the ticket dispenser, picked a number, and waited.

But nobody called Rowan's number—or any other number, for that matter.

After waiting for a few minutes, Rowan's sense of unease grew thicker, and the panic that he'd experienced earlier began welling up again. He walked back along the line of red masking tape to door number twelve.

Just like last time, the door opened into pitch-darkness. And again, like last time, when the door closed behind him, the room was illuminated.

But something was different.

The first thing Rowan noticed was that the hallway that had been there just moments earlier was somehow now a medium-sized rectangular room, and the carpet that had once featured the iconic orange, red, and brown hexagonal design from *The Shining* was now a slightly higher pile, design-free goldish-yellow color, blackened around the edges by age or water damage or whatever else.

Everything felt wrong.

When Rowan walked through the hallway earlier, it had smelled like brand-new carpet and fresh paint. This room smelled old. Rowan could almost feel the mold spores clawing their way into his lungs. And it was dark—or, rather, dim was a better word. It felt unnatural, as if somebody had turned down the brightness of the world.

As he moved farther into the room, Rowan noticed the odor getting stronger. It smelled like the hot metallic steam that would rise as you walked across a city sidewalk grate above whatever nightmare was going on deep below the surface of the city. The smell wasn't overpowering, but Rowan found it extremely unsettling.

He felt like he was going to throw up.

It was at this point that he noticed something else had changed from earlier.

Instead of a door at the end of a hall, there was an opening that led to another room—very similar to the room he'd just left, but just a bit smaller. And instead of plain yellowish paint, this room had torn black-and-white wallpaper covering the walls. The floor was different in this second room as well. It was covered with a tightly woven, low-pile industrial carpet in a bland blue that existed somewhere between navy and sky, but was missing the charm of both. The stains around the edges of the carpet remained, as did the increasingly obnoxious smell.

And still, no door.

Just another opening that entered into a similar room, and then another, and another.

Rowan mapped the size of the rooms in his head as he walked—an occupational hazard directly connected to people who design buildings and rooms for a living.

It didn't make sense.

The floors of these rooms didn't appear to be angled upward or downward, which meant that Rowan should have come to a wall or a door leading to the original waiting room a long time ago. But he just kept moving forward, from one empty, windowless room to another.

The rooms appeared to be located in the basement of some long-abandoned industrial office building. There was nothing like this in any of Rowan's designs. The rooms themselves were creepy— a perfect example of the horror movie feel of liminal space that Rowan had been trying to explain to Julie. But it wasn't just the smell or the dim lighting or the airlessness. They were something else, something more elemental.

They were wrong.

Moving through the seemingly endless series of rooms, Rowan imagined how a pet owner might feel looking at the taxidermied version of their beloved family dog. When looking at the taxidermy dog for the first time, the owner immediately recognizes that the essential essence of the thing is missing. What had once been alive and connected to the world has been replaced by something else, something that isn't simply uncanny or unfamiliar.

It's unreal.

It was the same with the endless rooms. They looked like rooms that might actually exist in real life, in any basement of any abandoned office building in America. But these were not those places. These places were something else.

Rowan wanted to get out of there as fast as he could.

He started to run.

He ran for what felt like forever, through room after room, over endless yards of stained carpet and scuffed linoleum until he finally came to a door. He almost missed it because it was located in the corner of a wood-paneled room and had been painted to match the fake wooden panels that lined the walls.

Rowan sprinted toward the door and yanked it open.

He felt a momentary burst of light and electricity, then fell into the waiting room from earlier, almost knocking Julie over.

"I'm sorry," Rowan said as he made sure Julie was okay. "I'm not sure what happened."

"Where did you go?" she asked.

He turned around and opened the door he'd just come from.

It was the hallway featuring the carpet from *The Shining*.

"I'm not sure," Rowan said, then he turned to Victor. "What's going on?"

"That's what I was talking about," Victor said. "The scale and layout doesn't feel like it makes sense, does it?"

"No. It sure doesn't."

"What do you mean?" Julie asked.

"Could you describe what happened?" Victor asked.

"I went through the hallway," Rowan said. "Then I entered another waiting room that was the mirror image of this one, but then, when I moved through the door to the original hallway, something was different."

"It felt like you were someplace else," Victor said.

"Yes. I was moving through a series of empty rooms."

"Liminal space," Victor replied, as if that was enough to explain what had happened.

Rowan nodded. "I got lost a few times. I'm glad you waited."

"What are you talking about?" Julie said. "You were gone for maybe five minutes."

"What? No. I was lost, for almost an hour."

Julie looked concerned.

"Wasn't I?" Rowan took a look at the time on his phone. Julie was right. He'd stepped into the hallway less than ten minutes earlier. There didn't seem to be any point in asking Victor about stolen plans. There were more important things to consider, like what the hell had just happened. What were those rooms?

"It took me an entire day to figure out how to do it," Victor said, "to follow the red line, choose the proper door—and even then, it only works some of the time. You were lucky. You found the mysterious office on the first try."

Rowan didn't feel lucky.

"What's the mysterious office?" Julie asked.

Victor smiled. "It's a mystery. Full disclosure, there's a lot I don't understand about some of the more technically advanced aspects of the physics involved here. My engineers explained how the mechanics in this exhibit incorporate a gyroscopic elevator combined with a sophisticated sensation modification system, and that certain electromechanics in the design allow a high-tech elevator to operate without our physically feeling it. And then there are the quantum computers that control everything and the literal maze of mobile active panel wall displays. I'm afraid I don't know how two-thirds of this technology works. Physics was never my thing."

"Are the rooms always identical?" Rowan asked.

"There are actually two possible landing rooms. They're similar, but not identical. The furniture is a bit different."

"The furniture?" Rowan asked.

"In one of the landing rooms, the desk is a reproduction of the captain's desk from the *Titanic,* and, in the other, eight original de-sign Eames lounge chairs form a kind of flower design around an ottoman."

Those things had been included in Rowan's design. But Rowan hadn't seen any furniture where he'd landed.

"How many times have you done this?" Rowan asked.

"Just twice myself."

"How many others?"

"Two of my structural engineers went through the process when we first finished. I think they were freaked out by the whole experi-ence. They both quit shortly afterward."

Rowan was shaken. What just happened?

"Okay," Julie said, "this sounds fucking amazing. I wanna try."

"No," Rowan said. "You can't." As he spoke, he knew that his voice was too sharp, too demanding.

"Um, excuse me?"

"It's just that I thought we might go for a drink," Rowan lied.

"Come on, Rowan," Julie said. "It's just a game."

"It's not safe," Rowan persisted. "I think there's something wrong with the air in some of the rooms. Maybe something in the paint or mold or something."

"Fuck you," Julie said.

"You're not going in there."

"You know, you're acting like a real asshole right now."

Julie took a step away from Rowan.

"It's perfectly fine," Victor said. "We took a number of atmo-spheric readings. Everything is well within acceptable safety param-eters."

"I think there's something dangerous happening," Rowan said. "I don't think it's safe."

Julie ignored his warning. She took a number, sat down, and waited.

Rowan exhaled. "Okay. If you make it to the basement with the empty offices, there might not be any doors for a long time, but the first door that I did manage to find led me right back here, to this room."

"Jesus, Rowan," Julie said. "Could you please not spoil anything else?"

He didn't want her going in there, but unless he grabbed her and dragged her outside, there was clearly no way she wasn't going in. "Will you at least leave your phone on and promise to be careful?" he asked.

At that moment, the voice called her number.

Julie walked over and opened door number twelve. Then, after briefly turning to give Rowan the finger, she turned and entered the hallway.

Rowan watched as the door closed behind her.

Rowan and Victor sat in the waiting room for half an hour before they started looking for Julie. She wasn't in the hallway or in the waiting room on the other side, and there were no other doors anywhere. Rowan tried calling her phone, repeatedly, but there was no answer.

The two of them performed the ritual that involved walking the red line in an attempt to reenter the abandoned basement or office building or whatever it was, but they were unable to find their way back. Rowan demanded that Victor show him how to find those rooms, but Victor continued to insist that rooms like the ones Rowan had described didn't exist.

Victor called in four additional members of his team to help look for Julie. The six of them searched the entire building. There was no sign of her.

Julie Furuno had disappeared.

Again.

Finally, after searching the building for a second time, they called the police.

38

I NEED YOU TO PLEASE STOP ASKING QUESTIONS AND JUST FUCKING DRIVE

ALTHOUGH SHE'D INTRODUCED HERSELF using two distinctly separate names, Rowan had somehow managed to lose the same person twice.

First Eliza Brand, now Julie Furuno.

He tried to go back into The Hall of Incredible Possibilities after Julie had disappeared, but both Victor's legal team and the Las Vegas Police Department denied Rowan's requests for access to the building.

Victor couldn't understand why Rowan was so upset. As far as Victor was concerned, the two of them had a fight and Julie had taken off because she was pissed off at Rowan.

The Las Vegas police told Rowan they'd call if they heard anything about his friend, but when Rowan mentioned the fact that a woman named Eliza Brand had disappeared under similar circumstances in the past and that she looked exactly the same as Julie Furuno, Victor Garland had to step in and use his local influence—which was apparently considerable—to convince the police not to take Rowan into custody. It worked, but it meant that Rowan wasn't going to be able to go to the police and ask any more questions.

Back at the hotel, Rowan sat with his back against the headboard and scrolled through the pay-per-view movie options. He was exhausted, but there was no way he was going to be able to sleep. He was surprised to discover a listing for a movie that he really wanted to see, a film from 2018 called *The Favourite*.

Directed by one of Rowan's favorite directors, Yorgos Lanthimos, and starring Olivia Colman, Emma Stone, and Rachel Weisz, *The Favourite* was a black comedy that had been nominated for ten Academy Awards. Rowan had been meaning to watch the movie for quite a while, but he wasn't all that crazy about period pieces so he'd allowed it to slip through the cracks.

He was about ten minutes into *The Favourite* when Emily Connors popped into his mind. Being on the run with Emily felt like something that had happened ages ago. Rowan wondered how she was doing, and hoped that she was okay.

When he finally refocused his attention on the screen, Olivia Colman and Emma Stone were playing with a bunch of rabbits. Rowan remembered thinking that it was interesting—Emily Connors popping into his head followed by a bunch of rabbits—but as seventeen of the tiny furry creatures started to fill his television screen, he fell asleep.

Rowan woke up to the sound of beeping.

It was 4:44.

He felt terrible. He was shaking for some reason, and covered in sweat. The television was still on, but a documentary was playing—something called *Secrets of Playboy*. Hugh Hefner was talking about the birth of the brand. A bunch of half-naked young women were walking around the Playboy mansion. Rowan was about to switch it off when one of the young women turned around and the bunny logo on her T-shirt suddenly filled the screen. Rowan sat up with a start.

The bunny's head was facing to the right.

But when the camera filming the scene finally pulled back, Rowan saw that the young woman wearing the T-shirt had been standing in front of a mirror.

The bunny was facing the correct way.

Rowan took a look around. He'd thought there was no way he'd be able to fall asleep, but that must have been what happened. The movie had ended quite a while ago. The beeping that woke him up had come from his phone.

It was a message from the eBay seller who went by the username GiantNYCMouse. The lot of *Playboy* magazines was still available, if Rowan was still interested. The seller provided an address and told Rowan to show up any time after nine A.M. and to park behind the building.

Rowan got dressed and made his way down to the lobby.

He left his contact information and asked the concierge to call if Julie made an appearance, but he knew she wasn't coming back. He had no idea how he knew. He just did.

Less than an hour later, Rowan was on a flight home.

He was no longer worried about being followed. They could capture him, beat the hell out of him, or lock him up in any number of nondescript rooms. He didn't care.

He was altogether finished with this shit.

His apartment was as he'd left it. There were no bad guys waiting in the living room, and nothing appeared to be out of place. He ran a shower and just let the water wash over him in an attempt to clear his head. Whenever Eliza/Julie's face appeared in his mind, he dug his nails into his palms and the pain momentarily snapped him out of it.

Maybe she had simply taken off because they'd had a fight?

No.

He knew that wasn't true. Something had happened, and it was his fault.

After his shower, Rowan turned his attention to the eBay seller and the *Playboy* magazine he'd found online. He'd done his best to push the string of coincidences from his mind, but he'd fallen asleep to playful rabbits and woken up to *Playboy* bunnies.

Rabbits.

While out for dinner with Julie Furuno, he'd suddenly become obsessed with a *Playboy* bunny logo. Why did he care that the rabbit was facing the wrong way?

As he drove to the address he'd received from GiantNYCMouse, Rowan wondered what the hell he was doing. Had he somehow been infected by Emily Connors and her obsession with the game she called Rabbits? He'd never cared about *Playboy* bunnies—backward or forward—but for some reason he'd become fixated on them while on a date with Julie Furuno. And the fact that he couldn't remember any of it made him very uncomfortable. He didn't have any other avenue of investigation, so Rowan decided that it was finally time to deal with the backward bunnies.

As he pulled into the alley behind the building where the eBay person had told him to park, Rowan was picturing his reunion with Julie Furuno. He was thinking about dinner. He'd cook something romantic. Maybe jumbo scallops and risotto? No, risotto was too involved. Fingerling potatoes would be easier. That way they could drink wine and talk while he cooked.

He smiled and imagined Julie laughing as the two of them spoke about the crazy way their relationship began, ignoring the fact that Julie had told him she couldn't recall what had happened on their first date. He shook his head. He didn't want to think about that, or his time spent on the run with Emily, or getting kidnapped.

Emily.

What had happened to her?

No. She could take care of herself. He turned his attention back to Eliza. Julie.

Maybe they'd go for another walk after dinner.

He was imagining holding Julie Furuno's hand as the two of them jumped over a small puddle, when Rowan hit a woman with his car.

She'd come out of nowhere.

He'd managed to hit the brakes just before his car slammed into her, but it didn't sound good. As his car screeched to a stop, a second woman ran out and crouched next to the woman he'd just hit. Rowan opened his door to make sure the first woman was okay, but the second woman stood up and shook her head.

"Stay!" she yelled out as she opened the back door to Rowan's car and loaded the injured woman into the back seat.

"Is she okay?" Rowan asked.

"I don't know."

It was at this point that Rowan recognized the second woman. "Emily?"

She looked up from the injured woman in the back seat. "Rowan?"

"Yeah. What are you doing here?"

"Drive."

"We need to make sure she's okay."

"Rowan," Emily said, deadly serious. "I need you to please stop asking questions and just *fucking drive*."

Rowan opened his mouth to ask another question, when the injured woman raised her head and yelled from the back seat. "For fuck's sake, drive!"

Rowan put the car in gear and sped away from the building—and as he did so, he had the feeling that everything was about to change. Again.

39

I'VE NEVER BEEN HIT BY A CAR BEFORE

EMILY HAD SCREAMED as she watched the car slam into Pepper's thigh. It was true what they said about moments of extreme stress. She felt like she'd seen Pepper get hit in slow motion, the tires of the black Volvo screaming as the driver tried to stop and turn at the same time.

"Fuck," Pepper said as she stared down at her legs. "I've never been hit by a car before."

Rowan guided the car back out into traffic. "She might have internal bleeding."

"She'll be fine," Emily said as she pulled Pepper's jeans down over her hip bones and took a look at her injured leg. The entire top of her thigh was a deep reddish purple.

"Does it hurt?" Emily asked, but she already knew the answer.

"Yeah."

"Bad?"

"Yeah," Pepper said. "It's not great."

Emily took a look out the window. They were passing a series of roadside motels. The next motel in line featured a neon sign of a cowboy. "There." Emily pointed in the direction of the cowboy. "Turn in there."

Rowan pulled the car off the interstate and into the parking lot of the Midnight Rambler Motor Hotel. He switched off the engine and turned to face Emily and Pepper.

"Shit," Pepper said as she sat up with a wince. "You really fucked up my leg."

"I'm so sorry," Rowan said, "you ran right in front of my car. I tried to stop."

Emily held her phone up in front of Pepper's face. "I don't think you're bleeding internally, but take a look at this list of symptoms."

"Please don't," Pepper said, pushing Emily's phone away and then pulling up her jeans.

"Are your hands or feet tingling?" Emily asked.

"I thought you said she'd be fine?" Rowan said, alarmed.

Once she'd managed to get her jeans back on, Pepper sat up and opened the car door. "He stopped in time. I just need some ice for what is going to be an insane bruise. Other than that, I'm fine. They probably have an ice machine somewhere in the motel," Pepper said as she stepped out of the car.

"I'm not sure you should be—" Emily said as she watched Pepper try to put weight on her leg and then promptly crumble to the ground.

"Fuck," Emily said as she scrambled to help.

"Should I get us a room?" Rowan asked.

"No!" Emily and Pepper said in unison as Emily loaded Pepper back into the car.

"Fine, but I'm at least going to get you some ice," Rowan said.

"If this guy's name really was on The Index, we need to keep him close. Can we trust him?" Pepper asked as they watched Rowan walk across the parking lot to the motel.

"Yeah," Emily said, "he's cool."

"You sure?"

"We've been through some shit."

Emily tried calling Scarpio and MayDay, but there was no answer.

"How much longer until we're supposed to meet them?" Pepper asked.

"Twenty minutes," Emily said.

Pepper nodded. Her enthusiasm for tracking down the Quiet

Room, which hadn't been all that high to begin with, was clearly fading. Fast.

"We can find a way, Pepper. There's still time."

"Do you really believe that?"

Emily didn't answer. She had to believe. She really didn't want to disappear into nothingness.

Rowan got back into the car and handed Pepper a bottle of water, two ibuprofen tablets, and a reusable bright orange grocery bag filled with ice. "Thanks," Pepper said, wincing at the cold as she placed the bag against her thigh.

"What were you two doing back there when you ran in front of my car?" Rowan asked. "Were you playing Rabbits?"

Pepper glanced at Emily, then back to Rowan. "Why?" she asked. "Did something happen?"

"I don't know," Rowan said. "I mean, I can't be sure. But I started noticing weird things, things that might be part of the game or whatever the hell it is."

"What kind of weird things?" Emily asked.

He briefly considered sharing what had happened in Las Vegas, but that felt more like evidence that Rowan was completely losing his mind than anything related to Emily's game of patterns and co-incidences. "The *Playboy* bunny logo was facing the wrong way in two different places," he said, "and I saw it again on the television, and I don't know, but running into you the way I did. That was one hell of a coincidence."

"A painful one," Pepper added.

"I'm so sorry," Rowan said, for what felt like the hundredth time.

"What were *you* doing when you hit me with your car?" Pepper asked.

"I was going to that thrift store or whatever it was."

"Agatha's Used Furniture," Emily said.

"Yes."

"What for?"

"A *Playboy* magazine from 1973."

"Should we go back?" Pepper asked.

Emily bit her lip. If there was something in that magazine that could help them, the thrift store was only a few blocks away. But if the Rabbits Police were still there . . .

It was risky.

"As far as we know, they're not looking for Rowan or his car," Emily said, finally. "We can park a block away and he can walk in and buy the magazine."

Pepper nodded. "That could work."

"How's your leg?" Rowan asked.

Pepper forced a smile. "It's fine."

"You sure you want to go back?" Rowan asked.

Emily nodded. "I'll drive."

"But it's my car," Rowan said.

"Sure, but if the bad guys show up and we have to leave you behind, I don't want to have to switch seats."

Rowan smiled. He clearly thought she was joking.

Emily wasn't smiling back.

Emily wasn't smiling for two reasons: first, because she wasn't joking, and second, because the timer in her pocket had started vibrating, and when she pulled it out, she could see that there was something on the screen.

Emily held up the countdown clock so that Pepper could see it.

"Fuck," Pepper said.

Emily nodded. Fuck, indeed.

They had nine hours until the end of everything.

40

FASTEN YOUR SEATBELT AND CLOSE YOUR EYES, WE MIGHT BE IN FOR A BUMPY FUCKING RIDE

ROWAN STEPPED INTO Agatha's Used Furniture, and as he did he experienced a flash of something, a floating feeling, like all of the atoms in his body suddenly shifted. He started to sway and leaned against an old gumball machine in order to balance himself. He looked down at his hands. They were shaking.

"Everything okay?" a redheaded woman with a ponytail asked from where she was seated behind a long glass counter on the left side of the store.

Rowan smiled. "I'm fine, thank you. Just thought I might get some gum."

"It's fresh," she said. "I replaced it all yesterday."

"Great." Rowan checked his pockets, but he didn't have a quarter.

"There's a change machine in the back if you need it," she said.

Rowan thought he'd experienced this strange floating feeling before, but he couldn't remember when. Maybe when he was a kid? Maybe more recently? Had it happened with Emily? Eliza? Helena Worricker?

Whatever it was, the feeling passed and Rowan's hands stopped shaking. "Changed my mind." He approached the counter.

The woman behind the counter took off her reading glasses. "What can I do for you?"

"I called about some magazines."

"What kind?"

"Old *Playboys*."

"Really?"

Rowan nodded. "These ones." He pulled up the eBay listing on his phone.

"Oh my." The woman took a look at the listing. "I'm sorry, but somebody came in and bought those about half an hour ago."

"Oh," Rowan said. "I think those were meant for me. I spoke to somebody on eBay."

"Sorry," she said. "Nobody told me. They were a consignment thing."

"No worries. Do you happen to have any more?"

She shook her head. "Those were the only *Playboys*, but I think we have some *Hustlers* and a couple of French ones."

"That's okay," Rowan said. "Thank you."

"Any trouble?" Emily asked as Rowan slid into the back seat.

"The magazines were gone. Somebody beat me to it," Rowan replied. "Are you sure you don't want me to drive?"

But Emily had already pulled into traffic.

Rowan grabbed at some papers that were preventing him from fastening his seatbelt.

"Please be careful with that," Emily said, nodding toward the papers. "It's important."

After he'd finally managed to get his seatbelt fastened, Rowan took a look at the papers. It was actually a pamphlet, something titled "Museo del Futuro." On the cover was a sketch of a futuristic-looking building.

"Where did you get this?" Rowan asked, his voice suddenly thin and shaky.

"In an old washing machine coin box," Pepper said. "Why?"

"This is impossible."

"What?" Emily asked, pulling the car over to the side of the road. "Do you know this place?"

"This says the building was designed by Antonio Sant'Elia," Rowan replied.

"So? Who the hell is that?"

"He was a visionary futurist architect. They called him a prophet of the violent, industrial future."

"He's a famous architect. So what?" Emily asked.

"Sant'Elia died in 1916," Rowan said, ignoring Emily's question. "This pamphlet is dated 1957."

"So maybe he designed it decades earlier and it took them fifty years to finally get around to building it?" Pepper chimed in.

"He didn't design this building."

"What makes you so sure?"

"Because I did."

It looked old and authentic, but there was no way that pamphlet was created in 1957. The building on the cover was Rowan's. It was The Hall of Incredible Possibilities.

"What?" Emily asked.

"Wait, this place is real?" Pepper asked.

Rowan nodded. "It's currently sitting in the desert just outside of Las Vegas."

"Who built it?" Pepper asked.

"It's kind of a weird story," Rowan said.

"I think we might need to hear it," Emily said as she guided the car back into traffic.

Rowan exhaled, then he told them about a building he'd designed in his head that somehow now existed. He told them about the Liminal Space Exhibit and the seemingly endless rooms at the far end of an impossible hallway. He ended with everything that had happened after Julie Furuno had reentered the picture, from the *Playboy* bunnies facing the wrong way to the last time he saw her, waving at him from the waiting room with the tape lines on the floor.

"You saw Julie Furuno again?" Emily asked.

Rowan nodded.

"How?"

"I called her, and a little while later she showed up at my hotel."

"And then she disappeared?"

"Yes."

"Again?" Emily asked.

Rowan nodded.

"Shit," Emily said.

"What's liminal space?" Pepper asked.

"It's the spaces 'in-between,' like hallways, antechambers; transition places you move through on your way to a destination."

"That sounds like Betweenspace," Emily said.

Pepper sat up and turned to Emily. "You think this Liminal Space Exhibit might be connected to Betweenspace somehow?"

"I don't know," Emily said. "It sure sounds similar."

"What's Betweenspace?" Rowan asked.

"It's supposed to be some kind of transitional space between dimensions. It might be a way to reach the Quiet Room," Emily said.

"What's the Quiet Room?" Rowan asked.

"Shit," Pepper said. "You need to turn left at the next light."

"Why?"

"Just got a text from MayDay. Change of plans. They want us to meet them at the Gatewick place right now."

"Hang on," Emily said. The tires screeched as she guided the car through a yellow light.

"Jesus," Rowan said. "Slow down."

"Sorry," Emily said. "I can't slow down. We're trying to find a way home."

"What the hell does that mean? A way *home*?"

"Fasten your seatbelt and close your eyes, we might be in for a bumpy fucking ride."

Rowan didn't want to close his eyes.

He was looking for Eliza Brand, and there was no way he was going to miss anything that might help him find her again.

41

SHE'S PROBABLY NOT GOING TO SHOOT YOU

"What's so special about this place?" Rowan asked as Emily pulled the car over and stopped in front of a nondescript brownish-gray ten-story building.

"We think it might be connected to the Gatewick Institute," Emily replied.

"What does that mean, exactly?" Rowan asked.

"We're looking for answers." Pepper reached over to open her door.

"Let me get that." Rowan hurried out of the car and ran around to the passenger side to help her, but Pepper had already stumbled out and was standing on the sidewalk.

"How's the leg?" Rowan asked.

Pepper took a few steps. "It's fine."

She walked with a slight limp, but it looked like she was fine putting weight on it, which made Rowan feel a bit better about hitting her with his car.

The building was pretty beat-up, but appeared to be open for business, if only just. The windows of the lobby door had been smashed out and were covered by warped plywood. The door itself was stuck in a slightly ajar position.

Emily pushed the door open. "At least we don't need somebody to buzz us in."

"Shit," Pepper said as she pulled out her phone.

"What?"

"MayDay wanted us to text her when we got here."

Rowan led them over to a dilapidated elevator on the left side of the lobby. "Where are we going?" he asked as the elevator doors opened with a strained clank and wheeze.

"Tenth floor, room ten seventeen," Pepper replied.

Room 1017 was located at the end of a long hall directly opposite the elevator. As they moved down the hall, Rowan noticed that there were no names on any of the doors, just numbers. Aside from the sound of their footsteps echoing off the worn linoleum, the place was eerily silent. The entire building, or at least the tenth floor, appeared to be empty.

"Are you sure this is the place?" Rowan asked. "The building seems completely deserted."

"Sshhh," Pepper said as they approached room 1017.

Emily knocked.

No answer.

Pepper stepped forward and tried the door. It was locked.

"You texted MayDay?" Emily asked.

"Yeah."

Click.

Somebody unlocked the door from the other side.

"Somebody's in there," Rowan said.

"Hello?" Emily said.

No response.

Emily looked at Pepper, and then slowly opened the door.

It was dark.

Rowan followed Emily inside and squinted, doing his best to bring the contents of the room into focus. Slivers of daylight fought their way through tiny slats in the blinds, but it wasn't enough to illuminate the room.

"MayDay?" Pepper called.

Then somebody closed the door behind them and turned on the lights.

It was Helena Worricker.

She was holding a huge chrome revolver, which she pointed at Rowan and the others. She locked the door and then moved to the other side of the room to join Julie Furuno, who was standing beside two people who were gagged and zip-tied to chairs.

"Thank you for coming," Helena said.

Rowan recognized the people in the chairs. It was Alan Scarpio and MayDay.

"Julie?" Rowan said.

"Hey," she replied.

"What's going on?" Rowan took a step forward and then stopped. There was something about the expression on Julie's face. She looked different somehow.

"What the fuck?" Emily asked.

"Relax," Julie replied. "She's probably not going to shoot you."

"I thought you were dead," Rowan said to Helena. "What happened?"

"That was my idea," Julie said. "Those people with the masks had taken an interest. They were closing in."

"You faked her death?" Rowan asked.

"Don't make it sound so simple," Julie replied. "It was fucking hard."

"What are you doing?" Rowan asked.

"My job."

"Put down the gun," he said. "Let them go."

"That is not going to happen," Helena said.

"Why not?"

"Because that's not what we want," Julie replied.

"What are you talking about?" Rowan asked as a deep, painful throbbing ache started moving up the back of his neck and into his head.

Julie turned to face Emily and the others. "Give me your phones and the map."

They handed over their phones.

"The map."

"I don't know what you're talking about," Emily said.

Helena pointed her gun at Pepper and pulled the trigger.

From the corner of his eye, Rowan saw Pepper dive toward a dark corner of the room. "No!" he and Emily screamed together.

He had no idea whether or not Pepper had been hit. He lunged forward and tried to grab Helena's gun, but before he could reach her, Julie stepped between the two of them, and Rowan turned to avoid knocking her down.

He recovered his balance and took a step toward Helena.

"Please don't," Julie said.

"What's going on?" Rowan asked, doing his best to blink away the sudden pain in his head. "Why are you doing this?"

None of this made any sense.

What the hell was Helena Worricker doing with a gun?

"I'm sorry," Helena replied. "We're running out of time."

Scarpio and MayDay struggled against the zip ties, eyes wide, the legs of their chairs pounding the linoleum floor.

Helena took a step closer to Emily. "The map. Now."

"Just give her what she wants," Rowan said.

"Shut up, Rowan," Pepper said as she stepped out from the darkness.

Rowan was relieved to see that Pepper hadn't been shot.

"You don't talk to him like that," Julie said, glaring.

"You okay?" Emily asked.

"Fine," Pepper replied.

Emily turned to face Helena. "You're Hawk Worricker's daughter? What the hell are you doing here?"

"We don't have time for that," Helena said. "The map."

"Just calm down," Rowan said. "This can't be right. This doesn't make any sense."

"Shoot her," Julie said, nodding in Emily's direction.

Helena pointed the gun at Emily.

"If you don't put down that gun, I'm going to kill you," Pepper said.

Emily looked over at Pepper and then turned back and glared at Helena, defiant.

Helena stared at Emily for a moment, and then turned about thirty degrees and pointed the gun at Pepper.

"Don't do it, Em," Pepper said. "This bitch isn't going to shoot me."

"Oh," Julie said, "she's definitely going to shoot you."

Emily pulled the pamphlet they'd found in the washing machine at Agatha's Used Furniture from her pocket.

"Don't," Pepper said.

"You don't even believe it's real, Pepper," Emily said.

"But you do."

Emily handed the pamphlet to Julie.

Helena turned to Rowan. "Come on."

"What are you talking about?" Rowan said. "I'm not going *anywhere* with you."

Helena retrained her gun on Emily and pulled back the hammer with a click.

Rowan jumped in front of Emily. "Stop it with the fucking guns!" he yelled.

Emily walked over to Pepper, seemingly oblivious to Helena's gun. As Emily moved, Rowan kept himself positioned between her and Helena. He had no idea what the hell was going on. The pain in his head was now sitting right between his eyes. It felt like someone was pushing a hot blade into his skull. He did everything he could to ignore it and focus on what was happening in front of him. There was no way he was letting anybody get shot.

"You two okay?" Rowan asked.

"We're fine," Pepper said as she glared at Julie.

Helena motioned toward Rowan. "Let's go."

"No. You want to shoot them, you shoot me first," he said.

Helena rolled her eyes. "Seriously?"

"Come on, Rowan," Julie said, nodding in the direction of the door. "We have to get back, and we don't have much time."

"I already told you," Rowan said. "I'm not going anywhere with you, at least not until you tell me what's going on here."

"We don't have time for this shit." Helena fired two shots at Scarpio and MayDay. Both of their chairs hit the floor as their bodies were thrown back.

"No!" Emily and Pepper screamed in unison.

Then Helena swung her gun back around and pointed it at Emily.

"Stop!" Rowan yelled.

There were gurgling and rustling sounds coming from where Scarpio and MayDay were lying on the floor, still zip-tied to their chairs.

Helena pulled back the hammer of her gun with a loud click.

"Are you guys okay?" Emily called out.

No answer.

Helena exhaled and turned to Rowan. "Okay, how about this? I stop shooting people, and you come with us right now."

"What the fuck are you doing?" Rowan ran his hands through his hair as he tried to make sense of the situation. Why were Julie and Helena there together? The pain was a white-hot searing blast in his skull. Was he forgetting something that had happened? Was he experiencing some kind of mental break? "Why is this happening?" he asked as he took a step toward Julie.

As soon as Rowan started to move in Julie's direction, Emily dove past him and lunged at Helena. Emily caught her by the wrist as she was about to fire her weapon. Emily dragged her to the floor and reached up to wrest the gun from Helena's hand.

"Enough!" Julie yelled as she produced another gun from the back of her jeans and pointed it at the two women wrestling on the ground.

A loud gunshot reverberated through the room.

"What have you done?" Rowan asked.

"Nothing," Julie said, looking at the weapon in her hand. "The safety is still on."

Emily staggered back, shaking, as Helena's gun fell from her hand.

Helena was lying on the ground. She wasn't moving.

Pepper dove for Helena's gun, but stopped short as Julie pulled back the hammer of her own weapon.

"Don't even think it," Julie said as she reached down, picked up Helena's gun, and slipped it into the back of her jeans. Then, she pointed her gun at Emily. "Listen to me very carefully, Rowan. If you don't come with me, right now, I'm going to kill everybody in this room."

Rowan took another step toward Julie. "Please put down the gun," he said.

"I need you to come with me."

"That's not going to happen."

"I'll shoot her first," Julie said, "I swear."

Rowan looked at Julie. He could see it in her eyes. She wasn't going to hurt him, but she was definitely going to shoot Emily.

"Fine," Rowan said. "I'll come with you."

"She's going to kill you," Emily said.

Julie shook her head, exasperated. "Jesus, if I was going to kill him, I would have shot him already."

"She needs you because you're the only person playing the game," Pepper said.

"You have no idea what you're talking about," Julie said as she led Rowan toward the door.

"Get them help." Rowan nodded in Scarpio and MayDay's direction.

Then Julie Furuno pulled Rowan into the hallway and kicked the door shut behind them.

42

EMILY'S END-OF-THE-WORLD PLAYLIST

EMILY AND PEPPER RUSHED OVER to where Scarpio and MayDay were lying on the ground.

MayDay was slumped sideways in her chair, bright red blood pouring from a wound in her thigh, and Scarpio was a few feet behind her, lying on his back. Helena had hit them both.

Scarpio was alive, but his breathing was compromised. He'd been shot in the upper right part of his chest near the shoulder.

"You're gonna be fine," Emily said as she removed his gag and started to work on his restraints.

Scarpio tried to speak, but he winced in pain.

"Who was that bitch with Helena Worricker?" Pepper asked.

"That was the actor Julie Furuno."

"Why would she do this?" A tear rolled down Pepper's cheek as she kneeled next to MayDay.

"I have no idea," Emily said as she leaned down to take a look at Helena Worricker, who was lying in a pool of blood. Her eyes were closed.

"Is she dead?"

"I think so."

"How much time do we have left?"

Emily pulled out the timer Swan had given her. "Eight hours."

"We need to call an ambulance," Pepper said.

Scarpio was making gurgling noises and waving in Emily's direction.

"What is it?"

"Talk," he whispered as he removed a tiny receiver from his ear and handed it to Emily.

Emily slipped it into her ear.

"Hello?" she said.

"I work for Mr. Scarpio, and I'm going to send help. Do you need security, cleanup, or medical assistance?"

Emily looked at Scarpio and MayDay. "Better send all three."

Scarpio's people arrived less than ten minutes later. The person in charge of his team—a woman named Veruca—told Emily that Alan Scarpio and MayDay were both losing blood and if they didn't receive medical attention immediately, they would die. She didn't mention Helena Worricker or her condition.

Emily didn't bother telling Veruca that they were all going to die anyway, and that rushing Scarpio and MayDay to the hospital was essentially just prolonging the inevitable.

If Swan was right, the death of this dimensional stream was less than eight hours away.

"You're welcome to stay at the penthouse as long as you like, and if there's anything you need," Veruca said, "it's Mr. Scarpio's wish that we take care of it. Anything at all." She handed Emily a phone. "There's one number stored in this phone, and it goes straight to me."

"Thank you," Emily said. "What are you going to do about . . . all of this?" Emily motioned around the room.

"We'll take care of it," Veruca said.

Emily nodded, and pulled the countdown timer from her pocket. Seven and a half hours.

She swallowed the tears that had been welling up over the past few minutes and did her best to try to clear her mind. If they somehow managed to find their way out of this dimensional stub, she was going to be completely heartbroken about leaving her friends behind, but in that moment she needed to pull it together.

They were running out of time.

———

Back at the penthouse, Emily opened Scarpio's computer and searched for the building featured in that pamphlet, the Museo del Futuro. There was nothing. Then she looked up the architect listed on the cover, Antonio Sant'Elia. Rowan was right. He'd died in 1916. There was no way he designed a building in 1957.

Next Emily began collecting everything she could find that might help them figure out what to do next. There wasn't much, just the documents she'd found in her parents' secret office and a few sheets of paper they'd been using to take notes.

"What are you doing?" Pepper said as she watched Emily pace the room.

"There's nothing on the Museum of the Future pamphlet online," Emily said.

"Stop running around. You're making me dizzy."

"We have to find them."

"Why? In a few hours we're going to blink out of existence right along with everyone else."

Emily pulled out the timer. "We still have almost seven hours."

"For what?"

"They asked for the map. I think they know."

"I don't get it," Pepper said.

"Julie knew that pamphlet was a map."

Pepper walked over and grabbed two beers from the fridge and then sat down on the floor. "I think it's over," she said as she twisted off the caps and offered one of the bottles to Emily.

"Julie Furuno told Rowan 'We have to get back.' Do you remember?" Emily took the bottle from Pepper.

"Yeah? So?"

"I think I know where they're going," Emily said, and then took a long sip of beer.

"Where?"

"Las Vegas."

"Why?"

"What Rowan described in his place in Las Vegas sounded an awful lot like Betweenspace."

"Shit," Pepper said. "They're going after the Quiet Room."

"And so are we," Emily said. "Put on your fucking shoes."

Pepper just stared.

Emily could tell that she was losing her.

Pepper was clearly exhausted, quite possibly on the edge of a mental collapse. She'd either already given up, or was five minutes away from letting go of whatever thin emotional branch she was clinging to and falling into the metaphorical river of hopeless shit that had been rushing by nonstop ever since Emily had stepped into that Airstream in the woods.

Emily took Pepper's face in her hands and kissed her deeply. "I love you," Emily said, "and I know you're tired, but you have to trust me. Seven hours is plenty of time to get to Las Vegas, find the Quiet Room, and get the fuck out of this dying dimension." She pulled back and stared into Pepper's eyes. "Okay?"

Pepper smiled. "You know what, Connors?" she asked.

"What?"

"I love you too, but we can't control the end of the world."

"Maybe not, but we have to try."

"The world ended for me once already," Pepper said.

"What do you mean?"

"When I lost you."

"You didn't lose me, Pepper," Emily said, a sad smile crossing her lips. "You left me. There's a big difference."

"I came right back," Pepper said.

Emily shook her head. "I was right where you left me."

"Except that you weren't. Not for me."

Emily wiped away a tear.

"You can lose everything in a minute, in a second, in a day," Pepper continued. "Maybe we can find the Quiet Room and keep going, but maybe we can't. Whatever happens is what was always going to happen. For me? The world ended when I lost you, and that was way worse than blinking out of existence. Having the world end this way? Frankly, it's almost a relief."

"You could have told me," Emily said.

"I did tell you, well, another version of you. But in the end, it doesn't really matter. You were happy with K. I could see that."

She was right, Emily had been happy with K. Extremely happy.

But K was gone.

"It's okay," Pepper said. "There is nobody in the world I'd rather spend my last few hours of existence with than you."

"Fuck you," Emily said as tears streamed down her cheeks. "I just found you. I'm not letting you get away again."

"Technically, I found you," Pepper said.

Emily punched her playfully on the arm. "You know that I'm going to try to save us, and you also know that I'm not going to take no for an answer."

Pepper shook her head. "I don't know."

"Well, I do," Emily said. "But feel free to take a moment to wallow in your sad-girl bullshit for a few minutes if it makes you feel better."

Pepper laughed.

"After that you're going to stand the fuck up, give me a huge hug, and tell me that you're ready to keep trying."

Pepper stood up and the two of them embraced for a long moment. When they finally moved apart, Emily noticed an almost imperceptible change. Something small, electric, and familiar moved across Pepper's face, eventually landing in her eyes with a sparkle. This was followed by a very faint smile.

"Fuck you, Connors," Pepper said, finally, her smile widening.

"Good," Emily said. "I didn't want to have to knock you out and drag you to the airport."

Pepper grabbed the laptop, and after a few minutes spun it around and showed Emily the screen. "There's a flight leaving in an hour and a half."

They made it to the airport in record time. For some reason, they weren't able to print out boarding passes using the digital kiosk, so they were forced to visit the airline's physical check-in counter.

"Hi," said a bright-eyed young woman named Sylvia. "How can I help you today?"

"We're having a bit of trouble checking in," Emily said.

"Hmmm," Sylvia said as she typed away on her terminal. "This is really weird."

"What is it?" Pepper asked.

"I'm so sorry, but your flight has been canceled."

"What?" Emily asked. "When?"

"It looks like . . . ninety seconds ago."

"When's the next one?"

Sylvia typed some more. "Oh my gosh," she said.

"What?" Emily asked.

"They've all been canceled."

"All of the flights?"

She nodded. "Everything headed to Las Vegas today. But, if you like, I can get you there first thing tomorrow morning. We're happy to offer a discounted rate on a hotel both here in Seattle and in Las Vegas if you're interested."

"Fuck," Emily said.

The clerk leaned forward and whispered, "If you raise a fuss, they'll definitely comp you those rooms."

"Come on," Pepper said, "we'll find another airline. There must be a dozen flights from here to Vegas."

They found one that left around the same time and booked it online. But while Emily was reading the confirmation email, she received a second message indicating that flight had been canceled as well.

They checked with the airline and it was the same thing. Every flight to Las Vegas had been postponed until tomorrow. There was no reason given.

They tried booking flights through a few different apps, and it was the same thing every time. No flights to Vegas.

"What the fuck is going on?" Pepper asked.

"I think somebody doesn't want us going to Las Vegas," Emily replied.

"Who?"

"Rabbits."

"What?"

"I checked online and there's nothing happening on the Las Vegas side of things. Flights are leaving and landing from other cities around the world, right on schedule."

"That's weird."

"Super weird."

At that moment, Emily and Pepper were approached by airport security.

"What's going on?" Emily asked, but the two burly buzz-cut security guards didn't say a thing as they led Emily and Pepper through the airport's concourse and into a tiny interview room.

"Hello?" Pepper said.

The larger of the two men glared at Pepper and sniffed. "You two have been flagged as travel risks."

"What?" Emily said. "That's ridiculous."

The slightly less jacked security guard smiled. "Maybe there's a warrant for your arrest or something? Were you two being naughty?"

Emily glared. "I need to make a phone call," she said, finally.

"We'll get to that. You just hang tight."

"Did you just fucking tell me to hang tight?" Emily asked.

He smiled wide. Asshole.

"Really?" Emily asked.

He kept smiling.

"My lawyer is going to have a field day when I describe the way I was handled," Emily said, her voice suddenly shaky and scared, "the places I was inappropriately touched. And then, when I witnessed the same things happen to my best friend. I just don't think I'll ever be able to fly again."

"We didn't touch you," he said. "There's video."

"Do those video cameras cover everywhere? I didn't see anything in at least two of the halls we came through on the way here."

The bigger security guard looked over at his partner, who shrugged.

Emily smiled.

"Fuck," he said, "hold on."

A minute later the larger security guard came back into the room and handed Emily the phone that Veruca had given her earlier. "Keep it brief."

Emily and Pepper both glared.

"Please," the security guard added.

Emily called Veruca and explained the situation.

Ten minutes later, a fortysomething man in a charcoal suit stepped into the interview room and Pepper and Emily were released.

"My name is Nuno," he said as he opened the door to a large matte black SUV. "I'll be taking you to hangar seventeen where your flight will be departing in twenty minutes. Do you have any questions?"

Emily had a million of them, but the most pressing was the location of Rowan's mysterious building. "We're looking for something called The Hall of Incredible Possibilities," she said. "It's a mid-century modern–looking place, about the size of a department store. It's supposed to be out in the desert near Vegas."

"I'll look into it," he said.

"Thanks."

"Do you two have any special dietary requirements?"

"Umm . . . no," Emily said.

Pepper shook her head.

"Great," Nuno said, and then slid into the driver's seat and guided the SUV into traffic. "It's about six minutes to the hangar. The controls for the music and the temperature are located on the touch-screens on the backs of the seats."

The attendant told them they were on an incredibly fast aircraft, and that the flight to Las Vegas would take two hours and five minutes. She said they'd serve a meal in about half an hour. In the meantime, she offered them snacks and every type of beverage imaginable, from Dom Pérignon to a peach-flavored Japanese soft drink called Ramune. Pepper ordered a tea, and Emily said she'd wait for dinner.

Pepper fell asleep shortly before they reached cruising altitude. Emily thought about waking her up, but she knew that Pepper was exhausted. There were only four and a half hours left before the end of the world. Emily hated the idea of missing even a second of that time, but Pepper was different. Emily had always considered sleep an inconvenience—something her body required in order to function. Pepper was the opposite. Pepper lived for sleep. To her it was a luxury.

While Pepper slept, Emily thought about what was coming.

From the moment Swan handed Emily that countdown clock, everything had taken on a nostalgic heaviness. Would this be the last time she ever ate pasta? Last glass of wine? Final glimpse of the sun? Emily knew that Pepper had to be struggling with that stuff as well, but while Emily liked to confront difficult things head-on and get them out of the way, Pepper preferred to bury things like stress and emotional pain, tamp them down, crush them into something sharp that she could use later.

If Pepper wanted to sleep, that was her choice, but Emily was going to spend as much time as she could either desperately trying to escape this dying stream or listening to music.

Music was the thing that Emily was going to miss the most.

This was Emily's second time on a private jet. She wasn't shocked to learn that there were levels to these things, but she was a bit surprised by the comprehensive gift bag they found beneath their seats when they'd boarded, which included a sleep mask, slippers, a tablet, earbuds, makeup, a watch, and a designer robe.

Emily fished out the extremely expensive earbuds and opened the package, then spent a few minutes trying to come up with an end-of-the-world playlist. After five minutes or so, she gave up and just started playing the songs that popped into her head.

Had she written it down, Emily's End-of-the-World Playlist would have looked like this:

1. "The Killing Moon" by Echo & the Bunnymen
2. "Hazey Jane II" by Nick Drake
3. "Edie (Ciao Baby)" by the Cult
4. "Dream All Day" by the Posies
5. "On the Beach" by Neil Young
6. "Older Guys" by the Flying Burrito Brothers
7. "Range Life" by Pavement
8. "I Don't Believe in the Sun" by the Magnetic Fields
9. "See Emily Play" by Pink Floyd
10. "Oh Well, Okay" by Elliott Smith
11. "Paranoid Android" by Radiohead
12. "Everybody Knows" by Concrete Blonde

She was halfway through the thirteenth song, "Need You To-night" by INXS, when Pepper woke up. They still had an hour or so left before they were scheduled to land, so the two of them decided to use the remaining time to review what they'd learned so far and then try to formulate some kind of plan.

They went over everything, but the only thing they could think of that might help them find the Quiet Room was the map. They both remembered looking at the building's layout in that pamphlet, but neither of them could recall any concrete details about the pathway that had been drawn in black ink over the seemingly endless maze of rooms.

"What are we going to do?" Pepper asked.

"Well," Emily said as the captain announced that they'd begun their descent into Las Vegas, "the way I see it, all we really need to do is enter The Hall of Incredible Possibilities, find a magical pathway that leads to Betweenspace, discover the Quiet Room, then figure out how the hell to use the room's multidimensional powers to get home."

"When you put it that way," Pepper said, "it doesn't sound fucking bonkers at all."

"Admittedly, it's not much of a plan," Emily said.

"It certainly isn't."

Emily smiled. "But it's enough."

"Oh, really?"

"We do Rabbits things the way we always do Rabbits things—one step at a time. All we need to do is take the first step. After that, we do what comes next."

Pepper shook her head. "I fucking knew you were going to say that shit at some point."

Emily kissed Pepper, and then smiled.

"What was that for?"

"In case the whole world is about to end."

"Which it is," Pepper replied.

"Fasten your seatbelt," Emily said. "We're almost there."

43

SOMETHING VERY BAD

A CAR WAS WAITING for Emily and Pepper when they landed in Las Vegas. The driver held up a sign that read: EMILY CONNORS AND FRIEND. The driver told them he worked for Alan Scarpio and that he'd been sent there by Nuno. Emily asked to speak with Nuno before they got into the car.

"Hello?"

"Nuno?"

"You can trust the driver. We've booked you into the Wynn if you'd like to freshen up, otherwise, the driver has the address of the building you asked about."

"You found it?"

"We haven't been able to confirm the name, but this is the only structure that fits. It's an Italian neorealist building out in the middle of the desert that's been sitting dormant for a long time. The man who built it is responsible for a number of high-profile casino renovations, along with numerous escape room experiences and a dozen or so theme park attractions. He's recently dined with Rowan Chess. We're pretty sure it's the place. The driver has a key to the front door. There's no alarm registered with the city."

Emily thanked him and hung up.

"Where to?" the driver asked.

"Straight to that building, please," Emily said, and then squeezed Pepper's hand.

It wouldn't be long now.

———

The driver gave them the key and his phone number and then left them at The Hall of Incredible Possibilities.

It was incredible, as advertised.

The entire building was contemporary cutting-edge science center meets future-world Disneyland. The exterior reminded Emily of Jean-Luc Godard's *Alphaville*. It felt like a neo-noir authoritarian prison crossed with a museum of rocket-age desert flying saucer paranoia.

But inside, it was something else entirely. Stepping into the building felt like stepping into the future, or, perhaps more accurately, stepping into an optimistic and more user-friendly version of the future.

Emily knew it was nothing but theme park, escape room consumerist bullshit.

Still, it was singularly beautiful.

From animated video-screen floors to three-story-high fountains and every type of high-tech flourish in between, the space was amazing. Emily wanted to explore the entire building, to feel everything she imagined this space could make her feel, but a quick glance at the end-of-the-world timer in her pocket shut those thoughts down immediately. Time spent doing anything other than working to avoid oblivion wasn't an option.

They had ninety minutes left.

Everything inside the building was very clearly marked, so it didn't take them long to find the Liminal Space Exhibit. They just followed the signs, and in five minutes they were standing in the waiting room.

One side of the room was filled with red plastic chairs, and just like Rowan had described, the other side featured twelve doors. A line of red tape on the floor led to a smashed-up ticket dispenser on a stand.

"Somebody doesn't want us to get a ticket," Pepper said, nodding in the direction of the ticket dispenser.

"Sure looks like it," Emily said.

"Rowan said something about following the red tape," Pepper

said, but just as she was about to step onto the line, Emily grabbed her by the jacket and pulled her back.

"Wait," Emily said as she kneeled down and examined the tape. "Something's wrong."

"What is it?"

"I'm not sure, but look, part of the tape is scrunched up right here."

Pepper took a look at where Emily was pointing.

"I think they moved it," Emily said. "It looks like there's another line here, where the tape used to be."

"Shit," Pepper said. "I think you're right."

"Let's assume they fucked with the tape and follow the old marks instead," Emily said.

"Good call," Pepper said.

Emily wasn't sure why, but she had a strong sense that following the line was important somehow. The fact that somebody had clearly tried to prevent them from doing just that only reinforced those feelings.

"Didn't Rowan say that we need to open one particular door?" Pepper asked.

"Yeah," Emily said.

"Do you happen to remember which door?"

"I don't think he told us. I think he said we just need to pick a number and open one of the doors."

"But we have no idea which door?"

"Right."

"Great."

If following the proper path was important, choosing the door was probably not something they should leave to chance.

Emily got down on her hands and knees, turned on her phone's flashlight, and started examining the floor. "It's that one," she said finally, pointing to door number twelve.

"Are you sure?"

"I think so," Emily said. "There are more marks on the floor here. It looks like they peeled off another line of tape so we couldn't find it."

"Fuckers," Pepper said.

"Put your hands on my waist and make sure you follow the path I take exactly," Emily said as she carefully made her way along the remnants of the old tape marks on the floor.

When Emily felt Pepper's hands gripping her jeans, she wanted nothing more than to turn around and fall into Pepper's arms, to slip back into a world the two of them had left behind.

But there was no time.

Emily opened door number twelve and stepped into total darkness.

As soon as the door clicked shut behind them, the room was illuminated.

It was just like Rowan had described. They were standing in a long hallway with Native American art lining the walls. The floor was covered in orange, red, and brown carpet. It looked just like the hotel in *The Shining*. At the far end of the hall was another door.

There was something off about the floor. Emily felt like it was designed to appear flat, but she was pretty sure they were walking slightly uphill as they made their way toward the door at the far end.

As they moved through the hallway, Emily began to feel strange. She felt like she'd smoked a joint or something—nothing too overt, just a warm vibration. She thought about mentioning the feeling to Pepper, but it had taken everything Emily had to get them this far. The last thing she wanted to do was give Pepper something else to worry about.

They stepped through the door at the end of the long hallway into a room that was identical to the one they'd just left, except that it was flipped, the original waiting room's perfect mirror image.

"What now?" Pepper asked.

"Rowan said he went back through the same door, but that things had changed."

"Yeah," Pepper said. "I remember."

"Whatever happens, do not let go of my hand."

And then Emily guided Pepper back through door number twelve.

———

"Jesus," Pepper said. "Where the hell are we?"

Emily felt the warm vibration turn into a familiar tingling pressure at the base of her head. It was warm and itchy. She wanted to rip off her skull and scratch inside her brain.

She'd felt this way before, but was having a hard time remembering when.

She opened her eyes.

They were standing in a medium-sized rectangular room. Just as Rowan had described. *The Shining* floor was gone, and in its place was a sad goldish-yellow carpet with mold or something black around the edges.

"How the fuck is this possible?" Pepper asked. "We came through the same door."

"Maybe it's some kind of illusion?" Emily said.

But Emily didn't really believe it was an illusion. Wherever they were, it felt real.

"What is that smell?" Pepper asked. "It's like steamed dirty feet."

Emily thought it smelled much worse than that. She wrinkled her nose as she took a look around.

The room was cool and dim, as if a dusky film had been placed over reality. Shadows pooled and moved around the edges of Emily's vision, and that's when she remembered the last time she'd felt this warm, itchy feeling in her skull.

She'd experienced something similar in her last stream, when she'd woken up in a video arcade with K.

"Betweenspace," she said.

"I don't feel very well," Pepper said. "I think I might be sick."

"Whatever you do, don't let go of my hand." Emily didn't feel like anything bad would happen if Pepper let go, but there was no way she was going to lose Pepper the way that she'd lost K.

"You're squeezing a little tight, Em," Pepper said.

"Sorry," Emily said as she checked the countdown timer. "We've got forty-one minutes. We need to hurry."

"Can you remember anything at all about the map?"

"Not really," Emily said.

"How do we decide which way to go? Isn't the Quiet Room supposed to be impossible to find without directions?"

"You're not helping."

"How come there are no doors?" Pepper asked as they moved from one empty, windowless office space to another. "Each of these rooms is just another version of the last."

Pepper was right. The color and materials of the floors and walls changed a bit from room to room, but the layout was essentially the same.

They were either moving in circles, or deeper into nothing.

"I don't know," Emily said. "There has to be some kind of pattern we need to follow to escape the maze."

"Something like a map?"

"Again, not helpful," Emily said.

But Pepper was right. Without instructions, they were essentially lost.

"There has to be a way," Emily said, but she wasn't sure she actually believed it anymore.

"How do you propose we find the Quiet Room in forty minutes?"

"We just do," Emily said. "Come on."

Pepper leaned against the wall and slid down to the floor.

"We can't stop here. We need to keep moving."

"Look, the fact that we made it this far, to wherever the fuck this is, is amazing," Pepper said. "I'm just so tired."

"I'm not giving up. *We're* not giving up," Emily said. "If we can't find the Quiet Room, we can rest in oblivion. It's only forty minutes away."

Pepper closed her eyes and exhaled.

And then everything changed.

Emily was standing in the middle of a much larger room. It looked like some kind of a library. It took her a couple of seconds to realize that she recognized it. It was the large library from the enormous house on the lake that Emily had visited as a teenager. Or rather, what felt like a dim photocopy of that room. That original room had been bright, flooded with light from the library's large skylights. This version was dark—and even though it was full of books and furniture, it felt completely empty. And something else had changed as well.

Pepper was there, but she was hazy. She looked like a ghost.

"Pepper?" Emily said.

Pepper turned and opened her eyes—

—and then a blinding-white screaming pain filled Emily's head, and she was knocked to the floor.

"What the hell happened?" Pepper asked.

Emily was lying on the floor, looking up into Pepper's eyes. "What?" Emily said as she tried to sit up. Her head swam and she felt sick, but she eventually managed to make it to a sitting position.

"You called my name, and then you screamed and fell down," Pepper said. "Are you okay?"

"What did you do?"

"Nothing," Pepper said. "I just closed my eyes for a few seconds."

Emily felt weak, and her entire body was shaking. She imagined what she'd just experienced was probably similar to the pain of giving birth. She'd felt her entire body being ripped apart, muscles torn from bones. She had the feeling that she wasn't going to be able to survive that pain again.

"You don't look okay," Pepper said.

"I'm good. Just a bit dizzy," Emily said.

Pepper didn't appear convinced.

"I have an idea," Emily said. She tried to stand and failed.

"How about let's just sit for a minute?" Pepper said.

"We don't have time to sit. I'm going to ask you to do something," Emily said, "and I need you to trust me."

"Okay," Pepper said. "What is it?"

"I'm going to need you to wear a blindfold."

Pepper laughed. "Are you serious?"

"Yes."

"Why?"

"Please don't close your eyes until I explain."

"Okay." The sudden seriousness of Emily's voice made Pepper choke back the sarcastic comment she was about to utter. "What's going on, Em?"

"I don't have time to go into all of the details, but when I was a kid, I saw my parents perform some kind of weird experiment. I think they may have been looking for the Quiet Room."

"Gatewick Institute shit?"

Emily nodded. "My mom and dad were blindfolded in a room with these lines on the floor. I'm pretty sure their eyes were covered in order to stop them from looking at the subject of the experiment—a girl named Natalie. Natalie wasn't actually visible in the room, but I could feel her. I knew exactly where she was. I was able to sense her as she moved. When Natalie touched one of the other lines on the floor, she suddenly became visible. She began screaming in pain. I called out, and that's when my parents yelled at me to close my eyes."

"Whoa. That sounds intense."

"It was—but there's more."

"Okay."

"Before all of the screaming, I heard one of them mention that they were looking for a room of some kind. I didn't think anything of it at the time."

"Shit. The lines on the floor. Were they Meechum Radiants?"

"I think so," Emily said.

"What makes you think if I'm blindfolded you might be able to find the Quiet Room?"

"If those lines on that map we found were Radiants, I might be able to follow them."

"How?"

"I was in some kind of experimental protocol as a kid. My mom took a bunch of drugs when I was in the womb. If I focus, sometimes I'm able to sense the Radiants."

"And the blindfold?"

"I'm not sure, but I think it has something to do with quantum displacement or entanglements."

"Quantum superposition?"

"Maybe?"

"Every quantum state can be seen as a sum of two or more other distinct states. When a system is in one state, it can be seen as being partly in each of two or more other states, right?"

"Exactly. What if for someone in Betweenspace, it's like being in all the dimensions of the multiverse at once, but, like Schrödinger's cat, if you're observed, you get ripped out and back to one reality only: the observer's reality?"

"That's why you think I need to be blindfolded? So I can't be the observer?"

Emily nodded. "I think the blindfold is essential once I've discovered the proper path, but I don't know. I hate physics."

"I love your face when you try to deal with this stuff."

Emily smiled, her first genuine smile in a long time. "I love your face all the time," she said, "so I'm not going to enjoy covering it up."

Emily grabbed the bottom of her tank top and used her teeth to rip a six-inch strip along the edge, away from the rest. "Once I put the blindfold on, you can't take it off. You saw what happened to me. If you see me while I'm in the other state, I'm not sure I'm going to be able to make it back alive."

"I'll keep my eyes closed too, to be extra safe."

"Good idea," Emily said. "Ready?"

Pepper nodded. "I'll see you on the other side."

The two of them kissed deeply, and then Emily blindfolded Pepper.

"Hold my hand," Emily said.

Pepper grabbed Emily's hand, and the world changed again.

Emily was back in the large library.

"Something feels different," Pepper said.

"We're somewhere else."

"Where?"

"I'm not sure. It looks like a version of a library I visited once."

"What happens next?" Pepper asked.

"I'm going to try to follow the Radiants to the Quiet Room."

"What can I do?"

"Just don't let go of my hand."

"I think I can handle that."

"Okay, then," Emily said as she cleared her mind and began to concentrate.

It didn't take her long to pick up the first Radiant. It was located across a short hallway in a room directly in front of them. Then, just like she did all those years ago with her mother, Emily started walking the Meechum Radiants. She adjusted and readjusted her path whenever she felt the Radiant getting weaker, which was an indication that she'd strayed too far.

She checked the countdown timer.

Seventeen minutes.

Emily would have to hurry, but she'd known that before she checked the timer. She could feel it in the air, a new kind of atmospheric pressure. Something was changing. It wouldn't be long before whatever was going to happen to this dimensional stub happened.

She moved through one empty room after another, through kitchens, libraries, bedrooms, and foyers, all while following the Radiants, the change in atmospheric pressure growing stronger and more noticeable with each step.

There were seemingly endless rooms, but no doors.

Even though it's often difficult to feel, rooms have their own unique signatures, their own special rumble and hum. They breathe and sit and wait. Some of them are alive with crackles of electric possibilities, others almost churchlike in their deep and solitary silences.

Emily could tell that these rooms were different.

These rooms felt charged with something else, something beyond description. Emily felt overwhelmed with a feeling of powerless inevitability. As she moved through the space, following her own internal map, she had the sense that she was approaching something familiar—a dark and turbid maelstrom of energy that Emily couldn't help but feel was somehow connected to her family.

It was while she was thinking about her parents that Emily finally came to a door.

"What is it?" Pepper asked.

"A door."

"How much time is left?"

"Two minutes."

"I wish we had a gun."

"Me too."

"Are you going to open it?"

"Yes."

"Can I take off this blindfold?"

"Not yet."

"What are you waiting for?"

"I don't know," Emily said. "I feel like there's something bad waiting for us on the other side."

"Worse than the two of us disappearing into oblivion?"

"I think maybe, yes."

"We've come this far, Em. Just open it."

Emily took one last look at the countdown timer.

Five seconds. Four. Three. Two.

And then Emily Connors opened the door.

44

PURE ABJECT TERROR

"Fuck!" Rowan yelled. He'd just smashed his knee into the side of a wall. "Julie!"

"Call me Eliza. And we need to keep moving. It's not much farther."

"Can you slow down? I can't see a fucking thing."

"Just keep walking."

"Why do I need to be blindfolded again?"

"Because those were my instructions."

Julie Furuno had blindfolded him back in the Liminal Space Exhibit, and they'd been walking for hours. Rowan's face was sweating like crazy through the blindfold, his legs were killing him, and he was losing patience.

"We can't slow down," Julie said. "The last wrong turn took us too far off the path."

"I still don't understand where you're taking me," Rowan said.

"And I still don't care. You're going to find out really soon, and I promise you're going to be happy. Okay?"

"That's not very reassuring."

"It'll have to do," Julie said as she grabbed him and pulled him forward. "It shouldn't be too much farther now."

"You keep saying that."

"Let's change the subject," she said. "What else can we talk about?"

"How did you disappear from that bathroom in the restaurant?"

"I didn't disappear. That bathroom was located at a very special point. That's why we chose it as a meeting place."

"We?" As Rowan spoke, a searing pain erupted behind his eyes.

"You really don't remember?"

"Forget it," Rowan said.

His head was killing him. He was too tired to think about what had happened with Eliza at the restaurant, Alan Scarpio, Emily, or anything else. He rubbed his temples. All he wanted to do was lie down and sleep.

Julie led Rowan in silence for a few minutes, and then a low rumbling sound forced an image into Rowan's mind.

It was an airplane.

"I had a dream," Rowan said. "You were in it."

"What kind of dream?"

"We were on a plane."

"We've been on lots of planes. I'm afraid you're going to have to be more specific."

"What do you mean? We've flown to Las Vegas. That's it."

"Oh my god. This is so frustrating."

"What?"

"Describe the plane."

"It was big, a 777 I think. The seats were blue. It was bare-bones. Not a lot of technology."

"Blue seats with plant designs?"

"Yes. How did you know?"

"Malaysia Flight 370."

"What?"

"You don't remember? The flight that disappeared?"

"Of course I remember. Why would I be dreaming about that flight?"

"You weren't dreaming."

"What are you talking about?"

"You were remembering."

"That's ridiculous."

"You really don't remember?"

"What are you talking about?"

"It was a date."

"What?"

"That was when you revealed what was really going on, what this thing was doing to you. That was also the day you taught me that death wasn't the worst thing that could happen."

"I did?"

"Yeah. You told me that the worst thing was the *quality* of your fear right before death. That fear was the thing. Death was a relief."

"What are you talking about?"

"It was killing you."

"What?"

"Rabbits."

"That doesn't make any sense."

"Never mind," Julie said. "I was just trying to distract you. We're here."

Rowan wanted to believe her when she'd said that she was just trying to distract him, but there was something in her tone, and, more important, there had been something about the quality of that dream.

Suddenly, he was back on the airplane with Eliza Brand. He knew that she was Eliza and not Julie Furuno. He wasn't sure how he knew, but he just knew. It was the same plane Rowan had dreamt about earlier, with the blue seats and the text on the monitor that looked like Arabic. But this time Rowan understood that it wasn't Arabic. It was Malay. And he also understood something else.

It wasn't a dream.

The plane was Malaysia Airlines Flight 370.

And Julie was right. Rowan had taken her aboard that flight in order to show her something. His head felt like it was about to break apart. If only he could remember.

And then Julie opened the door.

And Rowan understood that he was about to remember.

Everything.

45

THE ENGINEER

When the Engineer awoke from what felt like an infinite number of deaths, he had no idea where he was. There was a pillow beneath his head, and he was lying on the floor. When his eyes finally adjusted and he was able to make out shapes in the darkness, he could tell that he was in a medium-sized room—possibly a bedroom—but based on the style and symmetrical organization of the furniture, he thought some kind of office was more likely. The only sound was the hum of an air conditioner coming from somewhere up near the ceiling.

He felt like he had been asleep for so long that he couldn't remember the details of his life, but that wasn't quite right. It wasn't that he'd been asleep for so long. It was something else.

He'd been away.

He sat up in bed and ran his hands through his hair. He could hear the sound of music coming from a radio or distant speaker somewhere. It took a moment for him to realize it was a song he recognized, but he couldn't quite place it.

The nearness of nameless things.

He felt the world shake and shiver, but that wasn't quite true. It wasn't the world that was vibrating. It was everything else.

Where was he?

Where had he been?

He rubbed his temples and lowered his head.

Think.

But it was no good. He couldn't remember.

"Oh good, you're awake."

He turned to greet the woman who had spoken. He didn't recognize her face, and he couldn't remember exactly when he began hearing her voice.

It started as an echo in the dark.

A long time ago, the Engineer had woken up at the bottom of a dark lake—or something that had taken the form and fundamental appearance of a lake. He was cold, and felt truly alone for the first time in as long as he could remember. Way up on the surface, he could make out something that looked like the shadow of a tower. But whenever he tried to swim up to the tower, the formless beasts in the muck pulled him back down.

And then he heard the echoes.

And the echoes finally became a word.

"Hello?"

And then the Engineer understood that the shadow on the surface of the lake wasn't a tower. It was a person.

And that person was calling his name.

He answered.

I'm here.

"Do you know where we are?" the voice asked.

"I don't know," he said, which was the truth. He knew that he'd been sleeping for a long time and that he had things to do. He'd been working on something, but what was it? Was it a tower?

Babylon.

Not a tower. A map to the tower.

The Engineer was going to speak with god.

But first he needed to find something.

First, he needed to find the game.

"Please tell me you know who the fuck I am?" the woman asked.

He didn't know who she was then, but he knew now. After the longest sleep he could remember, the Engineer was finally awake.

"Eliza," he said.

"It's about time." Tears started falling down her cheeks.

"How long have I been away?" he asked as she embraced him.

"Do I look like a fucking calendar?"

He smiled. "You look like a beautiful dream."

"Oh my god," she said. "You are really not yourself."

"I believe I'm still adjusting to the change," he said.

"No shit. But could you please hurry up? I think we might be lost, and we are definitely running out of time."

"You can relax," he said. "I know the way from here."

46

TINY METAPHYSICAL NEEDLES IN A GREAT BIG FUCKING HAYSTACK

EMILY LED PEPPER into a medium-sized room. It was dim, and it took her eyes a few seconds to adjust to the light. The room was square, with a ceiling that felt slightly higher than normal. A series of dark bookshelves covered the right-hand wall, and two large writing desks sat side by side in front of a large black rolling chalkboard on the left. Behind the chalkboard a narrow hallway led to darkness. The floor was covered with an amber-colored Persian rug beautifully detailed with tiny labyrinthian lines that appeared to be an intricate maze leading to a small circular design in the center. Directly across from them was a red door.

"Holy shit," Emily said.

"What?"

"I think we found it."

"You did," a man said as he stepped into the room from the dark hallway behind the chalkboard.

It was Rowan Chess. Julie Furuno was right behind him.

"You can remove your blindfold," Rowan said. "You're somewhere else now."

"Em?" Pepper asked.

Emily looked at Rowan. There was something different about him. He looked older somehow, more composed.

"It's okay," Emily said.

Pepper removed her blindfold.

"The fact that you made it here is . . . impressive," Rowan said.

There was definitely something off about him. His voice sounded different—maybe a bit deeper? Or perhaps he was just speaking slowly. Either way, he'd changed.

"How the hell did you find this place?" Julie asked as she produced a gun from the back of her jeans.

"Is this really the Quiet Room?" Pepper asked.

"It is," Rowan replied.

"How do you know?"

"Because I've been here before," he said. "Many times."

Rowan still sounded strange, but Emily felt strange as well. Ever since she'd stepped through the door, she'd felt incredibly clear and calm. She could feel endorphins flooding her brain as if she'd just gone for a long run. She felt like an opaque film or some kind of gauze had been pulled from in front of her eyes, and she could finally see clearly.

"You look so much like your mother," Rowan said with a slight smile. "It's uncanny."

"You knew my mother?"

He nodded. "Both of your parents. They were my friends."

And that's when Emily finally recognized him.

She pulled the photograph from her pocket and held it up. "It's you," she said.

The older man in the photograph with her parents was Rowan Chess.

The man standing in front of her now was decades younger, but he was definitely the same man.

He nodded.

"How is this possible?" Emily asked.

"Things are generally fairly uniform between adjacent dimensional streams, but when you move farther out, a lot can change. The passage of time is one of the big ones."

"So you're the Engineer," Emily said.

"Yes," Rowan replied.

"What kind of engineer?" Emily asked.

"I helped Crawford, your parents, and the others design the original research programs at the Gatewick Institute."

"My parents. They had titles as well, didn't they?"

"Of course. They were two of The Six," he said.

"What does that mean?"

"The original Gatewick dream team," he said. "When the six of us were assembled, we weren't allowed to use our real names or divulge any identifying information, so instead of choosing fake names, we decided to refer to one another using our occupations. It was your father's idea—a nod to his favorite movie, Andrei Tarkovsky's *Stalker*."

"Why didn't you come here earlier? Why go through all the rest of it?" Pepper asked.

"For his own protection, he couldn't know who he was," Julie said as she lowered her gun.

"When I finally discovered what was happening," Rowan continued, "what the game was trying to do, I didn't have much time. I did my best to make sure that there was a young enough version of myself hidden someplace safe. Sadly, the game ended up tracking me here and cutting off this stream before I was able to stop it."

"And The Hall of Incredible Possibilities? You built it to hide the Quiet Room?"

"The plans for this place were also hidden, decades ago."

"How?" Pepper asked.

"Helena Worricker understood that something was wrong with her father's AI. She wanted to help put things right. She was responsible for a number of things, but making sure this place was built without my knowledge was by far the most important."

"What about you?" Emily said, turning to Julie Furuno. "You must have known."

"It's complicated," Julie replied. "In order to keep this version of Rowan safe, Helena and I had to use the Quiet Room to move between dimensional streams. We did our best to figure out what the AI was doing out there in the multiverse, and tried to apply that information in order to try to stop it from happening here. But, once this dimension was cut off from the rest, dimensional drift prevented our memories from syncing properly. I was no longer able to remember Rowan at all, or, if I remembered, it was blurry, and hard to pin down. It was the same with Helena. Every time we used the Quiet Room, the drift got much worse and we were essentially starting at square one. It doesn't help that dimensional drift gets much worse the farther you move from your primary stream. We did our best to leave ourselves clues, but there was no way to know if we'd be able to find those clues once we left this room and reentered that stream. Every time we stepped through that door we were starting over. We were looking for tiny metaphysical needles in a great big fucking haystack."

"So what happens now?" Pepper asked.

"We leave this room, hop into a healthy dimensional stream, and get back to work," Julie said.

"Get back to work doing what?" Emily asked.

"Destroying the game called Rabbits," Rowan said.

"What the fuck are you talking about?" Pepper asked.

"Imagine a room the size of the entire cosmos filled with endless, vibrant, intelligent beings," Rowan continued. "You know everything they know, experience everything they do, and love everyone they love. These vibrant intelligent beings aren't just a part of you; they *are* you. Now picture those beautiful essential parts of you being snuffed out, one by one. Can you imagine what it might feel like to lose a loved one every day, every hour, every minute? When they're gone, only emptiness remains. Nothing takes their place. All that's left is pain and hopelessness. I've been murdered so many times I can't remember. I've been beaten, drowned, burned, starved, frozen, and shot. And every single time—after all of that immeasurable pain and terror—I wake up and discover that part of me is gone. A unique voice is silenced forever. That's what Worricker's game has taken from me. Over and over again."

"I'm sorry," Emily said. "That sounds incredibly painful. But what about the alternative? What if keeping you alive means the end of the entire multiverse, and every single soul within it?"

"What if it doesn't?"

"We were told that the game took action because it had determined you were going to destroy everything."

"And you're okay with that, morally?" Rowan asked. "Murdering every single instance of a human being in order to prevent something you're not sure is ever going to happen? Something determined by the questionable survival instincts of a game?"

Emily didn't know what to say.

"You know, I felt all of them—every single death—as if it were my own. But I think you'll be surprised to hear that the experience of being relentlessly pursued and needlessly murdered over and over wasn't actually the worst of it."

Emily could tell by the expression on his face that he had been through something terrifying and uniquely painful. If he was telling the truth, it was a wonder this man was still able to think or speak coherently at all. "How is it that you're able to feel all the other instances of yourself in other dimensions?" she asked.

"That gift came courtesy of the kind folks at the Gatewick Institute's predecessor," Rowan replied. "They fed me a wonderful cocktail of pre- and postnatal goodies. That's how you were able to find this place? You followed the Radiants?"

Emily nodded.

"You're lucky. Your parents gave you the new Gatewick drugs."

"I don't feel lucky."

"You might find this interesting," Rowan said. "Years ago, I, or rather, another version of myself, managed to capture one of the Wardens that the game had sent to kill me, and do you know what he said before I ended his life?"

Emily shook her head.

"He told me that Worricker's AI had determined the likelihood of my contributing to the destruction of the multiverse at roughly point zero two percent."

"That sounds wrong," Emily said.

"I'll say," Rowan replied. "Does that sound like reasonable risk assessment to you?"

Once again, Emily shook her head.

"Helena Worricker believed that her father's game would inevitably conclude that human beings are far too chaotic, that the danger our species represents to the planetary ecosystem is simply too great, and when that happens, the game will destroy us."

"That doesn't make any sense," Emily said. "The game is responsible for manipulating the Meechum Radiants, for keeping our dimensional streams healthy."

"Dimensional streams don't necessarily have to include human beings," Julie said.

"If you destroy the game, you destroy the multiverse."

Rowan smiled. "You Wardens really do make everything sound so simple."

"I'm not a Warden," Emily said.

Rowan nodded. "Sorry. I forgot."

"So that's it?" Pepper asked. "You're pissed off Rabbits wants to kill you, so you're going to destroy the multiverse?"

Rowan laughed. "Wow," he said. "What a wonderfully naïve explanation. But there's a problem with that theory, isn't there?"

"What's that?" Pepper asked.

"I live in the multiverse," Rowan said. "Why would I want to destroy it?"

"Maybe you're insane?"

Rowan raised his hand. "When I was targeted by Worricker's AI, all I was doing was trying to discover how the Meechum Radiants work. That's it. Does that sound like a crime worthy of the punishment I've endured?"

If what Swan had told Emily was right, Rowan Chess leaving the Quiet Room would result in the end of everything. But what if he was telling the truth? Point zero two percent? It just didn't seem fair.

"It sounds awful, truly," Emily said. "And I'm sure your suffering has been unimaginable, but what if destroying the game really does mean the end of everything? That feels like one hell of a huge risk. Is there maybe another way?"

"This is the only way," Rowan said as he and Julie started moving toward the red door.

"So what happens now?" Emily asked.

"We're going to open that door and step into another world."

"What other world?"

"It doesn't really matter," he said, and with that, Rowan Chess grabbed Julie Furuno's hand and opened the door.

A rush of color and light flooded the room, and Emily was almost knocked over as a low booming whooshed against her ears.

Everything started to shake.

Maybe it was because Julie and Rowan were closer to whatever was swirling around the other side of the door, but they were hit even harder. Rowan managed to hang on to the door, but Julie was thrown to the ground. She landed on her wrist, and as she did, the gun popped out of her hand and skidded across the floor, stopping right at Emily's feet.

Emily picked up the gun.

"We're going to step through the door now," Rowan said, lifting Julie up from where she'd fallen with his free hand.

"Stop," Emily said, raising the gun. "I can't let you go."

Rowan turned to face the door.

"You have to shoot him, Em," Pepper said. "Remember what Swan told us. It's the only way."

"I don't want to shoot you, but I will," Emily said.

"Then do it," Rowan said without turning around. "I've been killed before."

"Please," Emily said, pulling back the hammer of the gun with a click, "don't."

"Shoot him!" Pepper yelled.

Then Rowan yanked Julie through the door.

"No!" Pepper yelled as she lunged forward.

But she was too late.

The door slammed shut behind them.

They were gone.

Pepper slid down onto the floor, her back to the door.

The room was suddenly silent.

Emily sat down next to Pepper, and the two women embraced.

After a second or two, Pepper pulled away. "Em, why didn't you shoot?"

"You didn't believe what he said? That the game targeted him? Point zero two percent?"

"On the contrary," Pepper said. "I believe everything he told us. I feel like he was unfairly treated, but that doesn't change the facts."

"Unfairly treated? He consciously experienced the death and subsequent loss of every single instance of himself spread over the entire multiverse."

"Which is unspeakably awful, but whatever happened to all of those other instances of Rowan Chess has already happened. Before he stepped through that door, he told us that he was going to destroy Rabbits. And that means he's going to destroy everything. And 'everything' includes you and me and everyone else."

The two of them sat together for a long time, holding each other in silence. And then Emily finally stood up and stretched her neck.

"Come on." Emily held out her arms.

Pepper grabbed Emily's hands and Emily pulled her up.

They stood facing each other in front of the door that Rowan and Julie had just used to leave the room.

"Are you ready?" Pepper asked.

Emily just stared.

"What is it, Em?"

"Swan said that each of us is tethered to our primary stream."

"So?"

"What if this door sends us back to our primary streams?"

"What if it does?"

"I don't think we come from the same place," Emily said, finally.

"We don't know that for sure," Pepper said.

"You had a distinctly different experience in Greece."

"Dimensional drift," Pepper said. "We can't be certain about anything."

"When we step through that door, we're going to be separated."

"Maybe, maybe not, but either way, it's not going to matter," Pepper said as she swiped at a tear that began rolling down her cheek.

"How the fuck does that work?" Emily asked. "What if we forget? You know how dimensional drift works. Voices from the past can wane until they're almost completely inaudible. Some people I've known and loved are nothing more than faded outlines."

"Some people, sure, but not us. The way I understand it, every iteration of us is connected. When we slip streams, nothing is ever pushed out completely. The important stuff, like my love for you? That isn't going anywhere."

"What if you're wrong? What if I lose you again?"

"Listen to me," Pepper said as she gently placed her hands on Emily's face. "That is not going to happen. I'll find you."

"Let's say you do—against all wildly improbable astronomical odds. How will you know it's really me?"

"I know you." Pepper placed her hand against Emily's chest. "This you. This exact perfect fucking you that I'm deeply and hopelessly in love with, and always have been."

Emily laughed a little. "Okay then," she said as tears streamed down her cheeks.

"I'll find you," Pepper whispered.

Emily grabbed Pepper's hand, opened the door, and once again the Quiet Room was flooded with light and color and sound.

"You fucking promise?" Emily yelled over the loud rumbling and buzzing.

"I fucking promise," Pepper yelled back.

"I love you too."

And then, Emily and Pepper stepped through the door.

47

DANDELION

Emily opened her eyes.

She was in bed.

It took her a moment to acclimate to her surroundings. The weight of the air in the room seemed different—lighter somehow—and she felt rested in a way she hadn't felt for a very long time. She sat up and took a look around.

She was in a hotel room—and based on the state of the place, it looked like she'd been there for quite a while. A small suitcase sat overflowing on a nearby luggage rack, used drinking glasses and empty bottles of beer and soda littered the counters, and a small writing desk in the corner of the room was barely visible beneath a stack of newspapers, documents, file folders, and paper take-out coffee cups. The clock on the nightstand was face down. Emily picked it up. Seven o'clock in the morning.

How long had she been living here?

She got out of bed and stretched. She was in a hotel—four-star if she was to guess—but where? She walked over and pulled back the blackout curtains.

Downtown Seattle.

Staring out at the waking city, Emily felt a rush of relief. She watched for a long time as the rain fell over the familiar buildings and morning traffic, and then turned her attention to the window where a few thick drops of water slowly tumbled into tiny tributaries and then slid down the thick glass toward oblivion.

As she stared out the window, Emily thought about what had happened.

She could picture the expression on Helena Worricker's face as she shot Scarpio and MayDay, and she could hear the beeping and whirring of the machines surrounding Swan while she'd told Emily about the Quiet Room, but she couldn't *feel* those things—at least, not the way that she was able to feel the carpet beneath her feet or the slight chill in the air.

This hotel room was real. Those other things felt like they'd taken place in a movie.

Emily shook her head. What she was experiencing had to be dimensional drift. Things would eventually settle down like they always did. It was just going to take some getting used to.

Pepper Prince.

Emily stepped away from the window. She wasn't ready to think about Pepper. Not yet. While she stood there wondering what the hell this version of Emily had been up to, there was a knock at the door.

Emily was in her underwear. She ran over and dug through the suitcase until she found a T-shirt and a suitable pair of sweatpants and then made her way to the door.

"Hello?" Emily called out.

No answer.

She slowly opened the door.

There was a large tray sitting on the carpet directly in front of her room, but whoever had knocked was gone. The smell of toast and coffee filled the hall, and Emily realized she was starving.

She grabbed the large tray, set it down on top of a stack of papers on the desk, and turned on the television. She took a sip of coffee and then lifted the first of two cloches to reveal a cheese omelet, toast, and hash browns. She popped a piece of toast in her mouth and opened the second cloche.

It was a USB drive.

She looked around for a computer, and eventually found a laptop under one of the pillows. She booted it up and plugged in the drive.

There were two files on the drive titled "one" and "two." They had no extensions, so Emily couldn't tell what type of files they were.

She double-clicked the file titled "one" and a browser window opened. The URL section was blank, but the file had loaded what appeared to be some type of online form. There was a flashing prompt that read simply: *Choose a name for your adventure.*

"What the fuck?" Emily whispered through the piece of toast that was still hanging out of her mouth. It looked like somebody had sent some kind of text-based adventure game. Emily thought about it for a minute, then typed "Dandelion" and pressed Enter.

The form disappeared and Emily was directed to another website. This time there was a URL that she recognized in the address bar: abbeysskirt.com.

There, on the front page of the site, was a list.

It was The Circle.

    I: MICKIE MOUTH
   II: THE CONDOR
  III: ALISON CAT
  IV: RADIO KNIFE
   V: CARBON THING
  VI: CALIFORNIAC
 VII: NOVA TRAIL
VIII:
  IX: BISCUITHAMMER85
   X: CONTROLG
  XI: K
 XII: DANDELION

The name Emily had just entered was listed as the winner of the twelfth iteration of Rabbits. Someone had to be playing a prank.

Emily navigated back to the USB drive and double-clicked the file called "two."

Another browser window automatically opened. A few seconds later, she was looking at what appeared to be a bank account.

It took her a second, but she eventually realized that the bank account she was looking at was her own. The last time Emily had logged in, she'd had a six-digit balance and that had included the two digits after the decimal point. Things were a whole lot different now.

The decimal point was still there, but now there were eight digits to the left of it.

She hadn't realized the toast was still in her mouth until it landed on the laptop's keyboard.

She picked up the toast and set it down next to the uneaten omelet.

"What the fuck?" she whispered.

Emily slowly set the computer down next to a pile of documents. That's when she noticed something familiar.

The Hall of Incredible Possibilities.

The first document on the pile was a newspaper article about The Hall of Incredible Possibilities. Emily picked it up and started to read. At first she couldn't believe it, but then she dug up three more articles in that stack of pages, all from reputable news outlets, and all featuring the same story.

> The Hall of Incredible Possibilities, a brand-new escape room experience in Las Vegas, has been shut down indefinitely, pending an investigation into reports of people being drugged and hypnotized without their knowledge or consent. A man named Victor Garland is in custody pending arraignment.

"What the fuck?" Emily said.

At that point, there was another knock at the door.

"Hello?" Emily called out.

No answer.

She got up and took a look through the peephole. Standing in front of the door was a woman wearing a black leather motorcycle jacket and a vintage Seattle Mariners hat. Emily couldn't clearly make out the woman's face. At one point her eyes were blue, and then she thought they looked green.

The woman knocked again.

Emily opened the door.

When she finally saw the woman up close, Emily realized that the reason she couldn't tell what color the woman's eyes were was because she was wearing a mask. It was the kind of mask you'd see in a sci-fi movie. It had a reflective video surface that played a random shifting cycle of people's faces on a loop. They'd been designed to trick facial recognition software. Emily had seen masks like these before.

On the Rabbits Police.

Emily tried to close the door, but the woman's leg was already inside the room.

"Please," she said. "I'm not here to hurt you."

Something about the tone of the woman's voice made Emily believe she was telling the truth.

"May I come in?" the woman asked, although she was essentially already in.

Emily felt like maybe she recognized her voice, but she couldn't remember where. Dimensional drift was probably to blame, but Emily wasn't sure. This felt different. Emily stepped aside and let the woman into the room.

Her visitor was roughly five foot four. Wild tufts of dark brown hair poked out from beneath the baseball cap. She held a phone in one hand and a large black motorcycle helmet in the other. "Emily Connors?" she asked, but it wasn't a question.

Emily nodded.

"Normally this is where somebody might tell you that they're not here to take up much of your time," the woman said, "but I would be lying if I said that."

"Who are you, and what are you doing in my hotel room?"

"I'm not sure you're going to believe me when I tell you."

"Try me," Emily said.

"Okay." The woman pulled off her hat, then slowly removed her mask. She was in her mid to late thirties with wide, gray-green eyes.

But it wasn't until she smiled that Emily recognized her.

She felt the room begin to spin.

"Heya, sis."

Emily fell backward onto the bed.

"I knew I should have told you to sit," Annie Connors said as she rushed over and helped her sister up.

"Annie?" Emily barely managed a whisper.

She nodded. "I go by Max these days."

Annie's middle name was Maxine. She'd always hated it.

Emily wanted to jump up and hug her sister and never let go, but she wasn't sure she could trust her eyes. Was this actually happening? The last time she'd seen Annie was the night she died, when her sister was fifteen years old.

"Did you get the money?" Annie asked.

Emily pointed in the direction of her laptop.

"Good. We're going to need it."

"How?" Emily asked, finally.

"*How* is kind of a long story for right now, I'm afraid. *Why* is quicker. I came here because I need your help."

"What for?"

"I need you to help me find somebody and convince them to help us save the world."

"Who is it?"

"Hazel."

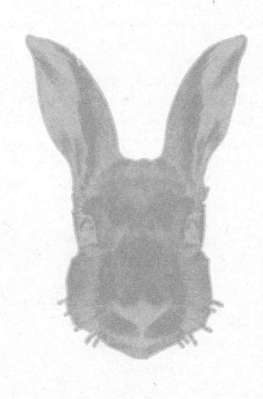

ACKNOWLEDGMENTS

This book is for those who are brave enough to play the game, to rush blindly forward into the mystery, often without properly considering the consequences, and perhaps, on occasion, even forgetting to pack a lunch.

And once again, although some names have been changed and some real-life incidents adjusted to protect certain individuals, and even though you probably found it in the fiction section, Rabbits is real.

With thanks to my brilliant agent, Marc Gerald, for continuing to support and encourage both me and my work, and to my equally brilliant editor, Anne Groell, for her incredibly helpful (essential) notes and thoughts, and for believing there was more story to tell in the world of Rabbits.

And finally, thank you to my family for supporting me through everything. It's not always easy to tell when a writer's working. Thank you to my wife, Isabel, for understanding that fact (even when I suspect you sometimes don't). Thank you to Luna, Maisie, and Aiden for the constant inspiration, and thank you to Bailey for being a good dog.

R U Playing?

ABOUT THE AUTHOR

TERRY MILES is an award-winning filmmaker and the creator of the Public Radio Alliance and that network's series of hit podcasts: *Tanis, Rabbits, Faerie,* and *The Black Tapes*. He splits his time between the dark emerald gloom of the Pacific Northwest and sunny Los Angeles.

terrymiles.com
publicradioalliance.com
rabbitspodcast.com
Twitter: @tkmiles
Instagram: @tkmiles

ABOUT THE TYPE

This book was set in Bembo, a typeface based on an old-style Roman face that was used for Cardinal Pietro Bembo's tract *De Aetna* in 1495. Bembo was cut by Francesco Griffo (1450–1518) in the early sixteenth century for Italian Renaissance printer and publisher Aldus Manutius (1449–1515). The Lanston Monotype Company of Philadelphia brought the well-proportioned letterforms of Bembo to the United States in the 1930s.